NA[
PAST AND

CU00866476

BY
ARTHUR H. NORWAY

PREFATORY NOTE

I have designed this book not as a guide, but as supplementary to a guide. The best of guide-books—even that of Murray or of Gsell-Fels—leaves a whole world of thought and knowledge untouched, being indeed of necessity so full of detail that broad, general views can scarcely be obtained from it.

In this work detail has been sacrificed without hesitation. I have omitted reference to a few well-known places, usually because I could add nothing to the information given in the handbooks, but in one or two cases because the considerations which they raised lay too far from the thread of my discourse.

I have thrown together in the form of an appendix such hints and suggestions as seemed likely to assist anyone who desires wider information than I have given.

A. H. N.

EALING, 1901

NAPLES
PAST AND PRESENT
CHAPTER I

THE APPROACH TO NAPLES BY THE SEA

On a fine spring morning when the sun, which set last night in gold and purple behind the jagged mountain chain of Corsica, had but just climbed high enough to send out shafts and flashes of soft light across the opalescent sea, I came up on the deck of the great steamer which carried me from Genoa to watch for the first opening of the Bay of Naples. It was so early that the decks were very quiet. There was no sound but the perpetual soft rustle of the wave shed off from the bow of the steamer, which slipped on silently without sense of motion. The Ponza Islands were in sight, desolate and precipitous, showing on their dark cliffs no house nor any sign of life, save here and there a seabird winging its solitary way round the crags and caverns of the coast. Far ahead, in the direction of our course, lay one or two dim, cloudy masses, too faint and shadowy to be detached as yet from the grey skyline which bounded the crystalline sparkles of the sea. And so, having strained my eyes in vain effort to discover the high peak of Ischia, I fell to wondering 2why any man who is at liberty to choose his route should dream of approaching this Campanian coast otherwise than by the sea.

For Naples is the city of the siren—"Parthenope," sacred to one of those sea nymphs whose marvellous sweet singing floated out across the waves and lured the ancient seamen rowing by in their strange old galleys, shaped after a fashion now long since forgotten, and carrying merchandise from cities which thirty centuries ago and more were "broken by the sea in the depths of the waters" so that "all the company in the midst of them did fail." How many generations had the line of sailors stretched among whom Parthenope wrought havoc before Ulysses sailed by her rock, and saw the heaps of whitening bones, and last of all men heard the wondrous melodies which must have lured him too, but for the tight thongs which bound him to the mast! So Parthenope and her two sisters cast themselves into the sea and perished, as the old prediction said they must when first a mariner went by their rock unscathed. But her drowned body floated over the blue sea till it reached the shore at Naples, and somewhere near the harbour the wondering people built her a shrine which was doubtless rarely lovely, and is mentioned by Strabo, the old Greek geographer, as being shown still in his day, not long after the birth of Christ.

There is now but little navigation on these seas compared with the relative importance of the shipping that came hither in old days. Naples is in our day outstripped by Genoa, and hard run, even for the goods of southern Italy, by Brindisi and Taranto. The trade of Rome goes largely to Leghorn. If Ostia were ever purged of fever and rebuilt, or if the schemes for deepening the Tiber so as to allow 3large vessels to discharge at Rome were carried out, we might see the port of Naples decline as that of Pozzuoli did for the selfsame reason, the broad facts which govern the course of trade being the same to-day as they were three thousand years ago. Even now it is rather the convenience of passengers and mails than the necessities of merchants which take the great ocean steamers into Naples. It is not easy for men who realise these facts to remember that the waters of the Campanian coast have more than once been ploughed by the chief shipping of the world. Far back in the dawn of history, where nothing certain can be distinguished of the deeds of men or nations, the presence of traders, Phœnician and Greek, can be inferred upon these shores. The antiquity of shipping is immense and measureless. Year by year the spade, trenching on the sites of ancient civilisation, drives back by centuries the date at which man's intellect began to gather science; and no one yet can put his finger on any point of time and say, "within this space man did not understand the use of sail or oar." The earliest seamen of whom we know anything at all were doubtless the successors of many a generation like themselves. It cannot be much less than a thousand years before Christ was born when Greek ships were crossing the sea which washed their western coasts bound for Sicily and the Campanian shores. Yet how many ages must have passed between the days when the Greeks first went afloat and those in which they dared push off toward the night side of the world, where the mariners of the dead went to and fro upon the sea, where the expanse of ocean lay unbroken by the shelter of any friendly island, and both winds and currents beat against them in their course, or even by coasting up and down the Adriatic set that 4dreaded sea between them and their homes! Superstition, hand in hand with peril, barred their way, yet they broke through! But after what centuries of fearful longing,—curiosity, and love of salt adventure struggling in their hearts with fear of the unknown, till courage gained the mastery and the galleys braved the surf and smoke of the *planctæ*, the rocks that struck together, "where not even do birds pass by, no, not the timorous doves which carry ambrosia for Zeus, but even of them the sheer rock ever steals one away, and the father sends in another to make up the number."

Then the rowers saw the rock of Scylla and her ravening heads thrust forth to prey on them, while beneath the fig tree on the opposite crag Charybdis sucked down the black seawater awfully, and cast it forth again in showers of foam and spray. These fabled dangers passed, there remained the Island of the Sirens, which legend placed near Capri, where Ulysses passed it when he sailed south again; and so the wonderful tradition of the Sirens dominates the ancient traffic of mankind upon these waters, and the harbour where the shrine of Parthenope was reflected in the blue sea claims a lofty place in the realms whether of imagination or of that scholarship which cares rather for the deeds of men than for the verbal emendations of a text.

The shrine has gone. The memory remains only as a fable, whose dim meaning rests on the vast duration of the ages through which men have gone to and fro upon these waters. But here, still unchanged, is the pathway to the shrine—the Tyrrhene Sea, bearing still the selfsame aspect as in the days when the galleys of Æneas beat up the coast from Troy, and Palinurus watched the wind rise out of the blackening west. Since those old 5times the surface of the land has changed as often almost as the summer clouds have swept across it. Volcanic outbursts and the caprice of many masters have wrought together in destruction; so that he who now desires to see what Virgil saw must cheat his eyes at every moment and keep his imagination ever on the stretch. Even the city of mediæval days, the capital of Anjou and Aragon, is so far lost and hidden that a man must seek diligently before he cuts the network of old streets, unsavoury and crowded, in which he can discover the lanes and courtyards where Boccaccio sought Fiammetta, or the walls on which Giotto painted.

But here, upon the silent sea, at every moment fresh objects are coming into sight which have lain unchanged under dawn and dusk in every generation. Already the volcanic cone of Monte Epomeo towers out of Ischia, a menace of destruction which not twenty years ago fulfilled itself and shook the town of Casamicciola in a few seconds into a mere rubble heap. It is a sad thing still to stroll round that once smiling town. Ruins project on every side. The cathedral lies shattered and untouched; there is not enough money in the island to rebuild it. The visitors, to whom most of the old prosperity was due, have not yet recovered from the attack of nerves brought on by the earthquake. But there remains wonderful beauty at Casamicciola and elsewhere on Ischia; the "Piccola Sentinella" is an excellent hotel; some day, surely, the lost ground will be recovered, and prosperity return.

The new town lies gleaming on the flat at the foot of the great mountain. Far away towards my right Capri, loveliest of islands, floats upon the sea touched with blue haze; and there, stretching landwards, is the mountain promontory of Sorrento, Monte St. 6Angelo towering over Monte Faito, and the whole mass dropping by swift, steep slopes to the Punta di Campanella, the headland of the bell, whence in the old days of corsairs the warning toll swung out across the sea as often as the galleys of Dragut or of Barbarossa hove in sight, echoing from Torre del Greco, Torre Annunziata, and many another watchtower of that fair and wealthy coast, while the artillery of the old castle of Ischia, answering with three shots, gave warning of the coming peril. Even now I can see that ancient castle, standing nobly on a rock that seems an island, though, in fact, it is united with the land by a low causeway; and it comes into my mind how Vittoria Colonna took refuge from her sorrows there, spending her widowhood behind the battlements on which she had played with her husband as a child. Doubtless the two children listened awestruck on many a day to the cannon-shots which warned the fishers. Perhaps Vittoria may even have been pacing there when, as Brantôme writes, a party of French knights of Malta came sailing by with much treasure on their ship, and hearing the three shots took them arrogantly for a salute in honour of their flag, and so, thinking of nothing but their dignity, made a courteous salute in answer, and kept on their way. Whereupon the spider Dragut, who at that moment was sacking Castellammare, just where the peninsula joins the mainland, driving off as captive all those men or women who had not fled up into the wooded hills in time, swooped out with half a dozen galleys, and added the poor knights and their treasure to his piles of plunder.

Many tales are told about that castle, so near and safe a refuge from the turbulence of Naples. But already it is dropping astern, and the lower land of Procida usurps its place, an island which in the 7days of Juvenal was a byword of desolation, though populous and fertile in our own. The widening strait of water between the low shore and the craggy one played its part in a tale as passionate, though not so famous, as that of Hero and Leander. For Boccaccio tells us that Gianni di Procida, nephew and namesake of a man whose loyalty popular tradition will extol until the end of time, loved one Restituta Bolgaro, daughter of a gentleman of Ischia; and often when his love for her burnt so hotly that he could not sleep, used to rise and go down to the water, and if he found no boat would plunge into the black sea, swim the channel, and lie beneath the walls of Restituta's house all night, swimming back happy in the morning if he had but seen the roof which sheltered her. But one day when Restituta was alone upon the shore she was carried off by pirates out of Sicily, who, wondering at her beauty, took her to Palermo and showed her to King Federigo, who straightway loved her, and gave her rooms in his palace, and waited till a day might come when she would love him. But Gianni armed a ship and followed swiftly on the traces of the captors, and found at last that Restituta was in Palermo. Then, led by love, he scaled the palace wall by night and crossed the garden in the dark and gained the poor girl's chamber, and might have borne her off in safety had not the King, suspecting that all was not well, come with torches in the darkness and discovered Gianni and cast him into prison, where he lay till he was sentenced to be taken out and burned at the

2

stake in the Piazza of Palermo together with the girl who had dared to flout the affection of a king. And burned they would have been had not the great Admiral Ruggiero di Loria chanced to pass that way as 8they stood together at the stake and known Gianni as the nephew of that great plotter who conceived the massacre of the Sicilian Vespers, whereby the crown of Sicily was set upon the head of Aragon. Straightway he hastened to the King, who forthwith released Gianni and gave him Restituta, and sent both home laden with rich gifts to Ischia, where they lived happy for many a year, till they were overcome at last by no worse fate than that which is reserved for all humanity whether glad or sorry.

No man can prove this story true; but it is at least so happily conceived as to be worth credence, like others told us by the same immortal writer, who, though a Florentine, knew Naples well, and doubtless wove into the *Decameron* many an anecdote picked up in the taverns which survives now in no other form. For there was no Brantôme to collect for us the gossip of the days when Anjou drove out Hohenstaufen from this kingdom; and if we would know what happened on the coast in those tragic and far-distant times we must take the tales set down by Boccaccio for what they may be worth.

I am not sure that Gianni, the hot-passioned lad who used to swim this strait by night, does not emerge out of the darkness of the centuries more clearly than his greater uncle—that mighty plotter who, using craft and guile where he had no strength, is fabled to have built up a conspiracy and engineered a massacre which has no parallel save in the St. Bartholomew. Yet it is not to be judged without excuse like that foul act of cold-blooded treachery, but was in some measure an expiation of intolerable wrongs, as may be discovered even now by anyone who will study the plentiful traditions of that March night when eight thousand French 9of every age and either sex perished in two hours, slain at the signal of the vesper bell ringing in Palermo. That bloodshed split the kingdom of the two Sicilies in twain. It did more: it scored men's minds with a memory so deep that even now there is no child in Sicily who could not tell how the massacre began. To men then living it appeared a cataclysm so tremendous that they must needs date time from it, as from the birth of Christ or the foundation of the world. In documents written full four centuries later the passage of the years is reckoned thus; and in Palermo to this day the nuns of the Pietà sing a litany on the Monday after Easter in memory of the souls of the French who perished on that night of woe. So memorable was the deed ascribed by tradition to the plotter, Giovanni di Procida, lord of that little island which is already slipping past me out of sight.

The steamer slips on noiselessly as ever. Procida falls away into the background, with its old brown town clinging to the seaward face of a precipitous cliff; and I can look down the Bay of Baiæ, where in old Roman days every woman who went in a Penelope came out a Helen, and almost catch a glance at Cumæ, where Dædalus put off his weary wings after that great flight from Crete which no man since has contrived to imitate. There lies the Gate of Hell down which Æneas plunged in company with the Sibyl; and round it all the land of the Phlegræan fields, heaving and steaming with volcanic fires. There too is the headland of Posilipo, where Virgil dwelt and where he wrought those enchantments concerning which I shall have much to say hereafter; for though Virgil is a poet to the world at large, he is a magician in the memory of the Neapolitans. And who shall say their tradition is not true?10

Next, sweeping round towards my right hand in a perfect curve, comes the shore of the Riviera di Chiaia, once a pleasant sandy beach, broken midway by the jutting rock and island on which stood the church and monastery of San Lionardo. It is long since church and island disappeared, and few of those gay Neapolitans who throng the Via Caracciolo, that fine parade which now usurps the whole seafront from horn to horn of the bay, could even point out where it stood. In these days the whole shore is embowered in trees and gardens skirting the fine roadway; and there stands the wonderful aquarium, which has no equal in the world, and where the wise will spend many afternoons and yet leave its marvels unexhausted.

My eyes have travelled on to the other horn of this fine bay, and are arrested by what is surely the most picturesque object in all Naples. For at this point the spine or backbone of land which breaks the present city into two, leaving on the right the ancient town and on the left the modern, built along the pretty shore of which I have just spoken,—at this point the ridge sweeps down precipitously from the Castle of St. Elmo on the height, breaks off abruptly in the sheer cliff of the Pizzo-Falcone, "The Falcon's Beak," and then sends jutting out into the sea a small craggy island which bears an old hoary castle low down by the water's edge. On this grey morning the sea breaks heavily about the black reef on which the castle stands, and the walls, darkened almost to the colour of the rock itself, assume a curious aspect of vast age, such as disposes one to seek within their girth for some at least among the secrets of old Naples. Nor will the search be vain; for this hoary fortress is Castel dell'Uovo, "The Castle of the Egg," so called, if we may lend an ear to Neapolitan tradition, because Virgil the Enchanter built it on an egg, 11on which it stands unto this hour, and shall stand until the egg is broken. Others again say that the islet is egg-shaped, which it is not, unless my eyes deceive me; and of other explanations I know none at all, so that any man who can content himself with neither of these may resign himself to contemplate an unsolved puzzle for as long as he may stay in Naples.

Apart, however, from the wizard Virgil and the idle tale of the enchanted egg, there is something so arresting in the sight of this ancient castle thrust out into the sea that I cannot choose but see in it the heart of the interest of Naples. It is by far the oldest castle which Naples owns, and as its day came earliest so it passed the first. Castel Nuovo robbed it of its consequence, both as a royal dwelling and a place of arms; and now the noisy, feverish tide of life that beats so restlessly from east to west through the great city finds scarce an echo on the silent battlements of the Egg Castle, where Norman monarchs met their barons and royal prisoners languished in the dungeons. Inside the walls there is nothing to attract a visitor but memories. Yet those gather thick and fast as soon as one has crossed the drawbridge, and there is scarce one other spot in Naples where a man who cares for the past of the old tragic city can lose himself more easily in dreams.

But again the steamer turns her course a little, and suddenly the Castel dell'Uovo slips out of sight, the old brown city passes across my line of vision like a picture on the screen of a camera obscura when the lens is moved, and I am gazing out beyond the houses across the wide rich plain out of which the vast bulk of Vesuvius rears itself dark and tremendous, towering near the sea. There are other mountains far 12away, encircling the plain like the walls of some great amphitheatre, but they are beyond the range of volcanic catastrophe, and stood unmoved while the peaks of Vesuvius were piled up and blown away into a thousand shapes, sometimes green and fertile, the haunt of wild boars and grazing cattle, at others rent by fire and subterranean convulsion so as to give reality to the most awful visions which the imagination of mankind has conceived concerning the destruction which befell the sinful cities of the plain.

The plain is the Campagna Felice, a happy country, notwithstanding the perpetual menace of the smoking mountain, which time after time has convulsed the fields, altered the outline of the coast, and overwhelmed cities, villages, and churches. Throughout the last eighteen hundred years a destruction like to that which befell the cities of Herculaneum and Pompeii has been overtaking hamlets and buildings of less note. The country is a palimpsest. What is now written on its surface is not a tithe of what was once inscribed there. In 1861 an earthquake at Torre del Greco made a fissure in the main street. Those who dared descend it found themselves in a church, long since buried and forgotten. So it is in every direction throughout the Campagna Felice. The works of man are overwhelmed in countless numbers by the ejections from Vesuvius, and the green fields of beans and lupins which stretch so pleasantly across the wide spaces between the Sarno and the Sebeto cover the ruins of innumerable homes.

It seems strange that a land exposed to such great and constant perils should be densely populated. The coast is lined with towns, all shining in the sun, and the first graceful slopes of Vesuvius itself are studded with white buildings, planted here and there in apparent oblivion of the floods of red-hot 13lava which have so often forced their way down the inclines towards the sea. There must be many dwellers in those towns who saw the lava break out from new vents in 1861 among the cultivated fields. Yet the fields are cultivated still, and in time of eruption the peasants will continue working in the vineyards within a few hundred yards of the crawling stream, knowing well how often its progress is arrested by the cooling of the fiery mass. There is, moreover, the power of the saints to be considered. How often has not San Gennaro arrested the outbreaks, and brought peace to the frightened city! On the Ponte della Maddalena he stands unto this day, his outstretched arm, pointing to the mountain with a gesture drawn from the mimic language of the people, bids it "Halt!" And then the fertility of the volcanic soil! Vesuvius, if a rough friend, is a kindly one. He may drive the people to their prayers from time to time, which is no great harm! but, if a balance be struck, his benefits are as many as his injuries, and the peasants, looking up, as they hoe their fields, at the coiling wreaths of copper-coloured smoke which issue from the cone, are content to take their chance that death may some day meet them too in a cloud of scorching ashes as it did those who dwelt in Pompeii so very long ago.

The great steamer is already near her moorings. The western or newer half of Naples is hidden by the hill, and I have before my eyes only the densely peopled ancient city, a rabbit warren of tortuous and narrow streets, unsavoury and not too safe, yet full of interest if not of beauty, and possessing a picturesqueness which is all their own. One salient feature only arrests the eye wandering over this intricate mass of balconies and house-fronts—the handsome steeple of the Carmine, a church sorely 14injured and defaced, but still abounding in romance. For there lies the boy-king Conradin, slaughtered by Charles of Anjou in the market-place just outside; and there, too, the fisherman Masaniello met his end, after a trick of fortune had made him ruler of Naples for eight days. There is no church in all the city so full of tragedies as this, which was founded by hermits fleeing from Mount Carmel twelve hundred years ago, and which ever since has been close to the heart of the passionate and fierce-tempered people dwelling round its walls.

I do not doubt there was a time when travellers, arriving at Naples by sea, found themselves greeted by persons of aspect more pleasing than those who accost the astonished pilgrim of to-day. There was surely an age when the lazzaroni were really picturesque, when they lay on the warm sand in the sunshine, while the bay resounded with the chant of fishermen, the light-hearted people beguiling their unbounded leisure with the tuneful strains of "Drunghe, drunghete," of "Tiritomba," or even the too familiar "Santa Lucia." It cannot be that travellers lied when they wrote of the amazing picturesqueness of the Neapolitans, that they painted brown purple, and put on their spectacles of rose as they approached the land! I wish I had those spectacles; for indeed the aspect of the quays and wharves of Naples is not attractive, while the people who throng the boats now pushing off towards the steamer are just such a crowd of expectant barterers as one may see wherever a great steamer touches. In the stern of the first stands a naked boy, brown and lithe. His accomplishment is to dive for pence, which he does with singular dexterity, cramming all the coins as he catches them into his mouth, which yet is not so full as to impede his bellowing like a bull in the effort to 15attract more custom. Did I complain of the lack of music? I was hasty; for there comes a second boat, carrying two nymphs whose devotion to the art has caused them to forget the use of water, unless it be internally. One has a hoarse voice, the other a shrill one;

4

and with smiles and antics they pipe out the cheapest of modern melodies, chanting the eternal "Funicoli, Funicola," till one wishes the writer of that most paltry song could be keelhauled, or taught by some other process of similar asperity how grave is the offence of him who casts one more jingle into the hoarse throats of the street musicians of to-day. If I flee to the further side of the steamer and stop my ears from the cacophony, my face is tickled by the foliage of huge nosegays thrust up on the ends of poles from a boat so low in the water that I cannot see it. The salt air grows heavy with the scent of violets and roses. None of my senses is at peace.

But in another hour the landing was happily accomplished. The recollection of the mob through which one struggled to the quay, the noise, the extortion, and the smells had faded away into the limbo of bad dreams, and I was free to go whither I would in the small portion of the day remaining and taste whichever sight of Naples pleased me first. There is nothing more bewildering to a stranger than to be turned loose in a great city with which he is imperfectly acquainted. I looked east towards the Carmine; but the handsome campanile lay far from the centre of the city. I gazed before me, up a long straight street which cleft the older city with a course as straight as any bow shot, the house fronts intricate with countless balconies and climbing plants. It is the Strada del Duomo; but I knew it to be new through all its lower length, and it leads into the 16very heart of the dense old town, where, lost in a maze of vicoli, I could never grasp the broad and general aspect of this metropolis of many kings.

At that moment I remembered the hill on which the Castle of St. Elmo stood; and turning westwards along the street which borders the quays, I came out in no great distance on the Piazza del Municipio, bordered on the further side by the walls and towers of Castel Nuovo, that old royal castle of Anjou and Aragon, which saw so many tragedies wrought within its walls, and holds some still, as I shall tell in time, for the better persuasion of any who may be disposed to set down the accusations of history as distant and vague charges, which cannot nowadays be brought to the test of sight. Before my eyes rises the white priory of San Martino topping the hillside high above the town, and it is to that point that I am hastening ere the gold light of the afternoon fades off the bay, and the grey shades of the early dusk rob the islands of their sunset colours. It is a long climb up to the belvedere of the low white building. The Neapolitans believed in days not long distant that vast caverns of almost immeasurable extent branched out laterally from the dungeons of St. Elmo and ran down beneath the city even to Castel Nuovo, making a secret communication between the garrisons of the two fortresses on which the security of Naples most depended. The story is not true. The vaults of St. Elmo do not reach so far, and are not more extensive than the circuit of the castle. But indeed these hillsides on which Naples lies are pierced so frequently by caverns, so many tales are told of grottoes known and unknown in every spine of rock, that the wildest stories of mysterious passages have found ready credence; and there are doubtless many 17children, old and young, in Naples who believe that one may walk beneath the earth from St. Elmo to Castel Nuovo no less firmly than they credit the existence of vast caverns filled with gold and jewels lying underneath Castel dell'Uovo, guarded for ever from the sight of man by the chafing of the waves.

Naples presents us with a strange blend of romance and common sense—the modern spirit, practical and useful, setting itself with something like the energy of the old Italian genius towards the gigantic task of acquiring the arts of government, and turning a people enslaved for centuries into one which can wield the hammer of its own great destinies. "L'Italia è fatta," said Massimo d'Azeglio, "ma chi farà ora gli Italiani?" It was the question of a patriot, and it may be that it is not wholly answered yet. The most careless of observers can see that some things still go wrong in Italy, that the Italians are not yet wholly made, and it is the easiest as it is the stupidest of tasks to demonstrate that thirty years of freedom have not taught the youngest nation what the oldest took eight centuries to learn. It galls me to hear the supercilious remarks dropped by strangers coming from a country where serious difficulties of government have not existed in the memory of man, the casual wisdom of critics who look around too carelessly to note the energy with which one by one the roots of evil are plucked up, and the refuse of the long tyranny cleared away. I am not writing a political tract; but I say once for all that the recent history of Italy can show more triumphs than its failures; and the day will surely come when the indomitable courage of her rulers shall purge the country of those cankers which for centuries ate out her manhood.18

"We do not serve the dead—the past is past.
God lives, and lifts his glorious mornings up
Before the eyes of men awake at last,
Who put away the meats they used to sup,
And down upon the dust of earth outcast
The dregs remaining of the ancient cup,
Then turn to wakeful prayer and worthy act."

Dear prophetess and poet, who once from Casa Guidi sang so bravely of the future, kindling the love of Italy in many a heart where it has since grown into a passion,—it is coming true! It may be that fulfilment loiters, but Heaven does not disappoint mankind of hopes so great as these. They are of the sort with which God keeps troth. The child who went by singing "O bella libertà, o bella!" does not flute so sweetly now he is a man, but his hands have taken hold, and his heart is set on the greatness of his motherland.

The sun lies thick and hot in the Toledo, that long and crowded street which is the chief thoroughfare of Naples. It is hotter still when, having toiled as far as the museum, I turn off along the Corso Vittorio Emmanuele, which winds along the hillside, giving at each turn grand views across the town and harbour

5

towards Capri shining in the west. A little way down the Corso is a flight of steps, long, tortuous and steep, yet forming much the pleasantest approach to the white priory whither every visitor to Naples goes once at least towards the hour of sunset. As one mounts, the city drops away, and the long semicircle of hills behind it rises into sight, green rounded hills, bearing on their summits palms which stand out sharp and dark against the sky. With every convolution of the stairs one sees more and more of the great plain out of which Vesuvius rises,— the Campagna Felice, a purple flat, stretching from the base of the 19volcano as far as that mountain chain which marks the limit of its power. Out of the mountains comes a fresh cool wind, and all the city sparkles in the sun.

So I went up among the housetops till at length I reached an open space bounded by a rampart whence one looked down upon the town. On the further side a gateway gave admission to a courtyard, and that again to a corridor of the old priory, through which a guide led me with vain pointings toward the chamber containing the "Presepe," a vast model of the scene of the Nativity. Mary sits upon a height under a fragment of an old Greek building; while all the valleys are filled with the procession of the kings. Their goods are being unloaded from the troops of asses which bore them. In the meadows sheep are grazing, cows are being milked; and the sky is filled with choirs of angels. It is an ingenious, theatrical toy, but not half so pretty as the sunset, which I came to see. So, with some indignation of my guide, I pressed on through an exquisitely cool arcaded courtyard of white marble, its centre occupied by a garden wherein palms and roses grew almost profuse enough to hide the ancient draw well, with its chain and bucket lying as if they waited for some brother told off by the Prior to draw water for the rest. In one corner of this courtyard a doorway gives admission to the belvedere, a little chamber with two windows, whereof one looks towards the plain behind Vesuvius, and the other gives upon Posilipo.

As I stepped out on the belvedere the sun was dropping fast towards Posilipo, and wide flashes of gold were spreading over all the cup-shaped bay. Far out at sea, between the two horns of the gulf, the dark peaks of Capri caught the light, and presently 20the glow blazed more brightly in the west, and all the shores where Sorrento lies began to quiver softly in the sunset. Vesuvius was grim and black; a pillar of dark smoke mounted slowly from its summit, and stretched across the paling sky like a banner floating defiantly from some tall citadel. Deep down beneath me lay the white city, a forest of domes and house-fronts which seemed at first impenetrable. But ere long the royal palace detached itself from the other buildings, and I could distinguish Castel Nuovo, with its old round towers, looking very dark and grim, while on the left a forest of domes and spires rose out of the densely crowded streets which have known so many masters and have allured conquerors from lands so very far away. A faint brown haze crept down from the hilltops, the first touch of evening chilled the air, but the seaward sky was marvellously clear, and the wide bay gleamed with gold and purple lights.

CHAPTER II

THE ANCIENT MARVELS OF THE PHLEGRÆAN FIELDS

21

It is a morning of alternate sun and shadow. The clouds are flying low across the city, so that now one dome and now another flashes into light and the orange groves shine green and gold among the square white houses. All the high range of the Sorrento mountains lies in shadow, but on the sea the colours are glowing warm and bright, here a tender blue, there deepening into grey, and again, nearer into shore, a marvellous rich tint which has no name, but is azure and emerald in a single moment. Away across the crescent of the gulf a crowd of fishing boats are putting forth from Torre del Greco or Torre dell' Annunziata. Even at this distance one can see how they set their huge triangular sails and scatter, some one way, some another, searching each perhaps for his favourite volcanic shoal; for the largest fish lurk always in the hollows of those lava reefs which have from time to time burst out of the bottom of the bay. Some, perhaps, are sailing for the coral fishery upon the coast of Africa, to which great numbers go still in this month of April out of all the harbours beneath Vesuvius, though the profits are not what they were, and the trade is falling upon evil days. As for the mountain, he has cleared himself of clouds, and from his summit a heavy coil of smoke uncurls itself lazily 22and spreads like a pennant stretching far across the sky.

All these things and more I have time to notice while I trudge along above the housetops of the city, those flat roofs named *astrici* which are such pleasant lounges on the summer evenings when the blue bay is dotted over with white sails and the shadows deepen on the flanks of Vesuvius or the distant line of the Sorrento coast. At length the road approaching the ridge of hill whose point forms the headland of Posilipo drops swiftly, and I find myself in face of a short ascent leading to the mouth of the very ancient grotto by which, these two thousand years and more, those who fared from Naples unto Pozzuoli have saved themselves the trouble of the hill.

It is absolutely necessary to pause and consider this hill, to which so much of the rare beauty of Naples is to be attributed. For the moment I set aside its legends and traditions, and turn my attention to the eminence itself. It is a cliff of yellow rock, whose consistency somewhat resembles sandstone, evidently worked without much difficulty, since it has been quarried out into vast cavities. The rock is tufa. It is a volcanic product, and forms the staple not only of the headland, but also of all the site of Naples and the rising ground behind it up to the base of the blue Apennines, which are seen continually towering in the distance beyond Vesuvius.

6

Thus at Naples one may distinguish between the eternal hills and those which have no title to the name. Of the latter is Posilipo, formed as I said out of volcanic ash. That ash was ejected underneath the sea, and having been compacted into rock by the action of the water was upreared by some convulsion long since forgotten. It is an intrusion on the landscape—a very ancient one, certainly—but it has 23nothing to do with the great mountain-chain which hems in the Neapolitan Campagna and ends at last in the Sorrento peninsula and Capri. All the most fertile plain which lies within that barrier was once beneath the sea, which flowed up to the bases of the mountains. There is no doubt about it. The rock of Posilipo contains shells of fish now living in the bay. From Gaeta to Castellammare stretched one wide inlet of the sea. But underneath the water volcanic ash was being cast out, as it is still at certain spots within the bay; the heaps of ash and pumice stone grew into shoals and reefs, were uplifted into hills, the sea flowed back from its uptilted bed, and the coasts of Naples and of Baiæ assumed some outline roughly similar to that which they possess at present.

Of course all this is very ancient history, far beyond the ken of written records, or even the faintest whisper of tradition, unless, indeed, in the awe with which ancient writers alluded to the Phlegræan fields, fabled in old time to be the gate of hell, we may detect some lingering memory of the horrible convulsion which drove back the sea, and out of its deserted bed reared up this wilderness of ash and craters. But speculations of this kind are rather idle. We had better turn towards the grottoes, which are, at least in part, the work of men whose doings on this earth are known to history. The one, of course, is wholly modern, a construction of our own age for the accommodation of the steam tramway; but the other, through which one walks or drives, is certainly as old as the Emperor Augustus, and has sometimes been supposed to possess an antiquity far greater than that.

It seems remarkable that the Romans should have esteemed it easier to bore through the cliff than to 24make a road across the headland. Indeed, there were villas on Posilipo, and there must surely have been a road of some sort from very early times, though it must be admitted that the founders of Naples did not go to Pozzuoli by the coast as we do. The old road climbed up directly from the city to Antignano, in the direction of Camaldoli, and kept along the ridge as far as possible. The coast road began to be used when the tunnel had been made. Still there must have been at least a track across the headland, and one wonders why the Romans did not improve it, in preference to boring underground. The ease with which the soft stone can be worked may account partially for their choice; but it is not to be forgotten that numberless caves, whether natural or artificial, exist in the cliffs at Posilipo and Pizzofalcone, giving occasion to the quick fancy of the Neapolitans to devise wild tales of buried treasure and of strange fierce beasts which guard it from the greed of men. The old legends of the Cimmerians who dwelt in dark caverns of the Phlegræan fields present themselves to mind in this connection, and without following out this mysterious subject further into the mists which envelope it, we may recognise the possibility that some among these caverns are far older than is commonly believed. Of course the preference of the Romans for tunnelling is explained at once, if we may suppose that by enlarging existing caverns they found their tunnel already partly made.

POZZUOLI.

"I do not know," cries Capaccio, an ancient topographer who may yet be read with pleasure, though the grapes have ripened three hundred times above his tomb, "I do not know whether the Posilipo is more adorned by the grotto or the grotto by Posilipo." I really cannot guess what he meant. It sounds like the despairing observation of a writer 25at a loss for matter. We will leave him to resolve his own puzzle and go on through the darkness of the ill-lighted grotto—no pleasanter now than when Seneca grumbled at its dust and darkness— sparing some thought for that great festival which on the 7th of September every year turns this dark highway into a pandemonium of noise and riot. The festival of Piedigrotta is held as much within the tunnel as on the open space outside, where stands the church whose Madonna furnishes a devotional pretext for all the racket. Indeed it is almost more wild and whirling within than without; for one need not become a boy again to understand that the joys of rushing up and down, wearing a fantastic paper cap, blowing shrieks upon a catcall, and brandishing a Chinese lantern, must be infinitely greater in the bowels of the hill than in the open air. Of course it is not only, nor even chiefly, a feast for children. All the lower classes rejoice at Piedigrotta, and often with the best of cause; for it happens not infrequently that the sky, which for many weeks has been pitiless and brazen, clouds and breaks about that time, the welcome rain falls, the streets grow cool again, and laughter rises from end to end of the reviving city.

Of Fuorigrotta, the unpleasing village at the further end of the grotto, I have nothing to say, unless it be to express the wish that Giacomo Leopardi, who lies in the church of San Vitale, lay elsewhere. That superb poet and fine scholar whose verses upon Italy not yet reborn rank by their majesty and fire next after those of Dante, and who yet could produce a poem rendering so nobly the solitude of contemplation as that which commences—

"Che fai tu luna in ciel, dimmi, che fai,
Silenziosa luna!"
26

this man should have lain upon some mountain-top, among the scent of rosemary and of fragrant myrtle, rather than in such a reeking dirty village as Fuorigrotta.

7

But I forget!—the compelling interest of this day's journey is not literary. A short walk from Fuorigrotta brings me to a point where the road turns slightly upward to the right, leading me to the brow of a hill, over which I look into a wooded hollow—none other than the Lago d'Agnano, once a crater, then a volcanic lake. Oddly enough, it is not mentioned as a lake by any ancient writer. Pliny describes the Grotta del Cane, which we are about to visit, but says not a word of any lake. This fact, with some others, suggests that the water appeared in this old crater only in the Middle Ages; though it really does not matter much, for it is gone now. The bottom has been reft from the fishes and converted into fertile soil. The sloping heights which wall the basin have a waste and somewhat blasted aspect; but I was not granted time to muse on these appearances before a smiling but determined brigand, belonging to the class of guides, sauntered up with a small cur running at his heels and made me aware that I had reached the entrance of the Dog Grotto.

I might have known it; for, in fact, through many centuries up to that recent year when it pleased the Italians to drain the lake, the life of the small dogs dwelling in this neighbourhood has been composed of progresses from grotto to lake and back again, first held up by the heels to be stifled by the poisonous gas, then soused head over ears in the lake with instructions to recover quickly because another carriage was coming down the hill. Thus lake and grotto were twin branches of one establishment, now dissolved. Perhaps the lake was the more important 27of the two, since it is easier to stifle a dog or man than to revive him; and on many occasions there would have been melancholy accidents had not the cooling waters been at hand. For instance it is related by M. de Villamont, who came this way when the seventeenth century was very young indeed, that M. de Tournon, a few years before, desiring to carry off a bit of the roof of the grotto, was unhappily overcome by the fumes as he stood chipping off the piece he fancied, and tumbled on the floor, as likely to perish as could be wished by the bitterest foe of those who spoil ancient monuments. His friends promptly dragged him out and tossed him into the lake. It is true the cure found so successful with dogs proved somewhat less so with M. de Tournon, for he died a few days later. Yet had the lake been dry, as it is to-day, he would have died in the cave, which would surely have been worse.

The little dog—he was hardly better than a puppy—looked at me and wagged his tail hopefully. I understood him perfectly. He had detected my nationality; and I resolved to be no less humane than a countrywoman of my own who visited this grotto no great while ago, and who, when asked by the brigand whether he should put the dog in, answered hastily, "Certainly not." "Ah!" said the guide, "you are Englees! If you had been American you would have said, 'Why, certainly.'" I made the same condition. The fellow shrugged his shoulders. He did not care, he knew another way of extorting as many francs from me; and accordingly we all went gaily down the hill, preceded by the happy cur, running on with tail erect, till we reached a gate in the wall through which we passed to the Grotta del Cane.

A low entrance, hardly more than a man's height, 28a long tubular passage of uniform dimensions sloping backwards into the bowels of the hill—such is all one sees on approaching the Dog Grotto. A misty exhalation rises from the floor and maintains its level while the ground slopes downwards. Thus, if a man entered, the whitish vapour would cling at first about his feet. A few steps further would bring it to his knees, then waist high, and in a little more it would rise about his mouth and nostrils and become a shroud indeed; for the gas is carbonic acid, and destroys all human life. King Charles the Eighth of France, who flashed across the sky of Naples as a conqueror, came here in the short space of time before he left it as a fugitive, bringing with him a donkey, on which he tried the effects of the gas. I do not know why he selected that animal; but the poor brute died. So did two slaves, whom Don Pietro di Toledo, one of the early Spanish viceroys, used to decide the question whether any of the virtue had gone out of the gas. That question is settled more humanely now. The guide takes a torch, kindles it to a bright flame, and plunges it into the vapour. It goes out instantly; and when the act has been repeated some half-dozen times the gas, impregnated with smoke, assumes the appearance of a silver sea, flowing in rippling waves against the black walls of the cavern.

With all its curiosity the Dog Grotto is a deadly little hole, in which the world takes much less interest nowadays than it does in many other objects in the neighbourhood of the Siren city, going indeed by preference to see those which are beautiful, whereas not many generations ago it rushed off hastily to see first those which are odd. For that reason many visitors to Naples neglect this region of the Phlegræan fields and are content to wait the natural occasion 29for visiting the mouth of Styx, over which all created beings must be ferried before they reach the nether world. It is a pity; for, judged from the point of beauty solely, there is enough in the shore of the Bay of Baiæ to content most men. The road mounts upon the ridge which parts the slope of Lago d' Agnano from the sea. One looks down from the spine over a broken land of vineyards to a curved bay, an almost perfect semicircle, bounded on the left by the height of Posilipo, with the high crag of the Island of Nisida, and on the right by Capo Miseno, the point which took its name from the old Trojan trumpeter who made the long perilous voyage with Æneas, but perished as he reached the promised land where at last the wanderers were to find rest. The headland, which, like every other eminence in sight, is purely volcanic, is a lofty mass of tufa, united with the land by a lower tongue, like a mere causeway; and on the nearer side stands the Castle of Baiæ, with the insignificant townlet which bears on its small shoulders the burden of so great a name. Midway in the bay the ancient town of Pozzuoli nestles by the water's edge, deserted this long while by all the trade which brought it into touch with Alexandria and many another city further east, filling its harbour with strange ships, crowding its quays with swarthy sailors, and with silks and spices of the Orient. All that old consequence has gone now like a dream, and no one visits the cluster of old brown houses for any other reason than to see that which is still left of its ancient greatness. But before going down the hill, I turn aside towards a gateway on my right, which admits me to a place of strange and curious interest. It is the Solfatara, and is nothing more or less than the crater of a half-extinct volcano, which, having lain torpid for full seven centuries, is now a striking proof of the fertility of volcanic soil, and the speed with which Nature will haste to spread her lushest vegetation even over a thin crust which covers seething fires. It was so once with the crater of Vesuvius, which, after five centuries of rest, filled itself with oaks and beeches, and covered its slopes with fresh grass up to the very summit.

Indeed, on entering the inclosure of the Solfatara, one receives the impression of treading the winding alleys of a well-kept and lovely park. The path runs through a pretty wood. The trees are scarcely more important than a coppice; but under their green shade there grows a wealth of flowers of every colour, glowing in the soft sunshine which filters through the boughs. There is the white gum-cistus, which is so strangely like the white wild rose of English hedges, and the branching asphodel, with myriads of those exquisite anemones, lilac and purple, which make the woods of Italy in springtime a perpetual joy to us who come from colder climates; and among these, a profusion of smaller blossoms trailing on the ground, crimson, white and orange, making such a mass of colour as the most cunning gardener would seek vainly to produce. One lingers and delays among these woods, doubting whether any sight which may be shown one further on can compensate for the loss of the cool glades.

But already over the green coppice bare grey hillsides have come in sight. They are the walls of the old crater, and here and there a puff of white smoke curling out of a cleft reminds me that the flowers are only here on sufferance, and that the whole hollow is in fact but waiting the moment when its hidden fires will break forth again, and vomit destruction over all the country. A few yards further on the coppice falls away. The flowers persist in carpeting the 31ground; but in a little way they too cease, the soil grows grey and blasted. Full in front there rises a strange scene of desolation. The wall of the crater is precipitous and black. At its base there are openings and piles of discoloured earth which suggest the débris of some factory of chemicals, an impression which is driven home by the yellow stains of sulphur which lie in every direction on the grey bottom of the crater. From one vast rent in the soil a towering pillar of white smoke pours out with a loud hissing noise, and blows away in wreaths and coils over the dark surface of the cliff.

There is something curiously arresting in this quick passage from a green glade carpeted with flowers to the calcined ash and the grey desolation of this broken hillside. Of vegetation there is almost none, except a stunted heather which creeps hardily towards the blast hole. A little way off, towards the right, lies a level space sunk beneath the surrounding land, not unlike the fashion of an asphalt skating rink, so even in its surface that it resembles the work of man, and one strolls towards it to discover with what purpose anyone had dared to tamper with the soil in a spot where so thin a crust lies over bottomless pits of fire. But when one steps out upon the level flat, it reveals itself at once to be no human work. The guide stamps with his foot, and remarks that the sound is hollow. It is indeed, most unpleasantly so. He jumps upon it, and the surface quivers. You beg him to spare you further demonstrations, and walking gingerly on tiptoe, wishing at each step that you were safe in Regent Street once more, you follow him out towards the middle of this devilish crust, which rocks so easily and covers something which you hope devoutly you may never see. Midway in the expanse the fellow pauses in 32triumph—he has reached what he is confident will please you. He is standing by a hole, just such an opening as is made in a frozen lake in winter for the watering of animals. From it there emerges a little vapour and a curious low sound, like that which a child will make with pouting lips. The guide grins, crouching by the opening; you, on the other hand, hang back, in doubt whether the crust may not break off and suddenly enlarge the hole. You are encouraged forwards, and at last, peering nervously down the hole, you see with keen and lively interest that the crust appeared to have about the thickness of your walking-stick, at which depth there is a lake of boiling mud. The grey mud stirs and seethes in the round vent-hole, rising and falling, while on its surface the gas collects slowly into a huge bubble, which forms and bursts and then collects again.

For my part I do not deny that the sight fascinated me, but it deprived me of all wish to tread further on that shaking crust, and I sped back as lightly as I might, wishing all the way for wings, to where there was at least sound, green earth for a footing, in place of pumice stone and hardened mud, which some day, surely, will fly into splinters, and leave the seething, steaming lake once more open to the heavens.

POZZUOLI.

From the hillside just beyond the gate of the Solfatara one gazes down on the town of Pozzuoli, brown and ancient, looking, I do not doubt, much the same unto this hour as when the Apostle Paul landed there from the *Castor and Pollux*, a ship of Alexandria which had wintered in the Island of Melita. But if the town itself, the very houses clustered on the hill, preserve the aspect which they bore twenty centuries ago, so much cannot be said for the sea-front, which is vastly changed. Pozzuoli in those days must have rung with the noise of ships entering or departing.33Its quays were clamorous with all the speeches of the East; its great trade in corn needed long warehouses near the water's edge; its amphitheatre was built for the games of a people numbering many thousands. But now the little boats which come and go are too few to break the long silence of the city, and

9

there are scarce any other noises in the place than the shout of children at their games, or the loud crack of the vetturino's whip as the strangers rattle through the streets on their way to Baiæ.

It was the fall of Capua which made the trade of Pozzuoli, and it was the rise of Ostia that destroyed it. Capua, long the first town of Italy by reason of its commerce and its luxury, lost that pre-eminence in the year 211 B.C., when the Romans avenged the adhesion of the city to the cause of Hannibal. That act of punishment made Rome the chief mart of merchants from the East, and the nearest port to the Eternal City being Pozzuoli, the trade flowed thither naturally. Naples no doubt had a finer harbour; but Naples was not in Roman hands, while Pozzuoli was. Ostia, before the days of the Emperor Claudius, who carried out great works there, was a port of smallest consequence. Thus the harbour of Pozzuoli was continually full of ships. They came from Spain, from Sardinia, from Elba, bringing iron, which was wrought into fine tools by cunning workmen of the town; from Africa, from Cyprus, and all the trading ports of Asia Minor and the isles of the Ægean. Thither came also the merchants of Phœnicia, bringing with them all those gorgeous wares which moved the prophet Ezekiel to utter so great a chant of glory and its doom. "Tarshish was thy merchant by reason of the multitude of all kinds of riches; with silver, iron, tin, and lead they traded in thy fairs.... These were thy merchants in all sorts of things, in 34blue clothes and broidered work and in chests of rich apparel, bound with cords and made of cedar among thy merchandise. The ships of Tarshish did sing of thee in thy market. Thou wast replenished and made very glorious in the midst of the seas." All that most noble description of the commerce of Tyre returns irresistibly upon the mind when one looks back on the greatness of Pozzuoli, where the Tyrians themselves had a mighty factory and all the nations of the East brought their wares for sale. Most of all the town rejoiced when the great fleet hove in sight which came each year from Egypt in the spring. Seneca has left us a description of the stir. The fleet of traders was preceded some way in advance by light, swift sailing ships which heralded its coming. They could be known a long way off, for they sailed through the narrow strait between Capri and the mainland with topsails flying, a privilege allowed to none but ships of Alexandria. Then all the town made ready to hasten to the water's edge, to watch the sailors dancing on the quays, or to gloat over the wonders which had travelled thither from Arabia, India, and perhaps even far Cathay.

Well, all this is an old story now—too old, perhaps, to be of any striking interest—yet here upon the shore is still the vast old Temple of Serapis, the Egyptian deity whom the strangers worshipped. One knows not by what slow stages the Egyptians departed and the ancient temple was deserted. The only certain fact is that at some period the whole inclosure was buried deep beneath the sea, and after long centuries raised up again by some fresh movement of the swaying shore.

COLUMNS IN THE SERAPEON, POZZUOLI.

Strange as this seems to those who have not watched the perpetual heavings and subsidences of a volcanic land, the testimony of the fact is 35unmistakably in sight of all. For the sacred inclosure once hallowed to the rite of Serapis is still not allotted to any other purpose; and the visitor who enters it finds many of the ancient columns still erect. It is a vast quadrangle, once paved with squares of marble. There was a covered peristyle, and in the centre another smaller temple. Many of the columns of fine marble which once adorned the abode of the goddess were reft from her in the last century, when the spot was cleared of all the soil and brushwood which had grown up about it; but three huge pillars of cipollino, once forming part of the pronaos, are still erect; and what is singular about them is that, beginning at a height of some twelve feet from the ground and extending some nine feet further up, the marble is honeycombed with holes, drilled in countless numbers deep into the round surface of the columns.

There is no animal in earth or air which will attack stone in this destructive manner; but in the sea there is a little bivalve, called by naturalists "lithodomus," whose only happiness lies in boring. This animal is still found plentifully in the Bay of Baiæ. His shells still lie in the perforations of the columns; and it is thus demonstrated that the ancient temple must have been plunged beneath the sea, that it lay there long ages, till at length some fresh convulsion reared it up once more out of the reach of fish. Surely few buildings have sustained so strange a fate!

The holes drilled by the patient lithodomus, as I have said, do not extend through the whole height of the column, but have a range of about nine feet only, which is thus the measure of the space left for the operations of the busy spoiler. Above the ring of perforations one sees the indications of 36ordinary weathering, so that the upper edge of the holes doubtless marks the level of high water, and the summit of the columns stood up above the waves. But one does not see readily what protected the lower portion of the marble. Possibly, before the land swayed downwards something fell which covered them.

In the twelfth century the Solfatara broke forth into eruption for the last time. The scoriæ and stones fell thick in Pozzuoli, and they filled the court of the Serapeon to the height of some twelve feet. Probably the sea had then already stolen into the courtyard; and it may be that the earthquakes attending the eruption caused the subsidence which left the lithodomus free to crawl and bore upon the stones which saw the ancient mysteries of Serapis. At any rate it was another volcanic outburst which raised the dripping columns from the sea in 1538, since which time the land has been swaying slowly down once more, so that now if anyone cares to scratch the gravel in the courtyard he will find he has constructed a pool of clear sea water.

10

It is a strange and terrible thing to realise the existence of hidden forces which can sway the solid earth as lightly as a puff of wind disturbs an awning; none the less terrible because the ground has risen and fallen so very gently that the pillars stand erect upon their bases. Once more, as at the Solfatara, one has the sense of treading over some vast chasm filled with a sleeping power which may awake at any moment. Let us go on beyond the city and see what has happened elsewhere upon this bay, so beautiful and yet so deadly, a strange dwelling-place for men who have but one life to pass on the surface of this earth.

In passing out of Pozzuoli one sees upon the right 37the vine-clad slopes of Monte Barbaro. That also is a crater, the loftiest in the Phlegræan fields, but long at rest. The peasants believe the mountain to contain vast treasures—statues of kings and queens, all cast of solid gold, with heaps of coin and jewels so immense that great ships would be needed to carry them away. These tales are very old. I sometimes wonder whether they may not have had their source in dim memory of the great hoard of treasure which the Goths stored in the citadel of Cumæ, and which, when their power was utterly broken, they were supposed to have surrendered to the imperial general Narses. Perhaps they did not; perhaps—but what is the use of suppositions? Petrarch heard the stories when he climbed Monte Barbaro in 1343. Many men, his guides told him, had set out to seek the treasure, but had not returned, lost in some horrible abyss in the heart of the mountain. They must have neglected the conditions of success. They should have watched the moon, and learnt how to catch and prison down the ghosts which guard the precious heaps, otherwise the whole mass, even if found, will turn to lumps of coal!

What a wilderness of craters! Small wonder if wild tales exist yet in a district which in old days, and even modern ones, has been encompassed with fear. One volcano is enough to fill the country east of Naples with terror. But here are many—active, doubtless, in very different ages—Monte Barbaro, Monte Cigliano, Monte Campana, Monte Grillo, which hems in the more recent crater of Avernus much as Somma encircles the eruptive crater of Vesuvius. What terrible sights must have been witnessed here in those far-distant days when these and other craters were in action!—"affliction such as 38was not from the beginning of the creation which God created" until then! But a few miles away across the sea is Monte Epomeo, towering out of Ischia. That was the chief vent of the volcanic forces in Roman times; and then the Phlegræan fields were still. Epomeo has been silent for five centuries; but that proves nothing, and there are people who suggest that the awful earthquake which destroyed Casamicciola may be just such a prelude to the awakening of Epomeo as was the convulsion which shook Pompeii to its foundations sixteen years before its final destruction. *Di avertite omen!*

We need not, however, go back five centuries for facts that bid men heed what may be passing underground about the shores of this blue bay. Here is one too large to be overlooked, immediately in front of us—no other than the green slope of Monte Nuovo, a hill of aspect both innocent and ancient, ridged with a few pine trees by whose aid the mountain contrives to look as if it had stood there beside the Lucrine Lake as long as any eminence in sight. This is a false pretension. There was no such mountain when Petrarch climbed the neighbouring height, nor for full two centuries afterwards. What Petrarch saw exists no longer. He looked down upon the Lucrine Lake connected with the sea by a deep channel, and formed with Lake Avernus into one wide inlet fit for shipping. This was the Portus Julius, a harbour so large that the whole Roman fleet could manœuvre in it. The canals and piers were in existence less than four centuries ago; and this great work, so remarkable a witness to the sea power of the Romans, would doubtless have lasted unto our day had it not been for the intrusion of Monte Nuovo, which destroyed 39the channels and reduced the Lucrine Lake to the dimensions of a sedgy duck pond.

The catastrophe is worth describing, for no other in historic times has so greatly changed the aspect of this coast or robbed it of so large a portion of its beauty. For full two years there had been constant earthquakes throughout Campania. Some imprisoned force was heaving and struggling to release itself, and all men began to fear a great convulsion. On the 27th of September, 1538, the earth tremors seemed to concentrate themselves around the town of Pozzuoli. More than twenty shocks struck the town in rapid succession. By noon upon the 28th the sea was retreating visibly from the pleasant shore beside the Lucrine Lake, where stood the ruined villa of the Empress Agrippina, and a more modern villa of the Anjou kings, who were used, like all their predecessors in Campania, to take their ease in summer among the luxuriant vegetation of the hills whose volcanic forces were believed to be lulled in a perpetual sleep.

For three hundred yards the sea fell back, its bottom was exposed, and the peasants came with carts and carried off the fish left dry upon the strand. The whole of the flat ground between Lake Avernus and the sea had been heaved upwards; but at eight o'clock on the following morning it began to sink again, though not as yet with any violence. It fell apparently at one spot only, and to a depth of about thirteen feet, while from the hollow thus formed there burst out a stream of very cold water, which was investigated cautiously by several persons, some of whom found it by no means cold, but tepid and sulphurous. Ere long those who were examining the new spring perceived that the sunken ground was rising awfully. It was upreared so rapidly that by 40noon the hollow had become a hill, and as the new slopes swelled and rose where never yet had there been a rising ground, the crest burst and fire broke out from the summit.

"About this time," says one Francesco del Nero, who dwelt at Pozzuoli, "about this time fire issued forth and formed the great gulf with such a force, noise, and shining light that I, who was standing in my garden, was seized with great terror. Forty minutes afterwards, though unwell, I got upon a neighbouring height, and by my troth it was a splendid fire, that threw up for a long time much earth and many stones. They fell back again all

11

round the gulf, so that towards the sea they formed a heap in the shape of a crossbow, the bow being a mile and a half and the arrow two-thirds of a mile in dimensions. Towards Pozzuoli it has formed a hill nearly of the height of Monte Morello, and for a distance of seventy miles the earth and trees are covered with ashes. On my own estate I have neither a leaf on the trees nor a blade of grass.... The ashes that fell were soft, sulphurous, and heavy. They not only threw down the trees, but an immense number of birds, hares, and other animals were killed."

Amid such throes and pangs Monte Nuovo was born, and the events of that natal day suggest hesitation before we label any crater of the Phlegræan fields with the word "extinct." It is granted that in the course of geologic ages volcanic forces do expend themselves. The British Isles, for instance, contain many dead volcanoes, once at least as formidable as any in the world. But the exhaustion has been the work of countless ages, and many generations of mankind will come and go upon this planet before the coasts of Baiæ and Misenum are as safe as those of Cumberland.41

While speaking of these terrors, I have been halting by the wayside at a point, not far beyond the outskirts of Pozzuoli, where two roads unite, the one going inland beneath the slope of Monte Barbaro, the other following the outline of the curved shore on which Baiæ stands. The inland road is the one which goes to Cumæ, and is entitled to respect, if not to veneration, as being among the oldest of Italian highways, the approach to the most ancient Greek settlement in Italy, mother city of Pozzuoli and of Naples, not to mention the mysterious Palæopolis, whose very existence has been disputed by some scholars. Some say it was more than ten centuries before Christ's birth that the bold Greeks of Eubœa came up this coast, where already their kinsmen were known as traders, and having settled first on Ischia moved to the opposite mainland, and built their acropolis upon a crag of trachyte which overhung the sea. Their life was a long warfare. More than once they owed salvation to the aid of their kinsmen from Sicilian cities, yet they made their foundation a mighty power in Italy. With one hand they held back the fierce Samnite mountaineers who coveted their wealth, and gave out with the other more and more freely that noble culture which has had no rival yet.

One must wonder why these strangers coming from the south passed by so many gulfs and harbours shaped out of the enduring rock only to choose a site for their new city at the foot of all these craters. It may be that chance had its part in the matter; in some slight indication of wind or wave they may have seen the guidance of a deity. Indeed, an ancient legend says their ships were guided by Apollo, who sent a dove flying over sea to lead them. But again, the fires of the district were sacred in their eyes. The 42subterranean gods were near at hand, and on the dark shore of Lake Avernus they recognised the path by which Ulysses sought the shades. The mysteries of religion drew them there, and the cave of the Cumæan sibyl became the most venerated shrine in Italy. Lastly, one may perceive that the volcanic tract, full of terrors for the Etruscan or Samnite mountaineer who looked down upon its fires from afar, must have made attack difficult from the land.

Greek cities, such as Cumæ, studded the coast of southern Italy. "Magna Græcia" they called the country; and Greek it was, in blood, in art, and language. How powerful and how rich is better understood at Pæstum than it can be now at Cumæ, where, with the single exception of the Arco Felice, there remains no dignity of ruin, nothing but waste, crumbling fragments, half buried in the turf of vineyards. Such shattered scraps of masonry may aid a skilful archæologist to imagine what the city was; but in the path of untrained men they are nothing but a hindrance, and anyone who has already in his mind a picture of the greatness of Eubœan Cumæ had better leave it there without attempt to verify its accuracy on the spot.

Observations similar to these apply justly to most of the remaining sights in this much-vaunted district. The guides are perfectly untrustworthy. They give high-sounding names to every broken wall, and there is not a burrow in the ground which they cannot connect with some name that has rung round the world. It is absolutely futile to hope to recapture the magic with which Virgil clothed this country. The cave of the Sibyl under the Acropolis of Cumæ was destroyed by the imperial general Narses when he besieged the Goths. The dark, wet passage on the shore of Lake Avernus, to which the name of 43the Sibyl is given by the guides, is probably part of an old subterranean road, not devoid of interest, but is certainly not worth the discomfort of a visit. The Lake of Avernus has lost its terrors. It is no longer dark and menacing, and anyone may satisfy himself by a cursory inspection that birds by no means shun it now.

The truth is that this region compares ill in attractions with that upon the other side of Naples. In days not far distant, when brigands still invested all the roads and byways of the Sorrento peninsula, strangers found upon the Bay of Baiæ almost the only excursion which they could make in safety; and imbued as every traveller was with classical tradition, they still discovered on this shore that fabled beauty which it may once have possessed. There is now little to suggest the aspect of the coast when Roman fashion turned it into the most voluptuous abode of pleasure known in any age, and when the shore was fringed with marble palaces whose immense beauty is certainly not to be imagined by contemplating any one of the fragments that stud the hillside, though it may perhaps be realised in some dim way by anyone who will stand within the atrium of some great house at Pompeii, say the house of Pansa, who will note the splendour of the vista through the colonnaded peristyle, and will then remember that the Pompeiian houses were not famed for beauty, while the palaces of Baiæ were.

Baiæ, like Cumæ, is lost beyond recall. Fairyland is shattered into fragments; and the guides who baptise them with ridiculous names know no more than any one of us what it is they say. Really, since the tragedy of that first great outbreak of Vesuvius did, as Goethe said, create more pleasure for posterity than any other which has struck mankind, one is 44disposed to wish that it had been more widespread. If only the ashes had rained down a trifle harder at Misenum and at Baiæ, what noble Roman buildings might have survived unto this day, conserved by the kind wisdom of the mountain! What matter if more of that generation had been left houseless? It nearly happened, if Pliny's letter is not exaggerated. "The ashes now began to fall on us," he says, of his escape with his mother from the palace at Misenum, "though in no great quantity. I turned my head, and observed behind us a thick smoke which came rolling after us like a torrent. We had scarce stepped out of the path when darkness overspread us, not like the darkness of a cloudy night, nor that when there is no moon, but that of a closed room when all the lights are out. Nothing was to be heard but the shrieks of women, the screams of children, and the cries of men, some calling for their children, others for their parents, others for their husbands, and only distinguishing each other by their voices.... At length a glimmering light appeared, which we imagined to be rather the forerunner of an approaching burst of flames, as in truth it was, than the return of day. However, the fire fell at some distance from us. Then again we were immersed in thick darkness, and a heavy shower of ashes rained upon us, which we were obliged every now and then to shake off, otherwise we should have been crushed and buried in the heap...." It is an awful tale. Anyone can see how nearly all this region escaped the fate of Pompeii, and how narrowly the modern world lost a greater joy than that of contemplating the city by the Sarno.

CASTLE OF BAIÆ.

However, it did not happen so, and there is comparatively little satisfaction in describing all the melancholy scraps of what was marvellously beautiful. I have nothing to say about them which 45is not said as fully in the guide-books. There is, however, something which more piques my interest in the narrow tongue of land parting the Lucrine Lake from the sea. There is, or was, a causeway here so ancient that even the Greeks, who settled at Cumæ so many centuries before our era, did not know who built it; and being in the dark about the matter, put down the construction to no less a person than the god Hercules, who made it, they declared, for the passage of the oxen which he had taken from Geryon, the monster whom he slew in Gades. It was no small work, even for Hercules. The dam was eight stadia long, nearly a mile, made of large stone slabs laid with such skill that they withstood the sea for many centuries. Who could have been the builders of this dam in days so ancient that even the Greek settlers did not know its origin? Rome was not in those days. There were factories and traders on the coast,—Phœnicians perhaps. But why guess about a question so impossible to solve? The curiosity of the thing is worth noting; for the age of civilisation on these coasts is very great.

At this spot beside the Lucrine Lake, where the sea is lapping slowly, almost stealthily, on the one hand, and the diminished waters of the lake lie still and reedy on the other, one memory, more than any other, haunts my mind. It cannot have been far from this very spot, certainly in sight of it, that there stood in old Roman days the villa of the Empress Agrippina, mother of the Emperor Nero, and it was at Baiæ, lying just across the blue curved bay, that he planned her murder, as soon as he discovered that she loved power, like himself, and stood in the way of certain schemes on which he set great store.

The fleet which lay at Capo Miseno, the great naval station of those days, was commanded by one 46Anicetus, a freedman, who, being of an ingenious mechanical turn of mind, devised a ship of a sort likely to prove useful to any tyrant anxious to speed his friends into the nether world without suspicion. It had much the same aspect as other ships when viewed from without; but a careful observer of its inward parts might notice that the usual tight boltings were replaced by movable ones, which could be shot back at will, so that on a given signal the whole ship would fall to pieces. This pretty toy was of course not designed to make long voyages—it was enough if it would reach deep water.

Nero was delighted. He saw now how to avoid all scandal. The Empress was at that moment on the sea, homeward bound from Antium, and designed to land at Bauli, which lay near Baiæ on the bay. The ship was prepared, the bolts were shot, and the pretty pinnace lay waiting on the beach at Bauli when the Empress disembarked. And there too was Nero, come from Baiæ on purpose to pay duty to his mother and invite her to spend the Feast of Minerva with him at Baiæ, whither he hoped she would cross over in the boat which he had had the pleasure of fitting up with the splendour which was proper to her rank.

Agrippina knew her son, and was suspicious. She would go to Baiæ, but preferred to follow the road in a litter. That night, however, when the festivities at Baiæ were over, her fears vanished. Nero had been affectionate and dutiful. He had assured her of his love. It would be churlish to refuse to enter the boat which he had fitted out for her, and which having been brought over from Bauli now lay waiting for her on the sands. It was a bright night, brilliant with stars. The bay must have looked incomparably peaceful and lovely. On the shore there were crowds 47of bathers, all the fashionable world of Rome, drawn thither by the presence of the Emperor, and attracted out by the beauty of the night. At such a time and place nothing surely could be planned against her. She went on board with her attendants. The rowers put off from land. They had gone but a little way when the canopy under which Agrippina lay crashed down on her and killed one of her waiting women. A moment's examination showed that it had been weighted with pigs of lead. Almost at the same moment the murderers on board withdrew the bolts. The machinery, however, refused to act. The planks still held together; and the sailors despairing of their bloodmoney, rushed to the side of the ship and tried to capsize it. They

13

succeeded so far as to throw the Empress and her attendants into the sea. Agrippina retained sufficient presence of mind to lie silent on the water, supporting herself as best she could, while the sailors thrashed the sea with oars, hoping thus to make an end of their victim, and one poor girl who thought to save herself by crying out that she was the Empress had her brains beaten out for her pains. At last the shore boats, whose owners could not know that they were interrupting the Emperor's dearest wish, arrived upon the scene, picked up the Empress, and carried her to her villa on this Lucrine lake.

It would have been wiser to flee to a greater distance, if indeed there was safety in any Roman territory for the mother of the Emperor when he desired to slay her. That night, as she lay bruised and weak, deserted by her attendants, a band of murderers rushed in, headed by Anicetus, who thus redeemed his credit with his master when his more ingenious scheme had failed. "Strike the womb that bore this monster!" cried the Empress, and so died.48

"Then," says Merivale, from whose most vivid story this is but an outline, "began the torments which never ceased to gnaw the heart strings of the matricide. Agrippina's spectre flitted before him.... The trumpet heard at her midnight obsequies still blared with ghostly music from the hill of Misenum."

CHAPTER III

THE BEAUTIES AND TRADITIONS OF
THE POSILIPO

WITH SOME OBSERVATIONS UPON VIRGIL
THE ENCHANTER

49
It was setting towards evening when I turned my back on Baiæ and drove through Pozzuoli along the dusty road which runs beside the sea in the direction of Posilipo. All day I had seen the blunt headland of tufa lying like a cloud on the further side of the blue bay; and from hour to hour as I plodded through the blasted country, my thoughts turned pleasantly to the great rampart which stood solid when all the region further west was shaken like a cornfield by the wind, and beyond which lies the city, with its endless human tragedies and its fatal beauty unimpaired by the possession of many masters. "Bocca baciata non perde ventura...," the scandalous old proverb has a sweet application to the city, and the mouth which has been kissed by conquerors and tyrants is still as fresh and rosy as when first uplifted for the delight of man.

I think this angle of the bay more beautiful than Baiæ or Misenum. In Roman times the opposite shore may have excelled it; but one does not know the precise form of the ancient coastline. As I advanced towards the headland, leaving behind the bathing-place of Bagnoli, and passing out on the wide 50green flats which at that point occupy the valley mouth, the lofty crag of Nisida began to detach itself from the mainland, and a channel of blue sea shining between the two glowed sweetly in the increasing warmth of evening light. The island is a crater, a finely broken mass of volcanic rock and verdure, flecked here with light and there with shadow. One side of the crater lacks half of its rim, so that there is a little port. Down by the edge of the many-coloured water is a pier, where half a dozen boats lie rocking; and from a similar landing-place upon the shingly beach of the mainland a fisherman is hailing some comrade on the island. The answering shout floats back faint and distant through the clear air, and a boat pushes off, sculled slowly by a man standing erect and facing towards the bow, in the ancient fashion of the Mediterranean. At this point I dismiss my carriage, for I have many things to think about, and do not want the company of the chattering, extortionate vetturino. Having seen him go off up the hill, cracking his whip like pistol shots, and urging on his eager pony in the full hope of a fare at the Punta di Posilipo, I stroll on up the long ascent towards the shoulder of the hill, stopping often to watch the gold light grow warmer on the sea, tinging the volcanic crags of Ischia, until my enjoyment of the view is broken by an uninvited companion, who thrusts himself upon me with a reminder that I have reached the opening of the Grotto of Sejanus.

I had forgotten all about the grotto, though indeed it was the point for which I should have made, and but for the interruption of the lively little Tuscan who acts as custodian, I might have walked by without going in. I accepted gratefully the voluble assurances that this is indeed the most wonderful 51and authentic grotto on the Posilipo, far surpassing those twin tunnels through which one goes from Naples to Pozzuoli; and the guide, having caught up a torch of smouldering tow, and vented a few hearty curses on the Neapolitans, who lie, he says, without recollection of eternity, conducted me into a long passage of utter and palpable darkness.

"Nè femmena nè tela a lume di cannela," say the Neapolitans—You must not judge either a woman or a weft by candlelight. This is very true, and many a man has suffered from forgetting it. But when it is a case of grottoes, there is no choice; and accordingly I delivered myself over to the chatter of the Tuscan.

The lively little man was extolling the superior character of his own countrymen of Tuscany; and when his torch flickered out with no warning, leaving us in sudden blackness in the bowels of the earth, his indignation blazed out fiercely against the worthless knaves who sold such tow in Naples. I paid little heed to him, for the grandeur and the silence of the place appeal to the imagination. I was treading on a smooth and even floor, between walls of tufa which had been chiselled out so straight that whenever I looked back the entrance shone behind me like a star across a vast dark sky. The air was sweet and fresh, filtering through some

14

hidden openings of the rock. The relighted torch flashed now on Roman brickwork, now on arches of massive stone built to increase the strength of the vault, and fit it the better for those great processions of chariots and horsemen which came and went to the villa at the further end, returning from a hunting party with dogs which had wearied out the game on the hills of Astroni, or escorting the gladiators landed at Pozzuoli for some combat in the theatre which now lies so waste and 52desolate amid the vineyards. How this passage must have rung with shouts and laughter in old Roman days! But now it is as silent as the tomb; and one passes on a full half-mile in darkness, to emerge at length with heated fancy and high memories of Roman splendour, on nothing but a ruinous cottage, a starved vineyard, and a paltry garden-ground of common vegetables!

It is not possible, one thinks impatiently, that this trumpery of vines and cabbages can be all there is to see at the further end of a passage so ancient and hewn with such vast labour through the solid rock; and indeed, when one's eyes are used to the sunshine, one perceives that the garden plot lies like a dust heap on the ruins of a splendid palace. Treading across a patch of vegetables, covering I know not what remains of marble portico or colonnade, I peered down through the trails of budding vines into a hollow where some fragments of old masonry project still from the earth, and after much gazing perceived that the sides of the hollow rise in tiers, one bank above another, to the height of seventeen rows. So that here, on this now lonely creek of the Posilipo, in face of Nisida and all the blue reach of the Bay of Baiæ, there was once a theatre, ringing with shouts and applause, and by it all the other buildings of a noble mansion. It is a poor ruin now, stripped of the marbles which once made it splendid. There are vast structures on the slopes and in the sea itself: an Odeon, another building seated like a theatre, and relics innumerable of one of the greatest of all Roman villas, which must have been incomparably lovely. If only one such might have lasted to our day!

The long darkness of the grotto, the exit on the hillside, where the ancient splendour is so shattered, 53combine to create a sense of mystery which one never loses on the Posilipo. The sea frets and chafes about the jagged reefs at the base of the headland, echoing and resounding in caves of vast antiquity, where broken marbles and defaced inscriptions give substance to the tales of treasure which the fishers say lies hidden in them to this hour. The dullest of mankind would be smitten with some touch of fancy on this spot, much more the quick-witted Neapolitans, whose rich imagination has run riot among the relics of a splendid past.

The impression of this lonely cliff is characteristic of all the headland. I send away my guide, who can do nothing more for me, and perch myself upon a scrap of ancient wall, whence I can look past the green island of Nisida, full in the warm light of the westering sun, over the wide bay to where the black peak of Ischia, towering into the clear sky, begins to shine as if some goddess had brushed it with liquid gold.

There is a cavern in the cliff at no great distance which the fishermen call "La Grotta dei Tuoni" (The Cave of Thunders); I scarcely know why, unless it be because the sea bellows so loudly when it is driven by the storm wind round the vaults and hollows of the rock. The cave is accessible only by boat; and, like many another cleft in the soft tufa of this headland, it is believed to hide immeasurable riches, left there since the days when every cliff bore its white Roman villa, and all the shady caverns were the cool arbours of their pleasure grounds. From the creek of Marechiano, which cleaves the Posilipo in half, up to the very spot on which I sit, there is no break in the succession of the ruins. Ancient cisterns lie upon the beaches, the green tide washes over shattered colonnades, the boatmen peering down 54through the translucent water as they sink their nets see the light waver round the foundations of old palaces, and the seaweeds stir fantastically on the walls. It is little wonder if no one of them can rid himself of the belief in spirits wandering yet about the wreck of so much splendour, or shake off the fear

"Lest the dead should, from their sleep
Bursting o'er the starlit deep,
Lead a rapid masque of death
O'er the waters of his path."

As for this cave of the thunders, the story goes that one day certain Englishmen presented themselves before a boatman who was lounging on the quay of Santa Lucia at Naples and demanded whether he would take them on his skiff into the grotto.

Pepino had seen the cavern many times, and did not fear it. "Why not?" he said, and the bargain was struck. As they rowed across the crescent bay of the Chiaia, past the Palazzo di Donna Anna, and under the hillside where the whispering pines grow down the high cliff faces, and golden lemons glow in the shade of marble terraces, the Englishmen were very silent; and Pepino, who loved chatter, began to feel oppressed. He did not quite like the zeal with which they sat studying a huge volume; for he knew that great books were of more use to magicians than to honest people, who were quite content with little ones, or better still with none at all. So he looked askance at the English students as he guided his boat to the mouth of the grotto of the thunders, and ran in out of the sunshine to the cool green shades and wavering lights among which the old treasure of the Romans lies concealed.

FISHING STAGE, SANTA LUCIA, NAPLES.

The Englishmen rose up, and one of them, taking the book in both hands, began to read aloud. Who 55can tell what were the words? They were strange and very potent; for as they rolled and echoed round

15

the sea-cave it seemed as if the vaulted roof rose higher, and Pepino, glancing this way and that in terror, saw that the level of the water was sinking. Shelf by shelf the sea sank down the rock, leaving dripping walls of which no living man had ever seen the shape before; and Pepino, keeping the boat steady with his oars, shook with fear as he saw the top of a marble staircase rear itself erect and shiny out of the depths of the ocean. Still the English student rolled out the sonorous words, which rang triumphantly through the cave, and still the water sank stair by stair, till suddenly it paused—the readers voice had stopped, and slowly, steadily the sea began to rise again.

The spell was broken. A page was missing from the book! The Englishman in despair clutched at the pages as if he would tear them piecemeal. Instantly the crash of thunder rang through the cave, the sea surged back to its old level, the marble staircase leading to the treasure was engulfed, and the boatman, screaming on the name of the Madonna, was whirled out of the cavern into the light of day again.

Close below me is a little reef or island of yellow pozzolano stone, jutting out from the Punta di Coroglio, which is the name of the most westerly cliff of the Posilipo, that through which the tunnel runs. Under the island there is a tiny creek with a beach of yellow sand; the spot is so silent that I can hear the ripple plashing on the beach. That rock is a famous one. It is the "Scoglio di Virgilio," the Rock of Virgil, by all tradition a favourite haunt of the great poet, and the spot in which he practised his enchantments.56

Petrarch said he did not believe in those enchantments. But then King Robert questioned him about them at a moment when both were riding with a gallant party, and the joy of life was surging high enough to make men doubt all achievements but those of battle or of love. Had Petrarch sat alone watching the sunset bathe the Scoglio di Virgilio with gold, he might have judged the matter differently. At any rate twenty generations of Neapolitans since his day have accepted the beliefs of thirty more who went before them, and set down Virgil as a magician. Why must we be wiser than fifty generations of mankind?

To be a wizard is not to be wicked! Virgil's fair fame is in no danger. There was no malignity in any of the spells wrought out on that little headland. Each of them conferred a benefit on the city which the poet loved. One by one the woes of Naples were assuaged by the beneficent enchanter; its flies, its serpents, the fatal tendency of butcher's meat to go bad, exposure to volcanic fires, all were held in check by the power of the enchanter.

A stranger visiting Naples ten centuries ago would have found it studded with the ingenious inventions of the wizard. Perhaps the device for bridling the audacity of Vesuvius might be the first to strike him. It was nothing less than a horse of bronze bestridden by an archer, whose notched arrow was ever on the string, its point directed at the summit of the mountain. This menace sufficed to hold the unruly demons of the fire in check, and might do so to this hour were it not that one day a countryman coming into Naples from the Campagna, and looking at the statue for the hundredth time felt bored by seeing the archer had not fired off his arrow yet, and so did it for him. The shaft sped through the air, striking the rim of 57the crater, which straightway boiled over and spouted fire, and from that day to this no man has found the means of placing another arrow on the string. It is a thousand pities. San Gennaro has taken up the duty now, and stands pointing imperiously with outstretched hand bidding the volcano halt. He had some success too. In 1707, when the fires of the volcano turned night into day, and its smoke converted day into night, San Gennaro was carried in procession as far as the Porta Capuana, and had no sooner come in sight of the mountain than the thunders ceased, the smoke was scattered, the stars appeared, and Naples was at peace. But as a rule the holiness of the saint impresses the demons less than the menace of the arrow, and the mountain goes on burning.

As for the bronze fly which the good poet made and set high on one of the city gates, where it banished every other insect from the town, it certainly is not in Naples now. Many people must have wished it were. The story runs that the young Marcellus was intercepted by Virgil one day as he was going fowling, and desired to decide whether he would rather have a bird which would catch all other birds, or a fly which would drive away all flies. Nobody who knows Naples can doubt the answer. Marcellus, it is true, thought fit to consult the Emperor Augustus before replying; but that fact only adds to the weight of his decision. He decided on the fly, and many a man listening in the midnight to the deadly humming outside his mosquito curtains will lament the loss of Virgil's fly.

It is an Englishman, one John of Salisbury, who collects these pretty tales for us; and he has another which, as it supplies a reason for an historical fact which must have puzzled many people in the history 58of Naples, is the better worth recording, and may indeed have the luck to please both clever and stupid people in one moment.

The puzzling fact is to discover how on earth it happened that the city which in Middle Ages bore a somewhat evil reputation for surrendering itself light-heartedly at the first summons of any conqueror, yet held such a different repute in earlier days, having remained faithful to the Greek Empire in Constantinople when Amalfi had fallen and Salerno received a stranger garrison, which resisted heroically every attack of Lombard or of Norman, and saw army after army retire baffled from before its walls. Whither had all that stout-heartedness fled in the days when French, Spanish, and German conquerors found no more resistance in the Siren city than in a beautiful woman to whom one man's love is as much as any other's? How came that old glory to sink into shame, to accept slavery and to forget faith? The answer is that in the old days the city was kept by a spell of the enchanter Virgil.

16

Virgil, it seems, musing on this point of rock throughout long moonlight nights, had constructed a palladium. It consisted of a model of the city, inclosed in a glass bottle, and as long as this fragile article remained intact the hosts of besiegers encamped in vain beneath the walls. The Emperor Henry the Sixth was the first who managed to break in. The city fathers rushed to their palladium to discover why for the first time it had failed to protect them. The reason was but too plain. There was a crack in the glass!

Through that crack all the virtue went out of the palladium, and until the great upstirring of heroic hearts which the world owes to France at the close of the eighteenth century, Naples was never credited 59again with any marked disposition to resist attack or to strike courageously for freedom. I am not sure whether those who know best the inner heart of Naples would claim that the great deeds wrought since then are to be attributed to any new palladium; but, for my part, if spells are to be spoken of, I prefer to hold that the long age of sloth and slavery is that which needs the explanation of black magic, and that neither the loyal Naples of old days nor the free Naples of the present time owes any debt to other sources than its own high spirit and its natural stout heart, which slept for centuries, but are now awake again.

The setting sun has dropped so far towards the sea that the tide begins to wash in grey and gold around the yellow cliffs. The bay is covered with dark shades falling from the sky in masses, and a little wind rising from the west ruffles the water constantly. Only the ridge of Ischia yet holds the light, and there it seems as if a river of soft gold flowed along the mountain-top, vivid and pure, turning all the peak of Epomeo to a liquid reflection, impalpable as the sky itself. But the glow fades even as I watch it; and the approach of chilly evening warns me not to loiter on the lonely hillside. I wander down across the hollow, passing near the broken theatre, and so strike a path which climbs up the further hill between high walls and hedges, where it is already almost dark, bringing me out at length on the main road which crosses the headland, just where a row of booths is set to catch the soldi of those Neapolitans who have strayed out here in search of evening freshness. There is a clear, sharp air upon this high ground; and the young moon climbing up the sky sends a faint, silvery light upon the sea. The road winds on as beautifully as a man 60need wish. On the left hand rises the hill, on the right the ground drops in sharp, swift slopes, cleft with deep ravines where the cliff is sometimes sheer and sometimes passable for men. All these hollows are filled with vegetation of surpassing beauty—here a belt of dark green pines, there a grove of oranges thatched over to protect them from the sun. Golden lemons gleam out of the rich foliage, hanging thick and numberless upon the trees. The bare stems of fig trees are bursting out into their first yellow leaf; and the hedges of red roses and abutilon fill every nook with masses of bright colour unknown except in lands where spring comes with gentle touch and warm, sweet days of sunny weather. Far down amid the depths of this luxuriance of fruit and flowers the sea washes round some creek or curved white beach, and there built out with terraces and balconies of pure white stone are villas which repeat the splendour of those Roman homes over whose ruins they are built and whose altars lie still in the innumerable caverns which pierce the base of the old legendary headland.

In the silvery dusk of this spring evening the beauty of these ravines brimming over with fruits and flowers is quite magical. I pause beside a low wall, over which a man may lean breast high, and gaze down through the shadows spreading fast among the trellised paths below. The fading light has robbed the lemons of their colour; but the crimson roses are flaming still against a heavy background of dark firs, and beyond them the path winds out upon a little beach, where the tide breaks at the foot of yellow cliffs, and a boat is rocking at her moorings. Beyond the outline of the wooded cliff the grey sea lies darkening like a steely mirror; and lifting my eyes I can see the spit of rock on which 61stands the enchanted Castle of the Egg, black and grim as ever, and higher still Vesuvius towering amid the pale sky and the stars, its slowly coiling pillar of dark smoke suffused with a rosy glow, the reflection of the raging furnace hidden in its cone. Already one or two lamps are flashing on the shore. The day is nearly gone, and the beautiful Southern night is come.

Many people had wandered up from Naples to enjoy the taste of approaching summer on this height, where surely the scent of roses is more poignant than elsewhere and the outlook over land and sea is of incomparable beauty. As I walked on slowly down the road my ears caught the tremulous shrill melody of a mandolin, and a man's voice near at hand trolled forth the pretty air of "La vera sorrentina." I stopped to listen. The voice was sweet enough, and some passion was in the singer.

"Ma la sgrata sorrentina

Non ha maje di me pietà!"

The music came from a little roadside restaurant, half open to the sky, where a few people sat at tables overlooking the sea. I strolled in, and sat sipping my vino di Posilipo while the mandolin thrummed till the singer grew tired, took his fees, and went off to some other café. The wine is not what it was in Capaccio's days. "Semper Pausilypi vigeat poculum!" cries the jolly topographer, "and may Jupiter himself lead the toasts!" By all means, if he will; but I fear the son of Saturn will not be tempted from Olympus by the contents of the purple beaker set before me at the price of three soldi. "It is pure, it is fragrant, it is delicious," Capaccio goes on, waxing more eloquent with every glass. "In the fiercest heat it is grateful to the stomach, it goeth down easily, it 62promoteth moisture, it molesteth neither the liver nor the reins, nor doth it even obfuscate the head! Its virtue is not of those that pass away; for whether of this year, last year, or of God knows when, it hath still the scent of flowers, and lyeth sweetly on the tongue." I think Capaccio must have had a vineyard here, and sold his wines by auction. Far beneath me I could hear the washing of the sea, and the moon climbing up the sky scattered a gleam of silver here and there upon the water. Naples stretched darkly round the curving shore, while high upon the ridge the Castle of St. Elmo stood out black and solid against the night sky, with the low priory in front, sword and cowl dominating the city, as ever through her history, whether for good or ill.

In dusk or sunshine no man who looks upon this view will need to ask why Virgil loved it, and desired to be buried near the spot whence he had been used to watch it. Not far away upon my left, above the grotto which leads to Pozzuoli, is the tomb traditionally known as his. There are many who believe and some who doubt; but there is a mediæval tale about the matter which is well worth telling. It was commonly reported in the days of Hohenstaufen and Anjou that the bones of Virgil were buried in a castle surrounded by the sea. There is no other fortress to which this could apply than the Castle of the Egg.

In the reign of Roger, King of Sicily, a certain scholar—they are always English, in these legends!—who had wandered far in quest of learning, came into the royal presence with a petition. The King, who found him wise and grave, and took pleasure in his conversation, was willing to grant his wish, whatever it might be; whereon the Englishman replied that he would not abuse the royal favour, nor beg for any 63mere ephemeral pleasure, but would ask a thing which in the eyes of men must seem but small, namely, that he might have the bones of Virgil, wheresoever he might find them in the realm of Sicily. It was even then long since forgotten in what spot precisely the body of the great poet had been laid; and it seemed to the King little likely that a stranger from the north should be able to discover what had remained hidden from the Neapolitans. So he gave consent, and the Englishman set forth for Naples, armed with letters to the Duke, giving him full power to search wherever he would. The citizens themselves had no fear of his success in a quest where they had often failed, and so made no effort to restrain him. The scholar searched and dug, guiding his operations by the power of magic. At last he broke into the centre of a mountain, where not one cleft betrayed the existence of any cavity or tomb. There lay the body of the mighty poet, unchanged and calm as if he slept. Full eleven centuries he had lain silently in a rest unbroken by the long-resounding tread of barbarous armies from the north, flooding and desolating the fair empire which must have seemed to him likely to outlast the world. I wish that some one of those who broke into the sepulchre, and shed the light of day once more upon those features which had slept so long in darkness, had told us with what feelings he looked upon them and saw the very lips that had spoken to Augustus, and the cheek which Horace kissed. I think the men who found themselves in the sudden presence of so much greatness must have stood there with a certain tremor, as those others did who not long afterwards disturbed the bones of Arthur and of Guenevere at Glastonbury, daring to lift and touch the long fair tresses which brought Lancelot to shame.64

These men who found the tomb of Virgil would have done well if they had sealed it up again and lost the secret, so that the bones might lie unto this hour on the spot where the spirit is so well remembered. But the English scholar had the King's warrant, and claimed at least the books on which the wizard's head was propped. Those the Duke of Naples gave him, but the bones he refused, and had them taken for greater safety to Castel dell'Uovo, where they lay behind an iron grating and were shown to anyone who desired to see them. But if they were at any time disturbed, the air would darken suddenly, high gusts of storm would roar around the battlements of the castle, and the sea beating heavily about the rocks would rage as if demanding vengeance for the insult.

Such is the tale told by Gervasius of Tilbury, who has been dead almost half as long as Virgil. It may be true or untrue. I am not fond of climbing up into the judgment seat, or attempting to recognise white-robed truth in the midst of the throng of less worthy, though more amusing, characters which throng Italian legend. Least of all on such a night as this, when the soft wind blowing over the sea from the enchanted Castle of the Egg fills the air with whispering suggestions of old dead things and calls back many a tale of inimitable tragedy wrought out upon the shore of the gulf which lies before me—a furnace in all ages of hot passions and sensuous delights such as leave deep marks upon the memory of man. That most wilful quality is not unlike the echo in the hollow of some overhanging rock. It will repeat the sounds that please it, but no others, while even those it will distort, adding something wild or unearthly to every one, however ordinary. So the memory of the people selects capriciously those circumstances which it 65cherishes; and even while it hands them on from generation to generation it is ever adding fact to fact with the cunning of him who writes a fairy tale, casting glamour round the sordid details, struggling towards the beautiful or terrible—even not seldom towards the scandalous.

A little lower on the slope of the hill, well in sight from the point at which I sit, there is a vast and ruined building on the very margin of the sea. In the dusk light I can clearly see its two huge wings thrust out into the water, and the broken outline of its roof breaking the pale sky. The tide washes round its foundations. The whole mass lies black and silent, except at one point where a restaurant has intruded itself into the shell of a once splendid hall, and lights flicker round the empty windows which were built for the pleasure of a court. Three hundred years ago this palace was begun for the wife of a Spanish viceroy, Donna Anna Carafa. It was never finished, and has been put to a number of degrading uses, being at one time a quarantine station, at another a stable for the horses of the tramway, while a few fishermen have always housed their wives and children in its old ruined chambers, undeterred by the tales which associate the ruin with the spirit of the Queen Giovanna.

Queen Giovanna is so great a personage in Naples that it is worth while to consider her particularly. There are few spots within thirty miles of Naples where one does not hear of her too amorous life and her tragic death. I doubt if there are half a dozen guides or vetturini in all the city who, if asked the name of this great building, will not answer that it is "Il Palazzo della Regina Giovanna," and on being further questioned will not tell a doleful story of how she was strangled in one of the deserted chambers. 66The stranger, ignorant of Naples, will perhaps set down this fact, pleased to discover a trace of history yet lingering in the recollection of the people, and will cherish it carefully until he is told the same tale at Castel Capuano, on the other side of the city, with the addition of certain particulars which, by our narrow northern way of thinking, are damaging to Queen Giovanna's character. For instance, it is said of her that she was in those early days so convinced a democrat as to choose her lovers freely from among the sovereign people. They were doubtless gratified by her choice; but the pleasure faded when they discovered in due course of time that each favourite in turn, after the fickle Queen grew tired of him, was expected or compelled to leap from the top of a high tower, thus carrying all his knowledge of the secret scandals of a court by a short cut into the next world. A cruel Queen, it is true; but how prudent! Any one of us might leave a marvellous sweet memory of himself in the world, if only he could stop the mouths of—But that has nothing to do with Queen Giovanna.

This sweet memory, however, this fruit of prudence, is precisely what the Queen has attained in Naples and in all the surrounding country. I have questioned many peasants who spoke to me about her, and received the invariable answer that she was a good Queen, a very good Queen—in fact, of the best. Now history, listening to this declaration, sighs and shakes her head despairingly. There were two queens named Giovanna— leaving out several others who, for various reasons, do not come into the reckoning. The first was certainly a better woman than the second, but she is credibly believed to have begun her reign when quite a girl by murdering her first husband, after which she departed in 67various ways from the ideal of Sunday-schools. The second was an atrocious woman, concerning whose ways of life it is better to say as little as possible. The first was strangled, though not in Naples, or its neighbourhood, but at the Castle of Muro, far down in Apulia. The second had innumerable lovers, and was, perhaps, one of the worst women ever born.

The Queen Giovanna of tradition seems to be a blend of these two sovereigns, laden with the infirmities of both, and loved the more for the burden of the scandals which she bears. It is a charming trait, this disposition of poor humanity to glorify dead sinners! Conscious of their own imperfections, mindful of the condescension of a queen who steps down to the moral level of her people, the Neapolitans welcome her with outstretched hands, and love her for her peccadilloes. Legend confers a pleasanter immortality than history, earned less painfully, bestowed more charitably, and quite as durable.

<h2 style="text-align:center">CHAPTER IV</h2>

<h3 style="text-align:center">THE RIVIERA DI CHIAIA
AND SOME STRANGE THINGS WHICH OCCURRED THERE</h3>

68

In bright sunshine I came down the last slopes of the Posilipo, wending towards the Riviera di Chiaia. The bay sparkled with innumerable colours; the hills lay in morning shadow; Vesuvius was dark and sullen, and the twin peaks of Capri rested on the horizon like the softest cloud. The sun fell very sweetly among the oranges in the villa gardens, lighting up their dark and glossy leaves with quick-changing gleams which moved and went as lightly as if reflected from the restless waters of the bay. Out on the sea there was a swarm of fishing boats, each provided with a rod of monstrous length; while as I reached the level of the sea, and entered on the winding road that goes to Naples, I found myself skirting a long, narrow beach, of which the reeking odours proclaimed it to be a landing-place of fishers. There, under the shadow of the towering cliff, boats were hauled up, nets were drying, fish frails were piled in heaps, and close to a small stone pier which jutted out into the water a couple of fishing-wives were scolding each other much in the same way as two dames of Brixham or of Newlyn, while a small urchin prone upon the sand, watched the encounter of wits with 69eager curiosity to know whether more was to come of it or not.

STRADA DI CHIAIA, NAPLES.

More did not come of it. The strife sank into silence, and as I paced along the margin of the little beach, glancing now at the wide curve of the bay, now at the dark fortress of the enchanted Castle of the Egg upon its further horn, I found myself in a strange medley of ancient thoughts and modern ones, the old world wrestling with the new, tales of the kings of Aragon mingling with the cries of cabmen and the whirring noises of the tramways.

This little beach by which I stand is all that is now left of the Marina di Chiaia, which once ran round the bay up to the rocks and caverns of the Chiatamone, where the Egg Castle juts out into the sea. It was all a sandy foreshore, with boats hauled up and nets set out to dry, just as one may see them on this scrap which still remains. It was renowned as a place of ineffable odours. Indeed, an ancient writer, seeking a simile for a certain very evil smell, could think of none more striking than "that which one smells on the Marina di Chiaia in the evening." It is to be gathered that the women were in large measure responsible for this—as for most other things that go wrong in Naples. "'Tutt'e' peccate murtali so' femmene," says the proverb—All the mortal sins are feminine; and if those, why not the smells also? But it is not to be supposed that the women of the Chiaia were the less attractive. Far from that. We have the word of the poet del Tufo that they were so gracious and

19

charming that even a dead man would not remain insensible to the desire of loving them. What can have become of these houris? I did much desire to see them, but I searched in vain. I found none but heavy, wide-mouthed women, owning no charm but dirt, and no attractions save 70a raucous tongue. Perhaps the disappearance of the smells involved the loss of the beauty also. If so, another grudge is to be cherished against the sanitary reformers, who so often in the history of mankind have proved that they know not what they do.

But I was about to speak of King Alfonso of Aragon, a monarch whose story can be forgotten by no one who has given himself the pleasure of reading the superb work in which Guicciardini has told the story of his times, a tale of greatness and of woe immeasurable, having in itself every element of tragedy, with a human interest which throbs even painfully from page to page. Macaulay, by giving currency to a stupid tale about a galley slave who chose the hulks rather than the history, has contrived to rob many of us of a pleasure far greater than can be derived from the antitheses in which he himself delights; and has spread abroad the impression that this prince among historians, this dignified and simple writer, this unsurpassed judge of men whom he himself in a wiser moment compared to Tacitus, was dull! It is but one more injustice done by Macaulay's hasty fancy, serving well to prove what mischief may be wrought by a man who cannot deny himself the pleasure of a quirk until he has reflected what injury it may do to another's reputation.

Alfonso of Aragon was King of Naples when the French, led by their King Charles the Eighth, were advancing through Italy to the attack of Naples. The old title of the House of Anjou which reigned in Naples for near two centuries, was in the French judgment not extinct; and Charles, called into Italy by Ludovic the Moor, Duke of Milan, and one of the greatest scoundrels of all ages, was pressing on through the peninsula faster and with more success 71than either his friends wished or his enemies had feared. One by one the obstacles which were to have detained him in northern Italy crumbled at his approach. Florence was betrayed by Piero di Medici; the Neapolitan armies in the Romagna were driven back; the winter was mild, offering no obstacle to campaigning; the Pope was overawed; and at length Alfonso, seeing the enemy victorious everywhere, and now almost at his gates, fell into a strange state of nerves. The first warrior of his age broke down like a panic-stricken girl. The strong, proud King fell a prey to fear. He could not sleep, for the night was full of haunting terrors, and out of the dark there came to visit him the spectres of men whom he had slain by treachery, each one seeming to rejoice at the vengeance of which Heaven had made the French King the instrument.

Yet Alfonso had large and well-trained armies at his command, and the passes of the kingdom were easily defended. The French were no nearer than at Rome; and anyone who has travelled between the Eternal City and Naples must see how easily even in our own days a hostile army could be held among the mountains. Had there been a resolute defence, many a month might yet have passed before a single Frenchman reached the Siren city. But Alfonso could give no orders; and his terrors were completed by a vision which appeared to one of his courtiers in a dream repeated on three successive nights. It was the spirit of the old King Ferdinand which appeared to the affrighted Jacopo, grave and dignified as when all trembled before him in his life, and commanded, first in gentle words and afterwards with terrifying threats, that he should go forthwith to King Alfonso, telling him that it was vain to hope 72to stem the French invasion; that fate had declared their house was to be troubled with infinite calamities, and at length to be stamped out in punishment for the many deeds of enormous cruelty which the two had committed, but above all for that one wrought, at the persuasion of Alfonso, in the Church of San Lionardo in the Chiaia when he was returning home from Pozzuoli.

The spirit gave no details of this crime. There was no need. The mere reference to it completed Alfonso's overthrow. Whatever the secret may have been, it scored the King's heart with recollections which he could not face when conjured up in this strange and awful manner. There was no longer any resource for him. His life was broken once for all, and hastily abdicating his kingdom in favour of his son Ferdinand, whose clean youth was unstained by any crimes, he carried his remorse and all his sinful memories to a monastery in Sicily, where he died, perhaps in peace.

No man who reads this tale can refrain from wondering where was this Church of San Lionardo on the Chiaia, and what it was that King Alfonso did there. The first question is easier than the last to answer, yet there are some materials for satisfying curiosity in regard to both.

NAPLES—PORTA MERCANTILE.

It is useless to seek for the Church of San Lionardo now. It was swept away when the fine roadway was made which skirts the whole sea-front from the Piazza di Vittoria to the Torretta. But in old days it must have been a rarely picturesque addition to the beauty of the bay. It stood upon a little island rock, jutting out into the sea about the middle of the curve, near the spot where the aquarium now stands. It was connected with the land by a low causeway, not unlike that by which the 73Castle of the Egg is now approached; and it was a place of peculiar interest and sanctity, apart from its conspicuous and beautiful position, because from the days of its first foundation it had claimed a special power of protection over those who were tormented by the fear of shipwreck or captivity, both common cases in the lives of the dwellers on a shore haunted by pirates and often vexed by storms. The foundation was due to the piety of a Castilian gentleman, Lionardo d'Oria, who, being in peril of wreck so long ago as the year 1028, vowed a church in honour of his patron saint upon the spot, wherever it might be, at which he came safely to land. The waves drove him ashore upon this beach, midway between Virgil's Tomb and the enchanted Castle of the Egg; and here his church stood for seven hundred years and more upon its rocky islet—a refuge and a shrine for all such as went in peril by land or sea.

Naturally enough, the thoughts of Neapolitans turned easily in days of trouble to the saint whose special care it was to extricate them. Many a fugitive slipped out of Naples in the dark and sped furtively along the sandy beach to the island church, whence, as he knew perfectly, he could embark on board a fishing-boat with far better hope of getting clear away than if he attempted to escape from Naples. Thus at all moments of disturbance in the city the chance was good that important persons were in hiding in the Church of San Lionardo waiting the favourable moment of escape. King Alfonso must have known this perfectly. One may even surmise that his journey to Pozzuoli was undertaken with the object of tempting out rebellious barons and their followers from the city, where they might be difficult to find, into this solitary spot, 74where he could scarcely miss them. If so, he doubtless gloated over the first sight of the island church as he came riding down from the Posilipo and out upon the beach towards it, knowing that the trap was closed and the game his own.

Alfonso was a man who never knew mercy. Who the fugitives were whom he found hidden in the church, or in what manner they met their death, is so far as I know, recorded nowhere. But this we know, that it was no ordinary death, no mere strangling or beheading of rebellious subjects that the King sanctioned and perhaps watched in this lonely church which was built as a refuge for troubled men. Of such deeds there were so many scored up to the account of both kings that the spirit of the elder could hardly have reproached his son with any one of them. What was done in the Church of San Lionardo was something passing the common cruelty of even Spaniards in those ages, and it is perhaps a merciful thing that oblivion has descended on the details.

I shall return again to King Alfonso and his family, for the city is full of memories of them, and in the vaults of the Castel Nuovo there are things once animate which throw a terrible light upon the practices of the House of Aragon. But for the time this may be enough of horrors; and I turn with pleasure to the long sea-front against which the tide is breaking fresh and pleasantly, surging white and foaming over the black rocks which skirt the foot of the sea-wall. The wind comes freshly out of the east. Capri is growing into a wonderful clearness. Even the little town upon the saddle of the island begins to glow white and sparkling, and the limestone precipices show their clefts and shadows in the increasing light. The soft wind blows in little sunny gusts, 75which shake the blossoms of wistaria on the house-fronts, mingling the salt and fishy odours of the beach with the scent of flowers in the villa gardens. There is scarce a sign of cloud in the warm sky, and all the crescent bay between me and the city takes colours which are perpetually changing into deeper tints of liquid blue and rare soft green, with flashes here and there of brown, and exquisite reflections which are but half seen before they yield to others no less beautiful. The long white sea-wall gleams like the setting of a gem, and the warm air trembles slightly in the distance, so that the Castle of the Egg looks as if it were indeed enchanted, and might be near the doom predicted for it when its frail foundations shall be broken.

I had meant to spend an hour this morning in the Church of Sannazzaro, on the slope of the hill, at no great distance from this spot. He who does not see churches betimes in Naples may chance to miss them altogether, and will waste much temper during the hot afternoon in hammering on barred doors with vain effort to rouse sleepy sacristans. Heaven knows I am not indifferent to church architecture, and had the morning been less beautiful I should certainly have described learnedly enough, the building preserving the memory of the quaint and artificial poet whom Bembo, as frigid and unnatural as himself, declared to be next to Virgil in fame, as he was also next in sepulture. I often wonder whether Bembo really meant anything at all by this judgment, except an elegant turn of verse. If he did—But I am straying away from the lights and shadows of this magic morning, which are far more delightful than the arcadian rhapsodies of Sannazzaro and of Bembo. Let me put them both aside. Or stay, one observation of the former comes into mind. He said the 76Mergellina was "Un pezzo di cielo caduto in terra"—a scrap of heaven fallen down on earth. He had blood in him, then, this worshipper of nymphs and classicism; let us go and see his Mergellina. It will not take us far from the sea-front, to which it once lay open, in the days when there were no grand hotels nor ugly boarding-houses blocking out the sweet colours and the clean air of the sea.

As I turn inland, my eye is caught by a tablet on a house-front to the left, which has a melancholy interest for all Englishmen:—

"IN QUESTA CASA NACQUE FRANCESCO CARACCIOLI
AMMIRAGLIO
IL 18 GUIGNO 1752
STRANGOLATO AL 29 GUIGNO 1799"

"Strangolato"—ay, hung at Nelson's yardarm, while his flagship lay off Naples, and sunk afterwards in the sea, whence his naked body was washed up on shore. It is a tragic tale; but to use it as an imputation on Nelson's honour is unjust. Caraccioli was a rebel, and paid the penalty of unsuccessful revolution. He was brave and unfortunate, he resisted manfully an evil government; but he was not unfairly slain.

In a few yards further the whole charming length of Sannazzaro's bit of heaven lies spread out before me. A wide, straight street, a paradise of yellow stucco, stained and peeling off, a wilderness of sordid shops and dirty children running wild, a solitary tramcar spinning on its way to Naples, a creaking cart with vegetables, a huckster bawling fish—I have not patience to catalogue the delights of the Mergellina of to-day, but turn my

21

back on them and flee to the sea-front again, where I can look out on what is still unspoiled, because man has no dominion over it.77

BOATS AT THE MERGELLINA—NAPLES.

A short stroll towards the city within reach of the lapping waves restored my temper, and I remembered that as I fled from the Mergellina I saw over my shoulder a halting-place for tramcars, well known to all who visit Naples by the name of the "Torretta."

I hardly know how many of those visitors have asked themselves what this Torretta was, to which they have so often paid their fares of twenty-five centimes, or have connected it in memory with the other towers of which they hear upon the further side of Naples. But since Naples is a seaborn city, and a wealthy city by the shore of ocean attracts pirates as naturally as flies flock to honey, it may be as well to explain why the Torretta was built.

The tale goes back as far as the days of Don Fernando Afan de Rivera, Duca d'Alcala, who did Naples the honour of condescending to govern it as Viceroy to His Most Catholic Majesty of Spain from the year 1629 to 1631. He was an old and gouty viceroy, but not lacking in energy or courage. Those were times in which infinite numbers of Turkish pirates hovered round the coasts of Italy; and week by week the warning cannon roared out from Ischia, and the heavy toll of the alarm bells rolled along the shore from Campanella and Castellammare to the harbours beneath Vesuvius, waking all the fishermen to watchfulness and rousing the guards within the city walls.

"All'arme! all'arme! la Campana sona
Li Turche so' arrivati a la marina!"

The terror-stricken refrain is still on the lips of the peasants in the coasts which were harried by Dragut and Ucchiali.

One night a band of these bold corsairs struck 78suddenly in the darkness, and landed on the western end of the Chiaia, well outside the limits of the city. There were among their numbers certain renegades of Naples, and using the local knowledge of these scoundrels, they had conceived the design of capturing the Marchesa del Vasto, whose palace stood in this somewhat unprotected region, and whom they intended to surprise in her sleep. So rich a prisoner would have brought them a vast ransom; but the scheme turned out disappointing. The Marchesa had gone to take the waters, over the hills at Agnano, whither greedy Turks could not pursue her. Nothing remained but to bag as many people of inferior consequence as time permitted; and the renegades, turning to their advantage the alarm which was already spreading among the inhabitants, rushed about knocking at every door and imploring the people in anguished tones to come out at once and save themselves from the Turks, who were landing at that moment. Some poor frightened souls were simple enough to accept this invitation, and were made prisoners for their pains the moment they crossed the threshold. Others, more wisely, suspecting the trick, made rude replies, and barred their doors and shutters, knowing that at dawn, if not before, help must surely come from the neighbouring city.

NAPLES—GRADONI DI CHIAIA.

They were not mistaken in their faith. Naples was astir, and the guards were mustering by torchlight in the streets. The Duca d'Alcala was at the Palazzo Stigliano, near the Porta di Chiaia. Old and gouty as he was, he had set himself at the head of his men, the city gate was flung open, and in the grey light of morning the Turks saw a considerable force advancing on them. They did not stay to fight, but pushed off their ships, carrying with them 79twenty-four prisoners, whom next day they signified that they were willing to ransom. Accordingly parleys were held upon the Island of Nisida; the Viceroy himself paid part of the sum demanded, while the rest was contributed by the Society for the Redemption of Captives, a useful public institution whose income was heavily drawn upon in those days. Probably neither one nor the other was entirely pleased at having to pay out a large sum for the redemption of people living almost under the walls of the city. It was to guard against such mishaps in future that the Torretta was built, and garrisoned as strongly as its size permitted.

What old tales these seem, and how changed is all the aspect of this bay! San Lionardo gone as completely as the shadow of a drifting cloud! The Torretta degraded to a halting-place of tramcars! The Mergellina stripped of all that made the poet Sannazzaro love it! Only on the sea-front the same beauty of heavenly blue still shimmers on the waters, breaking into bubbles of pure gold where the soft tide washes up amid the rocks. The fishing boats slip to and fro under their large three-cornered sails. There is more wind out there upon the bay; it strikes in sharp puffs on the bellying canvas, and the light craft heel towards the land. One of them has put in beside the stairs not far from where I am loitering. The bottom of his boat is alive with silvery fish; and on the cool stones of the landing-place, just awash with clear green water, stand the barelegged fishermen, stooping over the still living fish, cleansing their burnished scales from the soil of the dirty skiff, laughing and chattering like children, as they are. Suddenly one of them snatches at a little object which the others had not noticed, and holds it up to me in gleeful expectation of a few 80soldi. "Cavallo di mare!" A tiny sea-horse, already stiff and rigid, a clammy and uncomfortable curiosity. My good man, if I desire to look at sea-horses I have but to cross the road to the aquarium, where I can watch them in the grace and wonder of their life and shall not be asked to cumber myself with their dead bodies. Salvatore shrugs his shoulders. If I am mad enough to miss this chance, it is my own affair; the Madonna will scarce send me another. In the midst of the diatribe I stroll across to the aquarium.

Rarely, if ever, have I passed by this storehouse of great marvels without regretting it, for indeed it has no equal in the world. Tanks of fish are kept in many cities; the only aquarium is at Naples. There alone can one stand and watch the actual stress and movement of the life which passes in the sea, that animal life of myriad shapes and colours which is so like the plants and which while rooted to a rock, and spreading long translucent tendrils like a frond of seaweed, will yet curl and uncurl, swaying this way and that in search of food, or in the effort to escape some enemy it fears. For the depths of the sea are full of enemies, and every sense of those which dwell beneath it is alert. There one may see the tube-dwelling worms, thrust out from the mouth of their tall cylinders like a feathery tuft of tendrils, a revolving fan, which spins and spins until some sea-horse floating up erect and graceful comes too close, and instantly the fan closes, the tendrils disappear and lie hidden till the danger has gone by. Far along the rock clefts, high and low throughout the pools, there is a perpetual watchfulness and motion, a constant stir and trembling; and the provision which the lowest animal possesses for the protection of its life is in quick and momentary 81use, laying open such a revelation of the infinite resources of nature as itself makes this cool chamber one of the most interesting places in the world.

But if a man go there for beauty only, in what profusion he will find it! The green depths of the tanks are all aglow with soft rich colour. The sea beneath the cliffs at Vico is not more blue on the softest day in spring than the fish which glide by among these shadows; nor are the lights seen from Castellammare when the sun drops down behind Ischia and the rosy flushes spread along the coast, more exquisite than the soft pink scales which glance through the arches of the rocks. Turquoise and pearl, emerald and jacinth, the gleams caught from the hidden sun above reflect the hues of every gem. The strange, dense vegetation, the quick flash of moving gold and purple, reveal a world of marvellous rich beauty; and if it be indeed the case that those bold divers of past days who dared to plunge out of the bright sun into the dusk and dimness of the ocean depths saw there the orange sponges, the waving forests of crimson weed, and all the myriad colours of the moving fishes glinting through them, it is no wonder that they came back into the world of men spreading tales of countless jewels, and unnumbered treasures, which lie buried in the caves and grottoes of the sea.

Naples is alive with stories of this sort; and not Naples only, but all Sicily and southern Italy share the tales of the great diver, Nicolò Pesce, who is sometimes a Sicilian and sometimes a dweller on the mainland, but is claimed by Naples with good reason, as I shall show presently. The mere sight of things so like those which Nicolò must have seen calls up all the rare stories told of him; and I go up into the Villa Garden, which skirts the long sea-front, and 82having found a seat beneath a shady palm tree, whence I can watch the blue sea lying motionless around the dark battlements of Castel dell'Uovo, while the wind makes light noises in the feathery boughs above me, I fall to thinking of the diver who, at the bidding of the king, searched the caverns underneath the castle, which no man has ever found but he, and came back with his arms full of jewels. Any child in Naples knows that heaps of gems are lying in those caverns still.

Who was Nicolò Pesce? Ah! what is the use of asking such questions about a myth? He was once, like all of us, a thing which crept about the earth—it matters little when, *nei tempi antichi*! But now he is a butterfly fluttering in the world of romance, a theme for poets, and cherished in the heart of children. If you must know more about his actual existence, catch a child and give him a few soldi to escort you to the foot of the Vico Mezzocannone, away on the further side of the city, where the lanes drop steeply to the harbour. There, built into the front of a house, you will see an ancient stone, on which is carved the figure of a shaggy man grasping a knife in his right hand, while his left is clenched in the air. That is Nicolò Pesce, so called because he was at home in the water as a fish is; and the knife is that which he used to cut himself out from the bellies of the fish when he had done the long swift journeys which he was wont to make in the manner of which no other man had experience but Jonah.

You may get much more than this from the child, though confidence is hard to gain, and soldi will not always buy it. One day the King bade Nicolò find out what the bottom of the sea is like. The diver plunged, and when he came up gasping he said he had seen gardens of coral and large spaces of ribbed 83sand strewn with precious stones, and piled here and there with heaps of treasure, mouldering weapons, the ribs of sunken ships and the whitening skeletons of drowned mariners. I well believe it! Ave Maria, Stella Maris, Star of the Sea, be gracious to poor sailors in their peril!

But another time the King bade Nicolò dive down and find out how Sicily floated on the sea, and the man brought up a fearful tale. For he said that groping to and fro in the dim abysses he saw that Sicily had rested on three pillars, whereof one had fallen, one was split and like to fall, and one only stood erect and sound! The years have gone by in many hundreds since that plunge; but no man knows whether the shattered pillar is erect.

Now the King desired to be sure that Nicolò did actually reach the bottom of the sea, and accordingly took him to the summit of a rock where the water was deepest, and there, surrounded by his courtiers, hurled a gold cup far out from the shore. The goblet flashed and sank, and the King bade Nicolò dive and bring it back.

The diver plunged, and the King waited, watching long before the surface of the sea was broken. At last Nicolò rose, brandishing the cup as he swam, and when he had reached shore and won his breath again he cried, "Oh, King, if I had known what I should see, neither this cup nor half your kingdom would have tempted me to dive." "What did you see?" the King demanded, and the diver answered that he found on the floor of the ocean

23

four impenetrable things. First the great rush of a river which streams out of the bowels of the earth, sweeping all things away before the might of its resistless current; and next a labyrinth of rocks, whose crags overhung the winding ways between them. Then 84he was beaten hither and thither by the flux and reflux of the waters out of the lowest parts of ocean; and lastly, he dared not pass the monsters which stretched out long tentacles as if to clutch him and draw him into the caverns of the rocks. So he groped and wandered in mortal fear, till at last he saw the gleam of gold upon a shelf of rock and grasped the cup and came up into the world again.

Now the King pondered long upon this story, and then taking the cup flung it into the sea once more, and bade Nicolò dive again. The fellow begged hard that he might not go, but the King was ruthless, and the waters closed over the diver. The day waned, the night came on, and still the King waited on the crag beside the sea. But Nicolò Pesce the diver was never seen again.

Many a child has thrilled over this story as told in Schiller's verse,—"Wer wagt es, Rittersman oder Knapp...." You ask—What is the truth of these old stories? I answer that they have neither truth nor falsity, and that is enough for most of us in this dull world, of which so much has to be purged away before the beauty can appear. The flower-laden boughs in this Villa garden go on rustling in the sunny wind; the Judas trees are gay with purple blossoms, and from the long, straight avenue, where white marble statues gleam in the cool shades, the cries and laughter of the children ring out merrily. Tell a child these tales and he will doubt nothing, reason over nothing, but accept the beauty and talk of it with quickened breath and glowing cheeks. That is the wisdom of the babes. Let us be content to copy it.

CHAPTER V

THE ENCHANTED CASTLE OF THE EGG
AND THE SUCCESSION OF THE KINGS
WHO HELD IT

85

In Naples one is never very far from history, and when I arose from my pleasant seat beneath the palm tree, plodding on down the long and beautiful avenue of the Villa garden I came out at no great distance on the sunny Piazza della Vittoria—a name which, I suspect, connects itself in the fancy of many visitors with some of the wild triumphs of Garibaldi. But the piazza has an older history than that. It commemorates the sea battle of Lepanto, in which Don John of Austria, the youthful son of the great Emperor Charles the Fifth and of Barbara Blomberg, washerwoman of Ratisbon, led the united fleets of Venice, Spain, and Rome into the Gulf of Lepanto as the Turks were coming out and administered a drubbing under which the throne of the Caliph rocked and tottered, all so long ago as the year 1576. Naples had the best of reasons, as I have said already, for rejoicing over any event which reduced the sea power of the Turks, and I do not doubt that the child of Kaiser and of washerwoman had an intoxicating triumph on this spot which has so long forgotten him.

At this point I hesitate, as the ass did between 86two bundles, a dilemma often thrust on one in Naples. For if I turn towards my left and mount the hill, I reach the Piazza dei Martiri and the pleasant strangers' quarter. But since my aim is not to describe things known easily to all who visit Naples, but rather to talk at large of what the guide-books do not mention, I take the other way and move out on the sea-front again, just where the Via Partenope, a new road, runs towards the ancient castle at the point.

As I approach the centre of this ancient city, scene of so many bitter conflicts, it becomes the more needful to select those epochs which are most worthy to be remembered, to let all the ghosts of great names flutter by except a few, and those the few whose memories rise oftenest. The choice is easy. All the deepest tragedy of Naples closes round the fall of the House of Hohenstaufen and the fall of that of Aragon. I must explain briefly how these houses held the throne of Naples and of Sicily.

The Normans founded that kingdom in the year 1130. They won it by conquest from Lombards and from Saracens; and they placed their capital at Palermo, where their rule on the whole was just and splendid, and their throne gained lustre from Arab art and Arab learning, so that those were happy days for Italy and Sicily, held by strong sovereigns who kept in check all dangers from without. But even in the good times the seed of trouble was sprouting fast; for the first Normans, superstitious in their piety, and anxious to obtain a legal title to the lands their swords had won, accepted the feudal lordship of the Pope; and thus originated the papal claim to alter the succession of the realm at will.87

The male line of the Normans failed. Constance, the heiress of the house, carried the throne to the Emperor Henry VI., son of the great Barbarossa, and as resolved as he to turn into realities the shadowy claims of the Emperors to the overlordship of all Italy. But the Popes already claimed the universal spiritual dominion, as the Emperors claimed the temporal; and since in the rough-thinking minds of men there was but little comprehension of the theoretical distinction between the dominions of spirit and of matter, it happened often that even in the understanding of Pope and Kaiser themselves the difference was lost, and the two claims worked out to rivalry and the clash of interests which wrought much bloodshed.

There was not room in Italy for two universal rulers, both holding of God, even though one ruled spiritual things and the other temporal. The theory was clear, but who could interpret the practice on all occasions? Every Pope was greedy for temporalities; and no Kaiser, unless wholly occupied in taming rebellious barons beyond the Alps, could refrain from meddling with spiritual affairs. Thus arose two parties throughout

24

Italy, and all the land was cleft with the feuds of Guelf and Ghibelline, the former holding to the Pope, the latter dreaming, as Dante did, of the days when the Emperor should descend from the Alps again brandishing the sword of judgment, and purge away the foulness from the lovely cities which stood oppressed and mourning. Day and night, in the fancy of the great Florentine, Rome lay weeping, widowed and alone, calling constantly, "Cesare mio, why hast thou deserted me?"

More often than not the Emperors did not come, and the Pope grew ever stronger. But when the successor of St. Peter saw his great rival established 88by natural inheritance in the territory which was not only the fairest of all Italy, but also the one over which he claimed feudal rights, it was certain that there could be no peace; and the conflict might have broken out at once had not the Emperor died and his widow granted the Church great power over her young son, whom the Pope might naturally hope to mould into what he would.

But the lad grew up strong and self-reliant, a noble and a splendid monarch, worthy of the fame which clings to this day about the name of the Emperor Frederick the Second. Alone of all the line of Western Emperors this one lived by choice in Italy. He loved the blue sea and the purple mountains which guard the land of Sicily. His heart was in the white coast towns of Apulia and the ranges of long low hills which look towards the Adriatic over the flat plains of Foggia, where the hawks wheel screaming in the clear air and the great mountain shrine of Monte Gargano towers blue and dim above the heel of Italy. He loved the Arab art and learning. He was no mean poet—a troubadour, moreover; and withal a just and upright ruler, with aims far greater than those of the age in which he lived, a monarch born for the happiness of nations, had only the Pope been able to bate a little of his pride and tolerate the rival at his gates.

But those were days in which the Popes would endure no compromise; and from the hour in which he entered man's estate to that in which he laid down his weary life in an Apulian castle, Frederick was in continual warfare with the Church. Had he lived, who knows how that struggle might have ended, or by what devices the prince who was Emperor as well as King, and had the prestige of the Holy Roman 89Empire at his back, might have met the dangers gathering round his kingdom? For the Pope was negotiating with other princes, offering them the inheritance of Naples if they would but turn the Hohenstaufen out; and at length, after an English prince had refused the enterprise, Charles of Anjou took it up, brother of St. Louis, and a man accounted the first warrior of his age. By this time the kingdom of the Two Sicilies had passed to Manfred, the favourite child of Frederick the Second, though born of an unlawful union. There was a child in Germany of lawful blood, one Conradin; but he was still playing with his mother, and of no age to stem the troubles of the kingdom. Moreover, he was reported dead, and Manfred seized the throne with the goodwill of the people, who loved him well, and keep his memory unto this day; for he was handsome and gallant, "Bello e biondo" the Apulians call him still, a king whom a man might follow and a woman love, and, but for the Pope and his restless enmity, Manfred also, like his father, might have made the happiness of a whole people.

But Charles of Anjou descended suddenly and met Manfred in battle outside Benevento. It was the 26th of February, in the year 1266. Manfred, watching the battle from a hillock, saw his troops waver; and suspecting treachery, which was indeed abroad that day, he rushed into the thickest of the fight, and was slain by an unknown hand as he strove to rally his Apulians.

That day there fell before the French spears not only a noble king, but the peace and happiness of southern Italy. Charles of Anjou was a grim and ruthless tyrant, whose conceptions of mercy and justice were those of a hawk hovering above a hen-coop. He denied burial to the body of his enemy, 90and caused it to be flung naked on the banks of the river, where every soldier as he passed cast a stone at it. He seized Manfred's luckless queen, Helena, and kept her prisoner with her children until death released them. He overthrew good laws and set up bad ones. He sought to stamp out loyalty to the old kings by exile and the sword. In Sicily he wrought unutterable woe, such as in the end turned the blood of every islander to fire and his heart to stone, and produced a massacre from which no Frenchman escaped. All the world knows that great act of retribution by the name of the Sicilian Vespers.

But in the meantime Conradin had grown up to tall boyhood, and his heart was already brave enough to rage when he saw his kingdom in the hands of a cruel conqueror, and his own subjects slain and banished because they loved his house. His mother wept, but the boy did what any brave boy of kingly blood would do. I will tell the tale of that great tragedy later, when I reach the square outside the Carmine where the last scene was played out, and the boy-king lost the game, but carried all the honours with him from the world, leaving eternal infamy for a heritage to the foe who slew him.

So Charles of Anjou possessed the kingdom. But it brought no happiness to him or to his race. His own days were tortured by the loss of Sicily, and every one of those who followed him reigned uneasily. Even his grandson Robert, called "The Wise," is suspected of having won the throne by murder. Robert's granddaughter, Queen Giovanna, whose sweet memory we found on the slopes of the Posilipo, was privy to the murder of her husband, and was herself smothered with a pillow. The other Joanna, who followed her, was the most profligate 91woman of her age, and in her ended, meanly and sordidly, the line of Anjou sovereigns.

NAPLES.

Then came the House of Aragon, which had reigned in Sicily ever since the Vespers, and now expelled the last scion of Anjou and established a kingdom which seemed likely to be stable. But the claims of the royal

25

house of France were only dormant; and before the end of the century they started up again, eager and adventurous, in the heart of the young King, Charles the Eighth. It was the wily Duke of Milan, Ludovic Sforza, named the Moor, who incited this young man to lead the French chivalry through the passes of the Alps. He was the warder of Italy, and he betrayed her. It would be hard to name any one act of man since God divided light from darkness which has let loose upon the world such tremendous consequences of woe.

It is not my duty here to describe those consequences, nor to tell how the French invasion resulted very shortly in riveting on Naples the long Spanish slavery, which in the middle of the last century became a monarchy again, and in 1860 was torn from the hold of the Bourbons, and made free at last, by the grace of God and the valour of true heroes, each one of whom dared all for Italy.

"Blessed is he of all men, being in one
As father to her and son,
Blessed of all men living, that he found
Her weak limbs bared and bound,
And in his arms and in his bosom bore,
And as a garment wore
Her weight of want, and as a royal dress
Put on her weariness.
"Praise him, O storm and summer, shore and wave,
O skies, and every grave;
O weeping hopes, O memories beyond tears,
O many and murmuring years."
92

I will quote no more, even of these immortal verses. Since it was given to an English singer to voice the rapture with which all good men hailed the salvation of Italy, it is but just that every visitor should read the "Song of Italy" himself. I would that everyone among them had it by heart and could catch some thrill from the noble passion of the verses.

This has been a long discourse. But if certain things happened a great while ago, is it my fault? Or again, am I to blame for the strange neglect of Italian history in schools? The lesson is done now, and the sun is still bright and hot on the Via Partenope. Even the enchanted Castle of the Egg, black and grim as it usually looks, has caught the glow, and is steeped and drowned in warm light. A quiver of haze hangs over the sea, tremulous and burning. The wind has dropped, and a midday silence has descended upon Naples. It is the hour when sacristans bar the church doors and seek the solace of slumber, when the vetturini congregate on the shady side of the piazza and cease to crack their whips at the sight of strangers. On the castle bridge a sentry paces to and fro. There are one or two restaurants below him in the shadow, neither good nor bad, but good enough; and I order my colazione in one which looks towards the sheer cliff of the Pizzofalcone, and from which towards my right I can look out upon the harbour, can catch a glimpse of the Castel Nuovo, the old royal dwelling of the Houses of Anjou and Aragon, and see beyond it the old city bathed in sunshine sloping to the curving sea.

The Pizzofalcone is the Falcon's Beak. If it were not too hot to think much about anything, I might perhaps detect the resemblance. But at this hour, in this city, and in face of this sun, one does not think; 93one sits and lets half realised ideas drift past as they will. The Pizzofalcone looks to me much like any other cliff, rather dangerously near the castle, which could easily be dominated from the height by even the smallest modern guns. There was once a villa of the Roman Lucullus on that height. Statesman and epicure, he had another on this island; or perhaps the two formed part of a single domain, which must have been rarely lovely in those days when waving pine trees filled the hollows of the cliff and the sea broke white and creamy on the strand of Santa Lucia. It was not this handsome quay stretching on beyond the castle which set the Neapolitans singing—

"Oh, dolce Napoli,
Oh, suol beato."

For the truth is that modern works of engineering have not yet proved as prolific in poetry as the abuses they replace, and the Neapolitans have not written about their sea-wall any song one half so sweet as that which was inspired by the pretty, solitary creek outside the city bounds, bad as it is understood to have been in morals. There were, and are still, caverns all along the cliffs of Santa Lucia which were sad places in the old day, full of riotous and evil people who resorted thither for the worst of ends. For this reason Don Pietro di Toledo, when he was Viceroy, ruined some and closed others, by which act he at once improved the morals of Naples and enriched its folklore, for nothing stimulated the imagination of the people so much as the idea that their caverns were lying empty and silent. They believe now that some are the haunt of witches, while others are filled with treasure. One or two are worth seeing still if a guide can be found to show them.94

But I sat down here to talk of tragedies connected with this castle. Some people may think it would be better to do so within and not without the walls, and they are welcome to their opinion; but I have tried both courses and think not. The interior of the castle is badly modernised. The custodian is stupid and knows nothing. The old chapel is a kitchen, and when I went to see the spot where the spirit of Queen Helena wrote the word "revenge" upon the altar I found it full of soldier cooks washing potatoes for the garrison. The prisons are either forgotten or not shown. Inside the walls there is nothing but disillusion and regret.

Queen Helena was the young wife of Manfred, who, as I said above, was slain at Benevento, defending his kingdom against the butcher, Charles of Anjou. The poor girl was at Lucera with her children, when they brought her news that her husband, kingdom, and home were all lost; and her first natural impulse was to flee to the protection of her father, the Greek Emperor in Constantinople. So she took to horse, and rode down out of the hill country through the coast plains of Apulia, where but a few weeks earlier she had hunted and feasted with her lord, and so came to the port of Trani, where she had touched land and met the King in all the splendour of his retinue when she came from the east a happy bride. One can fancy with what fearfulness this little band of fugitives rode towards the sea, carrying with them the children of the slain King, and how often they must have turned their heads to watch lest they might see the spearpoints of Anjou flashing among the defiles of the mountains. At Trani surely they would find servants loyal enough to speed them on board ship before they cast themselves at the feet of the conqueror; and as she rode 95beneath the gateway of the white-walled town and saw the green Adriatic stretching far towards the shores of Greece, the Queen's heart must have leapt amidst its sorrow at the thought that she had brought her dead lord's boys in sight of safety and of freedom.

Alas, poor Queen! The whole land was turning like a flower to the sun! The Castellan of Trani spoke her fair. A month before he would have given all he had to gain her favour, and now—he did but beg her rest until a ship could be got ready, and instantly sent off tidings to the French. Ere morning mother and children were riding once more across the plain, their horses' heads turned from the sea, and their bridles guided by French hands. Neither the sorrow of the Queen nor the youth of the children touched the heart of Charles. He would have none of the blood of Manfred left in freedom, and Queen and children died after many years in prison.

Queen Helena was shut up in this castle for some years. Men say it was at Nocera that she died, but it must have been here that her noble spirit fretted most sorely against fate, bruising itself like a poor lark flapping against its prison bars. For in the corridors of this old castle her spirit used to walk on the eve of Ascension every year, pacing slowly from her cell to the chapel of the castle, where she wrote upon the altar the word "revenge" with finger dipped in blood. Nothing could erase those letters till the night of the Sicilian Vespers, when the French were hunted and slain in every street and alley of Palermo. After that dread act of vengeance wrought in her own capital city, the spirit of Queen Helena was never seen again.

It is in sight of these grey walls, which stood here 96before Naples was a kingdom, certainly in the year 1140, that every pageant and almost every tragedy in the long story of the city has passed by. In those days when dukes ruled Naples, and the age of Greek dominion was but just over, the castle was called "Castello del Salvatore," the Castle of the Saviour, with the addition of the words "near Naples," for the old walled city which made such valorous defences lay beyond the ridge. Sometimes, again, it is spoken of as "Castello Marino," a name which sufficiently explains itself; but nowhere is its present designation used in ancient documents until the year 1352, when it appears in the rules of the Order of the Holy Spirit, founded by Louis of Anjou, and appears, moreover, not only as "the Castle of the Egg," but as "the Castle of the Enchanted Egg," thus showing that the legend concerning the magical foundation of the fortress had gained strength enough to displace one, if not two, ancient titles, and attach itself inseparably to the spot.

There is in this fact something very singular; and one would willingly ask the dead centuries why they left us the heritage of this mysterious name. Of itself, the ancient castle must remain in all men's minds as the chief interest in Naples, the most marked object on its beautiful shore, and the central point of its romantic story. But beyond the beauty and the interest, one is piqued with curiosity; and the sense of mystery clinging to the castle lends it a charm to which no one can remain insensible. There are few points near Naples, whether on hillside or in valley, from which one does not see the enchanted castle low down by the water's edge, swept by cloud and sunshine, or wet with spray, when the storm wind drives along the shore, a witness of past ages, the one thing in Naples which has not changed, 97except only the blue sea and the contours of the everlasting hills.

NAPLES—CASTLE OF ST. ELMO.

No castle builder of the days when artillery had come into use would have set this fortress on the shore beneath the Pizzofalcone, whence it could be so easily bombarded. It is rather curious to sit under these old walls, and turn one's eyes in succession to the three castles of the city. This is much the oldest, and the least defensible. Then came Castel Nuovo, a little higher in the town; Charles of Anjou founded it; and lastly St. Elmo, high upon the hillside, in a perfect situation, of all others best suited to be the *arx*, or citadel. Why, one wonders, did not the first builders use it, and let the city grow around it? or at least, why did they not place their keep and fortress on the Pizzofalcone? an eminence well suited for defence. Surely those first Greek settlers who came across the hills from Cumæ could not have overlooked the merits of this site! Perhaps, as some scholars hold, Neapolis, "the new city," could not be built upon the Pizzofalcone because Palæopolis, "the old city," was already there. I cannot tell. There are no answers to these questions, which recur again and again as one wanders round these coasts, none the less absorbing because one must speculate on them in vain.

But in Naples one must not spend time in chasing shadows. I have still to speak about the French bombardment of the enchanted castle; but first I will take up the tale of the fall of the House of Aragon where I left it in my last chapter, when King Alfonso, terrified and broken by nameless fear, leapt down shuddering from his throne, and fled from royalty and kingdom, to die a penitent monk in a monastery in Sicily.

27

It was a well-nigh hopeless task for his son 98Ferdinand to maintain the sceptre thus hastily thrust into his hands. The French were already over the borders of his kingdom. They had stormed and sacked the Castle of Monte di San Giovanni, putting the garrison to the sword. "This," says Guicciardini with scornful bitterness, "was the sum of the opposition and trouble which the King of France met with in the conquest of a realm so noble and so splendid; in the defence of which there was shown neither skill, nor courage, nor good counsel, no desire for honour, no strength, no loyalty." The Neapolitans were strongly posted at San Germano, the River Garigliano flowing like a moat in front, and their flanks guarded by lofty mountains; but they fled without a blow, before they even saw the French, leaving their guns behind, and falling back on Capua.

At Capua, that ancient city of delights, which turned the strong Carthaginian invaders into feeble voluptuaries, cowardice was fitly followed up by treachery. The troops were under command of Gianjacopo Triulzi, a captain of repute, "accustomed to make profession of honour," observes Guicciardini, in his dry, contemptuous way. This honourable captain seized the moment when his young master had been called back to Naples by disorders in the city, to deliver over his whole command to the French. Ferdinand hurried back; but arrived too late. He returned with a few followers to Naples. The whole city was in an uproar, the mob was already sacking the stables of the Castel Nuovo. There was no more hope of stemming the tide. The young king, brave, just, and personally popular, was overwhelmed by the misdeeds of his house. The very guards of his palace were inclined to seize his person; but he distracted their attention by admitting them to sack the castle, and while they were quarrelling 99over their booty, he left the castle by the secret postern towards the sea, and embarked on a light galley bound for Ischia. There as he stood in the stern, and through the black smoke of the burning ships, destroyed by his orders, saw home and kingdom lost by the sins and dishonour of other men, he repeated over and over, as long as he could still see Naples, those words in which the psalmist tells us that except the Lord keep the city, the watchman waketh but in vain.

But the Castle of the Egg still held out for him, and the French, having seized a little tower on the height of Pizzofalcone, bombarded the fortress from that eminence. King Charles the Eighth himself was there watching the practice of his gunners, when two light galleys ran across from Ischia, touching shore at the old mole, and from one of them landed Don Federigo of Aragon, uncle of the King, who had dwelt at the French Court, and knew both Charles and his barons. They took him up to the height, and when the French King saw him coming, says Passaro, that most gossipy of chroniclers, "he leapt down from his horse and bowed down to the ground, and embraced Don Federigo with the greatest pleasure, and took him by the hand and led him apart to a spot beneath an olive tree, where they began to talk together, but of what they said I know nothing, though many supposed that King Charles was trying to treat with King Ferdinand, offering him great lordships in France, but he would not, and Don Federigo left him and went back to his ships."

A strange interview, surely, between King and Prince, while the French gunners stood waiting with their matches burning, and the standard of Aragon still flew over the enchanted castle. It fell ere long, 100and the whole kingdom was in the hands of Charles. It is true he had not the wit to keep it. But anyone who wants to know that story must seek it in Guicciardini, and may live to thank me for referring him to one of the greatest and most interesting writers whom the world can show.

CHAPTER VI

THE BARBARITIES OF FERDINAND
OF ARAGON
WITH CERTAIN OTHER SUBJECTS WHICH PRESENT
THEMSELVES IN STROLLING ROUND THE CITY

101

It is not possible to stroll along the sea-front much further than the Castle of the Enchanted Egg, because the inclosures of the arsenal occupy the foreshore. Thus the only course open is to turn inland, and, retracing one's steps a little, to pass up beneath the shadow of the great cliff of the Pizzofalcone into the Strada Santa Lucia, which has always borne the fame of exhibiting at a glance more of the highly coloured, if uncleanly, life of the poorer Neapolitans than any other district of the city. I suspect its proximity to the hotels had something to do with this high reputation, for crowded as the winding roadway is at times with fishermen and peasant women, there is, I maintain, incomparably more of uncivilised and ancient Naples to be seen in the Strada de' Tribunali, or around Castel Capuano, than is now presented to the eyes of the astonished visitor in Santa Lucia. However, the wide pavement on the side of that highway which opens towards the sea—for the famous creek is filled up now—is at all times a standing-place for booths, chiefly for the sale of the "frutti del mare," edible or not; and there one may see both young 102girls and ancient hags proffering their wares with clamorous pertinacity, making use of a vocabulary which is piquant, if not sweet, and soaring up into howls such as only a Neapolitan throat can execute.

The charm of Santa Lucia is largely of the past. Naples is suffering a change; and at this point one realises for the first time that the old city of dirt and laughter is being swept and garnished. The "piano di risanamento," that much-needed scheme of resanitation which was conceived in Naples after the dread outbreak of cholera had scourged the narrow alleys in a way to make the most careless people think—that great conception of broad streets to be driven through the crowded quarters, letting the sweet and healing sea air course to and fro between the houses, has brought health and may bring cleanliness, but it seems to be expelling gaiety and picturesqueness with the mephitic vapours which have wrought such woe. Naples may be an idle city still, but it is not so idle. It is disorderly and not too safe, yet is more reputable than it was. The rake is contemplating better things, and by-and-by may actually achieve them—an anticipation over which good men must rejoice. But visitors who come to play may lament the increase of seriousness and the vanishing faith that life begins and ends with laughter.

A traveller approaching Naples from this side must needs be struck by the narrowness of the close alleys which pierce the houses of Santa Lucia. Standing in the middle of any one of these vicoli, a man might almost touch both house-fronts, while the walls tower up so high on either hand that only a mere strip of sky is visible, and that with effort. No breeze but one which blew directly on the mouth of these 103alleys could reach the windows of the dense population which inhabits them. Disease stalks unimpeded, beyond the power of science to restrain. The reason for building these lines of houses so close together was, of course, to secure shade, that priceless blessing throughout the burning dog days in southern Italy. No man can have strolled about Italian towns even in fine spring weather without feeling grateful for the shadows which fall on him from some overhanging house-front. Under shelter from the sun the very smells seem less; and in August scarce any price in health may appear too high to pay for a patch of shade which lasts throughout the day.

The curved roadway of Santa Lucia mounts the hill on which the kings of Anjou, having resolved to take up their residence in Naples rather than in Palermo, which was the former capital of the Two Sicilies, built their new castle—Castel Nuovo—still a fortress, though untenable in modern war. This eminence lay outside the city then. Centuries later the town had not absorbed it, and the castle on the knoll remained surrounded by vineyards and the palaces of those princes of the blood who were entitled to dwell in the immediate neighbourhood of the King. Eastwards lay the city, much as one may see it now, filling the hollow of the coast and stretching some way up a hill.

The royal palace, which stands now upon the right, hiding the front of the Castel Nuovo, is of course a modern building. It has no beauty, and I have naught to say concerning it. The handsome piazza laid out before the palace is a pleasant place to stroll in, especially on warm evenings when the lights are glittering and there is music at Gambrinus' Café at the corner. But it has no special interest, 104and I go on therefore round the corner of the piazza past the halting-place of tramcars, past the little garden of the palace and the colonnade of the San Carlo Theatre, till I reach the Piazza del Municipio, where a gateway in the long wall admits to the castle precinct. Admission is free. The sentry at the gate merely nods when I declare my business to be curiosity and nothing more, and leaves me to stroll unchecked up the ascending causeway till I enter the quadrangle of the castle, where a squad of soldiers are drilling awkwardly.

It is strange that many visitors to Naples omit this castle from the sights they see. It is well to spend hours and days in the museum and aquarium, or in wandering from church to church, spoilt as is almost every one among those sacred buildings by the corrupt taste of the eighteenth century, which daubed over noble gothic arches with unmeaning Barocco ornament, and left Naples degraded among Italian cities by the loss of almost all that was once done nobly within her walls in stone or marble. But here is the very fount and centre of the sovereignty of Naples, the home of all its kings since Manfred, the Palace of Anjou and Aragon. In these walls their secrets were deposited, and some to this day remain open to the curious. Here was the chief theatre of their pomp, and here, on the knoll above the shore among the olive groves and orchards that fringed the city walls, unnumbered tragedies occurred.

The castle has two courtyards. The portal leading from the outer to the inner is dignified by what is probably the finest piece of building now left in Naples, the triumphal arch erected by Alfonso of Aragon—first of the two kings who bore that name—to celebrate his conquest of the city and the downfall 105of the last adherents of the old House of Anjou. "Pious, merciful, unconquered": such were the terms in which his character was described upon the arch beneath which he rode in and out in triumph. Mercy was an attribute uncommon in his family; of that all men can judge unto this day. Piety is estimated differently from age to age. In monarchs, at least of mediæval times, it was a virtue of outward observance, and in this Alfonso did perhaps excel. As for the third merit which he claimed, it is not on record that anyone tried to conquer him, except the barons of the kingdom, who were suppressed with a ruthless cruelty which forecast the tyranny of his son and grandson, who wrought the deed of terror in the Church of San Lionardo on the Chiaia.

The archway is chiefly the work of Pietro di Martino of Milan, though it is said that Giuliano da Majano also laboured on it, if not others also. It possesses a noble pair of bronze doors of even greater interest than the archway; for not only is their workmanship extremely fine, but also the figures possess the interest of portraiture. The scenes depicted are the triumphs of King Ferdinand, second of the five monarchs of Aragon, over his revolting barons. There is Ferdinand upon his war-horse talking to the Duke of Taranto, his thin, cruel face recognisable at a glance by the high nose which he derived from his father, King Alfonso, builder of the arch. In the medallions of the door the same sharp face appears; while his son, afterwards Alfonso the Second, bears a shorter, thicker face, which is suggestive, though very falsely, of more kindness.

Let us go into the castle and see what remains there to explain the reputation of inhuman cruelty which history has conferred on these kings. A small 106boy armed with keys is already hovering about expectant; and though it is his purpose to show only the Chapel of Santa Barbara, the slightest hint of a desire to see the subterranean chamber will cause him to lead you through the sacristy, where he will produce a couple of candle ends, and throw open a small doorway hidden in the wall. A winding stair of perhaps twenty steps conducts to a little chamber, faintly lighted by a deep-set window. At first the room seems empty, but as one's eyes adjust themselves to the dim light four coffins become visible, each lying on a shelf, two open and two closed.

Surely, one thinks, this must be a place of private sepulture for the Royal Family or for their servants, and the stair giving access from the chapel was built for the convenience of mourners who wished to stand beside their dead. But the boy, with a chuckle of amusement, lifts the lid of one of the closed coffins. Within lies the mummy of a man, fearfully distorted by his agony, his cramped hands clutched desperately, as if fighting with all his strength against those who held him down. His mouth is contorted, his whole body heaving with a last struggle for life and breath. The man was strangled, there can be no doubt of it; and there he lies to this hour, fully clothed in the garments which he wore when he came down that little winding stair, hose, buttons, and doublet still intact.

Each of the other coffins contains the body of a man slain in his clothes, the head separated, and lying by the shoulders.

Who were these men, and how has it happened that they lie here all together? What made mummies of them, and with what object were their bodies preserved? The answer must be sought in history. The *Diario Ferrarese*, printed by Muratori, tells us 107that "it was the constant habit of King Ferdinand and King Alfonso, when their enemies, whether barons or people, had fallen into their hands, to cut off their heads and keep them salted in chambers underneath their palace." Not content with having dismissed the spirits of their foes to another world, these kingly Aragons must needs have, close by the scene of their continual sports and labours, so many secret pleasure chambers into which they could withdraw at leisure moments and gaze in rapture on the very features of the enemy whose turbulence was stilled and whose wits would never be turned against his king again. Doubtless these visits renewed the joy of killing!

So in this chamber where King Alfonso or his father stood and gloated, one may stand to-day and look down on the same bodies still unmoved—a strange step back into the Middle Ages, and a more revealing glimpse than any other known to me of what Naples was in old days, when its kings—yes, even the best of them!—were tigers, and the seeds were sown of that contempt for life which is to this hour a chief difficulty of those who govern Naples. Who were these men? Surely, one thinks, their rank and importance must be measured by the care with which the King bestowed their bodies in such close neighbourhood to the royal chapel and to his own apartments!

Probably we shall not miss the truth by very much if we conclude them to be some among those barons of the kingdom who, incensed by the harsh government of Ferdinand, and furious beyond all measure with his more hateful son, gave rein to their old affection for the House of Anjou, and conspired with the Pope to confer the realm on a prince of that royal house. It seems strange that even under 108the afflictions of the Aragon sovereignty men should have looked back on the days of Anjou with affection. But the fact is that Alfonso, Duke of Calabria, whose power as the eldest son of the aged King grew stronger daily, was such a ruler as must needs rouse regrets for other days even in a patient generation, much more in one so proud and turbulent as the Neapolitans. Harshness and cruelty they understood; but Alfonso did what no nation will endure. He took the women, even of the noblest houses, at his will. Of this came unquenchable hatred, and in the end the ruin of his house.

The conspiracy was a terrible one. Half the great officers of the kingdom were involved in it, and King Ferdinand knew not where to look for loyalty. The Prince of Salerno, Lord High Admiral of the realm, and the Prince of Bisignano were among the leaders—members both of that great family of San Severino, whose palace is known to every visitor as the Church of the Gesù Nuovo. The Grand Constable, the Grand Seneschal, the King's Secretary—there was no end to the men of note and consequence who joined in the appeal to the Pope to dethrone the tyrants of the House of Aragon, and give the kingdom to René of Lorraine, last descendant of the ancient kings.

Ferdinand was a prince whose sagacity is extolled by all men. He was wise as is the serpent. His statesmanship was of the type made widely known twenty years later by Cæsar Borgia, and in this emergency he practised the same arts as enabled that accomplished dissimulator to strangle his four chief enemies at once. The two occasions deserve close study from those who would understand the statecraft of the fifteenth century. Each was indeed a masterpiece of that art which Machiavelli calls 109"virtù," and it is difficult to decide where to award the palm.

Ferdinand negotiated. It was indeed his only course, for time must be gained at any cost. This was in the regular routine of kings in difficulty. De Comines, in a memorable passage, explains how useful it is to send ambassadors to meet one's enemies; they see so much even while they are treating. Ferdinand negotiated with such skill, such open frankness and goodwill, showed such a broad and merciful spirit, and was so ready to forgive, that the conspirators, who had waited in vain for their new king, accepted the accord and returned sullenly to their castles, doubting and fearing sorely.

"Let no man think that present kindnesses lead to the forgetting of past injuries," says Machiavelli, laying bare the roots of human nature in his incisive way. To do them justice, the barons supposed no such thing. The Prince of Salerno was missing one fine morning. On the gateway of his palace was a card, on which were inscribed the mystic words—"Passero vecchio non entra in caggiola" (An old sparrow does not go into the cage). He is said to have got out of the city disguised as a muleteer. Other sparrows were less prudent or more unfortunate. The cage doors were wide open, and the King and Duke sat piping so prettily that any bird might have thought it safe to flutter in. Towards the Count of Sarno Ferdinand showed particular affection. His son Marco Coppola was betrothed to the daughter of the Duke of Amalfi, the King's nephew. The wedding was at hand. It must be held in the Royal Palace, in Castel Nuovo, if only to mark the royal favour. There were great festivities. The pomp of the Court was boundless. But the wedding 110garments which the King was preparing were not of this world. Midway in the feastings and the music, when all men were confident and careless, the stroke fell. How, one wonders, did Ferdinand and Alfonso look at that moment when, sitting at the head of the tables, gazing down upon their guests, bridegroom and bride and relatives trusting in the royal honour, they gave the signal and called in the soldiers who turned that feast to terror? How did the guests look when the guard went round arresting every man of mark or consequence within the hall? Surely since Belshazzar was King in Babylon no feast has been broken up more awfully!

The craft and treachery of this great stroke fixed once for all the reputation of Ferdinand and Alfonso. The nice taste of Renaissance Italy revolted, giving voice to loud condemnation. King and Prince, surprised at the outcry, paused, and held back the secret executioner. It would be safer to have a show of justice; so a court was nominated, the prisoners were tried, and when they had been despatched from the world in this unexceptionable manner, one by one the other dukes and barons were caught and led into the secret pleasure chambers, whence they never more emerged. The Prince of Bisignano, the Duke of Melfi, the Duke of Nardo, counts and knights innumerable disappeared. Their children and their wives were treated in like manner. Few escaped; but for many a day Neapolitans told the tale how Bandella Gaetano, Princess of Bisignano, a woman of high courage and resource, fled with her young children to the Church of San Lionardo in the Chiaia; and there, profiting by the old fame of the saint as the guardian of fugitives, bribed a boatman to take her on to Terracina, and so sought refuge with the 111Colonnas. Ferdinand would have given much to stamp out the brood; and had he been able to turn the pages of the book of fate he would have given even more.

What happened to the prisoners was never known. For some time the fiction was kept up that they were alive, and food was even sent daily to their cells, set down perhaps beside the salted bodies in mockery. But the executioner was seen wearing a gold chain which had belonged to the Prince of Bisignano; and ere long it was known that every one was dead.

There is no doubt that in these awful days the Church of San Lionardo was filled with fugitives. It was there that Alfonso wrought that nameless deed of terror which dwelt so heavily upon his conscience as to destroy his nerves and send him fleeing from the kingdom. We have seen what things his conscience would endure; perhaps it is as well we remain in ignorance of what it would not. But if we argue from the known to the unknown we may form a surmise of the nature of that act which is enough to banish sleep, and may well make us grateful that the walls of that old sanctuary which concealed so terrible a secret stand no longer on the smiling shore which is the chosen parade of Neapolitan society of our own day.

There are two chapels in the castle, one opening from the other; but both lost whatever beauty they once had by the deplorable passion for Barocco, which wrought such evil in Naples. Two great beauties still remain, though not inside the chapels. One is the doorway, a lovely work of Giuliano da Majano, mercifully left untouched, I know not by what happy chance; the other is a winding staircase behind the choir, consisting of a hundred and fifty-eight 112steps, each formed of a single block of travertine, and so arranged that their inward edges form a perfect cylinder. There is no end to the scenes of history and tragedy which are recalled by these old walls and chambers, in which the hottest passions of life in Naples have spent themselves so often, even from the first coming of Charles of Anjou down to the creation of the Parthenopean Republic, when Nelson received the surrender of the Revolutionists, driven to despair by the arrival of his fleet. But these are tales which visitors must find out for themselves. If they will not go to Castel Nuovo on the inducement which I have given them, neither will they if I should write a volume.

NAPLES—OLD TOWN.

When I emerge from the old palace fortress I hesitate, being, in truth, half inclined to turn directly to the Carmine, the strongest point of interest in Naples. But a man will fail to comprehend the relation of the Carmine to ancient Naples if he goes to it by the broad street along the quays which lay outside the mediæval city. It is better to plunge into the maze of narrow ways which still, unto this hour, retain the general aspect of the city wherein Boccaccio rambled, picking up in I know not what haunt of roysterers those sad tales which beguile one yet in the pages of the *Decameron*. Who has not read of the nocturnal adventures of Andreuccio, who came from Pisa to Naples to buy horses with twenty gold florins in his pocket? Who would not wish to see the very lanes through which he wandered naked in the night? Who has not felt the charm of that naïve irresponsibility which pervades the tales of Naples in old days? Does it still exist? Are the narrow lanes athrob even now on summer nights with the thrumming of the lute, with 113the patter of girls' feet, made musical by wafts of song blown down from lofty windows?

"Flower of the rose,
If I've been merry, what matter who knows?"

31

Well, let us go and see; and first we will turn up the Toledo, now rechristened "Via Roma," that long straight street which the Viceroy Don Pietro di Toledo made without the city wall, and which is still the chief artery of life and fashion.

The narrow vista, made picturesque by hanging balconies and green shutters, is bathed in sunshine—not the fierce glare which even in early summer brings out the awnings used to convert the footways into shaded corridors, but the pleasant golden glow of an April Eastertide, carrying with it the reek of violets and early roses. It is no wonder that the street is odorous of flowers; for at any corner a few soldi will buy them by the handful, fresh and dewy, redolent of summer, though indeed summer never flees far from this sunny coast, and even in midwinter she will slip back for a while, bringing golden days. It is on the stroke of noon, noon of Holy Thursday, and in another hour the roadway will be closed to vehicles. For on this day, by custom old enough to be respectable, the Neapolitans go on foot to visit the sepulchres of Christ in the churches, combining this exercise of devotion with the more worldly solaces of friendship and social intercourse. There was a time when princesses came down and mingled with the throng, the royal ladies of the House of Bourbon going to and fro on foot; while the rustling of their long dresses of black silk gave the ceremony its picturesque title of "Lu Struscio." There being no princesses in Naples now, the old ceremony has lost some of its attractions for the nobly born; but it is still honoured, 114and already the carriages are growing thin, while in every part of the long street men armed with long brooms are reducing the whole width to the same state of cleanliness as the footpaths. With the disappearance of the vetturino a blessed peace steals down upon the air. This is, I should suppose, the one day in the year on which a man can hear himself speak in the Via Roma. But Naples, passionate for noise, is never long without it. Fast as the vetturini go the hawkers come, hoarse and raucous; men with strings of chestnuts, boys holding tiny Java sparrows on their finger-tips, women thrusting at you trays of "pastiere," without which no good citizen of Naples would dream of passing Easter, any more than he would go through Christmas without "capitoni." It is rarely wise to apply to local delicacies any other test than that of sight. The women push past me with their trays, knowing well that their market does not lie among the strangers. Meantime the Via Santa Brigida, which crosses the Via Roma, has broken out into a jungle of standing booths, on which are displayed proudly cheap playthings for the children, sweetmeats and other paschal joys, mingled with combs, shirtings, and suchlike useful articles, to which attention is drawn by huge placards.

OCCASIONE!

FERMATEVI! TASTATE! GIUDICATE!

while the seething crowd which hustles round the stalls is animated by any but a feeling of devotion.

So the throng gathers, till by-and-by the Via Roma is a sea of moving heads. The church doors stand wide open, of itself an unusual sight in Naples, where the churches are closed at noon, and reopen only for an hour in the evening. Their doorways are 115curtained heavily in black, and beneath the hanging folds a ceaseless stream of people are passing in and out, pressing forward to where the recumbent figure of our Lord lies at the foot of a blazing trophy of flowers and wax lights, kissing the contorted limbs fervently, then hurrying away. A large proportion of these devotees are dressed in black, especially the older women, but among them are many who seem more anxious to display their bright spring toilettes, and the crowded street assumes the aspect of a drawing-room, in which greetings and laughing salutations fly freely on all hands. It is all picturesque enough, and a relic of old life in Naples which is worth seeing.

In the absence of the usual street noises, in the solemn trappings of the churches, and yet more in the tramp of crowds so largely clad in mourning, there is not wanting a suggestion of funeral pomp; and as I stand apart and watch the throng go by, there comes into my mind the memory of a solemn procession which once came down this famous highway, bearing to the grave the body of a lad whom the city, by the strangest freak, had raised in one day from the lowest to the highest station, and cast down as suddenly into a bloody grave, one who had enough heroism in his ignorant mind to resent oppression, and might—who knows?—have proved an earlier Garibaldi, had he been supported by the nobles. It was Mas'aniello who was thus borne dead down the slope of the Toledo, honoured by the weeping people who were little likely to find another leader bold enough to head them, honoured even by the Church, which rarely refuses outward show of honour to the men she has destroyed. First came a hundred boys of the conservatorio of Loreto, then all the brothers of the monasteries, to the number of 116four hundred, and then the body of the fisherman dictator, wrapped in a white shroud folded so that all might see the head—I hope it had not that hideous look of death and anguish from which one shrinks on seeing the wooden model in the museum of San Martino! After the bier walked great crowds of Mas'aniello's followers, those ragamuffin soldiers who but a few days earlier had stormed down this street in triumph, sacking and destroying where they pleased. Now they walked mournfully and slow, as well they might, for liberty lay upon the bier they followed, and the Spanish tyranny was about to close over them again. Behind them trailed their flags, and they marched to the soft beat of muted drums all hung with crape. But last of all came those who made this great procession memorable beyond all others. The soldiers were followed by a countless throng of women of the people. Out of every lane and alley of the swarming city they had come to bid farewell to their defender, to the one man who in many generations had dared to show them that they were not worms. Many of them carried lighted candles, weeping bitterly as they went slowly by; while others sang in tearful voices the "Santissimo Rosario," in trust that the brave soul of the departed might find peace.

So through this outskirt of the city the funeral train of Mas'aniello came from the Carmine and went back to that centre of the life and tragedy of Naples. We too will go there presently, and then will talk the more about Mas'aniello. But first we must walk through the ancient city, and that is now quite close at hand. I have traversed almost half the length of the Toledo—the ancient name comes more readily than the modern—passing by the little Largo della Carità, where in the shadow of the tramcars green 117bays hang around the tablet that protests against forgetfulness of Felice Cavallotti. I am in sight of the Piazza Dante, and a little more would show me the red walls of the museum, when I halt beneath the vast and heavy front of the Palazzo Maddaloni, and turning round into the shadow of the Strada Quercia, I see the fine courtyard and loggia of the palace, eloquent of pomps and ceremonies which find no match in the Naples of to-day. Some hundred and fifty yards beyond the palace the old line of the city walls crossed the street at right angles. There is not a sign of walls or towers now. The ancient quadrangle of streets and alleys, the old Greek city which held out so stoutly generation after generation when besieged by Lombard or Imperialist, lies open now to strangers of every nation. On entering its precinct one appears to have found a new world, albeit an unsavoury one. For here, in place of the irregular and curved vistas in which the builders of modern Naples have delighted, is a long narrow street of exceeding straightness, cleaving like an arrow-flight through the close-packed houses. Irresistibly it brings to mind the long straight streets of Pompeii, so far as a thoroughfare seething with crowded life can recall one which lies silent and open under the winds of heaven. It is a just comparison; for indeed Pompeii still retains the very aspect which Naples must have borne. In size, in manner of construction, in defences, the two towns were closely similar, and this long street which under several names pierces the ancient city from side to side, was one of the three Decuman ways which every visitor to the buried city traces out and follows. A little higher up the hill is the Decumanus Major, now called the Strada de' Tribunali, and still by far the most interesting street in Naples, while higher yet 118upon the slope the third of the Decuman streets runs parallel to the other two under the name of Strada Anticaglia, and in it stood the ancient theatre, some remnants of which still exist between the Vico di S. Paolo and the Vico de' Giganti. These three Decuman streets are the arteries of ancient Naples. In them, and in the countless alleys which unite them, are to be found almost all the relics of the mediæval city; and indeed a man wandering about beneath those unmodernised house-fronts, elbowing his way through crowds of ragged peasants and of burly priests, might well doubt in what century he found himself, so unlike the scene is to the trim world which he has known elsewhere.

But these are quarters in which it is not prudent to wander when the night is falling. Naples is not a safe city, and travellers would do wisely to realise the fact. Even in broad daylight caution and good sense are needed more than in most other cities. Ladies will show it by removing from their dress all ornaments of the slightest value, and men by refusing absolutely all inducements to enter houses, whether offered by small boys professing to find sacristans—a not uncommon trick—or by any other person not known and vouched for. After dark, if a man must walk alone, he should walk carefully on the light side of the street and restrain any curiosity he may feel to see the effect of moonlight on the houses until he can watch it safely from his own window. These are not unnecessary cautions. Neapolitans themselves do not neglect them, though strangers do; and many have found cause to regret it. I myself, while walking with a lady in the immediate neighbourhood of the cathedral, have seen her caught by the waist by a burly brute and shaken as a terrier shakes a rat in the effort to unclasp 119a handsome silver buckle which she wore. The rascal failed, and was gone again before he could be seized. But the experience is one which few men would desire their wives or sisters to undergo. Complaint is useless. It is even doubtful whether, in a city where almost every robber has a knife, worse things may not happen to those who meet such attacks in the customary English manner. But the remedy is simple. Carry nothing which is of any obvious value. Avoid unnecessary conversation with poor boys, who are not safe guides. Go home while it is still light. With these plain rules men and women equally may explore the recesses of old Naples with pleasure and with almost perfect safety.

It is out of these teeming quarters, packed with a population as dense and fetid as that of Seven Dials, that the Camorra, the great secret society of Naples, drew the strength and vigour which enables it still to defy the law. There would be no exaggeration in saying that hardly a full generation has passed by since in all the lower quarters of the city the Camorra ruled with an audacity so high that there was neither man nor woman, boy nor girl, who did not know he must obey it rather than the law. The law was blind and deaf. The Camorra had eyes and ears in every vicolo and every cellar. It discovered all things; it struck heavily and secretly at those who tried to thwart it. A fruitseller who resisted payment of dues to the Camorrist would find his custom disappear. Accident upon accident would happen to his goods. Ere long he would be a ruined man. The Camorra might accept his submission, if proffered humbly and accompanied by a fine; but any active resistance, any communication with the police, would be repaid by a knife-thrust 120in the stomach some dark night. Fishermen, street hawkers, vetturini, guides—all were under the thrall of the ruthless organisation, all paid tribute in return for its protection, and executed its orders without remorse.

So far as is known to outsiders, the aims of the Camorra—which still exists, and wields considerable power yet—were not mainly political, though it was certainly at one time a powerful engine in the hands of those who desired the return of the Bourbons. That desire, once passionate in Naples, has almost died away. Francis the Second is dead, and there is none who can breathe life into the dry bones of his party. If the devotion to the old Royal House exists, it is kept alive by the exertions of the priests, who would make a hero of Apollyon if he came down on earth and showed a disposition to unseat the present king. The lower orders are still as clerical as in the days of Mas'aniello. Turbulent and fierce as are their passions, they are capable of high devotion; and a spiritual ruler who exerted the whole influence of the Church might turn them into a great people. But here too, as at every turn in Italy, the task of government is checked and hampered by the hostility of Church and Crown. No foreigner can appreciate the chances of this struggle, or even apportion fairly blame between the combatants. It is enough for those of us who love Italy to sit and watch the unrolling of the future, lamenting that from the outset of her career as a united nation she has been wrestling with a Church whose traditions lie in the humbling of emperors and kings.

CHAPTER VII

CHIEFLY ABOUT CHURCHES
WITH SOME SAINTS, BUT MORE SINNERS

121

He who will see the churches of Naples must rise betimes, since ancient custom closes them, for unknown reasons, from eleven o'clock till four. Some say the poor man will get nothing for his pains. But this is not so. It is indeed impossible that sacred buildings in a city so old and famous as Naples should be devoid of interest. Here, as elsewhere, they reflect the strong emotions of the citizens, their sorrows and their aspirations; and though it is true that many a once noble building has been daubed over with unmeaning ornament so freely that one has trouble in discovering the pure taste with which the builders wrought it, yet there is not a church in Naples which does not set vibrating some chord either of beauty or poignant association. No man can know the city or its people if he neglect the churches. Past and present jostle each other perpetually there, and the effigies of kings look down with fine grave eyes on the filthy peasant women lifting up their children to kiss the feet of the dead Christ.

I have paused in the Strada Quercia opposite the Gesù Nuovo, once, as I have said before, the palace of the San Severini, Princes of Salerno. It was on 122that fine doorway that the Prince affixed the inscription "An old sparrow does not enter into the cage," as he stood beneath his ancestral gateway listening for the mule team with its jingling bells which gave him his chance of life and safety. Perhaps he waited under this old archway till he saw the beasts with high-piled burdens coming up this way from the Mercato, and slipped in silently among the swarthy knaves who led them, and so forth from the city and away to France, where he hatched a scheme of vengeance which destroyed the King, his enemy. The tinkling of those mule-bells as they went up this narrow street in the night fell on no ears that heeded them, yet in truth and earnest they were ringing the dirge of the House of Aragon.

The interior of the Gesù is among those which arouse the citizens of Naples to enthusiasm. It is not without grandeur, but over-decorated, and on my mind it leaves but little sense of pleasure.

But from this archway where I stand I can see a church far older and more interesting, one indeed which yields in fame to none in Naples. It is Santa Chiara, whose dignified façade rears itself with twin towers in the cool shadow of the courtyard, a name famous not only in the ecclesiastical history of Naples, but in the legal also, having given its title to a great body of state councillors which once met here. It was the royal chapel of King Robert the Wise, third among the monarchs of his house, and the only prosperous one out of the whole number, though even he was pursued by sorrows, and by remorse too, unless the constant suspicions of the centuries have erred.

For the tale goes that Robert knew better than any other the cause of that sudden illness which carried off his elder brother, Charles Martel, King of 123Hungary, when, towards the close of their father's life, he came to Naples to arrange for the succession. Stories of mediæval poisonings are to be received with caution. No man who glances round Naples to-day, swept and garnished as it has been by advancing science, will find it hard to understand how swiftly disease may—nay, must have struck in those crowded dirty streets six centuries ago. Yet Robert was believed to have seized the throne by fratricide. This Church of Santa Chiara was his atonement for the crime, and by its high altar he sleeps for ever, robed as a monk and throned as a king, beneath a monument of rare beauty, on which Petrarch wrote the jingling epitaph, "Cernite Robertum, regem virtute refertum."

"Chock full of virtue." Such was Petrarch's judgment on King Robert dead, and doubtless he believed it, for the King's Court was splendid, poets and scholars were held in honour, and Florentines especially. Innocent or guilty, Robert ruled with a magnificence which makes his reign the one bright spot in the troubled history of the Anjou sovereigns; and posterity, which has little good to say of any of them, remembers gratefully that he procured the laurel crown for Petrarch, and gave his protection to that rake Boccaccio.

Let us go in and see his church. It is rectangular, and has no aisles, while a long range of chapels upon either hand recall irresistibly the quirk recorded of King Robert's son, when his father, proud of the progress which the church was making, brought him in to admire its fair proportions. The graceless lad gazed round, and it struck him that the chapels were not unlike so many mangers. So when the King pressed him for his opinion he remarked airily that the church reminded him of 124a stable, whereupon the King said angrily, "God grant, my son, that you be not the first to eat in those stalls!"

34

It was a prophetic speech, and one which must have returned many times on the King's memory, for the historian Giannone assures us that the first train of royal mourners who entered the new church were following the coffin of this very lad, King Robert's firstborn, and the hope of the realm.

The chief artist selected to adorn Santa Chiara with frescoes was no other than the great Florentine, Giotto. Petrarch, Boccaccio, Giotto! How the best brains of Tuscany flocked to Naples in those days! The explanation of it was, apart from the natural attractions of a splendid Court, that when Charles of Anjou defeated and slew Manfred, he cast down by that act, and ruined throughout Italy, the party of Ghibellines, the Emperor's men, of whom Manfred, son of a great emperor, was naturally head. The Guelfs, the Pope's men, returned to Florence, whence they had been banished, and straightway the closest ties sprang up between the city on the Arno and the city of the Siren, so close that the money-bags of Florence saved Charles from ruin at least once.

So Tuscan poets and artists making the weary ten days' journey were assured that on the shores of the blue gulf they would find compatriots. Giotto came most gladly, and in the chapels of Santa Chiara he painted many scenes of Bible story, all of which were daubed over with whitewash by order of a Spanish officer a century and a half ago. He complained that they made the church dark. There is indeed one fresco left in the old refectory, now a shop. But Crowe and Cavalcaselle do not accept it as the work of the same hand.

So here, in the large, cool church, Giotto painted 125for many a day, alternating his labours perhaps with visits to Castel dell'Uovo, where he painted the chapel, now a smoky, useful kitchen! King Robert loved the man, so shrewd and cogent was his talk, and often came to chat with him in one place or the other. "If I were you, Giotto, I should stop painting now it is so hot," observed the King. "So should I, if I were you," returned the artist dryly. And one day, wishing perhaps to warn Robert by how frail a tenure he held his throne, he painted an ass stooping under one pack saddle and looking greedily towards another lying at his feet. Both saddles were adorned with crowns, and the explanation was that the ass typified the Neapolitans, who thought any other saddle better than the one they bore.

The most beautiful works of art in Santa Chiara, if not indeed in the whole city, are the eleven small reliefs which run as a frieze along the organ gallery. The scenes are from the life of St. Katherine, martyr as well as saint. Dignified and tender, wrought with the rarest delicacy, yet inspired with astonishing vigour, the graceful figures are in white relief upon a ground of black. Very memorable and lovely they appear, rebuking the corrupt taste which has begotten so much base ornament in Naples.

Next to this frieze the interest of Santa Chiara lies in its monuments, for in this Royal Chapel of Anjou many children of that house were buried. The King himself assumed the frock of a Franciscan monk before his death, craving for a peace which he did not find upon his throne, and lies recumbent therefore, attired humbly in his habit, while on a higher story of the monument he sits enthroned in all his earthly splendour, gazing down upon his church with those keen features which were characteristic 126of his house, the thin hooked nose, not unlike a vulture's beak, so strangely like that which one sees on the coins of his grandfather, murderer of Conradin. Uneasy were the lives of all the monarchs of that house; their throne was set in blood, and in blood it was perpetually slipping.

I left Santa Chiara by the northern door, which opens on a handsome double staircase descending to the courtyard. In this wide space there is fine shadow, and, by contrast with the noisy street outside, the square is almost silent—a wondrous thing in Naples! Across the court, beside the archway by which I entered, rises the noble campanile, once planned on Gothic lines, but interrupted by the death of King Robert, and finished two centuries and a half later by an architect who transformed it into the classic style. There are mean houses all around, occupied by people who care not one jot for King Robert or his lost design.

Down the incline of the courtyard, where Boccaccio may well have whispered guilty secrets to his Anjou princess, there loafs a hawker with his donkey, his head thrown back, his brown hat tilted picturesquely, bawling with iron throat the praises of his leeks and cabbages, while the donkey creeps on cautiously over the broken stones. In the Neapolitan speech he is the "padulano"—the man who comes from the swamp, by which is meant the low plain of the Sebeto, that muddy river which the railway to Castellammare crosses on the outskirts of the city. On this marshy ground grow quantities of early vegetables, and these it is which the padulano goes vaunting in his brazen voice. He needs his strength of lung, for see! on the highest story a woman has heard his bawling and comes out upon her balcony. At that height they do not bargain in 127words, but in signs, the universal language of the people. A few rapid passes of the hands and the business is done. The woman lets down a basket by a rope; a few soldi are jingling in the bottom; the basket goes up packed with green stuff, and the padulano loafs on beside his patient donkey.

It is in these crowded quarters of the ancient city, these streets through which the noisy, swarthy, dirty people were seething just as they are now when Pompeii was a peopled town and the hawkers went up and down the streets of Herculaneum,—it is here that one can grasp most easily those peculiarities which fence off life in southern Italy from that of other regions in the peninsula. Here is neither the dignity of Rome nor the gracious charm of Tuscany, but another world, a life more hot and passionate, more noisy and more sensuous, a character strangely blended out of the blood of many nations—Greek, Saracen, Norman, Spaniard—each of which contributed some burning drop to the quick glow of the Campanian nature, making it both fierce and languid, keen and subtle beyond measure when its interests are engaged, capable of labour, but not loving it, easily depressed, and when thwarted turning swiftly to the thought of blood. Here is difficult material for the statesman. Never yet, in all its vicissitudes of government, have these volcanic, elemental passions been concentrated on any one great object. In the War of Independence Milan had its "Cinque Giorni"; Venice, led by Manin, struck a glorious blow at the oppressor; but Naples effected nothing till Garibaldi came with armies from without.

How the street swarms with curious figures! I stand aside in the opening of a side lane, and there goes past me a man carrying in one hand a 128pail of steaming water, while on his other arm he has a flat basket, containing the sliced feelers of an octopus, and a tray of rusks. At the low price of a soldo you may choose your own portion of the hideous dainty, warm it in the water and devour it on the spot. Close upon his heels, bawling out his contribution to the deafening noises of the streets, comes the "pizzajuolo," purveyor of a dainty which for centuries has been unknown elsewhere. "Pizza" may be seen in every street in Naples. It is a kind of biscuit, crisp and flavoured with cheese, recognisable at a glance by the little fish, like whitebait, which are embedded in its brown surface, dusted over with green chopped herbs. I cannot recommend the dainty from personal knowledge, but Neapolitan tradition is strongly in its favour.

The pizzajuolo goes off chanting down a sideway, and I, moving on a little, still away from the Toledo and towards the older quarter of the town, find that the street has widened out into a small square, the Largo San Domenico, on the left of which stands the famous Church of San Domenico Maggiore, second in beauty to none in Naples, and perhaps less spoilt than many others by the hand of the restorer. The bronze statue of the saint stands on a pillar in the square, looking down on the palaces which were once the homes of Neapolitan nobles, dwelling gladly in this centre point of the great city. Neither cavaliers nor ladies live here now. The world of trade and civic institutions has slipped into their abandoned palaces, and enjoys the spacious rooms and frescoed ceilings which were designed for the splendour of great entertainments.

On the southern side of the Largo, sloping towards the sea, runs the Via Mezzocannone, which, if antiquaries 129are to be believed, was the ditch skirting the city wall upon the western side in Greco-Roman days. It is a lane worth following, though narrow and somewhat fetid, for by it one may reach not only a certain very ancient fountain, the Fontana Mezzocannone, which is of itself worth seeing, but also the Church of San Giovanni Pappacoda, and by careful search may even find the bas-relief of Niccolo Pesce, of whom I spoke at length in a former chapter. But my course is eastwards. I turn up the steps, and enter the Church of San Domenico Maggiore by a door admitting to its southern transept.

The cool and silent chapel into which one steps is the most ancient part of the church, massive and severe. The first glance reveals that the building must have been in a high degree esteemed a place of sepulture. The tombs are very numerous, and names of mark in the history of Naples appear on every side. Through the vaulted doorway leading to the main body of the church there stream long rolling melodies, the crash of a fine organ played triumphantly, and the grand music of a pure tenor voice, ringing high among the arches. The church is full of kneeling figures, among which others stroll about with little care for their devotions; while children, infinitely dirty, waddle up and down untended, as if the show were for their amusement only.

The chanting ceases, and the priests in their gorgeous vestments stream down the altar steps towards the sacristy. I have come at an unlucky moment! The sacristy at least will be closed till the priests have done unrobing! But no! The hawk-eyed sacristan has marked down the stranger, and hurries up obsequious and eager to detain me. I cannot think of leaving without seeing the most interesting sight in Naples—the coffins? "Si, sicuro! The very sarcophagi 130of all the princes of the House of Aragon." "But they are in the sacristy," I object, "and that is full of priests unrobing!" "Oh, you English, you odd people," hints the sacristan, with a shrug. "What does that matter?" If he does not care, why should I? And in another moment we are in the sacristy.

Clearly the sacristan knew his ground, and has committed no breach of manners; for among the crowd of ecclesiastics, young and old, which fills the long panelled chamber, some jovial, some ascetic, many chatting pleasantly, others resting on long seats, not one betrays the least surprise at the intrusion of a tourist bent on sightseeing. High dignitaries, arrayed like Solomon in his glory, make way courteously as the sacristan draws me forward, and standing in the centre of the vast apartment points out that the panelling ceases at half the height of the walls, leaving a kind of shelf, on which lie, shrouded in red velvet, to the number of five-and-forty, the coffins of the family of Aragon, and the chief adherents of their house.

Here, taking what rest remorse allows him, is that Ferdinand who trapped the barons in Castel Nuovo. His son Alfonso, who shared in that and other infamies, is not here. He lies in Sicily, whither he fled at the bidding of the furies who pursued him. But close by is his son, the young King Ferdinand, whose chance of redeeming the fame of his house was lost by death. And here is that luckless Isabella, Duchess of Milan and of Bari, whose husband, Duke Giovanni Galeazzo Sforza, was robbed of throne and life by his uncle Ludovic the Moor, the man who, more than any other, was accountable for all the woes and slavery of Italy. What bitter tragedies were closed when the scarlet palls were flung over those old coffins! Here, too, is the dust 131of the base scoundrel Pescara, archetype of treachery for all ages, at least of public treachery. In private life his heart may have been true enough, else how could his wife Vittoria Colonna have loved and mourned him as she did? It is no new sight to see a woman lay great love at the feet of a man who, on one view, is quite unworthy of it.

Her knowledge is the wider, and the account as she cast it may be the truer. Why need we be puzzled that we cannot make our balance agree with hers? How is it possible that we should?

On leaving San Domenico Maggiore, my desire is to pass into the Strada Tribunali, the largest and most important of the three streets which still cleave the city as they did in ancient days. The cross ways turning up by San Domenico are devious and narrow, evil alleys darkened sometimes by the high dead wall of a church or convent, at others bristling with life, from the foul "bassi," the cellars which are the despair of Neapolitan reformers, where ragged women crouch over a chafing-dish of bronze, their only fire, and all the refuse is flung out in the gutter, up to the high garrets where the week's wash is hung out on a pole to dry. Not the freshest wind which blows across the sea from Ischia can bring sweetness to these alleys, or expel the wandering fever which on small inducement blazes to an epidemic and slays ruthlessly. There were high hopes of Naples when the "risanamento" was begun, that great scheme of clearance which was to let in fresh air and sunshine among the rookeries. But already the new tenements begin to be as crowded and as filthy as the old ones, and the better era is soiled at its very outset. One cannot make a people clean against its will. And then the sunshine! Week after week it is a curse in Naples. The old narrow 132streets made shadow, the new wide ones do not. Who knows whether the city will escape more lightly when the next epidemic comes? God grant it may! For the days of cholera in 1884 were more awful than one cares to think about.

Among these devious lanes lies the Chapel of San Severo, a shrine which everyone should visit, but one concerning which I have nothing to say that is not set forth in the guide-books. Had it been the Church of San Severo and San Sosio indeed, I could have told a grisly tale of poisonings; but that lies far down towards the harbour and we shall not pass it. At length I emerge in the narrow Street of Tribunals, and turning eastwards behold it running straight and crowded further than the eye will reach, a wilderness of bustling figures, a maze of balconies and garrets, bright shops high piled with fruit and vegetables, and butchers' stalls dressed with green boughs to keep off the flies. At a corner stands the booth of a lemonade seller, one of the most picturesque of all street merchants in this busy city. His golden fruit is heaped up underneath a canopy which shades it from the sun. Brown water-jars are reared among the fruit and a jet of water sparkling up sheds a cool dewy spray over oranges and lemons, dripping off their dark green leaves like dew. Many a passer-by stops to look at the pretty sight, and the vendor's tongue is never still, "A quatto, a cinque, a sei a sordo, 'e purtualle 'e Palermo." In another month or two his stall will be far gayer, for the figs and melons will come in, and the "mellonaro" will pass the day in shouting "Castiellamare! che maraviglia! so' di Castiellamare! mellune verace! cu' 'no sordo vevo e me lavo 'a faccia!" With a water-melon one may drink and wash one's face at once! Who has not seen the street urchins gnawing at a slice of 133crimson melon, while the water streams out from among the black seeds, and does in truth make streaks of cleanliness at least upon their faces; for not the widest mouth can catch all the dripping juice.

In this ancient street one is at the heart of Naples. This strong pulse of life, this eager, abounding vitality has throbbed along this thoroughfare for more ages than one can count; and the sight on which we look to-day, the seething crowd, the straight house-fronts, the long street dropping to the east, is different in no essential from that which has been seen by every ruler of the city—Spaniard, Angevin, or Norman, yes, even by Greek and Roman governors—from days when the fires of Vesuvius were a forgotten terror, and the streets of Pompeii surged with just such another crowd as this. It is here, in this most ancient Strada Tribunali, that the traveller should pause before he visits the old buried cities. Here and here only will he learn to comprehend how they were peopled; and only when he carries with him in the eyes of memory the aspect of the cellars and the shops, the crowded side streets and the pandemonium of noise, will he succeed in discovering at Pompeii more than a heap of ruins, out of which the interest dies quickly because his imagination has not gained materials out of which to reconstruct the living city.

Neapolis, the old Greek city, was similar to Pompeii both in size and construction. Its situation, too, was not dissimilar. It stood near the sea, yet did not touch it, having a clear space of open ground between its strand and walls, perhaps because the sea was an open gateway into every town which stood upon it, though the nature of the ground partly dictated the arrangement. There is no building, even in the Strada Tribunali, which was standing when Pompeii 134was a city. The oldest left is near the point at which we entered the street—to be exact, it is at the angle of the Strada Tribunali and the Vico di Francesco del Giudice—a tall brick campanile of graceful outline which, in the confusion of the narrow street, one might most easily pass unobserved. That is the only portion still remaining of the church built by Bishop Pomponio, between the years 514 and 532; and not only is it almost, if not quite the most ancient building now extant in Naples, but it was the first of Neapolitan churches known to have been dedicated to the Virgin, and it is thus especially sacred in the eyes of the citizens.

Going eastwards still along this most interesting street I come ere long to a great church upon my right where I must pause, for there are associated with it closely the memories both of Petrarch and Boccaccio. Now of these two men I confess to a strong preference for the rake. He was a sinner, and a great one. But for that matter he was a penitent in the end, and had he not found grace, it is for no man to scorn him. Iniquitous though they be, I prefer the record of his warm human passions to the dry spirituality of Petrarch; and to me one tale out of the *Decameron*, with its high beat of joyous and exultant life, is worth all the sonnets in which the poet of Avignon bewailed the fact that the moon would not come down out of heaven.

37

No one who has turned over the works of Boccaccio is unacquainted with the name of Fiammetta. She was of course not least among the seven ladies of noble birth who met in the Church of Santa Maria Novella in Florence on that Tuesday morning when the tales of the *Decameron* begin. She, too, it was whose amorous musings Boccaccio published in a book which bore her name. In fact her warm-blooded 135personality pervades the writings of her lover; and it was in this Church of San Lorenzo that he saw her first, as he tells us himself in the *Filocopo*. The passage is well known to be autobiographical, though occurring in a tale of pure, or rather impure imagination.

"I found myself," he says, "in a fine church of Naples, named after him who endured to be offered as a sacrifice upon the gridiron. And in it there was a singing compact of sweetest melody. I was listening to the Holy Mass celebrated by a priest, successor to him who first girt himself humbly with the cord, exalting poverty and adopting it. Now while I stood there, the fourth hour of the day, according to my reckoning, having already passed down the Eastern sky, there appeared to my eyes the wondrous beauty of a young woman, come hither to hear what I too heard attentively. I had no sooner seen her than my heart began to throb so strongly that I felt it in my slightest pulses; and not knowing why, nor yet perceiving what had happened, I began to say, 'Oimè, what is this?'... But at length, being unable to sate myself with gazing, I said, 'Oh, Love, most noble lord, whose strength not even the gods were able to resist, I thank thee for setting happiness before my eyes!'... I had no sooner said these words than the flashing eyes of the lovely lady fixed themselves on mine with a piercing light."

There was sin in that look, though not perhaps by the standard of those days. It was an Anjou princess who won immortality in the Church of San Lorenzo on that Holy Thursday when she was dreaming of nothing but a lover—perhaps not even of so much as that. She was the Princess Maria, natural daughter of King Robert the Wise, he whose tomb we saw in the Church of Santa Chiara. She 136had a husband; but no one asks or remembers his name. It is with Boccaccio that her memory is linked for evermore. She was certainly of rare beauty. Her lover, than whom no man ever wrote more delicately, tries to fix it for all time. "Hair so blonde that the world holds nothing like it shadows a white forehead of noble width, beneath which are the curves of two black and most slender eyebrows ... and under these two wandering and roguish eyes ... cheeks of no other colour than milk." Item two lips, indifferent red! Why, what a shiver it gives one to realise that not Boccaccio himself can convey to us any real picture of his love! Even the magic of his style, informed by all the passion of his burning heart, can give us nothing better than a catalogue of charms such as any village lover of to-day might write! The dead are dead; and no wizard can set them before us as they lived.

Yet granting that, it is still the spirits of these lovers which haunt the Church of San Lorenzo, filling the large old temple with a throb of human passion to this hour. I saunter round endeavouring to fix my mind on the details of the architecture, which are worth more notice than they commonly receive from all save students. But it is useless. Every time I raise my eyes I seem to see the subtle radiance of sympathy flash across the church from the eyes of the princess, stirring strange, uneasy feelings, born of young hot blood, and the sensuous essence of the chanting heard in the restless days of spring.

The architecture may wait the coming of some cooler head. I stroll out into the courtyard, full of memories of kings and poets and of Anjou Courts, when the world was splendid, and life was full of colour, and the city not more unhappy than it is to-day.137

Among the letters of Petrarch is one written from the monastery attached to this church. The poet lodged there during a visit to Naples in 1342, after the death of King Robert, and gives a vivid description of a great hurricane which struck the city on the 25th of November in that year.

The storm had been predicted by a preacher, whose denunciation struck such terror into the Neapolitans, easily stirred to religious apprehensions, that ere dark a troop of women stripped half naked and clasping their children to their breasts were rushing through the streets from church to church, flinging themselves prostrate before the altars, bathing the sacred images with tears, and crying aloud to the Saviour to have mercy on mankind.

The panic spread from house to house. The city was alive with fear. Petrarch, not untroubled by the general consternation, went early to his chamber, and remained at his window till near midnight watching the moon sail down a ragged angry sky until her light was blotted out by the hills, and all the dome of heaven lay black.

"I was just falling asleep," he says, "when I was rudely awakened by the horrible noise made by the windows of my room. The very wall rocked to its foundation under the buffet of the gust. My lamp, which burns all night, went out; in place of sleep the fear of death came into the chamber. Every soul in the monastery rose, and those who found each other in the turmoil of the night, exhorted one another to meet death bravely.

"The monks who had been astir thus early for chanting Matins, terrified by the trembling of the earth, came to my room brandishing crosses and relics of the saints. At their head strode a prior named David, a saint indeed, and the sight of them 138gave us a little courage. We all descended to the church, which we found full of people, and there passed the rest of the night, expecting every moment that the city would be swallowed up, as foretold by the preacher.

"It would be impossible to depict the horror of that night in which all the elements seemed to be unchained. Nothing can describe the appalling crash of the storm wind, rain and thunder in one moment, the roar of the furious sea, the swaying of the ground, the shrieks of the people, who thought death here at every instant. Never was night so long. As soon as day came near the altars were made ready, and the priests attired themselves for Mass. At last the morning came. The upper part of the town had grown more calm, but from the seafront came frightful shrieks. Our fear turned into boldness, and we mounted on horseback, curious to see what was going on.

"Gods! What a scene! Ships had been wrecked in the harbour, and the shore was strewn with still breathing bodies, horribly mangled by being dashed against the rocks—the sea had burst the bounds which God set for it—all the lower town was under water. It was impossible to enter the streets without risk of drowning. Around us we found more than a thousand Neapolitan gentlemen who had come to assist, as it were at the obsequies of their country. 'If I die,' I said to myself, 'I shall die in good company.'"

If we may trust the story told by Wading, a great historical authority upon the deeds of the Franciscan Order, to which the monks of San Lorenzo belonged, this same prior David, whose aspect Petrarch found so comforting, was the instrument of a notable miracle on this occasion, having kept the impious 139sea out of at least some part of the city by boldly thrusting the relics of the saints in its track. Petrarch does not mention this, and indeed if Prior David could do so much he is to blame for not having done more, since he might as easily have prevented all the damage done while he was chanting in his church.

As for Petrarch, the storm impressed him so deeply that he told Cardinal Colonna he had resolved never to go afloat again, even at the Pope's bidding. "I will leave the air to birds, and the sea to fishes," he observed very sagely; "I know that learned men say there is no more danger on sea than on land, but I prefer to render up my life where I received it. That is a good saying of the ancient writer, 'He who suffers shipwreck a second time has no right to blame Neptune.'"

Are we not growing a little tired of churches? There are so many in this city, and in the next chapter I shall have to dwell long upon the Carmine, or rather on its manifold associations. Well, no great harm will be done if we pass by a good many of these temples; but one must not be left unmentioned, namely the cathedral, which we have almost reached. A few yards from San Lorenzo, the Strada del Duomo cuts across the old Decumanus Major at right angles, and if we descend it a little way towards the sea we have before us the fine front of the cathedral.

It will be expected of me here that in lieu of copying from Gsell-Fels all the interesting facts about the date of the building, describing the ancient fane of Santa Restituta which has already witnessed fourteen centuries, or detailing the arrangement of the chapels where so much of the noblest ever born in Naples lies mouldering into dust,—it is expected of 140me, I suppose, that I shall repeat once more the oft-told tale of the liquefaction of the blood of San Gennaro, that miracle and portent which brings luck to the city if it happens speedily, and is a presage of woe when it is delayed. We have heard the story all our lives. But no book on Naples is complete without it, and I will therefore take the description by Fucini, which has at any rate the advantage of being little known in England, to which I may add that it is the work of one who might very truly say what he did not know of Naples, at least in his own day, was not knowledge.

"In the church," says Fucini, "the crowd was dense. Around the altar crowded pilgrims, male and female, shouting, laughing, weeping, chewing prayers and oranges.... In the midst of deep silence begins the moving function. The officiating priest holding up to the people the vase, not unlike a carriage lamp, inspects it carefully, and beginning to twirl it in his hands, cries out with a stentorian voice, 'It is hard, the blood is hard!' At that fatal announcement the people break out into cries most pitiful. The pilgrims weep, some even are like to faint. The saint is slow. The miracle delays, the cries and tears redouble. A group of peasant women who stand near me pour out these prayers, 'Faccela, faccela, la grazia, San Gennarino mio bello!' And if the priest still shook his head they broke out again, 'It is hard! O, quanto ci mette stamattina, San Gennarino mio benedetto. Ah faccela, faccela, questa divina grazia, faccela, faccela, San Gennarino bello, bello, bello!'

"The pilgrims went on chanting, the people crowded round the chapel. In the nave a powerful preacher was relating the life and glories of the saint. The noise of voices rose or fell as the priest signified that 141the commencement of the miracle was still far off, or gave hopes of its speedy consummation.

"At last, when the suspense had lasted nine-and-twenty minutes, we saw the priests and those spectators who were nearest to them fix their eyes more intently on the vase, with beckonings and signs, as if to say, 'Perhaps—a minute more—I almost think—who knows?' Then followed a moment of great anxiety, a short interval of silence, broken only by sobs and stifled sighs. The emotion spread, tearful faces and trembling hands undulated in a kneeling crowd. Then suddenly all arms were flung in air, all hands were clapped, the priest waved a white veil joyfully, and like the outbursts of a hurricane the organs pealed out in crashing harmonies, the bells clanged and clamoured through the air, and the high roof of the cathedral rang with the triumph of the voices of the vast crowd chanting the Ambrosian hymn."

If the Duomo had no other interest, the emotion of this oft-repeated scene would create a fascination to which everyone must yield. But it teems with interest. It abounds in relics out of every age of Naples. I cannot convey its charm to any other man. For me the church is full of presences and shadows of the past, kings and cardinals, noble gentlemen and lovely ladies, hopes and aspirations, and feverish ambitions mouldering together beneath marble cenotaphs and stately wealth of gilding and of fresco. I stand before the monument of Innocent the Fourth, he who had no other word than "adder" to bestow on the great emperor whom he opposed and crushed; and straightway all the tragedy of that terrific strife absorbs my memory, and I am devoured by pity for the fair land of Italy which became the battlefield of two such powers, and which 142by the victory of the Church and the ruin of the Empire lost a family of rulers more apt for the creation of her happiness than any which has governed the Peninsula from the destruction of the Goths until our own day. To one who looks back across the years, desiring more the welfare of this queen among the lands than the triumph of any principle, it seems a base deed that was wrought by this fine-featured old man, lying here so peacefully in the contemplation of the centuries, his judges. One wonders if he ever saw as we do the rare and precious value of the thing he was destroying, whether the true nobility of Frederick, his culture, his wide humanity, his strong firm government were really worse than nothing in the judgment of the active brain which throbbed beneath that placid brow. The ruin of the Empire, the concentration of all power in the papacy, the expulsion of the Emperor and all his brood from Italy, it was nothing less than this that Innocent contrived. Not the great Hildebrand himself, whose tomb we shall visit at Salerno, did more service to the Church. The pity is that one should find it so hard to see how that service helped mankind, to whom no consequences seem to have come that were not dire and woeful. But whether good or evil, it was great. There was nothing paltry about Innocent. He was not of double heart. He found a great thing to do, and did it with all his might. In this world of futilities that is much, and very much, perhaps all that can be asked of man with his dim vision. The consequences must be left unto the care of those who see them.

<h1 style="text-align:center">CHAPTER VIII</h1>

A GREAT CHURCH AND TWO VERY NOBLE TRAGEDIES

143
There can be no question that the interest of Naples deepens as one goes through the ancient quarter in the direction of the east. In modern times the centre of the city is on the western side, but of old it was not so. Castel Nuovo stood outside the city among groves and gardens. The further one goes back in history, the more frequently the court is found at Castel Capuano, which fronts the bottom of this most picturesque of streets by which we have come almost the whole distance from the Via Roma.

In an irregular space, shapeless and crowded with stalls and booths, stands the ancient fortress, long since rebuilt and handed over to the law. The very name of the street in whose narrow entrance we still stand recalls the tribunals. They were all brought together in this castle by Don Pietro di Toledo, that active viceroy who stamped his memory on so many parts of Naples. But there was a place of judgment on this ground long before his day; and the thing is worth mention.

Opposite the gate of the castle, and within a stone's-throw of the spot on which we have halted, stood in former days a pillar of white marble on a squared base of stone. It marked the ground on which 144debtors were compelled to declare their absolute insolvency. The wretched men were stripped stark naked in proof of their inability to pay, and stood there exposed to the insults of their creditors. This custom, which existed in many Italian towns, was doubtless of great antiquity. The pillar was taken down in 1856, and is now in the museum of San Martino. The people called it "La Colonna della Vicaria." Similarly the Castel Capuano is spoken of as "La Vicaria," a name which gained a frightful notoriety in the days of the last Bourbon kings, by reason of the barbarity of the treatment shown to political prisoners confined there, and the infamous condition of the dens in which innocent and cultured gentlemen were shut up.

So many streets radiate from the Largo della Vicaria that numberless streams of passengers unite and separate there, while all day long a market goes on beneath the walls of the Place of Lamentations whose secrets Mr. Gladstone laid bare before the eyes of Europe. Nothing rich or rare or curious is sold. Old keys, rusty padlocks, shapeless lumps of battered iron, cheap hats and tawdry bedsteads, with the inevitable apparatus of the lemonade seller, brown jars, golden fruit, and dark green leaves, all dripping in the shade—such are the wares set out to attract the seething crowd which saunters to and fro. If the truth must be confessed the crowd looks villainous. The Neapolitans of the lower classes have not as a rule engaging faces. They are keen and often humorous, intensely eager and alive, eyes and lips responsive to the quickest flashes of emotion. But candid or inviting trust they are not; and as many scowls as smiles are to be seen on the faces of old or young alike. They have their virtues, it is true. They have boundless family affection. When 145misfortune strikes their friends, they are helpful even to self-sacrifice. They respect the old profoundly, and serve or tend them willingly. They are industrious and very patient in their poverty, devout towards the Church, especially to the Madonna, who from time to time writes them a letter, which sells in the streets faster even than the "pizza." There is perhaps in these and other qualities the foundation of a character which may some day place Naples high among the cities of the world; but before that day dawns, many things will have to be both learnt and unlearnt. In this region of the Porta Capuana one sees the people in what Charles Lamb would have called its quiddity. There are low taverns in the house-fronts, haunts of the Camorra and the vilest of the poor. Each has its few chairs set out upon the pavement, and its large shady room inside, with great casks standing in the background. Here and there a barber hovers in his doorway, chatting with a neighbour. At morn and even the tinkling bell announces the coming of the goats, and children hurry out with tumblers to the wayside where the bleating herd is stopped and milked as custom goes, while all day long the steps of Santa Catarina a Formello are crowded with dirty women sitting in the shade. High against the church towers the great archway of the Porta Capuana, a fit gateway for the

40

approach of kings. What pageants it has seen! The great Emperor Charles the Fifth rode in beneath it on his return from the Tunis expedition, by which he drove out the corsair Barbarossa from the kingdom he had seized, freed no less than twenty thousand slaves, and dealt the pirates one of the few heavy blows ever levelled at their force by Europe until Lord Exmouth three hundred years later smoked out the hornets' nest at Algiers.

The Castel Capuano did not stand directly on the 146street in those days when it was the home of kings. It had its gardens, which must almost have touched those of another royal palace, the Duchescha, of which all traces have been swallowed up by the growth of squalor which has claimed this region for its own. The gardens of the Duchescha were large and beautiful. It was the pleasure-house of Alfonso of Aragon, while yet he was Duke of Calabria, heir to the throne from which he fled in terror so short a time after he ascended it.

It was no mere archæological musing which brought this blood-stained tyrant back to my memory, but rather the trivial inconvenience of being trundled roughly towards the gutter by a half-grown lad who was hurrying along the causeway with a bundle of pamphlets, one of which, thrust into a cleft stick, he was brandishing high in the air with an alluring placard announcing that it was to be had by anybody for the price of one soldo. I pursued the boy, caught him under the Porta Capuana, and bought his pamphlet. The miscellaneous literature of the Neapolitan streets is not as a rule of a kind that makes for righteousness, but my ear had caught the sound of the word "martiri," and I had been half expecting some sign of public interest in martyrs on this spot.

The pamphlet gave a fairly accurate account of the massacre of Christians by the Turks who landed at Otranto in the heel of Italy in the year 1480. So old a tale of course much interest for educated people still; but what, one asks in wonder, makes it worth while to hawk the story round the squalid streets surrounding the Vicaria, where it evidently commands a sale as brisk as if it were "Vendetta di Tigre" or any other highly peppered work about the social vices of the rich.

The matter will become a little clearer if we push 147past the half-clad women who sit suckling babes on the steps of Santa Caterina a Formello, and go into that uninteresting church. At the altar rails a priest is preaching vehemently to a languid congregation, while in the empty nave four fat laughing children are toddling round the benches, playing games and calling to each other merrily. There are gaudy paintings and high silk curtains; but the only object that excites my interest is a printed card hung on the closed railings of the second chapel on the left of the nave, which appeals for "Elemosina pel culto dei bb, martiri di Otranto, dei quali 240 corpi si venerano sotto questo altare."

Alms for the worship of the blessed martyrs of Otranto! So some of those twelve thousand who were put to the sword by the Turks in cold blood on a hillside near the city have been brought to this small church in Naples. But why? The answer doubtless is that the Duke of Calabria, who led the mingled hosts of Naples and of Europe against the Turks, brought back these bones as a religious trophy, and placed them in Santa Caterina because it lay near to his own palace. He may have been the more eager about the pious trophy since he brought no military ones. It was the death of the Turkish Sultan, not the sword of Alfonso, which drove the warriors of the Crescent out of Italy.

It is thus clear why the boy was hawking his pamphlets outside Santa Caterina. But what gains a ready sale for them? Well, partly the strong clerical feeling among the lower orders of the Neapolitans, and partly the skill with which the priests play upon this feeling for political ends.

I open the pamphlet, and in its second paragraph I find these words:—

"By this story we shall show that the Catholics 148are the real friends of the country, that the true martyrs are not found outside the Church, that Catholicism is the true glory of Italy, and that the great days worthy to be commemorated are not those of Milan, nor those of Brescia in 1848, nor those of Turin in 1864, but the days of Otranto in August, 1480. May the tribute which we pay to-day to our true martyrs atone for the frequent sacrilege of giving that name to felons—"

No words could prove more clearly by what untraversable distance the Church of Rome is parted from all sympathy with the unity of Italy. That is why I have told this incident at length. I venture to say that in the length and breadth of Britain, where, if bravery is loved, right and justice are loved too, and felons are not exalted, there is scarce one man who can read the tale of the five days of Milan without feeling that there is one of the bright spots in the history of all mankind, one of those rare occasions when what is noblest leapt to the front, and a ray of true hope and sunshine fell on Italy. But in the eyes of the priests this light and glory were mere crime and darkness. Those who fought the Austrians were criminals. It is a hopeless difference of view, hopeless equally if sincere, and if not. I went on a little sick at heart, as any lover of Italy may well be when he contemplates the enmity of State and Church, and that Church the Papacy.

If I were not so eager to reach the Carmine, I should certainly retrace my steps a little and go up the Strada Carbonara to the Church of San Giovanni Carbonara, which contains much that is interesting, and leads one straight to the tragic days of Queen Giovanna. But that age of lust and murder, that perplexed period of woe and strife, does not allure me when I have the Carmine almost in sight; and 149I turn away past the railway station, and down the Corso Garibaldi till I come to the round towers of the Porta Nolana, the only one of the old city gates which still serves its ancient purpose and recalls the days of fortification. Its twin towers are named "Faith" and "Hope," "Cara Fè" and "Speranza," and when one passes in betwixt those virtues one plunges into a throng which is as animated as the Strada Tribunali, and considerably dirtier. The life of the people in this Vico

41

Sopramuro is elemental. It has but few conventions and disdains restraints. A tattered shirt, gaping to the waist, admits the free play of air round the bodies of boys and girls alike; the breeches or the gown which complete the costume recall the aspect of a stormy night sky when the rent clouds are scattered by the wind and the stars peep through. It is as well not to loiter among this engaging people. "The Neapolitans," said Von Räumer airily, "were invented before the fuss about the seven deadly sins." I have no wish to make a fuss about those or any other sins so long as they are practised upon other people, and I feel completely charitable to the human anthill when I emerge safe and sound in the wide square of the Mercato.

In this wide market-place, this bare spot of open ground which to-day lies cumbered with iron bedsteads, and piled with empty cases, the débris of last market day, the bitterest tragedy of Naples was played out, and a scene enacted of which the infamy rang through all the world. There is no spot in the whole city less beautiful or more interesting than the Mercato; and in the hot afternoon, while the churches are closed, and half the city sits drowsy in the shady spots, I know no better way of passing time than in recalling some of the poignant memories which haunt this place of blood and tears.150

In an earlier chapter of this book, when I gave a rapid sketch of the succession of Hohenstaufen, Anjou, and Aragon to the throne of the Two Sicilies, I passed on without pausing on the story of the boy-king Corradino, little Conrad, as the Italians have always called him. It is time now to tell the tale, for it was on this spot that the lad was murdered.

I need not go back on what I have already said so far as to repeat how Charles of Anjou defeated Manfred and slew him outside the walls of Benevento, nor how utterly the party of the Ghibellines, the Emperor's men, were cast down throughout Italy by that great triumph of the Guelf. When Manfred fell and his wife, Queen Helena, passed with her children into lifelong captivity, the House of Hohenstaufen was not extinct. There remained in Germany the true heir of Naples, a king with a better title than Manfred had possessed, Corradino, a boy of five, who grew up in the keeping of his mother, Elizabeth of Bavaria; and as year after year went by found his pride and fancy stimulated by many a tale of the rich heritage beyond the mountains which was his by every right, but was reft from him by an usurper, and lay groaning under the rule of an alien and an oppressor. Tales such as these must have had for the child all the fascination of a fairy story; but as his years increased, and he came to the comprehension of what wrong and injury meant, they touched him far more nearly, and all the courage of his high race, all the spirit which he derived from the blood of emperors and kings, urged him on to strike one stout blow at least for the recovery of that land which was his father's, that sunny kingdom where the blue sea kissed the very feet of the orange groves, and marble palaces gleamed 151out of the shade of gardens such as the boy had never seen except in dreams.

His mother did her best to scatter these dreams, and bring him back to the plain prose of life. Italy, she said, had always sucked the blood and strength of the Hohenstaufen, and if she could, she would stop the drain ere it robbed her of her only child. But the task was too great for her. Not from Naples only, which was really full of nobles ready to revolt against the tyrant of Anjou and return to their old allegiance, but from a dozen other cities in northern Italy, where the Ghibellines waited for the coming of a leader, the growth of Conradin to manhood was watched impatiently; and when he was turned fifteen, strong, handsome, and kingly in every act, the hopes of his partisans could be restrained no longer. Pisa sent her embassies to bid him hasten. Verona, ancient home of the Ghibellines, assured him of support. Siena, Pavia, implored him to come and free his people. The task they said was easy, and the glory great. More than that, it was a righteous duty to resume what was his own. Many a burning tale of wrong committed by the French was poured into the lad's ears; and the end was that little Conrad broke away from his mother's prayers and tears, and crossed the Alps in the autumn of the year 1267 at the head of 10,000 men, being then fifteen, and by the universal consent of all who saw him both handsome in his person and by his breeding worthy to be the son of many kings.

At first all went well with him. At Verona he was received with the honours of a conqueror. The mere news that his standard had been seen coming down from the high Alpine valleys drew the exiles of Ferrara, Bergamo, Brescia, and many another city in crowds to welcome him. Padua and Vicenza sent 152him greeting; and in January he moved on to Pisa, where the same joy awaited him. The Pisan fleet was of high power in those days, and it was sent at once to ravage the coasts of Apulia and Sicily, where it inflicted a sound drubbing on the French. Near Florence, too, Conradin's army gained a victory, and when he moved on to Rome, where Henry of Castile, who ruled the city in the absence of the Pope, had joined his party, the hopes of every Ghibelline in Italy were high and proud, while Charles of Anjou was seriously anxious for his throne.

It was on the 18th of August of the year 1268 that Conradin left Rome. Charles expected him by the ordinary route of travellers which lies through Ceperano, San Germano, and Capua. That route was studded with fortresses and was easy to defend—for which sufficient reason Conradin did not take it. His aim was not to make for Naples by the shortest way, but rather to get through the mountains, if he could without a battle, and to raise Apulia, where he was certain of support, not only from the Saracens of Lucera, but from many other quarters also. So he struck off from Tivoli towards the high valleys of the Abruzzi, through which he found a way not only unguarded, but cool, well watered and fresh, considerations of vast moment to the leader of an army through southern Italy in August. It was the line of the ancient Roman road, the "Via Valeria," and he followed it until on the 22nd of August as his troops came down from the hills of Alba, debouching on the plain

42

of Tagliacozzo, some five miles in front, they saw the lances of Anjou gleaming on the heights of Antrosciano, drawn up in a position which was too strong for attack.

Conradin's army lay across the road to Tagliacozzo, offering battle to the king, who looked down upon 153the host of the invaders, and liked not what he saw. He had pressed on from Aquila, and was uneasy about the loyalty of that stronghold in his rear. Night fell; but before dusk hid the long line of foes upon the plain, Charles had seen an embassy ride into their ranks, and men said it came from Aquila, offering the town to Conradin. This was what Charles chiefly feared. He would trust no man but himself to learn the truth; and spurring his horse across plain and mountain through the night, he rode back headlong till he drew rein beneath the walls of Aquila, and shouted to the warder on the walls, "For what king are you?" Sharp and quick the answer came, "For King Charles"; and the King, reassured, rode back wearily towards his camp sleeping round the fires on the mountains.

He slept long that night, notwithstanding the hazard which lay upon the cast of battle; and when at length he woke, the host of the invaders was already marshalled along the bank of the River Salto, which formed their front. Charles scanned their line, and his heart sank, so great was their multitude. In something like despair he turned for counsel to a famous warrior who had but just landed from Palestine, where he had won world-wide renown, Alard de St. Valery. The wary Frenchman did not question that the chances of the coming fight were against Anjou. "If you conquer," he said, "it must be by cunning rather than by strength." Charles allowed him to make those dispositions which he pleased; and thereupon St. Valery placed a strong force of lances, with the King himself at their head, in a hollow of the hills, where they could not be seen. Then he hurled against Conradin two successive attacks, both of which were repulsed with heavy loss. Charles wept with rage to see his 154knights so broken, and strove to break out to rescue them, but St. Valery held him back, and Conradin, seeing no more enemies, thought the battle won. His men unhelmed themselves. Some went to bathe in the cool river. Others, after the fashion of the day, plundered the fallen knights. One large body under Henry of Castile had pursued the fleeing French far over plain and mountain. All this St. Valery lay watching in dead silence from his hiding in the hollow of the hills.

At last the moment came, and the serried ranks of the fresh warriors rode down upon their unarmed and unsuspecting enemies. No time was given to arm or form up the troops. Some perished in the water. Others died struggling bravely against the shock of that horrible surprise. The trap was perfect. All either died or fled; and in one brief hour Conradin, who had thought himself the conqueror of his father's throne, was fleeing for his life across the hills, a fugitive devoid of hope. Never, surely, was there so sudden or terrible a change of fortune.

With Conradin fled Frederick of Baden, his close friend, not long before his playmate; and these two princely lads were accompanied by a few faithful followers, the last remnant of what so short a time before was a noble army. All that night they sped across the mountains in the direction of the coast, where they hoped to find some craft which would carry them to Pisa, a safe haven for them all. They struck the sea near Astura in the Pontine marshes. On the shore they found a little fishing boat; and having sought out the men who owned it, they offered large reward for the voyage up the coast. The fellows demurred that they must have provisions for the trip; and Conradin, taking a ring from his finger, gave it to one of them and told him to buy 155bread at the nearest place he could. It was a fatal imprudence. The sailor pledged the ring at a tavern in exchange for bread. The host saw the value of the jewel, and took it instantly to the lord of the castle near at hand.

Now this noble was of the Frangipani family, on which honours had been heaped by the grandfather of the boy-king, thus cast up a fugitive and in peril of his life in his domain. The only gratitude which honour demanded of him was to let the lad pass by and escape in his own way; but even this was too much for Frangipani. He saw at once that the ring must belong to some man of mark escaping from the fight, and he bade his servants launch a boat, and bring back the fugitive whoever he might be.

When Frangipani's boat overtook the other, Conradin was not much dismayed. He knew how greatly the Frangipani were indebted to his house, and he did not doubt they would show due gratitude. The poor lad did not know the world. Frangipani foresaw that no boon he could ask of Charles would be too great if he handed him his enemy; and thus not many days had passed when Conradin and Frederick were brought into Naples, and carried through the streets where they had hoped to ride as conquerors.

Even Charles, bloodthirsty as he was, shrank from taking his prisoners' life without some legal warrant. It was so plain that they had played no part but that of gallant gentlemen, striking a blow for what was in fact their right, however much the Pope might question it, or assert his title to bestow the kingdom where he would. He convoked an assembly of jurists, but found only one among the number obsequious enough to tax Conradin or his followers with any crime. Thus driven back on his 156own murderous will as ultimate sanction for the act he meditated, Charles himself pronounced the death sentence on the whole number of his prisoners.

On the 29th of October a scaffold was raised in the Mercato. The chronicles say that it was by the stream which ran past the Church of the Carmine, a humbler building than that which we see now, but standing on the same spot. They add also that it was near the sea, from which we may conclude that few, if any, houses parted the market-place from the beach in those days, and that the whole of the most exquisite coast-line of his father's kingdom stretched blue and fair before Conradin's eyes as he mounted the scaffold. Side by side with him came his true comrade, Frederick of Baden. The united ages of the boys scarce turned thirty. There was no nobler blood in Europe than theirs, and among the great crowd of citizens there were few who did not weep when they saw the fair-haired lads embrace each other beside the block. The demeanour of both was high and bold. Of Conradin, no less than of another king more than thrice his age, it can be said—

"He nothing common did or mean
Upon that memorable scene."

NAPLES—THE CHURCH OF THE CARMINE.

He turned to the people, and avowed he had defended his right. "Before God," he said, "I have earned death as a sinner, but not for this!" Then he flung his glove far out among the crowd, thus with his last defiant gesture handing on the right of vengeance and the succession of his kingdom to those who could wrestle for it with the French. The glove was caught up by a German knight, Heinrich von Waldburg, who did in fact convey it to Queen Constance of Aragon, last of the Hohenstaufen blood, of which bequest came many consequences.157

Having flung down his gage, Conradin was ready to depart. He kissed his comrades, took off his shirt, and then raising his eyes to heaven, said aloud, "Jesus Christ, Lord of all creation, king of honour, if this cup of sorrow may not pass by me, into Thy hands I commend my spirit." Then he knelt and laid down his head; but at the last moment earthly sorrows returned upon him, and starting half up he cried, "Oh, mother, what a sorrow I am making for you!" Having said this he spoke no more, but received the stroke. As it fell, Frederick of Baden gave a scream so pitiful that all men wept. A moment later he had travelled the same path, and the two lads were together once more.

So died these brave German boys, and so perished the last hope of happiness for Naples. For if anything in history is sure, it is as clear as day that Naples never afterwards was ruled by kings so strong and just as those whose blood was shed in the Mercato on that October day. As for the slayer, he has left a name at which men spit. Six centuries already have execrated his memory. It may well be that sixty more will execrate it. Yet even while he lived he ate the bread of tears, and the day came when in the anguish of his heart he was heard to pray aloud that God who had raised him to such a height of fortune might cast him down by gentler steps.

There are countless traditions connected with the death of Conradin. Men say that as his head fell an eagle swooped down from the sky, dipped its wing in the blood, and flew off again across the city. Another and more constant tale is that the poor boy's mother, when she heard of his captivity, gathered a great sum of money to ransom him, and came herself to Naples, but was too late, and landed in deep mourning from her ship, and came into the 158Church of the Carmine, poor and mean in those days, and gave the monks all the money she had brought to sing Masses for ever for her son's soul.

These may be fables. But to pass to truth, it is a fact that in the year 1631, when the pavement of the Church of the Carmine was being lowered, a leaden coffin was found behind the high altar. The letters R. C. C. were roughly cut on it, and were interpreted to mean "Regis Corradini Corpus," the body of King Conradin. The coffin was opened. It contained the skeleton of a lad, the head severed and lying on the breast. There were some fragments of linen, which turned to dust immediately, and by the side lay a sword unsheathed, as bright and speckless as if it had but just come from the maker's hands. One would give much to know that the boy-king still slept there with his sword beside him, but when the coffin was next opened, at the wish of one of his own family in 1832, the sword had gone.

The Church of the Carmine is, as I have said already, a vastly different building from that into which the body of Conradin was carried. Whether the tradition speaks truly of the benefaction of the unhappy mother or no, the fact remains that a splendid reconstruction of the church took place about that time. The origin of the church is curious. The records of the monks declare that towards the middle of the seventh century the hermits of the Mount Carmel, fleeing from the persecution of Saracens, came to Italy, some to one city, some to another. A handful of them rested at Naples, bringing with them an antique picture of the Madonna, said to have been painted by St. Luke, and established themselves in this spot close outside the city walls, near a hospital for sick sailors of which in later days they obtained the site. There they built a humble church, and either 159found or excavated a grotto underneath it, in which they placed their picture. The image became famous, and to this day is known amongst the people as "La Madonna della Grotticella," or more commonly as "La Bruna." Indeed there was no similitude of Our Lady of Sorrows in all south Italy which wrought more wondrous miracles or better earned her sanctity; and when the jubilee came round in the year 1500 the Neapolitans could think of no better deed than to take La Bruna out of her grotto and carry her in procession to Rome, which they did accordingly, and many were the marvels which she wrought upon the long journey through the mountains.

But in Rome La Bruna was not well received by the Vicegerent of God. That intelligent and subtle man Rodrigo Borgia was Pope, and his equally keen-witted son Cæsar Borgia was in fact, though not in name, chief counsellor. Both had schemes for which much money was needed, and that money they looked to make out of the jubilee. They looked about them with their practical clear sight, and took note of the fact that La Bruna was very active, working miracles in fact on every side. Had the proceeds fallen into their pockets this would have been well, but as they did not it was ill. Madonnas from other cities must not come emptying the pockets of the pilgrims in that style, or what would be left for the Holy Father and the ex-Cardinal, his son? So La Bruna was packed off home, and the procession went back through the mountains. I should think the Madonna was glad enough to get out of the Roman stews of the Borgia days, and the Fathers who accompanied her had cause for thankfulness that they escaped without tasting those chalices with which the Pope and Cæsar removed all such as stood in their way.160

The wonders of the Carmine do not begin or end with La Bruna. There is another miraculous image in the church, a large figure of the dead Christ extended on the cross. Now in the year 1439, when the House of Anjou was tottering to its fall, sustained only by the feeble hands of René, last sovereign of his house, Alfonso of Aragon was besieging Naples, pounding the city without much care for considerations other than mere military ones. His brother, Don Pietro of Aragon, seems to have suspected that the Carmine was a sort of fort, and indeed its conspicuous steeple was used as a battery. Accordingly he turned his guns upon it, and a ball flew straight towards the head of our Lord, which lay back slightly raised as if communing with heaven. The ball carried away the crown of thorns, and would certainly have destroyed the head also of the sacred figure had it not bowed suddenly, as if it were alive, and let the shot go by. But the miracle did not end there. The ball, though having struck nothing but the light tracery of the crown of thorns, was checked in midair, hung there for an instant, and then dropped within the altar rails.

This very striking miracle is famous yet in Naples. Brantôme records it, but in his careless way sets down the wonder as having happened in the days of Lautrec, and attributes it to a statue of the Madonna. King Alfonso when he took the city made a careful examination of the neck of the figure, to discover whether there were not some hidden mechanism, but found none, and became convinced that human agency had naught to do with it.

From every point of view this Church of the Carmine is to me the most interesting of all Naples, not by reason of its architecture, though even that, as I suspect and guess, was beautiful before the hideous 161Barocco passion ruined it. Every nook and corner of it has been filled with vulgar and unmeaning ornament, so that the old graceful outlines are lost for ever. But it is for the abounding richness of its life, both past and present, that I visit it again and again. Standing in the poorest quarter of the city, within sight of the swarming population which crowds the streets and alleys around the Porta Nolana and the ancient rookeries which abut upon the Church of St. Eligio, endeared to the people by the miracles of which I have just spoken, there is no feast or saint's day on which the popolane do not visit it in thousands. I go to see it in its Easter glory. The wide vestibule is packed with women of the people, vilely dirty; and inside the church one can scarcely move through the swarming crowd, surging this way and that, now pressing forwards to the altar rails, where a priest is chanting in a loud monotone, now clustering thick about the image of the Madonna, holding on her knees the lifeless bleeding body of the Christ. The women press forward, kissing her robe with passion and holding up the babies to do the like. The chairs are packed with men staring vacantly before them, as if they wondered what had brought them there, and over the feverish bustle of the throng the fine grave figure of Conradin rises carved in snowy marble.

The sanctity of this great and ancient church, its propinquity to the Mercato and to the teeming populations of the old alleys of the city, has made it in all ages a central point of that turbulent hot life which fills the history of Naples with tales of blood and terror. The associations of the place are infinite, and would in themselves fill a portly volume were they all set down with the detail which their rich interest demands. One tale there is which must be 162told in full, for its tragedy is too great to be forgotten, and has indeed rung round all the world.

In the year 1647, when England was convulsed by civil war, Naples had lain for near a century and a half beneath the Spanish yoke, governed by viceroys, some good, others saturated with the greed and covetousness which have made the name of Proconsul odious since Verres drained the lifeblood out of Sicily. Naples was rich, but not rich enough for Spanish greed. The huge, unwieldy Spanish Empire began to fall on troublous days. The old rivalry with France was pressing hard on the statesmen of Madrid. Europe was unsettled, and war was constant. Fleets and armies are the most expensive toys of nations, and all viceroys were given to understand that the only road to royal favour was to remit more and still more money. Unhappily at Naples the effect of this hint on the Duke of Arcos, who then ruled in the palace often occupied by wiser men, was to set him angling in a well of which his predecessors had fished out the bottom. It was really very difficult to see how another penny could be got out of Naples, but nothing was more certain than that the penny must be found. So the Viceroy, having called a Parliament which met, after the custom of that time, in the convent attached to the Church of San Lorenzo, persuaded that august body to announce a fresh gabelle, to be levied on all the fruit brought into Naples.

Nobody who has visited Naples in the summer, and noted the abounding plenty of the fruit stalls at every corner of the ancient streets—the ruddy grapes, the vast piles of blackening figs, the immense water melons, sliced so as to show their black seeds and their brimming juice, so cool and tempting when the August sun burns down upon the houses,—nobody 163who has seen how the Neapolitans feed on fruit throughout the scorching dogdays can doubt that to tax it must be dangerous. If the risk was not self-evident, there was example of it to be found in the memory of men then living. Not fifty years before the same expedient had resulted in riot. A prudent governor would have been warned; the more so as the people were already oppressed and sullen, restless and indignant under the unending exactions of the farmers of the taxes, and divided by the memory of

45

many bitter outrages from the nobles of native birth who should have been their natural leaders and protectors. Naples was full of a sullen, dangerous temper; but those who were responsible for the safety of the city had not wit enough to understand its state.

The gabelle on fruit was imposed early in the year; and on many days of spring, even before the burden of the tax was felt, crowds ran beside the Viceroy's coach demanding angrily that the duty should be repealed. As the warm days drew on, the angry temper rose. Every market day whipped it up to fever heat and set the people thinking of their miseries. It is said—and the thing is probable enough—that many days before the actual outbreak of revolt a rising was being planned by several agents, of whom one was a Carmelite monk. The day selected for its commencement was carefully chosen in such a manner as to secure the patronage and protection of the most popular Madonna of the crowded city; but before it came an accident precipitated the disturbance.

It was the custom in those days to hold a kind of popular game in the Piazza del Mercato, a few days before the Festival of the Madonna of the Carmine. The ragged population chose a captain, 164under whom they attacked and stormed a wooden castle reared in the centre of the piazza. In this year the lot of the people had fallen on Tommaso Anello, who in their contracted and musical dialect was known as "Mas'aniello," a native of Amalfi, by origin, if not by birth, driven perhaps into the city by fear of the constant incursions of the Turks, which went near to depopulate the coasts from Salerno to Castellammare. By one account Mas'aniello was thirsting to revenge an insult offered to his wife by one of the collectors. Other writers assert that chance alone thrust him into the foremost position in what followed.

On Sunday the 7th of July the Mercato was seething with life. Out of all the rookeries around the Porta Nolana, and behind the Church of Sant' Eligio, the people poured out intent on frolic. Festivity was in the air— that joyousness which in southern Italy is very apt to smear itself with blood ere night. The women crowded in and out of the churches. The bells chimed. From all the towns and villages on either side of Naples the peasant women had brought in their fruit, and the thirsty people bought it greedily. Among the crowd Mas'aniello and his army of ragamuffins were going up and down armed with canes; when suddenly there arose a loud and angry bawling, and everyone pressed forward to see what had happened.

It was a dispute between the peasants who brought in the fruit and the keepers of the stalls who sold it. They could not agree which should bear the burden of the new tax. The people's magistrate was called in and decided in favour of the stall men; on which a fellow who had brought in figs from Pozzuoli flung down his baskets on the ground, and trampled on them in a fit of rage. The guard, insulted by the 165act, and still more by the words which accompanied it, seized the fellow and beat him. His cries gathered more and more people. So did the figs, which rolled about in every direction, while the boys scrambled for them, and some laughed, while others shouted angrily, "Take off the gabelle!" The guard tried to disperse the crowd; but scattering in one place, it reassembled in another. Soon sticks and stones began to fly—even the fruit upon the stalls was used for missiles. The guard gave way. The magistrate fled to the beach, with a gang of angry ruffians at his heels, and got off with difficulty in a boat; while Mas'aniello, reuniting his forces, led them against the office of the Gabelle in the Mercato, wrecked it, and burnt the books.

By this time all the turbulence of the city was aroused; its suppressed passions had found a rallying point, and from every quarter there poured forth an army, ragged and dangerous, carrying for the most part no other weapons than sticks and stones, but roaring with a single voice for the abolition of the gabelle. Mas'aniello seized rapidly on these raw levies, ordered them into bands, and sent them in various directions through the city with orders to break down the stalls of the collectors wherever they found them; while he himself, at the head of a mighty crowd, marched up to the Toledo and down that famous street towards the palace of the Viceroy.

That feeble ruler had come out upon the balcony of his palace to behold the sight. As far as he could see there stretched a forest of angry men and women, a sight most terrible and menacing in the eyes of any ruler. The Spaniard's inclination would have been to soothe and quiet them with pikes; but he had not men enough at his command, and so tried cooing at them, professing his immediate willingness to do 166everything they wished. It is uncertain what the result of this accommodating policy might have been if only the people could have heard him or would have waited to attend to the written messages he sent them out. Unluckily neither words nor notes were heeded. The mob broke into the palace and swarmed up the stairs, sweeping away the guards. The Viceroy, impelled by prudence, slipped out down the secret stair, and entering a private coach, attempted to pass through the mob towards the Castel dell'Uovo. His carriage had not travelled far before he met a crowd which recognised him and threatened to drag him out of his carriage. A few handfuls of gold scattered in the air opened a lane through the dense ranks of the rioters, and the Viceroy, taking advantage of the momentary diversion, slipped into the Church of San Luigi and took refuge there. Meantime the mob went on to sack his palace.

It must appear passing strange that no effort was made by the Spanish soldiery in Naples to defend the authority of the Viceroy. There was a garrison in each of the three castles, and in the length and breadth of Naples there must have been a sufficient number of well-disposed persons to furnish valuable accessions of strength to any central body of trained soldiery. But whether it was that the strength of the garrison had been so far drained off for the wars in Tuscany and elsewhere that the remnant possessed no fighting power, or whether, as seems also possible, the very suddenness of the revolt had paralysed the regular troops, dreading as all soldiers do a conflict with an undisciplined and ardent enemy in the streets of a great city—whichever reason may be the true one, the fact remains that throughout the ten days of this revolt the mob was not attacked, and its disposition to excess was restrained by little else than 167by its own moderation, which by all accounts was conspicuous and wonderful.

If, however, the Viceroy took no steps to repress the rising by force of arms, it is not to be supposed that he lay idle in the Church of San Luigi grasping the horns of the altar. By no means. On the contrary, Don Gabriele Tontoli, an eye-witness of these disasters, assures us that the great man in this crisis, while the mob were battering and howling at the doors of the church, forgot nothing which was due to his exalted position, but climbed out nobly on the roof of the church and addressed the people in affectionate accents, seeking to draw them back to the duteous loyalty which they seemed for the moment to have forgotten. Oddly enough these paternal admonitions were little heeded by the mob, who, if they spared a look for the pleading Viceroy on the roof, only roared the louder and battered at the door the harder. Indeed, there can be little doubt that they would have battered down the door ere long, and the Viceroy's position was growing so perilous that Don Gabriele compares it aptly with that of the innocent Andromeda bound to the rock and awaiting the onset of the sea monster. But Perseus arrived, as in the classical tale, just in the nick of time, wearing the odd garb of a cardinal of the Roman Catholic Church. In fact, he was no other than the Archbishop of Naples, Cardinal Ascanio Filamarino, a man destined to play a considerable part in the coming troubles.

Perseus took in the situation at a glance, and being unluckily unprovided with a Gorgon's head with which to turn the monster into stone, he saw no other way of saving the rhetorical Andromeda discanting eloquently on the roof than by translating some of his promises into actions. Taking his stand, 168therefore, on the steps of the church, he sent up word through the grid that the Viceroy must instantly make out an order for the abolition of the gabelle and send it down to him. The Viceroy sent it without delay, and the Cardinal, who appears to have been one of the very few men of mark in Naples possessing any credit with the mob, produced an instant sensation by waving the paper in the air. With a singular good judgment he allowed no one to see it on that spot, but getting into his coach, still waving the document high above his head, he drew off the people from the church, and so opened a way for the escape of the Viceroy.

It was perhaps hoped that the remission of the duty on fruit would quiet the city; but greater purposes were already taking shape in the minds of those who led the people. The Spanish tyranny had bitten deep into their hearts, and the very promptitude of their success made them hope the moment had arrived to end many things. The Convent of San Lorenzo in the Strada Tribunali was an armoury well stored with pikes and harquebusses. The crowd, led by a Sicilian who had played a foremost part in a revolt upon his native island, attacked the convent, and fierce fighting took place between the citizens and the small body of defenders who had thrown themselves into the convent. The Sicilian was shot in the forehead, but the attacks continued, and a day or two later the arsenal became untenable, and was surrendered with the cannon and munitions which it contained.

IN THE STRADA DI TRIBUNALI, NAPLES.

The night of Sunday was full of terror. Throughout the hours of darkness mobs raged through the city; and the excellent Don Gabriele, after vainly endeavouring to sleep, tells us that he got up and looked out to see what they were doing. They were169going by in gangs, brandishing torches which flared and dripped with pitch. For standards they bore a loaf stuck on the point of a pike in derision of its tiny size, the result of the gabelle on flour. Of opposition from the guardians of order there was none at all, and had the mob elected to burn the city to the ground it is not clear what force could have restrained them. The strange thing was that the ragamuffins made so little use of their opportunities. It was as if already, in these first moments of the insurrection, the rule of the leaders was respected. Mas'aniello was busy throughout the night in the Mercato and the piazza of the Carmine, organising, directing, and restraining. He must have had some rare quality of command, some spark of that divine faculty for swaying men which is recognised and honoured instinctively in moments of sharp crisis. Otherwise it could not have happened that the mob, unbridled and passionate, would have gone through the streets by night chanting "Viva, viva il re di Spagna," and abstaining from gross outrages as they did. Even Don Gabriele, whose mouth is full of fulsome praises of the powers that were, asserts that among the rabble, needy and starving as many of them were, none plundered for himself without being repressed by his companions, while one who did so was instantly tossed into the flames of a burning house, in punishment for an offence which could but bring disgrace on the whole movement.

So Don Gabriele watched the crowds go by, and consoled himself amid his natural fears of what might happen next by the sage reflection that the whole disturbance had been foretold as long ago as in the days when the Book of Ecclesiastes was written. It may probably puzzle even well-read men to discover any reference to Mas'aniello in that 170sacred book; but Don Gabriele was convinced of the fact, and anyone who desires to verify his references will find the passages on which he relied in the tenth chapter.

When morning came all Naples was in arms, and the authority of Mas'aniello was supreme. In the Piazza di Mercato, opposite the house in which he lived, some rope dancers had erected a platform for their exhibition, and on this throne sat the fisherman's boy, in trousers and shirt, both torn and dirty, girded with a rusty sword, and delivering his orders like a conqueror, calm and confident in the knowledge of his strength. The business which chiefly occupied his mind was the discovery of fresh arms and munitions. Early in the day, by the secret

47

help of a woman, the rioters had discovered five cannon hidden in the city. Powder they also found, flooded by the Spaniards, but not beyond the possibility of being dried. Meantime most of the prisons were flung open. Hour by hour the forces mustering in the Carmine increased, and already bands were told off to destroy the houses and property of those nobles who were hated by the people.

As for the Viceroy, he saw no resource but in sending messages of peace. For this purpose he released from prison the Duke of Maddaloni, head of the Carafa family, who had incurred the displeasure of the Crown, and despatched him to the Mercato, with instructions to use his influence in any way which seemed to him most likely to disperse the people to their homes. But, as Don Gabriele remarks quaintly, the people obstinately refused to taste the perfect liquor out of this caraffe, esteeming it indeed rank poison. Nor was their refusal merely passive. On the contrary, they hunted the Duke through the piazza till he fled for his life to the 171shelter of the Carmine, convinced that he was sent to play them false and delude them with worthless promises, in place of the restoration of the privileges bestowed on Naples by the great Emperor Charles the Fifth, which charter they were resolved to obtain and re-establish.

It is quite clear that the nobles of Naples had no real sympathy with the mob in the most reasonable of their grievances. Had any one among them come forward to support and to restrain them, the issue of the revolt might have been very different. Indeed, the part played by the nobles rankled in the minds of the citizens for many a year; and when, in the next century, the nobles themselves sought to organise a rising, an old man who had been out with Mas'aniello cast it in their teeth and called upon the people to go to their homes, which they did.

But finding that the rioters would have naught to say to nobles, the Cardinal Filamarino went himself to the Mercato. He was received with deference, if not with enthusiasm. The Cardinal was a cunning statesman. "Like a skilful hunter," says Don Gabriele, who is lost in admiration of his wisdom, "he knew well how to whistle the birds into his net." A churchman trained at Rome was scarcely likely to be baffled by the rough sincerity of fishermen and fruitsellers, ignorant of all the niceties which salve the conscience of diplomatists. The Cardinal spoke as one of themselves, as a father to his dear and faithful children. He sympathised with their complaints. He admitted their grievances, even exaggerating them. He commended their courage, and assured them of entire success if only they would be guided by his advice. He showed no horror at the steps taken by the rioters, watching bands told off to destroy houses, or erect fortifications without 172remonstrance. All his efforts were exerted to gain dominion over Mas'aniello and his followers. To this end he took up his quarters in the Carmine, and admitted the fisher's boy to audience at all hours. He was aided by the natural piety of Mas'aniello, who looked up to him as little less than divine, and always fell upon his knees before he spoke to him, seeking counsel in every difficulty, with absolute confidence that the church in which he trusted could not delude or trick him.

It cost the cunning Cardinal but little pains to win over a man so reverential and so humble. At the Cardinal's bidding Mas'aniello laid aside his scheme of punishing the nobles by still further destruction of their property, and in reward for this mark of obedience the Cardinal produced the much-desired charter of Charles the Fifth, with an order of the Viceroy giving it validity. On the next day Mas'aniello was to go in state to the palace to receive confirmation of these privileges, and the night of Tuesday fell upon a pleasing scene, the good Cardinal receiving the thanks and blessings of his grateful flock.

During that night, however, somebody, vaguely described as "a personage," was devising an elaborate scheme of murder. Don Gabriele is sure it could not have been the Cardinal, but he does not tell us who it was. Perhaps some enemy of the worthy Cardinal, designing to filch his credit while he slept, posted the murderers in the very Church of the Carmine, without the knowledge of either the good Fathers or their excellent Archbishop! There at any rate they were, and in the morning Mas'aniello, going into the church, was greeted by a salvo of balls, every one of which, by a miracle naturally set down to the credit of the Madonna della Carmine, flew past him harmlessly. The people, having wreaked 173summary vengeance on the would-be murderers, were unreasonable enough to suspect the Cardinal of complicity in the crime. But that good man had abundant evidence that it was not so, and Mas'aniello, yielding to reverence again, publicly declared his contrition for the unworthy suspicion he had formed. Whereupon the Cardinal, who was too great to harbour resentment, mounted the steeple of the Carmine and blessed the crowd. But still the identity of the personage is not revealed. Don Gabriele is contemptuous of his folly in thinking to kill the hydra by a premature and badly devised attack. When the personage tried next his scheme was better laid.

Meantime all went on wheels. An audience with the Viceroy was appointed, and Mas'aniello, having with great difficulty been persuaded to array himself in garments of silver cloth, which splendour he considered quite unsuited to his humble origin, mounted a richly caparisoned steed and rode towards the palace at the head of an innumerable crowd of people. What a change of state was there! On Sunday morning this fellow was among the basest of a great city, not even a fish-seller, but the ragged attendant who provided scraps of paper in which to wrap up the fish. On Wednesday, clothed like an emperor and followed by a crowd which adored him, he rode in triumph to meet the Viceroy of the proudest monarchy on earth. Surely never, save in the wild fantasy of Eastern fairy tales, has fortune turned her wheel so swiftly, or given more lightly what she caught no less rapidly away.

48

Mas'aniello cast himself humbly at the feet of the Viceroy, who raised him in the sight of all the people and embraced him with tears of affection. Don Gabriele makes no reference to Judas at this point, 174which is odd, seeing how well equipped he was with apt references to Scripture. The crowd roared with pleasure at the great man's condescension, making such a noise that no one of the gracious words used by the Duke of Arcos could be heard. On this—and the fact was noted as a striking proof of the ease with which the people could be swayed by one they trusted—Mas'aniello turned towards them and laid his finger on his lip. Instantly the roars ceased, and all the vast crowd stood as mute as carven statues. He waved his hand, in sign that they should go, and as if by magic the wide piazza, crowded to suffocation only a moment previously, stood bare and empty. The Viceroy offered him a rich jewel, but he refused it, declaring that it was his set purpose to go back to his lowly station: and indeed, having obtained decrees which confirmed the ordinances of the previous day, Mas'aniello returned to the Piazza del Mercato, doffed his splendid raiment, and put on once more the rags he had been used to wear when he followed humbly in the rear of his master who sold fish.

The work of quieting the city was almost done. During Thursday and Friday the tumults were steadily repressed; and on Saturday the Cardinal, leaving his temporary quarters at the Carmine, returned to his own palace in solemn procession, followed by Mas'aniello upon horseback. The streets were decorated. The people thanked and blessed their saviours. But already the strain of his position was telling on Mas'aniello. It was noticed that he did not sleep, but was possessed by a feverish activity which kept him sitting all day long in the scorching summer sun, organising, judging, and directing. The constant apprehension of murder weighed upon him; and even on the Wednesday, after discovering the 175plot to kill him, he was disposed to credit a wild story that the Viceroy had caused the fountains to be poisoned, a belief which could only be dissipated when the Cardinal, sending for a great beaker of fresh water from the fountain of the Carmine, drank it off in full sight of the crowd. Fatigue, excitement, some natural fear of death—there was nothing more the matter with the lad than a day's rest with some peace of mind would have repaired. But fate gave him the opportunity for neither; and indeed, if one calculates the possibilities before him, the power of the forces which he had offended, and the treacherous nature of the popular favour which was his only strength, one may well ask whether fate, kinder to mankind than they ever realise, did not show charity and love when she gave him death as the meed of his unselfish service to the people.

It is certain that ere the week was over Mas'aniello began to show signs of unsettled brain, infirmity of temper, extravagance of manner. The people began to be impatient of him, turning rapidly as ever against those who serve them best.

"Amor di padrone, e vino di fiasco,
La sera è buono e la mattina è guasto."

The people were Mas'aniello's "padrone," and like the wine in the flask, their favour was sweet at night but sour in the morning. There is no need to tell the history of the next two days in full, or to drag out the obscure conspiracy which culminated on the Tuesday morning. The poor lad knew well what was in store for him, and the knowledge may have completed his mental agitation. The Feast of the Madonna del Carmine came at last, and Mas'aniello went early to the church to await the Cardinal. When he saw the great man coming he ran to meet 176him and broke out, "Eminence and Lord, I see already that my people are abandoning me and betraying me. Now for my consolation I beg that there may be public procession to this most holy Lady of the Carmine, headed by the Viceroy, and I desire that your Eminence will also join it." The Cardinal embraced the agitated lad, and praised his devotion, assuring him that all should happen as he wished.

The Mass began. The church was packed with people so close that one could scarcely breathe. In the face of this vast crowd Mas'aniello mounted into the pulpit, and in burning words reproached the people for their inclination to desert him, reminding them of all that he had achieved, not for himself, but for them. Then turning on his past life, with some passionate remembrance of the holy character of the day on which he spoke, he laid bare his sins, calling loudly on the people to do the like, confessing them humbly before God. Then as his passion and delirium increased, he lost control utterly of himself, stripped off his clothes, and threatened to dash himself down from the pulpit on the floor of the church. By sheer force he was restrained, and being led away into the cloister of the convent, leaned out of an open window which looked towards the sea, seeking to cool his head with the fresh breeze that blew from Capri or from Ischia.

But for the second time the murderers were hidden in the Carmine. In the cloister they lurked waiting for the order of the Viceroy. The order arrived. The murderers came out openly and went along the corridor, calling "Signor Mas'aniello." The lad heard them, and went towards them saying, "What is it, my people?" on which they shot him, and he fell, crying "Ah, traitors and unjust!"177

Such was the end of Mas'aniello, a death which at the moment it occurred seems to have caused no sort of sorrow to the people. In fact, when the head of the prince-fisherman was cut off and carried through the streets on a pike there were few found who did not curse it, while the headless trunk was dragged about the Mercato by children in derision. But not many days passed before the instable people discovered how great a loss he was to them. The gabelles were reimposed, bread grew dear again. There was no longer any protector for the people; and by a quick revulsion of feeling, when it was too late, the corpse was dug up, the head reunited to the body, and those funeral pomps accorded which I spoke of in a former chapter.

49

And so the Viceroy and the Cardinal won the game, as rulers often win it in this world when they cast aside both faith and honour. But for all such crimes history reserves its chastisement. She speaks without fear or favour, and declares that these two princes cut a sorry figure beside the fisher boy whom they betrayed and slew. Both alike, whether spiritual or temporal, are of that poor scum of humanity which merits nothing but contempt; whereas Mas'aniello is heroic, stained by no unworthy action, and bearing himself right nobly in a crisis as wondrous as any in the whole history of man.

CHAPTER IX

VESUVIUS AND THE CITIES WHICH HE HAS DESTROYED—HERCULANEUM, POMPEII, AND STABIÆ

178

It is to most strangers approaching Naples for the first time a matter of surprise to discover that Vesuvius has two peaks rising out of the same base, and that far removed from all the range of Apennines which, dim and distant, hedge in the wide fertile plain.

When viewed from Naples, Monte Somma, the landward peak, appears scarcely less conical than its neighbour, which contains the crater; but from the other side it has a wholly different aspect, and if one looks at it from the Sorrento cliffs one perceives that it is no peak, but a long ridge, the segment of a circle which, if completed, would enfold the present eruptive cone.

The fact is important, for not only is it the key to all the topography of the mountain, but it is essential to the comprehension of what happened on that August day of the year 79 A.D., when the dead volcano woke to life. The broken circle of Monte Somma was complete in those days; and men looking up from Pompeii or Herculaneum saw a mountain vastly different from that which we behold, yet one 179which, from the part before us, can be reconstructed by an easy use of the imagination.

If a man will take his stand on the lower heights of the hills behind Castellammare, he will find that he looks over Pompeii, over Bosco Reale lying on the first slopes which swell upward from the plain, into the mouth of the gap which parts Vesuvius from Somma. Even from that distance he will obtain a forcible impression of the black cliff of Somma, towering almost sheer to the height of a thousand feet above the bottom of the gap, while the outer face of the same rock wall slopes towards the sunny plain and the woods of Ottajano with an incline so gentle as to be comparatively easy of ascent.

Clearly the two faces of Somma have been differently formed. The sheer one was, at least in part, the actual wall of the prehistoric crater, that caldron in which the volcanic forces raged in days so ancient that they had been clean forgotten when the Romans ruled the land. The present cone did not exist. The circuit of Monte Somma was unbroken, and lay clothed with green meadows up to the very summit. But where, then, is the rest of that gigantic wall? It was blown away by the eruption that destroyed Pompeii.

This is the first tremendous fact which the visitor to Naples has to realise; and it is well worth while to absorb it thoroughly before setting foot upon the mountain, for nothing else seen there carries with it the same impression of overwhelming, cataclysmal awe. It is from a distance that the terror of the thing can be appreciated best. When one goes forward from the observatory on the mountain-side, skirting the flank of the eruptive cone, into that portion of the gap which is called the Atrio del Cavallo—though it would at certain times be found 180as safe to stable a steed in the Kelpie's flow as in this wilderness of burnt rock—the sight of the steep wall towering on one's left is infinitely striking. But at so close a distance, and in the immediate neighbourhood of so many other sights, it is scarcely possible to concentrate one's thoughts on the girth of the ancient crater. To comprehend the extent of the wall which has been blown away one must go further off, till one can distinguish the shape of Somma's wall, till one's eye can measure the vast size of the crater which would be formed by its completion, even allowing for the doubts which have been raised whether the circuit could have been so vast as this measurement would imply. There are some shattered fragments of the wall to be seen upon the south or seaward side of the volcano. The ridge where the white observatory building stands is one; another, named the "pedementina," appears as a shoulder of the mountain, clearly distinguishable from Naples. But these scattered remnants help little towards the general impression. It is by contemplating Somma that one learns to comprehend the appalling nature of the convulsion which, with little warning, blasted away so immense a portion of the mountain regarded by those who dwelt beneath it as one of the eternal hills.

Far from having any title to immortality Vesuvius is among the youngest and most mutable of mountains. The present cone is, as I said, the creation of the last eighteen centuries, piled up by successive eruptions to something more than the height of Somma, which once, as its name implies, towered far above it. Even though the antiquity of the mountain be reckoned by the age of Somma, or of some earlier cone, on the ruins of which Somma may have reared itself, it is as nothing when set beside the great wall 181of mountains which sweeps round the plain and ends in the great crags of St. Angelo and the cliffs of Capri. Those hills may be termed "eternal" by as true a warrant as any on the earth. But long after they were shaped and fashioned the sea flowed over the Campagna Felice and the site of Naples. Vesuvius was a volcanic vent-hole underneath the water, like many another which now seethes and hisses deep down in the blue bay, forming lava reefs about which the best fish always cluster. Then came the upheaval of the sea floor, and Vesuvius stood on dry land, no longer a sea-

50

drenched reef or islet, but a hill of ashes and of lava piled over a crack in the earth's crust, which belched forth fiery torrents for unnumbered years, and sank at last to rest after an outburst which, if one may judge by the hugeness of the crater it scooped out, must have been terrible almost beyond conception.

Yet it was completely forgotten! How many centuries of rest must it not have needed to erase from the minds of men all memory of a cataclysm so tremendous! In the days when doom was drawing near to the cities of the Campagna, an old tradition was current that fire had once been seen coming out of the summit of Vesuvius. Doubtless many people looking up at the green mountain pastures shrugged their shoulders at the tale. Yet Strabo, the geographer, remarked that the rocks upon the surface of the mountain looked as if they had been subjected to fire. It is difficult for us to detach the idea of terror from Vesuvius, and to contemplate it with thoughts at all resembling those which the dwellers in the buried cities bestowed upon it. There has, however, been one period when the summit of the mountain presented an aspect probably not far unlike that which a Pompeiian would have seen, had 182curiosity led him to the top after visiting his vineyards or his pastures on the lower slopes. That time was in the years immediately preceding the eruption of 1631. Vesuvius had been almost at rest for near five centuries, and there were many who believed its fires to be extinct.

The Abate Braccini ascended the mountain in 1612, nineteen years before the outbreak. Vesuvius was then, as it is now, somewhat higher than Somma, though the comparative level has been changed more than once in the last three centuries. On the summit Braccini found a profound chasm, a mile in circuit, surrounded by a bulwark of calcined stones, on which no vegetation grew. Having crossed it, he descended to a little plain, where he found plants of divers kinds, though in no profusion. But from that point there was a gulf of verdure. One could descend it by tortuous paths, which led to the very bottom of the abyss, and were used not only by woodcutters plying their trade among the dense forest trees which had grown up to maturity on the lava soil, but also by animals which strayed down to browse on the succulent, rich grass. Neither men nor cattle retained any fear of the green crater depths. Only the rim of calcined stones at the summit seems to have betrayed the volcanic fire of old days, except that here and there a wreath of smoke coiled away across the elms and oaks and the pleasant scrub of broom and other underwood.

About the same time a Neapolitan descended to the bottom of the crater. He found there a flat plain with two small lakes, the crater walls all pierced with caverns, through some of which the wind whistled with a noise which sounded awfully on that dim, lonely spot. There were tales of treasure hidden in the caves, but no man had dared explore them. The 183crater was so deep that the descent and ascent occupied three hours.

Such was the aspect of the mountain in days when it had certainly rested for a shorter space than in the great age of Pompeii and Herculaneum. All men must have known what none remembered in either of those doomed cities. The tales of terror spreading from the mountain were still fresh, yet they inspired no more fear than there is in Ischia to-day of Monte Epomeo; and the herdsmen sat and whistled all day long upon the slopes as they do now within an hour's climb of Casamicciola.

To this false security must be ascribed the fact that those who dwelt about the mountain paid little heed to the indications of an approaching break in its long rest. Profound changes were taking place within the abyss which Braccini has described; and on the 1st or 2nd of December, 1631, an inhabitant of Ottajano, visiting the summit, found the woods gone, the chasm filled up to the brim. A level plain had replaced the yawning gulf. The bold Ottajanese walked across from one side to the other, surprised, no doubt, to see what had occurred, but, so far as we can judge from Braccini's narrative, by no means afflicted with any sense of awe at the magnitude of the event, still less inclined to see in it a foretaste of danger for the country.

A few nights later the peasants of Torre del Greco and of Massa di Somma began to complain that the growlings of the demons confined within the mountain disturbed their rest. Religious ceremonies were carried out, but the growls continued. On the night of the 15th, the air being extraordinarily clear, there hung in the sky above the mountain a star of strange size and brilliance. Dusk fell upon that day, and still there was no alarm; but somewhat later in 184the evening, a servant crossing the Ponte della Maddalena, on his way home from Portici, saw a flash of lightning strike the mountain; while at Resina a deep red glow appearing on the summit perplexed the villagers, for no such sight had been seen within the memory of living man.

As night passed and day approached, the reports of those who had ventured up the slopes grew more awful. Peasants between Torre del Greco and Torre dell'Annunziata had seen smoke pour in volumes out of the Atrio del Cavallo. A herdsman on the mountain saw the pastures rent, and the sweet herbage turned into a raging blast furnace. Santolo di Simone ventured some way up to ascertain the truth. He saw the ground cleft in divers places, out of which poured smoke and flame, while all the air was filled with thunderous reports, and great stones cast out of the fiery gulfs were hurled about the slopes. Meantime dawn in Naples was at hand; and as the light increased, men going about the common affairs of their existence began to take note of an extraordinary cloud which hung above Vesuvius, having the precise shape of a gigantic pine tree. Some wondered and some feared, but none understood what was the terror which had come upon them, till Braccini, going into his library and taking down his Pliny, read them that vivid passage which describes the sight young Pliny saw when he looked towards Vesuvius from Misenum. "There," said Braccini, as he closed the book, "there, in the words of sixteen centuries ago, is depicted what you see to-day."

That pine tree has become awfully familiar to most Neapolitans now alive; and to some of those who visit the city during an eruption it seems as if familiarity had bred contempt, and caused the occasion to be

51

regarded as one for merriment, since it 185draws strangers there in countless numbers, and enriches every trader on the coast. But there is terror also in the streets when the shocks come rapidly, when doors and windows rattle with continuous concussions, and all the city reeks with sulphurous stenches coming one knows not whence. To this natural and human fear there was added, in the days of which Braccini wrote, the shock of a horrible surprise. The people were not dreaming of eruptions. They thought of them as little as did their far-distant kinsmen, who occupied the lovely shore when Pompeii was a city of the quick, not of the dead. That is what makes Braccini's tale so interesting. It reproduces for us, as nearly as is possible, a picture of what must have happened in the city streets on that morning when Pliny came sailing from Misenum at the urgent cry of Herculaneum for help, only to find his ships beaten off the coast by a hail of fiery stones.

The Cardinal Archbishop of Naples was at Torre del Greco on that fateful morning. He hurried back to the city, and having celebrated the Sacrament, and given orders for the rite to be solemnised throughout the city, he went up to the treasury where the relics of the saints were kept, intending to arrange a solemn procession. The blood of San Gennaro was found already liquefied and boiling! Great crowds accompanied the procession, the superstitious Neapolitans turned to their priests and saints at the first sign of danger, and marched behind the relics with effusion of piety, the men scourging themselves till the blood ran from their shoulders, the women dishevelled and weeping, while crowds of boys chanted the Litany with extraordinary tenderness. The shops were shut. Naples had become a city of devotees.

But San Gennaro, though his blood had boiled, 186was not ready to disperse the peril. The shocks of earthquake grew louder. The concussions rattled faster from the mountain. Towards noon thick darkness stole down upon the city, as it had upon Misenum sixteen hundred years before. The smell of sulphur in the streets was choking. Men asked themselves if so strong a reek could possibly travel from Vesuvius, and whether some vent had not opened close at hand. The houses, says Braccini, were swaying like ships at sea, and in the air there was a horrible roaring sound like the blast of many furnaces. The darkness grew more dense, and tongues of lightning flashed continuously out of the mirk sky. The crashes became quite appalling. Naples went wild with terror. The Viceroy sent drummers round the city appealing to the people to live cleanly in that which appeared to be the supreme moment of the created world. Men and women utterly unknown to each other ran up and embraced, seeking comfort, and crying, "Gesù, misericordia !"

So passed the first day of the reawakened activity of Vesuvius. The night brought no abatement of terror. Early in the morning the crashes redoubled. The whole mountain seemed to be springing into the air, and all the surface of the earth rocked like water in a vessel which is violently shaken. At the same moment the sea retreated for near half a mile, and then swept back to a point far above its level. At Naples nothing more than that was seen, but the miserable inhabitants of Resina perceived that those mighty birth throes had ended in the ejection of a vast flood of lava, which was pouring down the mountain on the seaward side. The fiery torrent came on with such speed that it had reached the sea in less than an hour from the outbreak. As it advanced it split into seven streams, each one of which 187took a different course of devastation. One flowed in the direction of San Jorio, which it destroyed, engulfing, it is said, no less than three thousand persons, including a religious procession. A second arm of the flood destroyed Bosco Reale and Torre dell'Annunziata, running out more than two hundred yards into the sea, where it formed a reef so hot that the water round about it boiled for days. A third wrecked Torre del Greco, a fourth poured over Resina, and a fifth, passing westwards, ruined San Giorgio a Cremano, and touched Barra and San Giovanni. Meantime a sixth stream, after filling the valleys divided by the ridge on which the observatory stands now, swept down on Massa di Somma, and reached San Sebastiano.

In this point the eruption of 1631 differed from that which destroyed Pompeii. In the latter there was no lava, but only falling stone and ash, either dry, or compacted into mud by storms of rain and showers of water thrown out of the crater. But it was not by lava only that the country was devastated three centuries and a half ago. Ashes fell also in such masses that near Vesuvius they were heaped up twelve feet deep, and great quantities of them drifting across southern Italy fell upon the shores of that lovely bay where Taranto looks across to the snow-topped mountains of Calabria. Stones fell also of astounding weight. One which was thrown into Massa di Somma is reported to have weighed 50,000 pounds; while another, which fell as far away as Nola, was of such dimensions that a team of twenty oxen could not stir it.

When this great eruption ended, the relative heights of Vesuvius and Somma were reversed, and the eruptive cone, which had risen 50 feet above its neighbour, stood nearly 200 feet below it. It is almost the 188rule that in great eruptions Vesuvius suffers loss of height, while the cone is piled up by smaller ones.

Such is the country in which a teeming population elects to live. It is said that no less than 80,000 persons have their homes on the slopes of the mountain—a fact which appears inexplicable to those who do not know by experience how small the loss of life may be in the greatest eruption. It is true that in 1631 a vast number of persons perished. But this was due probably in some measure to the fact that they did not know their danger and took no proper measures to avoid it. The men then living had seen nothing like the sudden peril which beset them. But every peasant of our day is well aware what lava floods may do, and how their course will lie. All have their little images of San Gennaro, which they set up in their cottages, and many can tell how the good saint has averted from his vineyard a fiery torrent which crawled on to the point when it seemed as if not even heavenly power could avert destruction, yet twisted off to one side and left him scatheless. At times, of course, the velocity of the lava is so great that no man can do aught but flee. In 1766 Sir William Hamilton saw a stream

52

which ran in the first mile with a velocity "equal to that of the River Severn at the passage near Bristol," while in 1794 the lava ran through Torre del Greco at the rate of one foot in a second. Yet the loss of life was small. "Napoli fa i peccati," say the people, "e Torre li paga !"—Naples commits the sins and Torre pays for them. It is true enough; yet the toll is taken more in property than life. Moreover, the after-fruits of an eruption are worth rubies to the people, so fertile is the soil created by the decaying lava.

CARD-PLAYERS—NAPLES.

That the loss of life remains so small is the more surprising in view of the fact that Vesuvius can by 189no means be trusted to discharge itself on all occasions by the main crater. In fact, the flanks of the mountain, strengthened and compacted as they are by the outflow of countless lava streams, are yet seamed and fissured by the rupture of the surface to form other vents. Occasionally these "bocche" mouths, as the Italians call them, have opened far down the slopes among the cultivated fields and vineyards. It was so in 1861, not fortunately one of the greatest of eruptions. The bocche of that year are on the hillside no great way above Torre del Greco. Nothing, in fact, is certain about the operation of volcanic forces, and this is a fact which may be borne in mind by those who elect to ascend the mountain during an eruption. Sir William Hamilton in 1767 had a narrow escape. "I was making my observations," he says, "upon the lava, which had already from the spot where it first broke out reached the valley"—that is, the Atrio del Cavallo—"when on a sudden, about noon, I heard a violent noise within the mountain, and at a spot about a quarter of a mile off the place where I stood, the mountain split, and with much noise from this new mouth a fountain of liquid fire shot up many feet high, and then like a torrent rolled on directly towards us. The earth shook, and at the same time a volley of stones fell thick upon us; in an instant clouds of black smoke and ashes caused almost a total darkness; the explosions from the top of the mountain were much louder than any thunder I ever heard, and the smell of the sulphur was very offensive. My guide, alarmed, took to his heels; and I must confess I was not at my ease. I followed close, and we ran near three miles without stopping."

To run three miles over the broken and uneven lava reefs of the Piano, with a fiery torrent hunting 190close behind, is not an experience which would be relished by the ordinary tourist, however far it might be sweetened in the retrospect to the adventurous man of science. Yet happy is the man who in such a case gets off with a sharp run. In 1872 a party of tourists were less happy. The terrible eruption of that year deserves attention, being certainly the greatest within the present generation, and fortunately it has been described with knowledge and precision by Professor Palmieri who, with noble devotion to the cause of science, had spent so many years in the observatory planted on the barren ridge of trachyte which divides the two valley-arms which the Atrio del Cavallo projects towards Naples. Those valleys receive the streams of lava which are ejected into the Atrio, and when the volume of the flow is large, it has happened that the observatory has been almost engirdled with the red-hot torrents—a position of which, if the danger may be exaggerated, the awe certainly cannot, and which must fill all men with admiration for the illustrious scientists who endure it.

Palmieri regarded the eruption as the last phase of a series of disturbances which began at the end of January, 1871. From November, 1868, until the end of December, 1870, the mountain had been almost quiet. Only a few fumaroles discharging smoke bore witness to the need for watchfulness. "Early in 1871 the delicate instruments of the observatory which register earth tremors were observed to be slightly agitated, and the crater discharged a few incandescent projectiles, detonating at the same time, but not remarkably. On the 13th of January an aperture appeared on the northern edge of the upper plain of the Vesuvian cone; at first a little lava issued from it, then a small cone arose which threw out incandescent projectiles and much smoke of a reddish 191colour, whilst the central crater continued to detonate more loudly and frequently. The lava flow continued to increase until the beginning of March, without extending much beyond the base of the cone, although it had great mobility. In March the little cone appeared not only to subside but even partly to give way, as almost always happens with eccentric cones when their activity is at an end.... A little smoke issued from the small crater, and a loud hissing from the interior was audible. By lying along the edge I could see a cavity of cylindrical form about ten metres deep.... The bottom of the crater was level, but in the centre a small cone of about two metres had formed, pointed in such a manner that it possessed but a very narrow opening at the apex, from which smoke issued with a hissing sound, and from which were spurted a few very small incandescent stones and scoriæ. This little cone increased in size as well as in activity until it filled the crater and rose four or five metres above the brim. New and more abundant lavas appeared near the base of this cone, and pouring continually into the 'Atrio del Cavallo' rushed into the 'Fossa della Vetrana' in the direction of the observatory, and towards the Crocella, where they accumulated to such an extent as to cover the hillside for a distance of about three hundred metres.... For many months the lava descended from the cone and traversed the 'Atrio del Cavallo.'... On the 3rd and 4th of November a copious and splendid stream coursed down the principal cone on its western side, but was soon exhausted. The new small cone appeared again at rest, but did not cease to emit smoke...."

In the beginning of January, 1872, the little cone again became active, the crater of the preceding October resumed strength, there were bellowings, 192projectiles, and copious outflows of lava. In February the action of the hidden forces abated somewhat; but in March, at the full moon, the cone opened on the north-western side, the cleavage being marked out by a line of fumaroles, and a lava stream issued from the lowest part without any

53

noise and with very little smoke, pouring down into the Atrio del Cavallo as far as the precipices of Monte Somma. This lava ceased flowing after a week, but the fumaroles still pointed out the clefts, and between the small re-made cone and the central crater a new crater of small dimensions and interrupted activity opened. On the 23rd of April, another full moon, the observatory instruments were agitated, the activity of the craters increased, and on the evening of the 24th splendid lavas descended the cone in many directions. The spectacle was of superb beauty. There was clear moonshine, and from Naples the outline of a vast fiery tree was seen to be traced on the black side of the mountain. Strangers poured into the city. The long period of activity without destruction disposed them to regard the show as a display of fireworks. Half Naples set its heart on ascending the mountain by night, and little wonder, for the moonlit bay reddened by the wide reflection from the burning breast of the volcano made a sight on which no man could look without the sense of witnessing a thing which was absolutely unearthly in the splendour of its beauty.

But on the following morning the flow was nearly spent. One stream only continued to flow from the base of the cone. And this one was almost inaccessible, by reason of the roughness of the ground. As night fell the visitors began to arrive. No less than 120 carriages are said to have passed the hermitage by dusk. Palmieri tried to dissuade the 193sightseers from going on, but in vain. The display of the previous night had been too splendid. They hoped continually that the show might be repeated. It was, but in a manner which they little looked for.

The crater was casting out huge stones, with detonations resembling the discharge of whole parks of artillery at once. From time to time the din ceased absolutely, then low and softly it began again, and gained force quickly till it crashed as loudly as before. When midnight was past, immense clouds of smoke began to pour out of all the craters, and lava broke out simultaneously from many points upon the slopes. Out of the chief crater rose the awful pine tree. The detonations grew more constant. There was still time to flee; but the spectacle was growing grander every moment, and inexperienced guides led forward a large party into the Atrio, where they stood watching such a sight as living men have rarely seen. At half-past three came the catastrophe. The whole of the great cone rent itself from top to bottom with an appalling crash, casting out a huge stream of fiery lava. At the same moment two large craters formed upon the summit, discharging showers of red-hot scoriæ, while the pillar of the pine tree rose up to many times more than even the vast height which it then stretched across the sky. A cloud of choking blinding smoke enveloped the visitors, a fiery hail rained down on them, the lava broke out immediately by them, and barred their retreat to the observatory. Eight medical students were engulfed by the fire, with others who were not known. Eleven more were grievously injured; and when the survivors were able to reach the observatory, it was in several cases but to die.

The lava flow from this grand fissure was restrained for some time within the Atrio; but issuing thence 194at last divided, one branch threatening Resina, but stopping happily almost as soon as it reached the cultivated ground, while the larger branch ran through the Fossa della Vetrana, traversing its whole length of 1,300 metres in three hours. It dashed into the Fossa della Faraone, then again divided, one arm of the diminished stream destroying a great part of the villages of Massa and San Sebastiano, and flowing on so far in the direction of Naples that had it continued but for four-and-twenty hours longer it must have flowed into the city streets.

It may be supposed that whilst this awful eruption was proceeding, the position of the courageous men of science in the observatory was rather glorious than safe. Nothing can exceed the value of the services rendered to science by these gentlemen who elect to spend their lives upon a spot which is always dreary and exposed to constant danger. They are of the outposts of mankind. I take my cap off to their stout hearts and their keen intellects. To them their danger is a little thing, and they would not thank me if I were to dwell too long on it. But I will take Professor Palmieri's own words, and beg those who read to ponder over what is involved in them. "On the night of the 26th of April the observatory lay between two torrents of fire. The heat was insufferable. The glass of the windows was hot and crackling, especially on the side of the Fossa della Vetrana. In all the rooms there was a smell of scorching."

NAPLES—A SLUM.

Meantime the spectacle of the mountain must have been bewilderingly grand. The cone was seamed and perforated on every side, and the fiery lava issuing from the vents covered it so completely that, in Palmieri's picturesque expression, Vesuvius "sweated fire." On the 27th of April the igneous 195period of the eruption was over, though the rain of ashes and projectiles became more abundant, the crashes were louder than ever, the pine tree was of a darker colour, and was continually furrowed by flashes of lightning; while on the 29th stones fell at the observatory of such size that the glass of the unshuttered windows was broken. By midnight, of that day, however, there was a marked improvement, and on the 1st of May the eruption was at an end.

The visitor who strolls to-day through the main street of Portici sees nothing but a continuation of the squalid life and poverty of building which have followed him continuously from the eastern quarters of the city. The mean aspect of the town is unexpected. One had not looked for any striving after the dream of classical beauty, once so frequent and so great upon the Campanian shore. But this was the chosen pleasure resort of the Bourbon kings; and some greater dignity might have been expected in the close neighbourhood of a palace.

The palace is there still. The noisy street runs through its courtyard. Poor deserted palace! It has lost its royalty of aspect, and for all one sees in passing by the discoloured walls and shuttered windows it might be any poverty-stricken crowded palazzo in Naples. But turn in beneath the archway on the right, and go by the large cool staircase, across the clanking stones, until you emerge into the hot spring sun again. There is a noble semicircular expanse, flanked by a terrace, adorned with busts and vases, and with stairs descending to the garden, which stretches down to a belt of pine trees, cut away a little in the centre to reveal that 196band of heavenly blue which is the sea. The young trees standing by the pine are in fresh leaf; the grass is full of poppies; white butterflies are skimming to and fro across it; all is silent and deserted. A bare-armed stable-boy comes out to train a skinny pony round the terrace. The stucco of the walls is peeling off; the long rows of windows are shuttered; the sentry boxes stand empty. It is forty years since any courtier came out to taste the evening freshness on this spot where Sir William Hamilton talked of the wonders of the buried cities so long and eagerly that he forgot to watch the wife and friend whose sins the world forbears to reckon when it remembers the beauty of the one and the valour and wisdom of the other.

It is but a little way beyond the palace to the spot where the Prince d'Elbœuf is said, while sinking a well in the year 1709, to have chanced on things of which he did not know the meaning. This is one of the fables which demonstrate the extreme difficulty of speaking the truth, even about important and world-famous matters. Nothing is more certain than that the prince sank his "well" with the hope and intention of drawing up not water, but antiquities. The fact is, that in the year just mentioned he bought a country house, which stood near the site of the present railway station. It was perfectly well known that Herculaneum lay buried underneath Portici or Resina, and the prince began excavating of set purpose. It was mere chance which guided him to a spot where his first shaft came right down on the benches of the theatre, thus letting in to Herculaneum the first gleam of daylight which had entered there for more than sixteen centuries. Not much more than that stray glimmer has enlightened the old academic city even now; for none of the 197energy and learned patience lavished daily on Pompeii has been expended here.

Herculaneum as it lies to-day, awaiting its turn for excavation, creates in one respect an impression which Pompeii excites in a far less degree. It retains the visible aspect of a buried city. The sense of overwhelming tragedy is never lost. Pompeii stands free and open under the clear sky; so large, so perfect, that in the fascination of its archæology one is somewhat led away from the disaster. It is a deserted city. One knows what it was that drove the people out, but it is easy to forget. Perhaps one cares more to gloat over the rich old life laid bare so freely than to burden one's mind with memory of that day when the glow of August sunshine turned to darkness "as of a room shut up," and death came down from the mountain into the crowded streets.

At Herculaneum the mere fragment of a street, the few half-buried houses, the pit in which they lie, the cavernous darkness which hides the amphitheatre, stimulate the imagination till it leaps to a sudden comprehension of what it was that happened on that day of woe. One passes from the dirty street of Resina into a building of no dignity, somewhat like the entrance to the public baths of some small English town. A guide appears and guides one down a flight of steps which are at first palpably modern. But ere long the tread changes. One is on an ancient stair, and almost immediately the guide pauses in a vaulted corridor running right and left through perfect darkness. The height is hardly more than permits a tall man to walk upright. Here and there an arched opening in the corridor goes one sees not whither. Passing under such an arch one may descend four steps, beyond which rises 198another wall. That wall is tufa; it is no part of the structure. It flowed or fell here when it was half liquid; it came out from Vesuvius, and it is what overwhelmed the city.

The steps, thus interrupted by the intrusion of what are now stone walls, are the upper tier of seats in the amphitheatre. A gleam of daylight breaks the darkness: it comes from the Prince d'Elbœuf's shaft, which pierces the stone steps and goes down far below them. One looks up the tubular wet boring and then plunges forward to the bottom of the theatre through blackness barely scattered by the candles which the guide carries.

A short descent of nineteen steps in all brings one to the floor of the theatre, at the spot appropriated to the orchestra. The stage is a low platform, approached on either hand by steps. It is deprived of some part of its original depth by pillars and barriers hardened out of that choking mud which poured down from the mountain. Such barriers present themselves on every side; they leave the theatre formless; they create gangways where none existed, walls where the spectators had clear line of vision, darkness where the sun shone freely eighteen centuries ago. In one of these gangways behind the stage the clear impression of human features looks down from the rough wet ceiling; it is the impression of a player's mask. There were doubtless many in the theatre when the seething flood rolled in.

Among this darkness and these sights the sense of tragedy tightens on the imagination. The cruelty of the ruin stands before one and is not to be set aside. There are remains of frescoes here and there; but they are almost destroyed, and serve only to increase the pity that a theatre which once rang with laughter and glowed so richly with soft light and 199colour should lie wet, buried and forsaken in the darkness.

It is sometimes said that Herculaneum was destroyed by lava—the guides use the word to this day. But Vesuvius threw out no lava in the great eruption which destroyed the cities. It ejected much in prehistoric times. Pompeii itself is built upon a lava ridge, which in the old days was quarried for millstones, thus giving rise to an important industry. But in historic times lava did not flow—if we may trust geologists—till the year 1036 A.D.

55

Herculaneum was destroyed by fragments of pumice stone and ashes, scarcely distinguishable from those which one may see raked away from the half-uncovered walls of some new house at Pompeii. With this storm of falling cinders—how dense and thick one may picture dimly by remembering once more that all the seaward wall of the vast old crater was being blown away—with this crushing, choking shower, came torrents of rain, enough to turn the falling ashes to a sort of mud, which hardened into tufa. Indeed, just as the yellow tufa of Posilipo is composed of volcanic ash ejected underneath the sea, and is thus formed of ash and water, such precisely is the crust which hardened over Herculaneum, and holds the city in its clutch unto this hour. Perhaps the mud formed on the mountain slopes, and came rolling down upon the town. Professor Phillips thought it formed within the crater. Some obvious warning of great peril there must have been, and that quite early on the fatal 24th of August; for it was not long past noon when a message reached Pliny at Misenum, begging for his ships, since escape was even then impossible except by sea. Already Pliny, looking from Misenum, saw the mountain topped by that vast and awful cloud shaped like a pine tree, out 200of which ashes were raining down on the three cities. His ships, approaching the coast towards evening, ran into a hail of pumice stone. The ashes fell hotter and hotter on the decks, and in continually larger masses. The sea ebbed suddenly. Ruins were tumbling from the mountain. There was no possibility of giving help to the doomed city, and Pliny gave orders to steer off the coast. No eye has seen Herculaneum from that day to this. What became of the citizens is not known. Comparatively few bodies have been found; but the excavations were too imperfect to prove that somewhere in the city bounds they do not lie in heaps.

Such was the end of Herculaneum, by ashes, not by lava. It is true that lava beds lie above the city now. Probably the lava of 1631 passed over it. Sir William Hamilton distinguished the débris of no less than six eruptions besides that which destroyed it. Sir Charles Lyell also thought that a large part of the covering of the city was subsequent to its first destruction.

At Herculaneum all that is most interesting lies underground, and nearly all is still invisible. But little effort has been made at any time to disinter the city. The searchers who dug there at the command of Charles of Bourbon between the years 1750 and 1761—to which period we must refer nearly all the most precious discoveries—contented themselves with sinking shafts in likely spots, from which they mined and tunnelled as far as seemed possible to them, and then filled up the shaft again and sank another. Thus the notices of what they found, and still more of how they found it, are imperfect. They have, moreover, been carelessly preserved. Some were even wantonly destroyed in the last century by men who did not appreciate their value. Yet 201enough has been retained to stimulate the highest interest in Herculaneum, if not indeed to justify the belief that whenever it shall be possible to overcome the obvious difficulties of excavation, treasures will be found which may far exceed in quantity and beauty those which Pompeii has yielded.

This will be better understood by considering what has been written by Signor Comparetti and Signor de Petra concerning a single villa of Herculaneum, now, alas! buried up once more in darkness. It stood between the "new diggings" and the royal palace of Portici. I will preface my abstract of the treatise of the two scholars by some passages taken from the letters of Camillo Paderni, director of the excavations, to Mr. Thomas Hollis, in 1754.

"This route," says Paderni, "led us towards a palace, which lay near the garden. But before they arrived at a palace they came to a square ... which was adorned throughout with columns of stucco. At the several angles of the square was a terminus of marble, and on every one of these stood a bust of bronze of Greek workmanship, one of which had on it the name of the artist. A small fountain was placed before each terminus, which was constructed in the following manner. Level with the pavement was a vase to receive the water which fell from above. In the middle of this vase was a stand of balustrade work, to support another marble vase. This second vase was square on the outside and circular within, where it had the appearance of a scallop shell; in the centre whereof was the spout which threw up the water that was supplied by leaden pipes within the balustrade. Among the columns ... were alternately placed a statue of bronze and a bust of the 202same material, at the equal distance of a certain number of palms.... The statues taken out from April 15 to September 30 are in number seven, near the height of six Neapolitan palms, except one of them, which is much larger, and of excellent expression. This represents a faun lying down, who appears to be drunk, resting upon the goatskin in which they anciently put wine.... September 27.—I went myself to take out a head in bronze, which proved to be that of Seneca, and the finest that has hitherto appeared.... Our greatest hopes are from the palace itself, which is of a very large extent. As yet we have only entered into one room, the floor of which is formed of mosaic work, not inelegant. It appears to have been a library, adorned with presses inlaid with different sorts of wood, disposed in rows. I was buried in this spot more than twelve days, to carry off the volumes found there, many of which were so perished that it was impossible to remove them. Those which I took away amounted to the number of 337, all of them at present incapable of being opened. These are all in Greek characters. While I was busy in this work I observed a large bundle, which from the size I imagined must contain more than a single volume. I tried with the utmost care to get it out, but could not, from the damp and weight of it. However, I perceived that it consisted of about eighteen volumes.... They were wrapped about with the bark of a tree, and covered at each end with a piece of wood.

"November 27th.—We discovered the figure of an old faun, or rather a Silenus, represented as sitting on a bank, with a tiger lying on his left side, on which his hand rested. Both these figures served to adorn a fountain, and from the mouth of the tiger had flowed water. From the same spot were taken out, 203November 29th, three little boys of bronze of a good manner. Two of them are young fauns, having the horns and ears of a goat. They have likewise silver eyes, and each of them the goatskin on his shoulder, wherein anciently they put wine, and through which here the water issued. The third boy is also of bronze, has silver eyes, is of the same size with the two former, and in a standing posture like them, but is not a faun. On one side of this last stood a small column, upon the top of which was a comic mask that served as a capital to it and discharged water from its mouth. December 16th.—In the same place were discovered another boy with a mask and three other fauns.... Besides these we met with two little boys in bronze, somewhat less than the former. These likewise were in a standing posture, had silver eyes, and had each a vase upon his shoulder whence the water flowed. We also dug out an old faun, crowned with ivy, having a long beard, a hairy body, and sandals on his feet. He sat astride upon a goatskin, holding it at the feet with both his hands...."

Thus far Paderni; and I have made this long extract to little purpose if the reader has not already recognised some among the finest objects in the great museum at Naples. This villa, with its garden full of statues, its cool peristyle all humming with the plash of falling water, its shadowy colonnade sheltering the marvellous bronzes, must have been a place of wonderful beauty. He was a rare collector who dwelt there. He had twenty-three large bronze busts and eight small ones, thirteen large bronze statues and eighteen small ones. In his garden stood not less than nine marble statues, and of marble busts he had certainly seven and probably seven more. Among these not one is of mean workmanship. The 204greater part are famous all round the world for beauty. They are unsurpassed, and they all came from a single villa just beyond the walls of this buried city.

Who was the man who made himself a home so splendid? The style of the decorations points to the latter years of the Republic. It is in marked distinction from the more ornate style which prevailed under the Empire, and of great mythological pictures there was none. One thing only enables us to guess with something like assurance who among the patricians of those days owned the villa—namely the library. The mode of inference is curious.

It was no small library which was lifted by Paderni from the presses where it had lain for seventeen centuries. The papyri numbered 1,806, though by no means all were separate treatises, while some were mere scraps. All were charred and damaged to such a degree as to render their examination a work whose difficulty baffled many men of science. At length the task was accomplished by an ingenious arrangement of silk threads, which unfolded the papyrus upon a false back made partly of onion skins, and laid it open to investigation. The results are curious. Indeed, they are something more than curious; and making due allowance for the fact that wise men do not permit themselves to be ruffled by the tricksy mockeries of time, it must be admitted that the story of this library is exasperating.

All the world knows how small a space the treasures of Greek and Latin literature occupy upon our shelves compared with that which they would fill were they intact. What melancholy gaps! How much pure delight has not been reft from us! Where is the scholar who in moments of low spirits has not roamed round his library reckoning up his losses? 205Livy shorn of more than half his bulk, Terence mangled, Cicero lacking heaven knows how many of his finest compositions! Petrarch had the treatise of the great orator "De Gloria," but nobody has seen it since. It is a painful subject—the canker at the heart of learned men, the skeleton at the feasts of all academies.

So much the greater, then, was the joy when the news ran round Europe that a library, formed in the best age of Latin literature, was discovered at Herculaneum. Now, surely, some of the lost treasures would be restored! All the universities chuckled and stood on tiptoe. Humanity, with the help of a volcano, had scored a point against time at last.

But the rolls of papyri were sadly like mere lumps of charcoal. Paderni saw a letter here, a letter there, but on the whole could make nothing of them. The smile died on the faces of the scholars. The trick was not won yet. Who would unroll these charred manuscripts, and who could possibly read them when unrolled?

Many people tried and failed, Sir Humphry Davy among the number. Learned hearts sank, and hope flickered almost to extinction. At length Padre Piaggi invented an ingenious arrangement of silk threads, whereby the charred and brittle rolls were unwrapped in the manner described above. It was a slow and weary process, but the wit of man has devised no better. One by one the treasures of the past were read. It took a century and a half, but we know the contents of some three hundred and fifty of them now.

Broadly stated, the outcome of all the pother has been to restore to an unthankful world what is probably a complete set of the works of Philodemus! "Philodemus!" gasp the scholars. "Who wanted 206him?" A fifth-rate Greek philosopher and a fourth-rate poet, who lived at Rome in the days of Cicero, better esteemed for his verses than his reasoning, and not much for either. But no Livy? No Terence? No Cicero? Not one line; hardly anything but the prose treatises of Philodemus, concerning which Signor Comparetti observes with emphasis that the oblivion they lay in was anything but undeserved.

Such is the greatest practical joke played on us by the Time Spirit in the present age. But now, laying aside our disappointment and bad temper, let us see what can be made out of this curious, if worthless, discovery. Who could have cared to collect the works of Philodemus, large and small, even to the notes he made from other books? The philosophy was Epicurean, but the chief works of the leaders of that school are with few exceptions not there. Who could it be but Philodemus himself, the only man, surely, for whom such a collection would have value? But what, then, was the library doing in this splendid and costly villa at Herculaneum? Philodemus was a poor Greek scholar, the last man who could have afforded to collect fine marbles or to house them nobly. The villa must have belonged to his patron and protector. Cicero names for us the patrician who enjoyed the privilege of hearing Philodemus reason when he would. It was Piso, Lucius Calpurnius Piso Cæsoninus, attacked by Cicero in one of the greatest of his orations. Piso had known this poor scholar from a boy, learnt the philosophy of Epicurus from him, and gave him rooms in his own house. To Piso, probably, belonged this villa. Here he may have ended his stormy life in the society of Philodemus; and when that learned man ascended to Parnassus, his books remained in what had been his study, preserved perhaps by some lingering attachment 207to his memory, perhaps by such a superstitious pride in what is never read as may be seen in certain country houses of to-day, where the squire believes the dusty volumes collected by his grandfather are a credit to the house, and chides the housemaid if he ever finds a cobweb on the peaceful shelves. It will also be remembered that, unless you want the space very much, it is easier to leave books alone than to destroy them. On the whole, I do not think the discovery of this library affords any evidence of the prevalence of cultivated taste in Herculaneum. Rather the opposite, indeed, for whatever value the owners of the house may have attached to the library the fact remains that they added to it nothing in the hundred years which followed the decease of Philodemus.

As for the statues and the bronzes, the finest were doubtless part of the spoils of Piso's proconsulate in Macedonia. Cicero taunted him with having stripped Greece of its treasures, as Verres ransacked those of Sicily. The conduct of both men was barbarous perhaps; but the candid visitor will look many times at the Sleeping Faun, or the Mercury in repose, before daring to ask himself whether he would have come home from Macedonia without them. If he discover that he would, he may yet find cause to rejoice that Piso was less virtuous; for a very short reflection on the state of Greece during the last twenty centuries suggests that if a moralist had been proconsul we should have lacked many pleasures which we now enjoy.

The "Scavi Nuovi" lie at a little distance from the theatre. One goes down a steep street sloping to the sea, the Vico di Mare. A gate in the wall gives admission to what seems at first a quarry, but a second glance shows one a short street of roofless208houses, emerging from the hillside and running straight in the direction of the shore until stopped by the opposite bank. Beneath and behind these walls, bright with mesembryanthemums and wild roses, lies all the city save this little fragment, this portion of a street, this poor two dozen houses, with the remnants of four insulæ, of which three are occupied by private houses and the fourth by some rooms belonging to the baths, of which the greater part are buried still. The houses of the south-west insula are the most interesting. At the corner is a shop with marble counter, and close to that is a dwelling of rare beauty, the so-called "Casa d'Argo." At the door there are four pillars, and on either side a bench. Out of this entrance one passes through a larger room into the xystos, colonnaded on three sides. A row of rooms open from it, all frescoed in the architectural style of which we shall see much at Pompeii, and giving on the garden. Beyond these rooms there is a second peristyle, all very beautiful—clearly the dwelling of a man of taste and means.

But in all this there is no source of pleasure which cannot be enjoyed far better at Pompeii. It is there and not to Herculaneum that the traveller goes to see the results of excavation. On this spot, I say again, it is the tragedy that counts; and as I turn in the warm sunshine and look up the broken street, where rose bushes bloom profusely in the untended gardens and the brown lizards slip in and out among the cold and empty hearths, I see above the houses of the dirty modern town the huge cone of Vesuvius fronting me directly. So he stands, looking down upon the ruin he has made, while the long train of sulky smoke which stains the clear blueness of the April sky flaunts itself like a warning to mankind that it is vain to set human forces against his, and 209that what he wills to hide shall lie lost and hidden in the earth for ever.

NAPLES—IN THE STRADA DI TRIBUNALI.

A man willing to go on foot from Resina to Pompeii might find much to amuse him by the way, especially if he have any care for tracing out the ravages of eruptions. The seashore is not unpleasant. The lava reefs that fringe it are curious, and the ports of Torre del Greco and Torre dell'Annunziata have their share of interest and picturesqueness. But the crumbs of knowledge to be picked up during such a walk seem insignificant beside the banquet which lies waiting at Pompeii; and only those who have already tasted the last dish of that banquet will care to loiter on the way.

I do not propose to add one more to the countless unscholarly rhapsodies which have been produced by visitors to Pompeii. Certain tragic feelings strike every one who enters the old grey streets. They are too obvious to need description. All else belongs to the domain of the guide-book or of the expert—to the latter more than to the former, since the best of guide-books is a sorry companion to a man who has neglected the works of Helbig or August Mau. It is not to be expected that the detailed descriptions of Murray or of Gsell-Fels can supply the broad principles and the general ideas which would have been a constant delight if acquired in advance. Many of the best intellects in Europe have been engaged in estimating the significance of the objects found from day to day in Pompeii. It is in their works that knowledge should be sought; for there is scarce any subject on which so much has been written, both so badly and so well, as on this lost city of the Campanian Plain.

It is, as I have said already, by wandering up and down the Strada Tribunali in Naples that one may 210prepare oneself to picture what would have struck a stranger on first entering Pompeii. A man passing to-day beneath the vault of the Porta Marina sees a grey street, its house-fronts perfect, but empty, and startlingly silent. This street runs into the Forum, and is in easy hearing distance of the babel of noise which issued constantly from that centre of the city. Under the colonnade of the Forum tinkers mended pots with clatter and din of hammers. Women hawked fruit and vegetables up and down, chanting their praises doubtless as loudly as the "padulani" of to-day in Naples. Ladies met their shoemakers under the cool shadows of the great arcade; and there, too, children chased each other up and down, screaming at their games like any urchins of to-day upon the steps of San Giovanni Maggiore. We know it, for they are all depicted in paintings found in neighbouring houses. There is the seller of hot food with his caldron, not unlike the stall at which the workman stops to-day in the Piazza Cavour and pays a soldo to have his hunch of bread dipped into hot tomato broth. What cheerful sounds must have risen up from all these occupations! How shall one picture them, except in the streets of some other crowded city? On the left, abutting on the south-west angle of the Forum, is the Basilica, a broad hall used as an extension of the market-place, and containing at the rear the tribunals of justice; while at the opposite, or north-east corner of the Forum, is the market proper, the Macellum, where the fish were sold. Certainly they were brought in by this Porta Marina, far nearer to the shore in those days than now. The scales scraped off the fish in the Macellum were found there in great numbers. Close by were pens for living sheep and counters for the butchers. What a reek of odours, what a hum of eager voices, 211must have risen up from this dense quarter of the busy, active town! The Pompeiians traded with their very hearts. "Lucrum gaudium!" "Oh, joyous gain!" such were the exclamations which they painted on their walls. And gain they did! Transmitting over the seas the commerce from Nola and Nocera, trading doubtless with ships of Alexandria, as Pozzuoli did; harbouring at their piers upon the Sarno, round which a suburb had sprung up, galleys of many a seaport city, Greek or Barbarian, carrying the industries, and not a few among the vices of the East. Both found a ready welcome in this full-blooded city, intensely alive to all delights and interests, whether pure or impure. Venus was protectress of the city, and was worshipped without stint. There were some within the city whom loathing of its wickedness had impelled to prophecy, so at least one must infer from the fact that the words "Sodoma Gomora" are scratched in large letters on one of the house-fronts.

To whom in that pagan city could Hebrew history have suggested so apt and terrible a foreboding? A Jew, perhaps, of whom there were multitudes in Rome; even possibly a Christian, but there is scant evidence of that. Doubtless the Pompeiians read those words without comprehending their horrible significance, and went their way to theatre or to wineshop, a laughing people, a gay, light-hearted nation, a mixed race, the blood of Oscans and of Samnite mountaineers mingling with the languid graces of the degenerating Greeks, loving easily, forgetting lightly, careless, passionate, and intensely human.

Such was Pompeii, a seething, noisy, eager city, filled with the reek of dense humanity. But now it is swept clean by winds and sunlight. Its very 212stews are fragrant. In the morning sweet air blows in from the sea; at night it steals down no less sweetly from the mountains. In all the city there is not one stench. The freshness and the silence of the long streets weigh upon the nerves. There is so little evidence of ruin, not an ash left, not a bank of earth in all the wide district which one enters first, nothing to remind us by the evidence of sight what it was that drove out the people from these once crowded streets and left the houses and the colonnades open to the whispering sea wind.

It was not so before the great director Fiorelli came. He it was who stopped haphazard digging, and cleared each quarter completely before beginning work upon another. Since, then, his methods have in great measure freed the city already of its débris, and set its inanimate life before us as it was, the wiser part at Pompeii is to try to grasp the arrangements of a Roman city, leaving the necessary musings on the tragedy to be got through elsewhere.

It is beyond my scope, as I have said already, to assume the authority of an expert on Pompeii. More experts are not wanted. The lack, at least in England, is of readers for those who exist. A man intending a tour in Italy will lay out ungrudgingly ten pounds upon his travelling gear, but he will scout the idea of spending the price of a new hat-box on August Mau's treatise, *Pompeii, its Life and Art*, though it would increase his pleasure tenfold more. Still less will he buy any book in a foreign tongue. I must, therefore, in my unlearned way, set down some few facts which will with difficulty be discovered in the guide-books or from the guides. And firstly as to the houses.

It will occur to any man that a town so large as Pompeii must have been built in many fashions, 213old and new. New types grew popular, while old ones still persisted. There is no town in the world in which many manners cannot be traced. At Pompeii, where building was arrested eighteen hundred years ago, the changes of taste are plain and interesting. Indeed, while the houses all possess the atrium, that is the large square or oblong hall in front, open to the sky, with chambers surrounding it on every side, and most have also the peristyle, the colonnaded court behind; yet there are some which are built without the peristyle, and which by other points in their construction give witness of belonging to an earlier and simpler age.

One of these antique houses is easily found by passing through the Forum, across the Strada delle Terme and up the Strada Consolare, almost to the Herculaneum gate. It is called the House of the Surgeon; and as in all the city there is no other which retains so largely the aspect and arrangements of the earlier time, before Greek influence was paramount, it should certainly be visited first.

It appears at once on entering the house that the peristyle is lacking. One may stand within the courtyard of the atrium, and, looking through the house, see no such vista of colonnaded quadrangle, of fountains, busts, and splendid distances, as gratified the eye within the larger and more modern houses. Those beauties were the contribution of the Greeks to the old simple Latin life. This was the abode of a "laudator temporis acti," a lover of the old homely times, when the single courtyard of the atrium sufficed alike for the master, his family and clients, when the wife sat spinning with her maidens by the scanty light, as in Ovid's immortal description of Lucretia, and the slaves came and went about the household duties close at hand. 214A colonnade there is certainly, but of only one arcade, and giving on the garden. There was but little splendour in such a dwelling. Only when Greek influence destroyed the simplicity of earlier life was the family quarter distinguished from that of slaves and clients and relegated to the peristyle, the inner courtyard. There is no trace in the Surgeon's house of the rich ornament which became so popular in Pompeii, neither mosaics nor wall paintings. The very building stone differs from that used in later years; for the house is built of large square limestone blocks, while the immense majority of houses in the city are constructed of tufa, quarried chiefly from the ridge on which the city stands. All these facts mark the Surgeon's house as belonging to the earliest Pompeiian age of which traces still exist. It is certainly older than the year 200 B.C., and we may picture the city, while still untouched by the rare sense of beauty which was flowering in the Greek coast towns, as consisting largely of houses on this model, with others of a fashion older and more humble, of which we now know nothing.

From the House of the Surgeon it is but a little way to that of Sallust, a larger residence, and one of later date, when tufa had displaced limestone as a building material. It belongs, therefore, to the same period as the vast majority of houses in the city, yet in that period it is of the most antique, the work of a day when Greek influence was not yet paramount in architecture or in private life. It has no peristyle, if a late Roman addition be excepted; the family life was not yet divided. From the atrium one looked through to colonnade and garden, much as in the Surgeon's house. The only paintings are in imitation of slabs of marble on the walls.

To reach the House of the Faun we must return 215to the Strada delle Terme and follow it towards the north-east until it merges in the Strada della Fortuna, in which, upon the left, stands the once magnificent dwelling which takes its name from the beautiful bronze of the Dancing Faun now in the Naples museum. It is much to be wished that the treasures of this noble house could have been left in it. It may in part be older than the house of Sallust, though belonging like it to the Tufa period, and possessing the additional apartments prescribed by the influx of Greek taste. Indeed the added rooms, like all the other portions of the house, were planned with magnificence; and as there are two atria, so there are two peristyles, each of singular beauty and built in the purest taste. There is no house in Pompeii in which a man should pause so long, or to which he should come back so often; for this is the most perfect specimen of the best age of building in the city. It is the fruit of a long age of peace, during which the people drank in thirstily the exquisite sense of beauty diffused from the Greek coast towns. It is not difficult to understand how these rough townsmen, bred of sturdy mountaineers, and inheriting no tradition of fine culture, must have been affected when they went across the sea to Cumæ or to Pæstum, saw the austere glory of the temples rising near the shore, talked with the men whose brains schemed out that splendour and whose hands learnt how to fashion it, craftsmen who wrought nothing destitute of loveliness, whose coins were as noble as their temples, whose hearts must have been afire to spread more widely their own perception of line and form, and who were doubtless no less eager to teach than the Pompeiians were to learn. There is nothing in the world to-day comparable to the magic of that 216influence which spread like sunshine out of the Greek cities on the Campanian coast, no teachers so noble, no scholars so devoted and receptive, no people who surrender themselves so absolutely to the dominion of beauty, and will have it pure, and none but it.

Under the first passion of this enthusiasm Pompeii was transformed. Almost all the public buildings received their present shape from this wave of pure Greek art. Almost every one is graceful and lovely, the columns and architraves were white, the ornament not overloaded, the decorations simple. The artists who tinted the walls confined themselves to producing masses of colour. Wall pictures there were none; but the mosaics of the floors were wrought with curious beauty, and reproduced the first compositions of great painters. The House of the Faun is beautified by no wall pictures, but it contained on the floor of the room which divided the two peristyles one of the finest mosaics ever found, that which depicts the battle of Alexander the Great upon the Issos.

The stream of Greek influence ran pure for some four generations. After that it was contaminated. Man can keep no beauty in his hands for long unspoilt. The change is manifest in Pompeii. The Roman influence stole in. A muddy taste obscured the simple grace of the Greek lines, tortured the architecture, piled up unmeaning ornament, and degraded all the city. There were many stages between the first step and the last, not a few still beautiful, though the downward tendency is plain. The house of the Vettii is the finest of the later period. There one may see wall-paintings of rare charm, mingled with others of far inferior taste, as if the gallery of some fine connoisseur had fallen by mischance into the hands of men who did not 217understand its worth, and placed the compositions of degraded artists side by side with the masterpieces of an olden time.

Exact descriptions of these houses are the business of the guide-book. But there are certain observations which I think it necessary to make about the paintings—though if anyone would read the work of Helbig on the subject, it would be much better.

No one who visits Pompeii, no one who has seen in the most hasty way the collections of the Naples Museum, can fail to be impressed, first with the worth of the pictures, their dramatic force, their exquisite grace, their rich and tender fancy; and next by their vast profusion. What manner of city was this which worshipped art so devoutly that scarce a single house is without pictures more beautiful than any save a few collectors can obtain to-day? Helbig, writing more than twenty years ago, described and classified two thousand. Others perished on the walls where they were found. More still are being dug up day by day. No ancient writer has told us that Pompeii was renowned for the multitude of its paintings. The city bore almost certainly no such reputation. It was a provincial town of little note, remarkable for nothing in the eyes of those who visited it. Yet what a world of beauty must have existed on the earth when these were the common decorations of a fourth-rate town, excelled by those of Rome, or even Ostia, in proportion to the higher wealth and dignity of those imperial haunts! What were the decorations to be seen at Baiæ, when Pompeii was adorned so finely! That group of palaces must surely have drawn more noble craftsmen, and in greater numbers, than ever visited the town of trade and pleasure on the Sarno. As in a great museum we stand before the gigantic bone of some lost animal, striving to picture in our minds the 218creature as he lived, getting now a dim conception of great strength and bulk which is lost again by the weakness of our fancy ere half realised, so in presence of these pictures at Pompeii we are tormented by flashing visions of the grace and splendour of the ancient world which so many centuries ago was shattered into fragments, and which it may be that no human intellect will ever reconstruct before the earth grows cold and man fails from off its surface.

Whence came these pictures, these noble visions of Greek myth, austere and restrained, these warriors, these satyrs, these happy, laughing loves? Is it possible that one small city can have bred the artists who dreamed all these dreams and yet have left no mark in history of such great achievement? Clearly not. The artists cannot have been Pompeian. The elder Pliny tells us that in his day painting was at the point of death, while Petronius declares roundly that it was absolutely dead. One walks round the Naples Museum and recalls these judgments with astonishment. Can this art be really moribund, this Iphigenia, spreading her arms wide to receive the stroke, this Calchas, finger on lip, watching for the fated moment, this Perseus, this Ariadne! If this is dying art, Heaven grant that English art may ere long die of the same death.

But it is not. No man can judge it so. Pliny and Petronius meant something else, and the key to their despondency is produced by the discovery that many of these Pompeian pictures are replicas. The same subjects recur, with almost the same treatment. Sometimes the figures are identical. Sometimes the painter has elected to reduce the composition. The painting of Argos watching Io occurs four times in Pompeii. It has been found also in Rome!—the same picture, but containing figures which the Campanian artist 219thought proper to omit. There is evidence, too, that the picture was diffused over an area far wider than that lying between Rome and Pompeii. It appears on reliefs, on medals, and on cameos. Lucian had it in his mind when he wrote a famous passage in his poem, and it suggested an epigram by Antiphilos. The case is similar with the fresco of Perseus and Andromeda. Both were world-known pictures, the composition of a great artist—Helbig suggests that it was the Athenian Nikias—and both were copied far and wide by craftsmen who could merely reproduce.

This is what Pliny and Petronius meant. They looked about them and found only copyists. The great school of painting was dead, and those who reproduced its works did so without heart or understanding. This was sorrowful enough for them; but we may regard their woeful faces cheerfully. Time and the volcano have done us the good service of preserving to our day copies of some masterpieces of ancient painting. The copyists were often treacherous. There is a fresco of Medea at Pompeii in which the figure of the mother brooding over the thought of murdering her children is weak and unconvincing. But at Herculaneum was found a Medea who is terrible indeed, wild-eyed and murderous, such a figure as none but the greatest artist could conceive and few copyists could reproduce. Set this Medea in her place in the Pompeian fresco and the result may well be the Medea of Timomachus, one of the most famous pictures of all antiquity.

The school in which these artists, Pompeians or travelling painters, found their models was Hellenist, Greek art of the period subsequent to Alexander the Great. They did not draw by preference upon its highest compositions. Serious treatment of the 220ancient myths, that treatment which revealed the great and elemental facts from which they sprang, was not popular in Pompeii, where the citizens appear to have preferred a lighter and more artificial view of life—love without its passion, the comedy of manners rather than the tragedy. These gay feasters desired to see no skeletons among their roses and their winecups. They preferred light laughing cupids, kind towards the human frailties of both men and women. It was a joyous, light-hearted, unreflecting society on which this terrible destruction fell, luxurious and vicious. The realisation of that fact tightens the sense of tragedy, as the sudden annihilation of a group of children playing with their flowers seems more pitiful than the death of men.

There are a thousand things still to say of Pompeii, but they are beyond my scope. The westering sun has turned all the hills above Castellammare into purple clouds. The heat lies among the broken city walls. It is enough. I turn away, and take up anew the course of my journey.

It is no long way from the turfed ridges which conceal Pompeii to the first rises of the Castellammare Mountains. The road crosses the Sarno, and cuts straight and dusty through wide fields of beans and lupins, with here and there a gaunt farmhouse, or massaria, bare of all attempt to make it pleasant to the eye. The bitter lupins are almost, if not quite, the cheapest food that can be bought in Naples, and are accordingly sold principally to the very poor by the "lupinaria," who may be seen any day in the precinct of the Porta Capuana, or in the byways round about the Mercato. Does anyone ask how the beans became so bitter? It was by the curse of our Lord, who was fleeing from the Pharisees, and hid Himself in a field of lupins. The beans were dry, 221and betrayed His movements by their rustling; whereupon He cursed them, and they have been bitter ever since.

PORTA CAPUANO—NAPLES.

There is no doubt that the Sarno was navigable when Pompeii was a living city, but these many centuries it has been a rather dirty ditch, unapproachable by shipping. Its chief interest for me lies in the fact that along its bank, and across all the fertile country up to the base of the great mountains, was fought the last great battle of the Goths, those brave Teutons out of whom, as Mr. Hodgkin says, "so noble a people might have been made to cultivate and to defend the Italian peninsula." Heaven had been very kind to Italy in this sixth century after Christ. It had sent down upon her from the north a race of conquerors, barbarian, it is true, but brave, honourable, sincere, and possessing every capability for government. They conquered Italy from end to end. No province, no city, held out against them. From the Alps to Sicily they were supreme, and their genius, humane and not disdainful either of the arts or Christianity, was rapidly fusing every warring element of the peninsula into a mighty nation—Germanic earnestness infused with Latin wit—when the lord of the world, the Roman Emperor in distant Constantinople, resolved to put forth his strength and drive out these strangers, these builders of a nation, who were tending what he had neglected, defending what he had left open to attack, and reaping harvests of which he, out of all men, was least entitled to proclaim himself the sower.

So the Emperor sent first Belisarius, and then Narses, and long and bitter was the war which followed. Mr. Hodgkin, in his fourth volume, has told it in a style which is beyond all praise. Upon these plains was fought out the last battle of the Goths. 222Here Narses brought them to bay. For two months they lay along the line of the Sarno, while Narses, baffled by the river, plotted how to take them in the rear. At last he won over some traitor of an admiral, who surrendered to him the Gothic fleet, lying, perhaps, at Castellammare; and the Goths, finding that the port was no longer theirs, fell back upon the hills, entrenching themselves upon the spot where the ruined castle of Lettere now stands. But their supplies were cut off—it was impossible to feed an army on the barren mountains—and adopting counsels of despair, they descended to the plain and gave battle to the Imperial troops.

It was a great and terrible fight. Goths and Romans fought on foot. Teias the king fell after bearing himself right nobly; but the Goths fought on, and when darkness interrupted the engagement they did but pause in order to renew it with no less desperation when the light returned. When both armies were nearly wearied out the Goths sent a messenger to Narses. They perceived, they said, that God had declared against them, and that the strife was hopeless. If terms were granted they would depart from Italy. The Imperial general accepted their proposals, and the Goths, the noblest invaders who ever entered Italy, turned their backs for ever on the fertile land where they had made their homes, crossed the Alps in order, and were never heard of in Italy again. So perished, until our day, the last hope of unity for Italy, and for full thirteen centuries that unhappy land was drenched in constant blood—the prey of conquerors who could not conquer, and the sport of statesmen who never learnt to govern. For the Roman Emperor could build no state comparable to the one he had destroyed, and what Italy owes to him is forty generations of unhappiness.223

In travelling through this country one is haunted by the perpetual desire to look back into past ages, and admonished almost as often that as yet one cannot do so. Indeed, one looks forward almost as often, anticipating that day when scholars will combine to assist in the excavation of all the buried regions, when every villa shall be disinterred, and the secrets hidden underneath the vineyards be exposed to the light of day again. Here on the first slopes of the hills around Castellammare lay the groups of country villas which formed ancient Stabiæ, and every man who goes this way longs to see them disinterred. For what is seen at Pompeii is but half the life of Roman days—a city stripped of its country villas and all its rustic intercourse. Pompeii stood in the heart of the country. Its citizens must have had farms upon the mountain slopes; they must have had concern in husbandry as well as trade; there must have been hourly comings and goings between the crowded streets and the sweet hillsides of Varano, where the grapes ripened and the wine-vats gathered the crushed juice, where the oil dripped slowly from the olive-presses, and the jars stood waiting for the mountain honey.

The day will come when all this great life of Roman husbandry will be disclosed to us, and we shall know it as we now know the city streets; for it is here still upon the mountain slopes, buried safe beneath the vineyards, waiting only till its vast interest is comprehended by people in sufficient numbers to provide the funds to excavate it. Stabiæ was by no means another Pompeii. It was no city, but a group of farms and country villas, and has countless things to teach us which cannot be seen or learnt beside the Sarno. The very houses were of other shapes and plans; for the Romans did not reproduce 224town houses in the country, but designed them for different uses, and embodied apartments which had no matches in the city. There are the residences of

62

wealthy men, adorned with noble peristyles, mosaics, and fine statues, and side by side with them the home farms—if one may use a modern term—the chambers of the husbandmen, and the courts in which they worked. There, too, are buildings far too large for any family and differing in arrangement from any private dwelling yet discovered. The use of these great buildings can only be conjectured. Ruggiero, whose self-denying labour has collected in one monumental work all the information now obtainable upon the subject, suggests that they may have been hospitals, a supposition probable enough when we remember that the Romans must have been no less aware than we ourselves how potent a tonic is the mountain air for patients suffering from the fevers bred upon the plains. In Ruggiero's pages one may see the scanty and imperfect plans sketched out by those who dug upon the site more than a century ago. Posterity owes those hasty workers but little gratitude. They were inspired by hardly more than a mean kind of curiosity. They were treasure-seekers, pure and simple; and what they judged to be of little value they broke up with their pickaxes. Swinburne, the traveller, watched a portion of the excavations, but without intelligence, and has nothing to tell us of much interest. "When opened," he says, speaking evidently of a villa on Varano, it may be the very one in which Pliny passed the last night of his life, "the apartment presented us with the shattered walls, daubed rather than painted with gaudy colours in compartments, and some birds and animals in the cornices, but in a coarse style, as indeed are all the paintings of Stabiæ. In a corner 225we found the brass hinges and lock of a trunk; near them part of the contents, viz. ivory flutes in pieces, some coins, brass rings, scales, steelyards, and a very elegant silver statue of Bacchus about twelve inches high, represented with a crown of vine leaves, buskins, and the horn of plenty." With this perfunctory account we must rest content, until some millionaire shall conceive the notion of delighting all the world instead of building a palace for himself. But the camel will have gone through the needle's eye before that happens.

CHAPTER X.

CASTELLAMMARE: ITS WOODS, ITS FOLKLORE
AND THE TALE OF THE MADONNA OF POZZANO

226

"Marzo è pazzo" ("March is mad") say the Neapolitans, contemptuous of his inconstancies. God forbid that I should try to prove the sanity of March; but it is long odds if April is one whit the better. His moon is in its first quarter, and still sirocco blows up out of the sea day by day. The grey clouds drift in banks across Vesuvius and hide the pillar of his smoke, dropping down at whiles even to the level of the plain. From time to time it is as if the mountain stirred and shook himself, flinging off the weight of vapour from his flanks and crest, so that again one can see the rolling column of dense smoke, stained and discoloured by the reflection of the fires far down within the cone, now rosy, now a menacing dull brown which is easily distinguishable from the watery clouds that gather in the heavens. Yet slowly, steadily the veil of mist returns, while mine host murmurs ruefully, "Sette Aprilanti, giorni quaranta!" But it is not the seventh of April yet, so we may still be spared the sight of dripping trees for forty days. An hour ago, when I ventured up the hill towards the woods, a tattered, 227copper-coloured varlet of a boy looked out of the cellar where his mother was stooping over the smoking coals in her brass chafing-dish. "Aprile chiuove, chiuove," he bawled, as if it were the greatest news in the world. He thinks the harvest will be mended by the April rains; though if he and others in this region knew whence their true harvest comes, they would humbly supplicate our Lady of Pozzano to give fine weather to the visitors.

To be stayed at the gate of the Sorrento peninsula by doubtful weather is by no means an unmixed misfortune. It may be that our Lady of Pozzano sometimes employs the showers to bring hasty travellers to a better way of thinking. Certainly many people hurry past Castellammare to their own hurt. The town is unattractive, and may, moreover, be reproached with wickedness, though it suffers, as is said, from the low morality of Greek sailors, rather than from any crookedness of its homeborn citizens. But the mountain slopes behind it are immensely beautiful. No woods elsewhere in the peninsula are comparable to these. No other drives show views so wide and exquisite framed in such a setting of fresh spring foliage, nor is there upon these shores an hotel more comfortable or more homelike than the "Quisisana," which stands near the entrance of the woods; and this I say with confidence, though not unaware that the judgments of travellers upon hotels are as various as their verdicts on a pretty woman, who at one hour of the day is ten times prettier than at another, and may now and then look positively plain.

Castellammare possesses an excellent sea-front, which would have made a pleasant promenade had not a selfish little tramway seized upon the side next the shore, guarding itself by a high railing from the 228intrusion of strangers in search of cool fresh air. Thus cast back on a line of dead walls, house-fronts as mean as only a fourth-rate Italian town can boast, one has no other amusement than gazing at the mountains, which in truth are beautiful enough for anyone. Very steep and high they tower above Castellammare; not brown and purple, as when I looked up at them across the broken walls of Pompeii, but clad in their true colours of green of every shade, dark and sombre where ravines are chiselled out upon the slopes, or where the pines lie wet and heavy in the morning shadow. Higher up, the flanks of the mountains are rough with brushwood, while on the summits the clear air blows about bare grass deepening into brown. Sometimes sloping swiftly to the sea, but more often

63

dropping in sheer cliffs of immense height, this dark and shadowy mountain wall thrusts itself out across the blue waters, while here and there a village gleams white upon some broken hillside, or a monastery rears its red walls among the soft grey of the olive woods. There lies Vico, on its promontory rock, showing at this distance only the shade of its great beauty; and beyond the next lofty headland is Sorrento, at the foot of a mountain country so exquisite, so odorous with myrtle and with rosemary, so fragrant of tradition and romance, that it is, as I said, a good fortune which checks the traveller coming from the plain at the first entrance of the hills and gives him time to realise the nature of the land which lies before him.

It needs no long puzzling to discover whence the importance of Castellammare has been derived in all the centuries. The port offers a safe shelter for shipping, which of itself counts for much upon a coast possessing few such anchorages; and it lies 229near the entrance of that valley road across the neck of the Sorrento peninsula, which is the natural route of trade between Naples and Salerno. The road is of much historical interest, as any highway must be which has been followed by so many generations of travellers, both illustrious and obscure; and any man who chooses to recollect by what various masters Salerno has been held will be able to people this ancient track with figures as picturesque as any in the history of mankind. He will observe, moreover, the importance of the Castle of Nocera, which dominates this route of traders. I confess to being somewhat puzzled as to the exact course by which the commerce of Amalfi extricated itself from the mountains and dispersed itself over the mainland. Doubtless the merchants of La Scala and Ravello followed the still existing road from Ravello to Lettere, and thence to Gragnano, whence comes the ancient punning jest, "L'Asene de Gragnano Sapevano Lettere." This road is certainly ancient, and early in the present century it was the usual approach to Amalfi, whither travellers were carried in litters across the mountains. The little handbook of Ravello, based on notes left by the late Mr. Reid, seems to account this road more recent than the age of Ravello's commercial greatness. Probably a recency of form rather than of course is meant; but in any case, I cannot believe that the merchants of Amalfi sent out their trade by a route which began for them with an ascent so very long and arduous. Possibly they approached Gragnano by a road running up the valley from Minori or Majori. Of course the traders of old days were very patient of rough mountain tracks, and did not look for the wide beaten turnpikes which we have taught ourselves to regard as essential to commerce. Doubtless, therefore, 230many a team of mules from Amalfi, laden with silks and spices from the East, came down through Lettere, where it would scarce get by the castle of the great counts who held that former stronghold of the Goths without paying toll or tribute for its safety on the mountain roads. And so, passing through Gragnano and beneath the hillsides where the palaces of ancient Stabiæ lie buried, the wearied teams would come down at last to Castellammare, where they would need rest ere beginning the hot journey by the coast road into Naples.

Both the roads which diverge from Castellammare, the one heading straight across the plains towards the high valley of La Cava, the other clinging to the fresh mountain slopes, are therefore full of interest. Of Nocera, indeed, its castle full of memories of Pope Urban VI., and its fine church Santa Maria Maggiore, some two miles out, any man with ease might write a volume. But we stayed long scorching on the plains among the buried cities; and the hill route is the more inviting now. The weather is disposed to break. A gleam of sun sparkles here and there upon the water. Let us see what the hillsides have to show us.

Castellammare is a dirty and ill-odorous town. As I hurry through its crowded streets, brushed by women hawking beans and dodging others who are performing certain necessary acts of cleanliness at their house doors, I occupy myself in wondering whether there is in all southern Italy a city without smells. From Taranto to Naples I can recall none save Pompeii. It is, doubtless, an unattainable ideal to bring Castellammare to the state of that sweet-smelling habitation of the dead; though it would be unwise to prophesy what the volcano may not yet achieve on the scene of his old conquests. There 231are so many things lost and forgotten upon this coast. I see that Schulz, whose great work still remains by far the best guide through the south of Italy, describes vast catacombs in the hillside at Castellammare. I must admit that I do not know where these catacombs are. Schulz, who visited them before 1860, found in them pictures not older than the twelfth century, and resembling in many details those which are seen in the catacombs of Naples. Certainly the old grave chambers are no longer among the sights of this summer city. But the whole region impresses one with the constant sense that the keenest interest and the longest knowledge spent upon this ground which is strewn with the dust of so many generations, will leave behind countless undiscovered things. The world seems older here than elsewhere. And so it is, if age be counted by lives and passions rather than by geologic courses.

As one goes on up the ascent, the narrow alleys break out into wider spaces, and here and there a breath of mountain air steals down between the houses, or the ripe fruit of an orange lights up a shadowy courtyard with a flash of colour; till at last the houses fall away, and one climbs out on a fresh hillside, where a double row of trees gives protection from the sun. Two sharp turns of the steep road bring one into a small village, of which the first house is the Hotel Quisisana. But I have nothing to say to hotels at this hour of the morning, and accordingly trudge on a little further up the hill, till I come to the Vico San Matteo, a lane branching off along the hillside on my right, which brings me to a shady terrace road, rising and falling on the hillside just below the level of the woods. At this height the air blown down from sea and mountain 232is sweet and pure. The banks are glowing with crimson cyclamen and large anemones, both lavender and purple, while the hillside on the right, dropping rapidly towards the town, is thick-set with orchards, through whose falling blossoms the sea shines blue and green, while across the bay Vesuvius pours out its rosy vapour coil by coil.

It is a wide and noble view, one of those which have made Castellammare famous in all ages, as the first slopes of the cool wooded mountains must needs be among all the cities of the scorching plains. In Roman days, just as in our own, men looked up from Naples long before the grapes changed colour or the figs turned black, pining for the sweet breezes of Monte Sant'Angelo, and the whispering woods of Monte Coppola, where the shadows lie for half the day, and the only sounds are made by the busy hacking of the woodcutters. There is no caprice of fashion in this straining to the hills, but a natural impulse as strong as that which stops a hot and weary man beside a roadside well. Every generation of Neapolitans has come hither in the summer; everyone will do so to the end of time. I shall go up this evening to the Bourbon pleasure-house; and here, set before me at the turning of the road, is the ancient castle of the Hohenstaufen, built by the great Emperor Frederick the Second, and added to by the foe who seized his kingdom and slew his son, yet came to take his pleasure on the same spot.

Underneath the round towers of the crumbling ruin an old broken staircase descends towards the town, skirting the castle wall. It is from this ancient ladder, ruinous and long disused, that Castellammare looks its best. The harbour lies below, and a fishing boat running in furls its large triangular sail and drops its anchor. The long quay is a mass of moving 233figures. The tinkle of hammers rings through the quiet air. Here in the shadow of the woods time seems to pause, and one sees the hillside, the staircase, and the old town below much as they must have looked when Boccaccio came out hither in his hot youth, inflamed with love for Marie of Anjou, and heard, perhaps, on some summer night within the woods the story which he tells us of the base passion which beset the fierce King Charles in his old age, and how he overcame it. The tale, though possibly not true, is worth recalling, if only because not many kingly actions are recorded of the monarch who slew Conradin.

An exile from Florence had come to end his days among these mountains, one Messer Neri Degli Uberti. He was rich, and bought himself an estate a bowshot distant from the houses of the town, and on it made a shady garden, in the midst of which he set a fishpond, clear and cool, and stocked it well with fish. So he went on adding beauty upon beauty to his garden, till it chanced that King Charles heard of it, when in the hot summer days he came out to his castle by the sea for rest, and desiring to see the pleasaunce sent a messenger to Messer Neri to say that he would sup with him next evening. The Florentine, bred among the merchant princes, received the King nobly; and Charles, having seen all the beauties of the garden, sat down to sup beside the fishpond, placing Messer Neri on one side and on the other his own courtier, Count Guido di Monforte. The dishes were excellent, the wines beyond praise, the garden exquisite and still. The King's worn heart thrilled with pleasure. Cares and remorse fled away, and the charm of the soft summer evening reigned unbroken.

At that moment two girls came into the garden, 234daughters of Messer Neri, not more than fifteen. Their hair hung loose like threads of spun gold. A garland of blue flowers crowned it, and their faces wore the look of angels rather than of sinful humankind, so delicate and lovely were their features. They were clad in white, and a servant followed them carrying nets, while another had a stove and a lighted torch. Now the King wondered when he saw these things; and as he sat watching the girls came and did reverence to the old, grim monarch, and then walking breast deep into the fishpond, swept the waters with their nets in those places where they knew the fish were lurking. Meanwhile one of the servants blew the live coals of the stove, while his fellow took the fish; and by-and-by the girls began to toss the fish out on the bank towards the King, and he, snatching them up with jest and laughter, threw them back; and so they sported like gay children till the broil was ready. Then the girls came out of the water, their thin dresses clinging round them; and presently returning, dressed in silk, brought to the King silver dishes heaped up high with fruit, and then sang together some old song with pure childlike voices, so sweet that as the weary tyrant sat and listened it seemed to him as if some choir of angels were chanting in the evening sky.

Now as the old King rode homeward to his castle, the gentle beauty of these girls stole deeper and deeper into his heart, and one of them especially, named Ginevra, stirred him into love, so that at last he opened his heart to Count Guido, and asked him how he might gain the girl. But the Count had the courage of a noble friend, and set the truth before him, showing how base a deed he meditated. "This," he said, "is not the action of a great king, but of a cowardly boy. You plot to steal his daughter from the poor knight 235who did you all the honour in his power, and brought his daughters to aid him in the task, showing thereby how great is the faith which he has in you, and how firmly he holds you as a true king, and not a cowardly wolf." Now these words stung the King the more since he knew them to be true; and he vowed he would prove before many days were over that he could conquer his lusts, even as he had trodden down his enemies. So, not long afterwards, he went back to Naples; and there he made splendid marriages for both the girls, heaping them with honours, and having seen them in the charge of noble husbands, he went sorrowfully away into Apulia, where with great labours he overcame his passion. "Some may say," adds Fiammetta, who told the tale on the tenth day of the *Decameron*, "that it was a little thing for a king to give two girls in marriage; but I call it a great thing, ay, the greatest, that a king in love should give the woman whom he loves unto another."

Fiammetta should have known of what she spoke—none better. I wonder why Boccaccio chose to put an impossible circumstance into this story. If the tale be true of anyone, it cannot be one of the Uberti family who settled in the territory and near the castle of the great Guelf king. For the Uberti were all Ghibellines, supporters of the empire and deadly enemies of him who slew Manfred. Not one of them ever asked or obtained mercy from Charles, who was the butcher of their family. Boccaccio certainly did not forget this. No

Florentine could have been ignorant even momentarily of circumstances so terrible, affecting so great a family. No carelessness of narrative could account for the introduction of one of the Uberti into the story. It must have been deliberate, though I do not see the 236reason. It may have been that he desired only to accentuate the magnanimity of Charles, to whose grandson, King Robert, he owed much, and chose the circumstances, whether true or false, which made that magnanimity most striking. I can find no more probable explanation.

The road which goes on past the castle undulates beneath an arch of beech trees, just unfurling their young leaves of tender green, and in half a mile or so comes out at the ancient monastery of Pozzano, a red building of no great intrinsic interest, but recalling the name of Gonsalvo di Cordova, "il gran capitano," to whose piety the foundation of the convent is frequently ascribed, though in truth there had been an ecclesiastical foundation on the spot for three centuries before Gonsalvo's time, and all he did was to restore it from decay. I doubt if many people remember the great soldier now. The peasants who go up and down the slope before the convent doors know far better the tale of the mysterious picture of the Madonna which was found buried in a well, but is now hung up in glory in the church.

It is worth while to stop and hear the story of this picture. Long before the present convent was built, when the hillside at this spot lay waste and covered with dense herbage, through which the mules going to Sorrento forced their way with labour, the people of Castellammare noticed a flame which sprang up night by night like a signal fire lit to warn ships off the coast. The people looked and trembled, for there were strange beings on the mountain, dwarfs, and what not! No mortal man would make a fire there. So the signal blazed, but none went near it, till at length some fishers casting their nets in the bay, and wondering among themselves what could be the meaning of the flame which 237was then burning on the hill, saw the Madonna come to them across the sea, all clothed in light. The radiant virgin stood looking down upon them kindly as they sat huddled in their fear, and bade them tell their Bishop to search the ground over which the fire hovered, for he would there find an image of herself.

The poor men took no heed of what they thought a vision of the night; nor did they obey the Virgin when she came again. But when on the third night the Queen of Heaven descended to this murky world, she towered above their boat incensed and awful, denouncing against them all the pains of hell and outer darkness if they dared neglect her bidding. The fear-struck fishers hastened to their Bishop on the first light of morning and told him their tale. He too had seen a celestial vision, warning him of the coming of the sailors. There was no room for doubt or hesitation. He put himself at the head of a long penitent procession, went up the hill, discovered a well just where the flame had burnt, and in the well the marvellous picture which now adorns the church.

How came the picture there? If one could answer that question some light would be thrown on the age of the relic. The country people when they see any work of ancient art are disposed to say, "San Luca l'ha pittato"! ("St. Luke painted it"), as he did the Madonna of the Carmine in Naples; and accordingly this picture also has been ascribed to the brush of the Evangelist. The priests themselves do not claim an origin so sacred for their canvas, but maintain that it is an early Greek work, buried for safety in the days when, at the bidding of the iconoclastic Emperor, Leo the Isaurian, an attempt was made to root out image worship from the land. I do not know whether any competent expert has 238pronounced the painting to be of an age which renders the story probable. Ecclesiastical traditions are frequently inspired rather by piety than truth, and for my part, when I remember what ravages the Turks committed along these coasts up to the boyhood of men not long dead, I can find no reason for going back to the eighth century to discover facts which may have led either priests or laymen to bury sacred things.

In these days the Madonna of Pozzano walks no more upon the sea. Yet she remains, in a particular degree, the protectress of all sailors; and one may very well suspect that the priestly tale of the miraculous light, the hidden well, and the long-forgotten picture, does but conceal some record of kindness done to mariners which we heretics might prize more highly. For in old days, when ships approaching Naples may have found it hard to set their course after the light faded, and harder still to anchor off a lee shore, a beacon fire on the monastery roof would have been a noble aid, such as must have saved many a tall ship and brought many a sailor home to his wife in safety. Surely in some such facts as these lies the explanation of the traditional attachment of the sailors to the Madonna of Pozzano. "Ave Maria, Stella Maris!"—a star of the sea indeed, if it was the beacon kindled by her servants by which poor mariners steered back to port.

It needs not much faith to believe some portion of this pretty story. Incredulity is generally stupid; but he who most sincerely desires to be wise must needs ponder when he finds that almost every town throughout the peninsula possesses a Madonna found in some wondrous way. At Casarlano, for example, Maria Palumbo was feeding a heifer when she heard a voice issuing from the bushes, which said, "Maria, 239tell your father to come and dig here, and he will find an image of me." Maria, seeing no one, did not understand, but the same thing happened on the next day and the next, while at length her comprehension was quickened by a light box on the ear, which might have changed into a heavy one had she waited for another day. But, growing prudent by experience, she told her father all; and he, knowing that it was not for him to reason concerning heavenly monitions, went and dug in the spot indicated, and there found an image which has been of peculiar sanctity ever since. In fact its sensibilities were so keen, that when the Turks ravaged the country in 1538 it wept tears mingled with drops of blood.

66

When speaking of these Madonnas it would be wrong to omit the one most honoured in Nocera, and in many other places round about. She is known as "La Madonna delle Galline"—the Madonna of the cocks and hens—and her image was found, according to one version of the tale, by the scratching of hens in the loose soil which covered it. Her feast is on Low Sunday, or rather on the three days of which that Sunday is the centre; and most visitors who stay at Castellammare in the spring must have seen some trace of the festa. The procession starts from Nocera, and as the crowds of chanting priests and pious laity go by, every good peasant woman looses a hen, or else a pigeon, which she has previously stained bright purple. The purple hens perch on the base of the Madonna's statue, made broad and large for their accommodation, and are then collected by the master of the ceremonies, who sells them to devout persons. In many a village from Gragnano to La Cava the purple hens may be occasionally seen pecking in the dust, a marvel and astonishment to English 240visitors, who, being unaware how much their plumage owes to the dye-bag, are disposed to barter at a high price for animals so certain to create sensation at the next poultry show.

At the foot of the slope which drops from Pozzano into the highway from Castellammare to Sorrento is a little roadside shrine, set deeply in the rock, over which pious hands have inscribed one of those pathetically appealing calls to wayfarers which seem to penetrate so rarely the hearts to which they are addressed—

"Non sit tibi grave
Dicere Mater ave."

"Let it not be a burden to say, Hail, Mother!" It is a gentle appeal, a light act of devotion, yet few there are who care to claim the blessing. The peasants, men and women, go by without an instant's pause in their chatter, or the slightest glance towards the shrine. They do not want even the human love which is offered to them so simply. In Naples, on the Corso Vittorio Emanuele, is another Madonna, who has put on even more passionately the accents of a human mother brooding over sorrow-stricken children, and all the strong feeling is expressed in verses, of which the burden runs—

"... C'è un'allegrìa
Incontrar la Madonna in sulla via"—

"It is a joy to meet the Mother of mankind beside the way." In the last verse the pleading becomes more eager, giving utterance to the cry of a lost and frightened child seeking the protection which will never fail it—

"... O mamma mia
Venite incontrarmi in sulla via!"

241

But neither does this call find a ready answer, and I think the appeal of the verses falls more often on the hearts of strangers and aliens in creed than on those which it seeks to comfort.

The steep slope before the convent at Pozzano was the end of the ancient mule track from Sorrento, the same, I imagine, by which St. Peter travelled after landing at Sorrento, as I shall tell in the next chapter. Anyone who cares to penetrate behind the convent can trace it still meandering up hill and down dale with a pleasant indifference to gradients which is characteristic of highways of measureless antiquity. Over the crest of Capo d'Orlando and many another headland it climbs, as if its main object were to take one up into the clear, silent air, over the sweet-smelling brushwood, where myrtle and rosemary scent the air, and the white gum-cistus grows like a weed. No one follows that lonely track in these days, yet it is worth while to walk along it, if only that one may see how easy it made the respectable, but now decadent, trade of brigandage, which in days not yet far distant was the sweet solace of all the men and most of the women in the towns, and yet more in the mountain villages of the peninsula. Castellammare, placed so as to command the highway from Naples to Salerno, as well as those coast roads which were more frequented by wealthy tourists of all nations, was in high favour with men who practised the gentle art of stopping travellers, and many a heavy purse was eased of its burden upon the lonely roads. Fra Diavolo was well known here; in fact, it was among the mountains above this very road to Sorrento that he tried his 'prentice hand at the profession in which he afterwards became so great a master.

The Convent of Santa Marta lies towards Vico Equense, high up in the olive woods, in a lonely 242situation, guarded by its sanctity. That had been quite enough, until Fra Diavolo came into the world, to keep safe not only the nuns, but even their gold statue of the Madonna, which is perhaps more wonderful, though both are sterling proofs of the excellent and reverential morals of the people.

One Scarpi dwelt in the woods above Castellammare, with a faithful band of followers who loved him. I fear he is forgotten now, which is scarcely just, for he was a bold and bloodthirsty bandit. But as is said in the *Purgatorio* on a similar occasion—

"... Credette Cimabue nella pintura
Tener lo Campo! ed ora ha Giotto il grido."

In Brigantaggio it is just the same, and Scarpi's just celebrity is obscured by the greater fame of Fra Diavolo.

Scarpi was torn two ways; cupidity reminded him that the golden statue was easily obtained, piety interposed that it would be a shocking crime. Nothing worse was set down against him than the usual tricks on travellers, slitting their ears, and dismissing them upon occasion to a better world. It was a pity to spoil so fair a record. But Fra Diavolo, boy as he was when he joined Scarpi's band, possessed the great advantage of a single heart. Cupidity was not thwarted by any opposing force of piety, and craft came to make the weak arm strong.

He dressed himself like a novice, and going up boldly to the gate of the convent proclaimed himself a penitent, and sought admission to the Order. I doubt not he had an innocent face. The mother superior welcomed him, and straightway shut him up in solitude for the usual three days' communing with heavenly powers, which was to prepare him for the 243spiritual life to which he aspired. The boy naturally wished to make this intercourse as direct as possible, and making his way unobserved into the chapel he seized the golden Madonna and hid her under some straw in a cart belonging to a peasant whom some lawful occasion had brought up to the convent. Having done this, he presented himself before the Mother Superior, telling her reflection had convinced him he was not fitted for a heavenly life—which was indeed no more than the truth— and so departed with her approval.

The poor peasant driving down among the olive woods somewhat later, all unconscious of the riches in his creaking cart, was probably at a loss to understand why Scarpi's faithful followers should stop him, and insist on rummaging in the straw. His emotions when he saw what they fished out would be a fit subject for a dramatic monologue. Horror at the sacrilege must have struggled with regret that he had not himself thought of fumbling in the straw. Had he done so, would he not have driven off the other way, and melted down the Madonna in his own cottage? To be made the tool by which sinners acquire wealth is surely bitter, and often in after life the poor man must have cursed the fate which did not whisper in his ear what it was he carried in the cart.

But Scarpi's bandits carried off the statue, and Fra Diavolo gained great honour with them. This early fame he never lost. And the common people, holding that priests and devils are, however opposite in all their qualities, the only classes of mankind who are uniformly cunning and successful in all they undertake, combined the titles into one cognomen, no whit too glorious for the chieftain, who in his untutored youth had proved greater than all the 244restraints which hamper greedy men, and had laid hands on the Madonna.

So Fra Diavolo became a mighty leader, and woeful are the tales which travellers told of him. Yet I should be unjust if I did not mention that his most brutal outrages were sometimes capable of being dignified by the name of politics, if not of loyalty to an exiled king. For Ferdinand of Bourbon when he fled from his throne of Naples at the end of the last century, skulking from revolutionary outblasts and the coming of the French, was not so far untrue to the traditions of his race as to despise the help of any agents, however rascally. It might have seemed incongruous if we had found the inheritor of the name of the constable Bourbon who led Frundsberg's Lanzknechts down on Rome in 1527, and cast the treasures of ages as a prey to the scum of Europe, if we had found this monarch saying to himself "Non tali auxilio," and indulging in the luxury of scruples. But Ferdinand despised no man who would help him; and so Fra Diavolo, the murderer and bandit, became a secret agent of the exiled king, working hand in hand with that even more atrocious scoundrel Mammone, whose habit it was to dine with a newly severed human head upon the table, and whose cold-blooded assassinations were more in number than any man could count. So these murderous devils cut off French couriers on the mountain roads, attacked small parties in overwhelming numbers, and performed other gallant deeds in the service of their king, who was not ungrateful, but rewarded them after his kind and theirs.

I can find but little in the streets of Castellammare which invites me to linger in them. There are mineral baths just outside the town, but Providence gave me no occasion for visiting them, and I dislike 245the apparatus of ill-health. I went past the baths, therefore, and strolled on through the crowded, evil-smelling streets till I came out again at the foot of the hill leading to the woods of Quisisana, and went up once more beneath the green arches of the budding leaves, till I saw from time to time a snatch of sea above the houses and the wide sunlit plain revealed itself stretching far and distant round the base of the great volcano.

As I went through the little village of which I spoke before, I noticed hanging on a wire which crosses the road a doll made in the likeness of an old grey-haired woman, adorned with a tuft of feathers growing somewhat bare. As it swung to and fro in the light wind it had the aspect of a child's plaything which had fallen there by chance; but I had seen a similar doll hanging from a balcony in Castellammare, and knew the thing to be no toy.

Such dolls are seen commonly hanging in the air at this season in the Sorrento peninsula. The old woman is Quaresima, or Lent, and she is provided with as many hen's feathers as there are weeks in that period of fasting. Every Sunday one feather is plucked out; and when the last is gone Quaresima is torn down with rejoicing. On the first Sunday of her exaltation a playful diversion is carried on at the cost of poor Quaresima. A boy or girl, chosen by lot, is blindfolded and armed with a long stick, with which he strikes in the air, groping after the swinging figure. At last he finds it, and a sharp blow breaks a concealed bottle, letting out a red fluid— the blood of Lent; the ceremony is diversified by a good deal of horseplay.

I know not how ancient these superstitious ceremonies may be. Italy, perhaps southern Italy in particular, is crowded with usages handed down 246from days so old that it sometimes causes me a shudder to remember how many ages of mankind have passed by them in procession off the earth. The toy, the trivial folly persisting still, more than half meaningless, century after century, while the bright eyes and laughing lips, all that we call life, pass on like shadows when the sun goes in. It is the doll, the grotesque Quaresima, which has life and endures, not we, however distasteful it may be to realise it.

But if our time be shorter, and we shall see fewer springs than the absurd Quaresima, we may at least rejoice in the beauty of this one. For as unsettled weather brings the loveliest days, so the country has put on its rarest beauty. The blue sky hangs like a tent overhead, the clouds are driven back behind the mountains and lie there piled in heavy ranks of tower and column; while through the brown trunks of the trees and the green mist of their lower twigs I can see all the mountains behind Nola and towards Caserta rise one above the other into the far blue distance. For from the clouds of heaven there dropped light on some peaks and shadows on the others, purple lights and dark brown shadow deepening into indigo, so that some looked near and others far away, and some were sulphurous and others green, while all the Campagna laughed in the sunshine, and the houses white and pink flashed on the margin of the turquoise sea.

There are lovely villas on these fringes of the wood, stately houses with terraced gardens occupying the high slopes. The road twists upwards by sharp inclines, catching at each turn more of the freshness of the mountain, till at length it runs into the gateway of the old royal villa, a refuge used when heat or pestilence made Naples unendurable by almost 247every sovereign since the days of Charles the Second of Anjou. It was once the property of that shocking scoundrel, Pierluigi Farnese, most unsavoury and least respectable even among Popes' children, who do so little credit to St. Peter's chair. But it was associated more particularly with Ferdinand of Bourbon, who rebuilt the place. He is said to have given it the name "Quisisana" ("Here one gets well"); but I think that name, or at least as much of it as "Casa sana," is found in records much older than his time.

The villa is no longer royal, but it retains the aspect of old splendour. In these spring days it is empty and silent, lying with barred windows in expectation of those guests who will climb up the hill in crowds when the figs ripen and the sultry weather comes, and all Italy begins to dream of cool, green shades. For three summer months the place is an hotel, the "Margherita"; but now, when I walk round towards the wide terrace which overhangs the grass-grown courtyard, the sound of my steps echoes through the still air, and the red walls are eloquent of vanished royalty.

A formal air of ceremonial stiffness clings about the garden walks, suggestive of hoops and powder, of polished courtliness, and the old, stately manners which vanished from the earth in the crash of the Revolution. I pass out through the gate by which the courtiers entered the woods, and have hardly gone a hundred yards beneath the tender green of the young beech trees when I come to a shady fountain set round with stone seats, a pleasant spot in which the court used to linger on hot summer days, greeting the riders who mounted at the moss-grown block, so long disused except by peasants going to and fro with their rough carts. There were lovely 248roads laid out for those royal pleasure parties; but as I plunge further into the woods courts and kings are driven out of my mind by a sharp whirring sound breaking the silence of the treetops. Across an island of blue sky, in an ocean of green boughs, a bundle of faggots was flying like a huge brown bird. I watched it going with extraordinary speed. Hard on its heels came another, and then a third, while by watching closely I perceived that slanting downwards through the woods from the height of the next mountain there ran a stout wire, to which the faggots were slung by hooked sticks cut on those high uplands where the woodmen were working. Presently a sharp turn of the path brought me out at the last station of the wire. The faggots were piled high in stacks, the air was full of the scent of fresh-sawn wood, and a fire burning by the wayside sent up coils of thin blue smoke among the trees. Half a dozen men were piling cut staves upon a cart; and from time to time there was a jangling of bells as the mules tossed their heads or shivered, and all the brass contrivances set upon the harness to keep off the evil eye clashed together in the sunlight. Far away across dipping woods the logs came whirring down from Monte Pendolo. All the mountain tops are connected by these wires, and in every direction as one wanders through the silent woods the strange and not unmusical humming of the flying faggots is the only sound audible.

A little further wandering brings me to a glen, whose steep slopes are brown with fallen leaves and green with budding brushwood. A stream runs down through the ravine, and a stone bridge is flung across it. Here the road divides, one branch going more directly to those uplands whence the faggots start upon their journey, and by this route bare-legged 249children hurry up carrying baskets of the forked sticks by which the bundles hang. But I go onwards by the other road, winding upwards by slow inclines, now deep in glades where large blue anemones glow in the long grass, and bee orchids hide among the shadows, now emerging in full sight of the wide blue gulf and the smoking volcano which towers over it, till at last I reach the top of Monte Coppola, where once more seats and tables set beneath the trees mark a spot at which the Bourbon court used to revel in the mountain breezes. I lean over the low breastwork, and enjoy the splendour of the prospect.

It is late afternoon, and the westering sun leaves the great bulk of Monte Faito in deep shadow, casting only here and there a fleck of warm gold light on the pines that clothe some shoulder, and throwing into deeper shade the ravines and scars which are chiselled out of his grey flanks. Yet even in the dark clefts there are gleams of yellow broom or cytisus; for the cuckoo is calling all over the sunny country, the trees are in their brightest leaf, and all the slopes of oak and chestnut that sweep down to the margin of the bay are like a cataract of vivid green tumbling down the mountain. Here, on the summit, it is very still. The silence of the mountains holds the air, and scarce a bird twitters in the gold light. The ridge of Faito, like a gigantic buttress, cuts off all the western promontory towards Sorrento, and falls into the sea across the peak of Ischia.

As the sun sank lower, and the warm light grew deeper and more golden, a great bar of cloud formed across the western sky. The sun was now above and now below it. Ischia grew shadowy, and then caught the most delicate light imaginable, swimming like an impalpable fairy island on a sea of darkest 250blue. Then, at some unseen change in the order of the heavens, suddenly the craggy island lost its colour, and Monte Epomeo stood out sharp and black against the flushed sky. So one saw it for a few brief moments. But all the while a rosy glow was spreading over Cape Miseno, it ran along the coast of Baiæ, and caught Posilipo with a delicate radiance. Then all at once Ischia sprang again into light, quivering with every shade of rose and purple, till the sun sank down behind its blackening peak, and the stars hung large and luminous in a space of clear green sky.

CHAPTER XI

SURRIENTO GENTILE: ITS BEAUTIES AND BELIEFS

251

I suppose I need remind no one that the coast roads between Castellammare and Salerno are famous round all the world for beauty. No great while ago there were but two. A third has placed herself between them now, and many are the disputes as to which bears off the palm. In these bickerings it is to be feared that the way from Castellammare to Sorrento must needs go to the wall; for indeed it does not possess the grandeur of the others. The northern face of the peninsula has an aspect wholly different from that of the precipices which look towards Pæstum and the islands of the Sirens. It is softer, more exquisitely wooded; its hillsides sink more often into valleys and ravines; its cliffs are certainly not awful; its mountain slopes are sweet and homely, clad with olive groves and pastures, studded with villas and with monasteries. It is a land which lies in the cool shadow of the mountains for full half the day, so that the scorching sun does not strike it until he is well past the middle of his course towards the Tyrrhene Sea.

I left Castellammare on an uncertain morning. Large grey clouds had sunk far down over the green slopes of Monte Faito; even the wooded cone of Monte Coppola had caught a wreath of vapour 252which lay drifting across the trees with menace of rain and mist. But here and there a gleam quivered on the woods; and presently far-distant Ischia was all a-glimmer, while the dark sea in between flashed into tender shades of blue. Then came the sunlight, warm and soft, casting sharp shadows in the gloomy town, while out on the low road beyond the arsenal the colour of the waves was glorious, and all the long beaches of the curving shore shone like silver. A heavy shower in the night had clogged the level road with white mud. Out of the quarry, half a mile beyond the town, came five men pushing a cart of stones through the slush—swarthy ruffians, clad in blue trousers, with coloured handkerchiefs knotted on their heads. And there, descending by a rocky path from the Monastery of Pozzano, was a solitary monk, with flapping hat, a grey old man with a bleached, sunken face, the very opposite of the bright, lusty day. It is thus, so slow and lonely, that "'O Munaciello" comes, that ghostly monk whom all the children hope and fear to see; for if they can but snatch his hat from off his head, it will bring a fortune with it. But "'O Munaciello" does not come down the mountain paths in this bright daylight; nor is there time to think of spirits at this moment. For the beauty of the road is growing strangely. Round the shoulder of a sheer grey cliff which overtops the road, there is suddenly thrust out into the sea a craggy precipice, in which one recognises the familiar face of Capri, unseen since we passed Torre dell'Annunziata. A moment later a long, sharp promontory like a tooth emerges in the nearer distance. That is "Capo di Sorrento," but one has scarce time to identify it when the far loftier cliff of "Punta di Scutola" appears, dropping from a vast height almost sheer into the sea, while on 253a nearer and a lower cliff rests the white town of Vico, flashing in the sun.

Among the pleasures of the road it is not the least that the traveller coming from Castellammare, as long as this most lovely scene extends before his eyes, is compelled to saunter. No man may hurry, for the road winds continually upwards, and one pauses, now to look down upon a little beach, where the blue tide washes in over white gravel, now to notice how the slopes are cut in terraces of vines; while in every sheltered cleft the golden fruit of orange trees hangs in the shadow of the brown screens put up to guard them from the sun. The vegetation is extraordinarily rich; as well it may be, for the limestone mountain is overlaid with volcanic tufa for full half its height—though Heaven only knows where the tufa came from. A hundred yards beyond the beach there is once more deep water, dark and unruffled, up to the very base of the high cliff; and further out the sea is stained with turquoise changing into green that recalls in some dim way the colour of a field of flax when the blue flowers are just appearing. But this is fresher, alive with light and sparkles, flashing with the soft radiance of the sky, while the olive woods upon the lofty headland behind the town change from grey to dusk as the shadows of the clouds are flung upon them or dispersed by the returning sun.

Vico, no less than Pozzano, has its miraculous Madonna. She was found long ago by one Catherine, a poor crippled girl, to whom the Virgin appeared in a dream, saying, "Go, Catherine, to the Cave of Villanto, and there, before my image, you will be healed." Now the Cave of Villanto was occupied by cows, and seemed a most unlikely place to contain even the least sacred statue. But Catherine did not stay to reason; she went and found it, was healed according 254to the promise, and now on the third Sunday in October the image is borne in solemn procession from the Church of Santa Maria del Toro through the streets of Vico, in glorious memory of this striking miracle.

There is no end to these marvels of Madonnas. At Meta, just where the road drops into the plain of Sorrento, an old woman, attending on her cow, was amazed to see the beast drop on its knees in front of a laurel tree. She kicked and poked the creature, but in vain; Colley continued her devotions with placid piety, and the natural amazement of her mistress was increased when she saw a flame spring up at the foot of the tree, in which flame presently appeared not only a statue of the Madonna, but a hen and chickens of pure gold!

70

It may be mere accident that, while the legend goes on to describe fully what became of the statue, it says nothing more about the golden hen and chickens—worthless dross, of course, yet surely not without some interest for the finder! Perhaps the silence hides a tragedy. It had been prudent if the old woman had allowed no mention of those gewgaws to be made. She was probably a gossip, and could not hold her tongue in season. These are fruitless speculations, and yet I think some charm is added to the loveliest of countries by the knowledge that such gauds as a hen and chickens of pure gold are to be picked up there by the piously observant.

But to return to Vico. I should do that townlet too much honour if I left it to be supposed that its only traditions are concerned with heavenly presences. The truth is otherwise, and it would be improper to conceal it. Vico, indeed, shares with no few other townlets on the peninsula the discredit of having been afflicted sorely by witches. Once upon a time 255the nuisance grew unbearable. A farm close to the town had long been the centre of uncanny noises, such as terrified the peasants almost to death, and might have gone near to depopulate the neighbourhood had not some very bold people gone over to inspect. There were the witches sure enough. They had bells tied to their heels, and were leaping like monkeys from one tree to another, while the bells tinkled and the air was full of weird noises. Fortunately the investigators carried guns, and the witches, seeing that their enemies were ready to shoot, decided to come down, whereupon they received such a trouncing with sticks that they learnt better manners and left the neighbourhood at peace.

If one is so defenceless, is it worth while to be a witch in Italy at all? The point is arguable, and it is important to be right on it; for many children of both sexes become witches without knowing it, by the mere fact of being born on Christmas night, or on the day of the conversion of St. Paul. If, therefore, the parents do not wish the bairns to retain the *entrée* of the witches' Sabbath—held always at Benevento—it behoves them to take prompt action. The remedy is simple. You cut a slip of the vine, set fire to one end, and pass it over the child's arm in the shape of a cross. The flame burns out, and Satan's spell is broken.

I do not find anyone who can tell me why the witches have bells on their heels. Bells throughout the peninsula are sacred to Sant'Antuono, called Antonio elsewhere. In old times the bell of Sant' Antuono was carried round from house to house, and mothers would bring out their sucking children to sip water from it, in the hope that they might learn to speak the sooner. Even now a little bell is often hung round a baby's neck, where it serves the purpose 256of the horn, the half-moon, or the hand with outstretched fingers; that is to say, it keeps off the evil eye. What can there be in common between the babies and the sinful witches that both should be followed by the same tinklings?

Vico, as I have said, lies on a plateau, and when the road has traversed the clean town—how different from the foulness of Castellammare or Nocera!—it drops into a ravine of very singular beauty, a winding cleft which issues from the folds of Faito and St. Angelo, brimming over with vineyards and orange groves, and opening at last upon the sea, where through the soft grey foliage one looks to Ischia, far away across the blue. Having traversed the bridge which spans this shadowy valley, the road mounts again, rising through dense woods of olive, till at last the summit of Punta di Scutola is won, and all the plain of Sorrento lies below.

There is no hour of dawn or dusk in which this view is otherwise than exquisite. In the morning light the plain is full of shadows, for the sun has not yet travelled westwards of St. Angelo, and the mighty mountain towers dark over the whole peninsula. It is the evening sun which shines most beautifully here, and no one who has climbed up this road when the plain is full of soft, gold light, when Ischia turns rosy and the jagged peak of Vico Alvano soars up dark against the pale green sky, is likely to forget it when he thinks of Paradise.

Sorrento lies upon the western side of the plain, almost touching the rim of the mountains that inclose it, so that one has hardly left the streets before the mountains close in and the plain is lost. A little way beyond the houses the hill upon one's left is already high and sheer, a broken outline of sharp limestone jags, clothed with cytisus and broom and slopes of 257sweet short grass, out of which rings the plashing of a stream, for there has been rain upon the mountains, and all the clefts and runnels are brimming over with fresh fallen water. So one goes on among the whispering sounds of tree and brook until a mightier noise surpasses them, and one pauses at the foot of the ravine of Conca to behold the waterfall.

So high and dark is this ravine that though the sun is almost exactly above it, its light catches only the bushes at the very top, and penetrates not at all into the sheer funnel down which the water plunges, scattered into spray by the force of the descent, until a hundred feet below it drops upon a jut of rock and so pours down in a succession of quick leaps from pool to pool.

It is a wild and beautiful sight to watch the downpour of this water on the days succeeding rain. But in the warm weather the ravine is dry, and an active climber might go up it without much trouble. There is some temptation to the feat; for men say a treasure lies hidden in a cave which opens out of the sheer walls, and the gold is enough to make a whole village rich. If any doubt it, let him go there on the stroke of midnight. As the hour sounds, he will see the guardian of the hoard appear at the top of the ravine, a dark mailed warrior, mounted on a sable steed, who leaps into the gulf and vanishes when mortal men accost him. There was once a wizard living at no great distance from Sorrento whose dreams were haunted by the craving for this treasure. He must have been a half-educated wizard, for he knew no spell potent enough to help him towards his object. One day there came to him three lads who had possessed themselves, I know not how, of a magic book, a work of power such as might have been compiled by the great enchanter, Michael Scot, 258who toiled in Apulia for the

71

welfare of the Emperor, reading the secrets of the stars with little thought of the pranks that would one day be played on him by William of Deloraine in Melrose Abbey. It is rather odd that though our generation turns out so many kinds of books, both good and bad, it seems unable to produce the magic sort. But the three lads got one, and they brought it to the wizard of Sorrento; and all together one May night, casting a rope ladder into the ravine of Conca, climbed down until they reached the entrance of the cave.

They found it buried in black darkness, and waited there trembling till the grey dawn stole down the rocks, and a gold beam from the rising sun quivered into the mouth of the grotto. As the light shot through the opening, all the treasure-seekers shouted together; for walls and roof were crusted over with gold and gems, and marvellous flashes of soft colour glowed in the heart of rubies and of emeralds. They stood and stared awhile, then one of them tried to break off a mass of jewels, but had no sooner touched it than the rocks rang with a crash of thunder, the magic book whirled away in a livid flame, wizard and lads fled trembling up the ladder. It was a melancholy rout. I fear the party was too large for prudence. The local proverb says, "When there are too many cocks to crow, it never will be day."

A little further up the road a stair ascends the fresh and sunny hillside. It winds upwards through green grasses and grey rocks till it attains a level plateau, where a few olives grow detached and scattered. At that point I turn to look down upon the plain and the long line of cliff which holds the sea in check, so black and sheer, so strangely even in its height. It is still early on this bright mid-April morning, but the sun has force and power, and all the 259sea is radiantly blue. Immediately below me is a little beach, the Marina Grande, the opening of the westerly ravine, small, yet much the largest which the town possesses, and there most of the boats lie hauled up on the black sand. Another fringe of lava sand runs under the dark cliff below the great hotels. Sometimes in the early morning the traveller, waking not long after dawn, may hear a low monotone of chanting down beneath his window, and flinging it open to the clean salt wind that breathes so freshly over the grey sea dimpling into green, ere yet the sun does more than sparkle on the water, he will see far down below him the barefooted women tugging in the nets, while the fish glitter silvery on the red planking of the boat that rocks on the translucent water twenty yards from shore.

ROOF TOP—MODERN NAPLES.

Beyond these beaches the straight sheer cliff sweeps on with what looks like an unbroken wall, though in truth it is gashed by creeks and inlets, while one beach, the Marina di Cassano, has in its time done yeoman's service to the trade of all the plain. There clings to it a tale of witches too. But really, I must turn aside less readily at these beckonings of Satan. Let the witches wait. It is the lava which attracts me now. Anybody else would have noticed it long since, and turned his mind to the wonders of creation first.

Most people expect to have done with volcanoes and their products when they climb up out of the Campagna Felice on to the hillsides of Castellammare. Yet we heard of lava soil at Vico; and here are the lava cliff, the lava sand, and the abounding vegetation just as lush as if Vesuvius, or some other like him, were close behind the hilltop. Was I not told that the peninsula is built of limestone, showing no trace of fire, shaped and chiselled as it stands to-day 260before the earth's crust broke at any spot in all Campania, or fire burst forth from any fissure? It is limestone too! What other rock could so ridge its precipices, or give so vivid a freshness to the green pastures on its slopes? Whence, then, came the lava?

Well, that is in some degree a mystery. Swinburne, to whose travels I have referred already, thought he had solved it, and declared that the Isles of the Sirens, commonly known as "I Galli," for reasons which we shall come to in good time,—he declared these islands to be nothing but the relics of a crater. The rocks were visited so seldom a century ago that no one could contradict him at the moment. But in Naples a geologist lay waiting disdainfully to demolish him. It was no other than Scipione Breislak, a formidable man of science, and an authority even now, which is something more than can be said of Swinburne. Breislak got a boat and went himself to the Galli to see what nonsense it was that the Englishman had been talking. Alas! he found no trace of fires or crater! Thus one more nail was driven into the coffin of English scholarship, and since that day no one has even guessed where the lava came from.

What may be regarded as fairly certain, however, is that it was not ejected on this spot. The Piano di Sorrento, sweet country of perpetual summer, of which more truly than of many parts of Italy, the poet might have written—

"Hic ver assiduum, atque alienis mensibus aestas,"

is in no danger of being blown to fragments. Perhaps the lava came from some volcanic outburst under the sea, from some islet formed and washed away again—it matters little. Somewhere underneath 261the soil lies the clean, firm limestone, and the volcanic matter, whencesoever it came, did no more than fill a hollow of the hills, and turn it into the loveliest valley in the world. Sorrento, the very name whispers of smiles and laughter, and the people, softening it still with the incomparable music of their speech, modulate it into "Surriento," just as they turn "cento" into "ciento," and drop a liquid vowel into the harshness of Castellammare, calling it "Castiellammare." "Surriento!" How it trembles on the air! Had ever any town a name so fit for love!

And was any ever set in a fairer country? It is a plain, yet no monotony of level, for a spine of the encircling hills tilts the gardens to the evening sun, while the shadow of the mountains wards off the fierce glare of the heat till long past noon. And what fertility! Is there on the surface of the earth such a lush wild glade of orange groves, three generations, "father, son, and grandson," as the Sorrentines say, hanging on a single tree; while as they hang and ripen, the scented flowers are continually budding in the shadow of the dark green leaves, and every waft of air is sweetened by the fragrance of the blossom. But at Surriento all the airs are sweet. If they do not blow across the orange groves they carry down the scent of rosemary and myrtle from the mountains, which are knee-deep in delicious scrub; or they come off the sea in sharp, cool breezes, bringing the gladness and fresh movement of the deep, scattering the stagnant heats and making all the plain laugh with pleasure in the joy of life. How long the lovely summer lasts at Surriento, and how short are the bad winter days! "A Cannelora," say the peasants, "state rinto e vierno fora!" What is "Cannelora"? It is the second day of February, 262when England still has full three months of winter! Then it is that summer returns to the Piano di Sorrento and chases winter away across the hills. Is it true? "Chi lo sa." Perhaps not quite, but what of that? The Sorrentines themselves have another saying, which runs thus: "A neve 'e Marzo nu' fa male,"—that is, "Snow does no harm in March." So the summer which comes at Cannelora is not incompatible with snow! Yet even in fibs there must be probability, or where would be the use of them? To declare that an English summer began at Cannelora would be simply dull.

The plain, I say, is not one unbroken level, nor is it wide enough to be monotonous. One cannot look out far in any direction over the olive woods which like a soft grey flood surge over the fertile country, without being checked by the cool, shadowy mountains, St. Angelo vast and lovely, Vico Alvano thrusting up an almost perfect cone; and many another peak showing towards Sorrento a slope of crag and pasture-land which on its other face drops in sheer precipices to the Gulf of Salerno. One knows that from the summit of the ridge there is an outlook over both the gulfs; and from my post, here on the hillside known as Capo di Monte, I can see the red monastery called the Deserto, because it was indeed erected in a solitary waste, where the soul of man might hope to tread down underfoot him who, in the language of the place, is rarely spoken of by name, but indicated more gently as "Chillo che sta sotto San Michele"—"He who lies beneath St. Michael."

The pleasantest way to the Deserto is on foot. One goes up the stairs from Capo di Monte, stopping gladly enough to chaffer with the children who offer flowers or early fruits, and are contented 263with so very little coin in exchange, then climbing on past hillside cottages and orange groves within high walls, which only now and then admit a glance across the sea to Vesuvius smoking, or the blue hills beyond Nola so far away, until at last the stairs are left behind and one passes on through vineyards into a wood which occupies the higher slopes of the open hillside, a mossy, fragrant wood, whose spring foliage is not yet so dense as to bar the sunlight from the anemones, lilac and purple, which grow in profusion out of the trailing ivy and the dead leaves of last year's fall. After the wood, the gate of the Deserto is close at hand: it gives access to a straight, steep drive, at the end of which stands a tower overtopping a red group of buildings, and on it the words—

"Ego vox clamantis

In Deserto

Tempus breve est."

An old monk admitted me, and without waste of words, pointed out the staircase which gave access to the upper story. He did not offer to accompany me, but went back along the silent corridor like a man contemptuous of earthly things, even of the immeasurable beauty which lay stretched out on every side of that high eminence. So I went up the stairs alone, listening to the echoes of my feet, until I came to a doorway whence I passed out on the wall which surrounds the garden quadrangle; and here I turned instinctively to seek for Capri, unseen since the glimpse I caught of its high precipices on approaching Vico Equense.

Looking northward from the monastery wall I had the island on my left, the sheer cliff called the Salto turned towards me, the island rocks of the Faraglioni 264standing out distinctly, the little marina sparkling in the sun, while high above it, like an eagle's nest, towered the crags of Anacapri and Barbarossa's castle. The morning sun had transformed the island wondrously. Grey and green by nature, some suffusion out of the warm sky had showered down deep purple on it, and from end to end it lay glowing with the colour of an evening cloud. Whence that light came was a marvel that I could not guess; for the nearer slopes of Punta di Campanella caught not a trace of it, but ravine and mountain pasture lay there in the sunlight grey and green as ever, while across the narrow strait Capri had all the tremulous beauty of the coasts of fairyland. Far away northwards, across a space of the loveliest sea imaginable, lay the craggy peak of Ischia, the low reef of Procida, and the mountains of the Campanian coast; while on the hither side of that blue land of cloudy peaks the sun had flung a heavy shadow over Monte Sant'Angelo, and all his towering slopes lay black and lurid.

The southward view is scarcely so fine. For the Deserto is built on the Sorrento side of the ridge, so that even from its roof one surveys a part only of the vast waters which owned the domination of Salerno, of Amalfi, and in far older days submitted to the rule of that great city Pæstum, whose shattered temples are still, unto this day, a prouder relic than any left by the commonwealths which rose in later times upon the gulf. One looks across the blue moving waters towards the flat where Pæstum stood. Behind it rise the mountain peaks in long succession, flashing here and there with fields of snow, while further off, scarce seen by reason of its distance, the headland of Licosia marks the limit of the bay.

Such is the Deserto, a solitude among the mountains. When I came down once more into the cool 265corridors, the old monk acknowledged my benefaction with a solemn bow, but let me go without a word. Silence hung over the building like a spell. It played its part in the great charm and beauty of the spot; and

73

I was well content that nothing broke it. It was past noon, and the sun was dropping westwards. All the hillsides were glowing in gold light. The budding woods, so shadowy as I climbed up, were full of glimmering radiance; and as I descended further, and all the plain lay before me, its olive woods, its orange groves, and the long line of white villas cresting the black cliff were suffused in one wide glory of warm colour. As I went across the bridge into the city, I turned off from the main street, and found what is left of the old wall, guarding the ancient ducal domain, though indeed one might have thought the deep ravines had fenced it sufficiently on three sides, while on the fourth the sea protects it strong and well. The gates have gone, under which in the old days of festival, when Carnival pranced up and down the streets, the grisly figure of death, "la morte di Sorrento," used to lurk, waiting to mow down the rioter as the hour struck which marked the approach of Lent. But there is still enough left of the massive fortifications to show that a rich city once occupied this site.

It is a pleasant spot at this hour of evening shadows. The deep ravine is filled with the whispering echoes of a stream, which does not fill the bottom of the hollow, but leaves space for orange groves, deep thatched with boughs. Cottages are built out on jutting rocks, overhanging the precipice with strange indifference to the probable results of even little earthquakes; and the lanes are alive with brown, half-naked children. The sheer rocky chasms, the swarming population, the ancient walls, recall 266memories of an older Sorrento than one can recover easily upon the sea-front, or in the tortuous streets which skirt it. One sees here the system of defence, and can believe that in its day Sorrento was a fortress, though its great days of independence passed so early, and its dukes were tributaries long ere the Normans came and coveted these shores. Yet the ducal days, the "Giorni Ducheschi," are by no means forgotten in Sorrento. Indeed, if their natural glories had passed out of mind, the nocturnal ramblings of Mirichicchiu would serve to refresh the memory of every man and child, terror being, as Machiavelli puts it, a better remembrancer than love.

Mirichicchiu, "the little physician," was a dwarf. He lived in the time of the dukes, and was unwise enough to conspire against his lord, who promptly cut his head off and caused the body to be thrown into the fields outside the castle walls, where its several parts appear to have been dispersed by the operations of husbandry, since Mirichicchiu to this day has not been able to recover them.

Night by night he goes searching up and down the fields, stooping with a lantern over the clods, until the cock-crow frights him back to the place from whence he came. Sometimes the lonely little dwarf will go up to a cottage and tap at the door. When that light knocking rings through the startled house the inmates know that Mirichicchiu is hungry, and they prepare his breakfast. The dish must be cooked specially for him, and no one else must taste it. If he finds it to his mind he leaves coins in the plate.

There can, I think, be few districts in which the folklore is richer or more romantic than in this region of Sorrento. The peasants are soaked in superstition. The higher classes are scarce more 267free from it. Those who loiter at midnight near the Capo di Sorrento, whither every tourist goes to see the ruins of the Villa Pollio and the great cool reservoir of sea-water known as "Il Bagno della Regina Giovanna," may see a maiden clad in white robes rise out of the sea and glide over the water towards the Marina di Puolo, the little beach which lies between the Punta della Calcarella and the Portiglione. She has scarce touched land when she is pursued by a dark rider on a winged horse, who comes from the direction of Sorrento, and hunts her shrieking all along the shore. There are spectres on every cliff and hillside, witches on the way to their unhallowed gatherings at Benevento, and wizards prowling up and down in the shape of goats or dogs. At night the peasants keep their doors and windows closed; if they do not, the Janara may come in and cripple the babies. You may sometimes keep out evil spirits by setting a basin full of water near the door; the fiends will stop to count the drops, which takes a long time, probably enough to occupy them until day drives them home.

If anyone be out after dark it is better not to look round. The risk is that one may be turned into stone.

Here and there one may see ruined churches in the country, but no peasant will go near them after nightfall; for he knows that spectral Masses are celebrated there, solemn services chanted by dead priests, who are thus punished for neglect of their offices in life, and whose congregation is made up of worshippers who forgot their religion while they lived.

The Italian fancy begets things terrible more easily than it conceives a lovely dream. Even the tales of fairies turn more readily on fear than on the merry 268pranks with which our northern legends associate the dwellers in the foxglove bells. But on a fine spring evening, when the sun is glowing over the plain, there are pleasanter things to think of in Sorrento than the spirits of the other world. I turn gladly away from the ravines into the broad main street, and passing by the cathedral, pause in the piazza, where the life of the pleasant little town is busiest and gayest. It is here that one should call to mind the poet Tasso, whose tragedy was cast into noble verse by Goethe; for his statue stands in the square, looking down gravely on the rows of vetturini cracking whips, the children coming or going to the fountain, the babble of strange tongues from lands which never dreamt of Surriento when he dwelt on earth. But I think the days are gone in which English people can delight in the sixteenth-century poets of which Italy was once so proud. Tasso and Ariosto may have every merit save sincerity; but that is lacking, and Italy has so many noble poets who possess it! I care little for the memories of Tasso, save in Goethe's verse, and as I go down to the marina it is of older visitors, welcome and unwelcome, that my mind is full—St. Peter, for example. There is a constant legend that he came this way after the death of Christ, landing perhaps from some galley of Alexandria that touched here on its way to Pozzuoli, and set down the apostle to win what souls he could among the rough dwellers in the mountains. The saint preached his first sermon by the roadside near Sant'Agnello, a village between Sorrento and the Marina di Cassano; and then went over the hills towards Castellammare, where he rewarded the hospitality of the dwellers at Mojano, near the roots of Faito, by making springs of water gush out of the thirsty rock.

NAPLES—COURTYARD IN THE OLD TOWN.

Doubtless the apostle was on his way to Rome. 269I know no reason why we should distrust the tale that he did indeed pass through this country. The water-way from the East around the coasts of southern Italy is of mysterious antiquity. Pæstum was a mighty trading city many centuries before St. Peter lived, and its sailors may well have inherited traditions of navigation as much older than their day as they are older than our own. I do not know whether it was indeed upon the islands under the Punta di Campanella that Ulysses, lashed to the mast, heard the singing of the Sirens, but the tradition is not doubted in Sorrento; and without leaning on it as a fact, one may recognise at least that the tale suggests the vast antiquity of trade upon these waters. Else whence came the heaps of whitening bones of lost sailors, among which the Sirens sat and sang? Here year by year we learn more of the age of man, and of the countless centuries he has dwelt by the shore of the great deep. We cannot tell when he first adventured round the promontories with sail and oar; but it is safe to believe that those early voyages were made unnumbered centuries before any people lived whose records have come down to us, and that those sailors whom we discern when the mists are first lifted from the face of history were no pioneers, but followed in a well-worn track of trade, beaten out who knows how long before their time.

It is said that in old days the city of Sorrento stretched farther out to sea than it does now. The fishers say they could once go dryfoot from one marina to the other. There are ruins underneath the water. The two small beaches have but cramped accommodation now, and if trade settled there, as it did in the days of Tiberius, a harbour of some sort must have existed. A city on the coast may last without a harbour which has once brought it 270consequence; but would it have grown without one to a place of power? It is profitless speculation, perhaps. But no one wandering along these coasts, which played so great a part in early maritime adventure, can easily refrain from wondering at the tricks of destiny which brought the stream of commerce now to one spot, now to another; and then, wresting away the riches it had given, left the busy quays to silence, and made one more city of the dead.

The hotels which line the summit of the cliff conceal the remnants of great Roman villas. The Hotel Vittoria is built over one of the finest. On that spot, in 1855, were found the remains of a small theatre, destroyed to make the terrace of the hotel. The tunnel by which one goes down to the sea is the same by which the Roman lord of the mansion descended to his boat. Beneath the Hotel Sirena there are large chambers which once formed part of such another villa. I cannot tell how many other traces of old days may be left scooped out of the black rock.

As the dusk descends upon Sorrento, and the sea turns grey, the narrow, tortuous streets resume an appearance of vast age. They are very silent at this hour; the shops are mostly closed; the children hawking woodwork have gone home. One's footsteps echo all down the winding alleys, and the tall houses look mysterious and gloomy. Such was the aspect of the town on the evening of Good Friday, when I took my stand in the garden of the Hotel Tramontano to see the procession of our Lady of Sorrows, who, having gone out at daybreak to seek the body of the Lord, has now found it, and is bearing it in solemn mourning through the city streets.

Along the narrow lane which passes the hotel a 271row of lamps has been set, and little knots of people are moving up and down, laughing and jesting, with little outward recognition of the nature of the rite. The procession has already started; it is in a church at the further end of the long alley, and every ear is strained to catch the first sound of the chanting which will herald its approach. Wherever the houses fall back a little the space is banked up with curious spectators. Some devout inhabitant hangs out a string of coloured lamps, and is rewarded by a shower of applause and laughter, which has scarcely died away when a distant strain of mournful music casts a hush over the throng. Far down the alley one sees the glittering of torches, and a slow, sobbing march, indescribably weird and majestic, resounds through the blue night, with soft beat of drum and now and then a clash of cymbals. Very slow is the approach of the mourners, but now there is no movement in the crowd. Men and children stand like ranks of statues, watching the slow coming of the torches and the dark waving banners which are borne behind them.

So the heavy rhythm of the funeral march goes up into the still air, knocking at every heart; and after the players, treading slow and sadly, come the young men of Sorrento, two and two, at wide intervals, hooded in deep black, their eyes gleaming through holes in the crape masks which conceal their faces. Each bears some one among the instruments of the divine passion—the nails, the scourge, and scourging pillar, the pincers— while in their midst rise the heavy folds of a huge crape banner, drooping mournfully from its staff. Next comes a silver crucifix raised high above the throng, and then, as the head of the procession winds away among the houses, the throbbing note of the march changes to 272a sweeter and more plaintive melody, while from the other hand there rises the sound of voices chanting "Domine, exaudi." In a double choir come the clergy of the city and the country round, all robed in solemn vestments, and between the two bodies the naked figure of our Lord is borne recumbent on a bier, limbs drawn in agony, head falling on one side, pitiful and terrible, while last of all Our Lady of Sorrows closes the long line of mourners.

When she has passed, silence drops once more upon the dusky alleys. Far off, the sound of chanting rings faintly across the houses, and the slow music of the march sighs through the air. Then even that dies away, and on the spot where Tasso opened his eyes upon a troubled world there is no sound but the wind stirring among the orange blossoms, or the perpetual soft washing of the sea about the base of the black cliffs.

CHAPTER XII

CAPRI

273

It is a common observation among those who visit Capri that the first close view of the island is disappointing. The distant lights and colours are all gone. The cliffs look barren. The island has a stony aspect, inaccessible and wild. The steamer coming from Sorrento reaches first the cliff of the Salto, concerning which I shall have more to say hereafter, and only when that tremendous precipice has been rounded does one see the saddle of the island, a neck of land which unites the two mountain peaks so long watched from the mainland, a continuous garden, at the head of which stands the town of Capri, while the Marina is at its foot.

It must be admitted that the landing-place of Capri is on the way to lose its quaintness, and is even in some danger of taking on the aspect of an excursionists' tea-garden. Hotels and restaurants spring up on every side, and a broad, winding road has been carried in long convolutions from the sea up to the town. Capri is striving hard to provide conveniences for her visitors, and no longer conducts them up the hill by the ancient staircase, which was good enough for friends and enemies alike in all ages till our own, and is still so broad and easy that a donkey can go up it with less distress than it will 274experience on the hot and dusty road. However, the staircase is still there, and as it is my odd whim to care nothing for the nice new road, but to prefer entering Capri by the old front door, I consign my luggage to the strapping, stout-armed sirens who pounced upon it as soon as the landing-boat touched shore, and go up the cool and shadowy steps between walls of ivy and deep-rooted creepers, over which the budding vines project their tendrils, and blossoming fruit trees send a drift of petals falling on the stair. From time to time I cross the noisy road, and go on in peace again with greater thankfulness, till, after some twenty minutes' climb, I emerge beneath an old vaulted gateway, from the summit of which defence unnumbered generations of Capriotes must have parleyed with their enemies, fierce Algerines, followers of Dragut or of Barbarossa, merciless sea-wolves who descended on this luckless island again and again, attracted, no doubt, by its proximity to the wealthy cities of the mainland and the streams of commerce which were ever going by its shores.

The gate is flung wide open now, and the group of women sitting in its shadow eye the coming stranger with a friendly smile. I step out of the archway on to the Piazza, the prettiest and tiniest of squares, bordered with shops on two sides. On the third side stand the cathedral and the post office, while the fourth is occupied by a wall breast high, over which one may look out across the fertile slopes bounded by the huge cliffs of Monte Solaro all burning in the midday sun.

From the Piazza two or three arched openings give access to narrow, shady lanes. One of these is the main street of the town, and meanders down the opposite side of the saddle, passing Pagano's Hotel and the "Quisisana," whereof the former is as old as 275the fame of the island among tourists; for they, although the great interest and beauty of Capri were well known, came here rarely before the discovery of the Blue Grotto caught the fancy of all Europe. I shall not go to see that marvel of the world to-day, for the hour of its greatest beauty is past already; and I will therefore spend the hours of heat in setting down how the grotto was recalled to memory some seventy years ago by August Kopisch. The story is sold everywhere in Capri, but as it happens to be written in German, hardly any English visitors take the trouble to look at it.

There can be no doubt that when Kopisch landed in Capri during the summer of 1826 the blue grotto was practically unknown. There are, it is true, one or two vague passages in the writings of early topographers—Capaccio, Parrino—which appear to be based upon some knowledge of it; and it is said that in 1822 a fisherman of Capri had dared to enter the low archway. If so, he kept his knowledge to himself; for when Kopisch landed, and went up the old staircase to Pagano's Hotel—a humble hostelry it was in those days!—he knew nothing of the grotto, and his host, though very ready to talk about the wonders of the island, required some pressing before he would explain the hints he dropped of an enchanted cave below the tower of Damecuta, a place which boatmen were afraid to visit in broad day, and which they believed to be the habitation of the devil. "But I," went on Pagano, "do not believe that. Many times, when I was a lad, I begged friends of mine, who were strong swimmers, to swim into the cavern with me, but in vain; the fear of the devil was too strong in them! But listen! I once learned from a very aged fisher that two hundred years ago a priest swam with one of his colleagues a little way into the cave, but turned 276and came out at once in a terrible fright; the legend says that the priests found the entrance widen out into a vast temple, with high altar, set round with statues of the gods."

Pagano's story fell on the enthusiastic fancy of the young German artist like flint on steel, and the Capriote, catching his guest's excitement, went on to say that he himself believed the tower of Damecuta to be a relic of one of the palaces built by the Emperor Tiberius, who constructed no pleasure-house without a secret exit. Might not the hidden way go through the grotto? And if so, what strange things might they not find if they dared explore it! Perhaps a temple of Nereus, the shrine of some sea deity, left unworshipped and forgotten through all the ages since the Roman Empire fell!

Both men had heart for the adventure, undismayed by prophecies of mischief from devils, mermen, or sea monsters, though quaking secretly at the recollection of the sharks, which, however, rarely come close into shore. Wondrous tales were told them of things seen near the fabled grotto. Sometimes the frightened fishers had watched the glow of fire from within trembling on the waves. Beasts like crocodiles were seen to look in and out; seven times a day the entrance changed its shape and windings; at night the Sirens sang there among dead men's bones; the screams of little children in agony rang often round the rocks, and it was no uncommon thing for young fishermen to disappear in the neighbourhood of the ill-famed cavern. Many an instance could be quoted, and one tale in particular was brought up to show how mad they were who loitered on that sea. A fisherman went out to spear fish near the grotto. It was a lovely morning, and he could distinguish the shellfish creeping on the bottom, though the water 277was ten fathoms deep. Suddenly he saw all the fish scurry away into hiding, and just underneath his boat came swimming in concentric circles a vast sea monster, rising at each turn nearer and nearer to the surface. The fisher was uneasy, but instead of calling on the Madonna as a Christian would, he trusted in his own strength, and hurled his spear at the monster in the devil's name. He saw it strike the creature's neck, but from the wound there came such a gush of blood as clouded all the water so that he could see nothing. He thought joyfully that he had killed the fish; but the thong of his spear hung slack, and when he pulled it in the point of the harpoon was gone—not broken off, but fused, as if it had been thrust into a furnace!

The poor fisherman, terrified to death, dropped the spear and seized his oars, longing only to get away from that accursed place. But row as he might he could not progress. His boat went round in circles, as the sea monster had swum, and finally stood still as if anchored, while out of the reddened water rose a bloodstained man, with the spear sticking in his breast, and threatened the fisher with his fist. The poor man sank down fainting, and when he came to life again he was being tended by his friends at the Marina of Capri. For three days he was dumb. When he could speak and tell what had befallen him he began to shrivel up. First his right hand withered, then his arms and legs, till finally, when he died, he had lost the aspect of a man, and was like nothing but a bundle of dried herbs in an apothecary's shop.

Such were the tales with which the Capriotes sought to dissuade Kopisch from paying heed to the suggestions of Pagano, but in vain. Early in the morning the party started, having with them Angelo Ferraro, a boatman, with a second boat in which they 278had packed a small stove, with all the materials necessary for kindling a fire. When they came to the low entrance of the cave not one of them was quite at ease, and Kopisch, who was in the water first, begged Angelo, the boatman, for a fresh assurance that sharks never came between the rocks. Angelo was labouring to kindle his fire, and gave a hasty confident reply, which provoked the German to the natural reflection, "It's all very well for him to be sure. His legs are in the boat!"

But when the resinous wood shavings caught and blazed up brightly all fear was gone. Angelo pulled in under the low archway, pushing the smaller boat with the lighted stove before him. Close behind came Kopisch, Pagano, and a second German traveller, half blinded by the smoke which blew back in their faces, and full of natural excitement and anxiety concerning what might befall them in this bold quest. For a time they could see nothing save a dim, high vault; but when Kopisch turned to look for his companions he, first of all men of our age and knowledge, saw that sight which for absolute beauty and wonder has no superior in all the world.

"What a panic seized me," he says himself, "when I saw the water under me like blue flames of burning spirits of wine! I leapt upwards, for, half blinded as I was by the fire in the boat, I thought first of a volcanic eruption. But when I felt the water cold I looked up at the roof, thinking the blue light must come from above. But the roof was closed.... The water was wonderful, and when the waves were still, it seemed as if I were swimming in the invisible blue sky...."

I have told this adventure at some length because, in mere justice, Kopisch and Pagano ought not to be forgotten by the crowds of pleasure seekers who 279visit Capri, and for whom, however much or little they may take pleasure in the other immense beauties of the island, the Blue Grotto still remains the chief delight. It may not be necessary to claim for Kopisch that he was indeed first of all men to see its marvellous beauty; nor even that, for his bold adventure, its low gateway would have remained closed to all the world. Discoveries such as this are made at their appointed time, and Kopisch may perhaps have had precursors. But it remains true that his audacity first threw wide the gate for us; and for my part I acknowledge gladly a deep debt of gratitude.

No wise man goes to the Blue Grotto from the steamer by which he travels from Naples or Sorrento. When one has crossed the ocean, and journeyed thousands of miles, to see a sight so wonderful, why should one be content to hurry round it in the few minutes given by a boatman eager for other fares? There is but one way to see the Blue Grotto, and that is by hiring a boat at the Marina on a still, sunny morning, bargaining carefully that there shall be no compulsion to leave before one wishes. Then as the boatman rows on slowly beneath the luxuriant vineyards and the green slopes of the saddle of the island, he will point out the baths of the Emperor Tiberius, low down by the shore, indeed, partly covered by the clear green water, and will go on to talk of the strange life led by the imperial recluse, who studded the island with palaces and left it teeming with unsolved mysteries. Twelve villas he built, so says Tacitus, upon this narrow space, and in these solitary palaces by cliff and shore he lived a life of nameless tyranny and wickedness. Who can tell the uses of the strange masses of broken masonry which one finds in climbing up and down the lonely cliff paths? With what object did he build tower 280and arched vault in spots where only sea-birds could have the fancy for alighting? What secret

77

chambers may not still be hidden in these ruins! What passages leading deep into caverns of the hillside! What mysteries! What treasures for those who have the heart and courage of the German artist! Such are the suggestions of the brown-faced boatman bending towards me across his oars, while in a hushed whisper he points out now one and now another chasm of the limestone which gives access, so he tells me, to a cavern of unmeasured size. And still, as he talks eagerly and low, the sheer cliff rises higher and darker overhead; for the saddle of the island is long past, the towering precipices of Monte Solaro are above me, and high up on some eyrie which the sight straining from the water cannot reach is the white mountain town of Anacapri.

Presently the coast-line sinks to a more moderate height. The tower of Damecuta is seen ahead, and below it a stair, cut in the face of the rock, leads down to a low arched opening, through which the blue sea is washing in and out. A couple of women in gay dresses are sitting in the shade upon the stair. A few boats are rocking on the blue water, strangely, intensely blue, even in the morning shadow which the cliffs fling out across the sea. It was not the rich, royal colour which one may see about the shores of western England, nor yet the exquisite soft turquoise which glows by all the bays and headlands of this coast, but a darker and more watery blue, verging on indigo rather than on any other single colour.

The boat approached the opening. The boatman, warning me to lie flat in the stern, shipped his oars, grasped a chain which was fastened to the rock, and, at the lowest point of the wet, winding entrance, 281 flung himself backward on my body, while the boat shot into what for an instant seemed a moonlit darkness. But on struggling up erect I became conscious of a strange, milky radiance, which grew and brightened as the sight adjusted itself, until I saw that the waves washing round the boat were of a silvery blue, which is like nothing else, lambent, incandescent, flashing with the softest glow imaginable. One thinks of the shimmering flashes in the heart of an opal, of the flame of phosphorus, of the most delicate colour on a blue bird's throat—there is no similitude for that which has no match, nothing else upon the earth which is not gross when set beside these waves of purest light, impalpable, unsubstantial, and radiantly clear. "Che colore?" I asked in wonder; and the boatman, no less awed by the strange beauty, answered very low, "Il cielo," and sat silent, stirring his oar gently, so as to make spouts of light among the blue reflections.

The roof of the Blue Grotto, low-spreading near the entrance, rises at the centre into a domed vault. It is not dark—nowhere in the grotto is it dark—it is neither light nor dark, but blue; blue pervades the air, and plays about the crannies of the roof like flame, far paler than the sea, yet quick and living.

Far back in the cave, where the blue shades are deepest, is a shelf of rock, the only place within the grotto at which one can land. It is usually occupied by a boy who pesters visitors by offering to dive in return for as many francs as he can extort. The sight of his body in the silvery water has excited various writers to high flights of eloquence, one of them indeed assuring us that here alone we can realise what we shall look like in heaven, when the grossness of our bodies has been purged away into the radiance of ethereal light. If this is so one 282should rejoice, though on more human grounds I regret the presence of the boy, whose avarice detracts from the charm of the grotto. The aspect of his body in the water is less wonderful than he believes. Moreover, the shelf which he has turned into a bathing board has a higher interest than any which it derives from him.

For at this spot, and this only, is conclusive evidence that other eyes, in ages far distant from our own, have beheld this grotto, though, for reasons to be given presently, it is practically certain that those eyes saw a different sight. It is easy to discern a squared opening, like a door or window, in the rock above the ledge. Probably such visitors as notice it regard this as a modern contrivance to serve some purpose of the guides; but it is not so. It stands untouched since Kopisch saw it when he swam in half blinded by the smoke. When he, first of all men of our age, climbed up on the rock ledge and peered through the opening he felt confident that he had found the secret exit from the palace of Tiberius at Damecuta; and nothing has yet been discovered which disproves the possibility of this.

The boatmen will have it that the passage goes to Anacapri. Mine was positive upon the subject, and though constrained to admit that his conclusion had not been proved, yet did not regard it as open to discussion. Tradition has a certain value where proof is not available; and as the passage is blocked at no great distance from the grotto, it may be long before the boatman's faith is shaken. Kopisch followed it as far as possible. He describes several corridors radiating in different directions through the hillside, forming a sort of labyrinth in which his party almost lost themselves, and in which they 283were finally checked by the presence of mephitic vapours.

Now, whatever may be the secret of these passages, it scarcely admits of doubt that they were designed for an entrance to the grotto from the island. Capri is so thickly studded with Roman works of the emperors Augustus and Tiberius, and possesses so few others, that there is little risk in attributing the construction of this passage to Roman hands. But what did the Imperial courtiers see, if they did indeed come down those winding passages and stand on the rock shelf where the greedy boy now bargains loudly for francs? Was it the same blue wonder that we see? The answer is certain. The miracle of colour depends directly on the level of the water, and in Roman days the arch was far too high to permit the necessary refraction or colouration of the rays of sunlight.

This is proved in two ways. Firstly, there is unanswerable evidence in the hands of geologists and naturalists that the level of the sea in Roman days was many feet lower than at present. Secondly, the fact that there was more of the archway to be uncovered has been proved by Colonel MackOwen, who explored it by diving, and who found not only that the original height of the entrance was six feet and a half, of which three feet are under water, but also that the base of the opening is formed by a flat, projecting sill, which appeared to have been set there by human hands. Moreover, this archway, which is now the sole entrance to the grotto, is but a poor substitute for a more ancient and incomparably larger doorway still existing, but now submerged, and measuring as much as fifty feet by forty feet, which must have let white sunlight into the cavern as long as it stood above the water.284

There is thus not much reason for supposing that Roman eyes ever beheld this wonder of the world. Whether seen or not seen by an occasional bold intruder, this unique marvel lay silent and unvisited through all the Middle Ages, accounted even by our grandfathers as a haunt of fiends and a centre of mysterious terrors. It is not easy now to catch a moment in which the cave is silent. Only early in the morning one may find its charm completely undisturbed, and carry away a recollection of unearthly mystery and beauty which will remain a precious possession throughout life.

There is much in Capri that is unparalleled. If I have set the Blue Grotto first, that is not because more beauty is found there than exists elsewhere upon the island. It may be beauty of a rarer kind; I do not know. All Capri is a gem, and that which one sees from the island is lovelier still than anything upon its shores.

Only one driving road exists in Capri, yet that one serves the purpose of a score, so rich is it in a charm that perpetually changes. It leads to Anacapri, and is cut along the precipices of Monte Solaro, doing violence to the face of those solitary cliffs on which the winding staircase offered until recently the only mode of approach. Here and there one may find a few yards of the stair still clinging to the front of the abyss, and by its narrow steepness it is possible to gauge the desperate courage of those Turkish rovers who, coming up this way, stormed and destroyed the castle overhead. Perhaps, however, what we should measure by the dangers of the approach is the faint spirit of the defenders, who could not even keep a path by which every enemy was under full arrowshot a dozen times while toiling up the cliff. One ought to visit Anacapri on a clear 285morning, early, because the sunshine is then softer; and having seen what is of interest in that whitewashed hamlet, leaving Monte Solaro for another day, it is well to loiter down the road on foot—the way is far too beautiful to drive.

UNLOADING BOATS, BAY OF NAPLES.

First, in coming down, one's eye is caught by the incomparable loveliness of the channel that parts the island from the peninsula. High on the right hand towers the dark headland named "Lo Capo," and when one has dropped upon the hillside to the point at which the strait appears about to close, and the height of Capri seems almost to touch the tower on the Punta di Campanella, just so much of the coast towards Amalfi has disclosed itself as looks like the shores of fairyland skirting a magic sea. Behind the green slope of the Campanella, with its humps close to the water's edge, drops the purple ridge of the St. Angelo, with an islet at its base, shadowy and having the colour of an amethyst. Upon the great slopes of St. Angelo one can see every jag and cleft, while further off lie the blue mountains, vague, soft, melting imperceptibly into the pale sky. Away beyond Salerno, where the mountains join the purple sea, a solitary snow-capped cone towers up radiant and flashing, while as one watches the changes of the light, now one peak and now another is lit up, and disappears again under the returning shadow.

But if I turn in the direction of the north, there lies extended the whole length of the Sorrento peninsula, the little town of Massalubrense exactly opposite, with the low point of Sorrento jutting like a tooth, while further off the Punta di Scutola rises out of the sea, all purple in the warm sun, with the further cliff that hides Castellammare—Capo d'Orlando the people call it talking still of a great sea 286fight that occurred there six hundred years ago, when the Admiral Roger di Loria shattered the fleet of Sicily, which in other days he had led to victory. There is all the curving strand of the Campagna Felice, backed by its mountains, brown and blue, ridged here and there with snow; and then one sees Vesuvius with his smoky pillar, the reflection of which lies across the bay, discolouring the water, and Somma, wonderfully shadowed by the clouds; while further north again, gleaming so splendidly, rising so pure and white into the heavens that one has to look more than once to make sure they are not piles of cumulus, stretches the snowy line of Apennines, peak rising over peak till the gleam upon their summits dissolves in the great distance. Lower down in the vast prospect is the chain of Campanian mountains, which seem so lofty when one cannot look beyond them; and at their feet lies Naples, that queenly city with the long sweep of coast from Posilipo to Miseno, where the flames rose from the pyre of the Trojan trumpeter. Further off again is craggy Ischia, while blue and infinitely vague upon the skyline one can see the mountains behind Gæta.

There is surely in the whole world scarce any other view at once so wide, so beautiful, and so steeped in the associations of romance. The sun climbs higher, the light increases, the coast towards Amalfi is as purple as a violet. The sea, unruffled by the lightest breeze, is of that nameless blue which seems to have been refined and purified from the colour of a turquoise. Far as one can see, from the headland which hides Cumæ to the farthest point of the Lucanian coast, scarcely one vessel is in sight. The ancient waterway is deserted by which Æneas came, which through so many centuries was ploughed by the galleys of Alexandria, and which in later days, when 287the power of Amalfi rose to its height, was crowded with the wealth of furthest India. From side to side of the great Bay of Salerno there is now no port of consequence. The coast is silent which once rang with the busy noise of arsenals; trade has departed; and the boats which slip in and out beneath the Islands of the Sirens are so few that Parthenope would have disdained them, not caring to uplift her song for so mean a booty.

This decay happened long ago. It was partly the work of pirates, who, as I have often said, swarmed upon these coasts up to that year of grace in which Lord Exmouth destroyed Algiers. The nest being dinged down, the crows flew away, or rather learnt better manners. But for many generations they hunted at their will along the coasts of Italy, counting the people theirs, as often as they chose to come for them—the men to slay, the women and children to be carried off.

The corsairs in all generations had a rendezvous at Capri, which served them much the same useful purpose as Lundy, at the entrance of the Bristol Channel, did to others of their breed. It was a turnpike placed across the track of shipping, and heavy tolls were taken there from the luckless sailors. Barbarossa has stamped his memory on the island more permanently than any other rover. Dragut was, perhaps, as terrible in life, and Occhialy can have met few men who did not fear him. But tradition makes less of them than of the red-bearded scoundrel who assumed the cognomen of an emperor. Barbarossa was indeed often at Capri. His armaments were colossal. One gasps in reading of a pirate who descended on Capri with a fleet of 150 sail! Yet such were the numbers with which Barbarossa arrived about St. Johns Day in the year 2881543. Happily we do not know the exact details of the woe he wrought upon the midsummer seas; but on this lofty road it is well to recollect him, for it was up the now fragmentary stair to Anacapri that his warriors swarmed, perhaps on this, perhaps on some other visit, and stormed the ancient castle overhead.

It is worth while to climb up this last flight of the old broken stair. One has free access to it from the modern road, and turning away from the sea-wall, over which one can distinguish the boats far down below on their way to the Blue Grotto, looking as small as beetles from this vast height, one may climb cautiously up the shattered steps, gaining continually wider outlooks until at last a level platform is attained, where the path winds round the face of the precipice. Sweet-scented shrubs and flowering plants are rooted in the crannies of the limestone, and next the path leads under an old gatehouse, spanning the whole width of the ground between precipice above and abyss below.

How, one asks, did the Turks get past this point? There is no way round, save for the birds. They must have stormed it, coming on in twos and threes—which is another way of saying that the defenders were either fools or cowards. The mere sight of a Turk turned men's hearts to water, it would seem. When the corsairs had won the gatehouse, they were still at some distance from the castle, which towers on a crag several hundred feet higher, strengthened with towers, and having guardrooms for a substantial number of defenders. It is not often that a castle wins and keeps the name of the enemy who stormed it. One may surmise that Barbarossa committed some atrocious deed when the fight was over. There is a dizzy precipice on the higher side of the castle. 289Probably all the garrison went over it who had not fallen by the sword. It is a grand and beautiful spot. There is no end to the pleasures of these mountain slopes; one may wander over Monte Solaro for many days, and yet remain in doubt from what point or in what light its wondrous views are finest.

NAPLES—ON THE MODERN SIDE—LOOKING TOWARDS CAPRI FROM THE CORSO VITTORIO EMMANUELE.

As one comes down the winding road, in the shadow of the high grey scars, discoloured with patches of black brushwood, the saddle of the island looks picturesque and homely. The white town nestles on the ridge between two conical hills, the Telegrafo and the Castiglione, the latter crowned by a small fort, the modern representative of an ancient stronghold which was the last defence of the Capriotes in the days of piracy.

It is a good and defensible position, but the stranger, remembering the almost inaccessible plateau of Anacapri, may wonder not unnaturally why all the inhabitants of the island did not retreat thither on the approach of danger. The answer is that on the small island there are two nations, despising each other like most other neighbours. To the undiscerning eye of the stranger the Capriotes are a pleasant, friendly race; but any child in Anacapri will declare them to be full of malice and deceit, unworthy neighbours of those who look down on them from a moral elevation no less remarkable than the physical. The Capriotes, on their part, would not have dreamt of taking refuge in Anacapri, knowing that here, as elsewhere, only bad men dwell in lofty places. They had a refuge of their own in times of danger—a vast cavern in the hill of Castiglione, where the women and children used to crowd together when the pirates came. It could tell woeful stories, but has not been examined with the care that its past history demands.290

As for the streets of Capri, they are always gay and charming, but to my mind they are most pleasing when the dusk descends, bringing not only cool fresh breezes from the sea, but also imparting a sense of space to vistas which under the garish sunlight seem a trifle cramped. Therefore I go on through the town towards the opposite height, where the villa of Tiberius crowns the hill; and here it is necessary to discourse of Carolina and Carmelina, the two sirens who lie in wait for travellers on the ascent.

These words are not a warning. It is no calamity for a traveller to fall into the hands of either nymph. It is a thirsty walk, and she will bring him wine. It is not a very beautiful walk; and she—yes, both of her!—is charming, attired in blue and scarlet, like the Capriote maidens of an olden day. She will, moreover, dance the tarantella gracefully and well, and talk even about archæology when she has done explaining volubly what a cheat the other girl is, and how false is her pretence to be custodian of anything worth seeing.

The whole of the weary climb is beguiled by the pretty rivalries and antics of these dancers. I have scarcely commenced the ascent, when a boy, starting up from the cover of a rock, thrusts upon me a notice gracefully written in three languages. It advertises the attractions of the restaurant of the Salto and Faro of Tiberio, and contains the following emphatic caution: "Visitors are requested to take careful note that certain unscrupolous (*sic*) persons do their best to misguide visitors in misnominating the real and authenticated position of the Tiberius Leap. Visitors are therefore warned not to be misguided by these unscrupolous persons who, for their own ends, falsely indicate an historical fact, etc., etc."

I hardly know what weighty accusations may lurk 291beneath the words "etc.," but I have hardly done reading this kindly caution when, at a turn of the path, I am confronted by the chief among the "unscrupolous persons" who debase historical truth. It is no other, indeed, than Carmelina herself, smiling all over her handsome face so pleasantly that I could forgive her a worse crime. She is unabashed by the knowledge that I have been put upon my guard as to her true character. She has a Salto, she informs me; and when I point out that it is not the true one, but a fraud, she directs my attention, with a charming shrug, to her own particular notice-board, whereon is printed in large characters a judicial statement to the effect that it is quite impossible for anyone to say precisely over which precipice Tiberius threw his victims. Thus, one being as good as another, it is the part of a wise man, without labouring further up the hill, to take the first which comes, at which, moreover, the Capri wine is of unequalled quality, and so forth.

I do not propose to discuss the rival merits of Carmelina and Carolina. No chart avails the mariner in danger of wreck upon the reefs of woman's beauty. Nothing will help him but a good stout anchor, and that I cannot give him, nor even indicate where he should cast it out. But if a man pass safely by these perils he will ere long attain the summit of the rock, whence he will find much the same view exposed before him as he saw from Anacapri, and thus may give his attention the more freely to the ruins of the "Villa di Tiberio."

None but an archæologist can derive much pleasure from these ruins. Eighteen hundred winters and the delvings of many investigators, whether pirates or men of science, have so shattered the buildings that a trained intelligence is required to comprehend their arrangement. Other eyes can see nothing but broken 292walls, grass-grown corridors, and vaulted basement chambers, which suggest but little splendour. Yet here, on the summit of the headland, stood beyond any doubt the largest and most magnificent of the palaces in which Tiberius secluded himself during the long years he spent in Capri; and with this spot most of the stories told by the guides are associated. These tales are grim and terrible. Tiberius, in the days he spent in Capri, was a tyrant and a debauchee. His palaces, which are now washed and blown clean by the pure rain and wind, were stews of lust and murder while he lived. It is not strange that he is well remembered in the island. His life was wicked enough to beget tradition—the surest way of earning long remembrance! When he saw Capri first it was occupied by a simple, laughing people, gracious and friendly as they are to-day. He left it full of agony and tears. No wonder that after eighteen centuries he is not yet forgotten!

Tiberius came first with the Emperor Augustus, an old man near his end, but joyous and frank, as was his nature.

It happened that a ship from Alexandria was lying at the Marina, bound for Pozzuoli; and the shipmen, desiring to do honour to Augustus, clad themselves in white, put garlands on their heads, and came to give him hail. The simple ceremony, the frank reverence of the sailors, pleased the Emperor beyond measure. He mixed freely with them, gave his attendants money to buy merchandise from the ship, put himself at the head of the revels; and left behind him when he went away a kingly memory. Perhaps the Capriotes hoped that when Tiberius came back those good days would return. But Tiberius was made of other clay, and brought only deepening terror to the island.293

Timberio, the islanders call him, and they believe that deep down in the bowels of this hill, where now his crumbled villa is slowly yielding to the weather, the Emperor sits to this hour upon his steed, both carved in bronze, and having eyes of diamond. Years ago,—no one can say how many!—a boy, creeping through some crevice of the rock, saw that sight, and lived to tell of it, but could never find his way into the vault again. Such tales of mystery are common all the world over; but there are few places in which, whether true or untrue, they have more excuse.

It is impossible to wander round the remnants of this gigantic building without suspecting that the hillside underneath it must be honeycombed with vaults and secret chambers, natural caverns, perhaps, which are so plentiful in Capri, adapted to the uses of the villa. There is a constant tradition among the peasants that from this palace as from all the others, Tiberius had a secret passage to the sea. The tremendous height of the cliff seems almost to forbid belief in the tale; but if it be true, corridors and stairs must exist in the hill upon a scale sufficient to warrant even stranger stories than those which circulate.

There is in the face of the Salto a cavern which, from its proximity to the ruins of the palace, has sometimes been regarded as a possible exit of the secret passage. In 1883 a gentleman of Capri named Canale, together with three peasants, climbed up to this grotto from the sea. It was a hardy feat; and the searchers were rewarded by the discovery of two chambers hewn by hand in the solid rock. Beyond them was an opening closed with fallen stones and earth; and having cleared away the rubbish, they penetrated into a large and lofty natural grotto, hung with stalactites; but found no exit from it. There 294was no trace of a staircase. The issue of the search seems unsatisfactory, and one can only wish that it may be resumed. Clearly there must have been some approach to these chambers otherwise than by climbing from the sea.

81

The day may come when on this spot, as elsewhere in Capri, more careful excavations and researches will be set on foot and continued until Time has either been compelled to yield up his secrets, or has been convicted of possessing none. At that day the archæologist will rejoice; but I think the unlearned man may rather grieve. For the abounding mystery of Capri is so inextricably woven with its extraordinary beauty that to touch either must be to reduce the strange fascination which conquers every visitor, which wakes enthusiasm even in those who do not love Italy, and makes this little island the one spot which no one sees without longing to return. How shall one explain this feeling? It would be as easy to analyse a caress. Not alone the mystery, the beauty, the aloofness from the world, the balmy air or the odorous vegetation of the hillsides,—all these elements exist upon the mainland, yet there is no town, not even Sorrento, which wins such instant or such enduring love. It is partly in the people that the secret lies. They have charm. They are simple, friendly, gracious; they accost the stranger from the outset as a kindly friend, who must mean well, and whom they are disposed to like. If they beg, which is but rarely, they ask without importunity, and accept refusal with good temper. The children run up as you cross the piazza, say "Buon Giorno," and run away smiling out of pure delight. The women sitting in their doorways, clean and industrious, look up and smile but ask for nothing. They are indifferently honest, paragons of every solid 295virtue, when compared with the denizens of Naples. But were it otherwise, were they unblushing rogues and knaves, I think one would love them still for their abundant charm and grace.

In Capri it is rare to see a plain girl; it is perhaps not very common to see a beautiful one. But between the two extremes lies something more attractive than regularity of feature, a thing without a name—charm, vivacity, a gracious radiance of manner which is lacking in scarce any girl or woman of the island. Their features are small and delicate, their heads well poised, their faces brown as berries, their large and lustrous eyes are sometimes pensive, but oftener sparkling with goodwill and merriment. They toil at heavy weights like men, yet do not grow coarse. They will work from dawn to dusk without complaining, without even dreaming that constant labour is a grievance; and at any moment they will return a pleasant word with one still pleasanter, not only responsive to kindness, but arousing it with all the frankness of a child who feels sure all people are as full of goodwill as he is himself.

It is this sense of simplicity and friendliness which, more than any other of Capri's rare attractions, wins the heart of every visitor. On the mainland no such sense exists, save perhaps in some degree on the Piano di Sorrento. Naples, even in broad daylight, is none too safe, and at night the citizens themselves walk cautiously. Castellammare is a wicked city. Amalfi puts the stranger on his guard instinctively. In Capri, from the very hour of landing, one drops precautions. Suspicions are cast off like bad dreams in this isle of laughter and goodwill; the women on the roads want nothing but a greeting, the men believe you when you say you do not need a carriage. If you lose your purse the loss is cried in church, 296and the odds are the purse comes back that day. Crimes of violence are very rare; and never has it been taught in Capri, as it is even in Sorrento, that he who licks the warm blood on his knife will not be troubled by remorse.

There is a hermit on the summit of the hill among the ruins of the villa. He is not poor, but prosperous. He keeps a visitors' book, a tap of wine, moreover, and though he has a chapel he did not interest me. Escaping him with some dexterity, I wandered along the cliff past the lighthouse, climbing over boulders, sometimes knee-deep in tuft grass and scrub, until I reached the brow of the valley on the hither side of the Telegrafo, and climbed down into it by a break-neck path. Having reached the bottom, I was in the main way from the town to the Arco Naturale, and a few turns of the path brought me to the verge of the cliff.

The sun had sloped far westwards, so that all this, the eastern face of the island, was in shade. The first steps of the rock staircase by which the gorge is descended lay in grateful shadow. There is a fine path along the northern slope, but it is better to plunge down the stair towards the level of the sea. After many flights had been descended I came out under a great arch, where cavernous vaults lined with Roman masonry awake once more the sense of mystery which is never far distant in this island. At the foot I found a rough path leading to the south, by which I clambered on until by backward glances I was assured that the Arco Naturale had freed itself from the labyrinth of spires and splintered jags of limestone over which it rises, and stood out clear and sharp against the sky.

The setting sun shone warm and soft on the top of the great cliffs, but all their vast height was 297covered with cool grey and brown, with here and there a green tuft of grass or trailing herbs. There is no end to the fantastic wonder of the crags rising out of the cliff slopes. The great loophole of the Arco Naturale is the loftiest and most striking, but there are countless others. The whole line of the cliff is pierced with cavities and grottoes, with many a sheer, smooth precipice, dropping steep and awful to the sea. Immediately opposite lay the bare headland of the Bell, bathed in golden sunlight, and the rocky coast towards Amalfi, purple and brown beneath the paling sky. Then a bar of cloud came and drew its wisps of vapour slowly across the sunset slope of the Campanella. Whence it came I know not; for the sky was clear, and the hill, both above and below the bank of mist, was bright. The ravines of St. Angelo grew sharper and the glow more purple. The sea was paling fast. One or two rosy clouds floated in the east, catching all the reflections of the sunset. Night was at hand; but as I climbed up the stair I turned often to look again upon that channel through which the Greek ships steered their way three thousand years ago, as they came or went between Eubœan Cumæ and the far-distant cities of the East.

Well, it is growing dusk in Capri, and the time has gone by in which one can see sights. The sea has turned grey and the colour has gone out of the coast. I turn back towards the town, and as I loiter down the steep hill paths I perceive by a growing brightness in the sky that the full moon is rising behind the Telegrafo. The April night has all the fine warm scents of summer. The blue darkness is dropping fast across both town and sea, while in the soft sky the small gold stars are trembling as they do in June in England.298

Ere long the silvery light begins to drive the shadows back; the bright disc climbs above the pointed hill, and floods all the Valley of Tragara. From hill to hill the old white town lies glowing softly. The sea is all a-shimmer, "Splendet tremulo sub lumine pontus"; the deserted cloister of the Certosa has the colour of old carved ivory; the Castiglione on the hilltop shines like steel. The tremendous precipice of Monte Solaro, a cliff wall severing the island in twain, is transformed most wonderfully. In the clear morning sun the heights are red and grey, chiselled into infinite crevices and clefts, awful and magnificent. But when the full moon sails clear of the Telegrafo all the rock face turns light and silvery, almost impalpable, towering up among the stars like a mountain of frosted silver rising out of fairyland. The small piazza is silent and empty, streaked with hard shadows flung by the rising moon. As I step out on it and pause in wonder at the beauty of the scene, the striking of the clock falls on the still air with a strange theatrical effect. Away over the houses comes a drift of music; for Schiano, the coiffeur, is giving a concert in his salon, and all the world has crowded down the street to hear it. At this distance the voices are softened, and blend insensibly with the magic of the summer night, across which, trembling like a star fallen out of the blue sky, shines the light hung over the great figure of the Madonna set in a cleft of the rock on the road to Anacapri.

CHAPTER XIII

LA RIVIERA D'AMALFI, AND ITS LONG-DEAD GREATNESS

299

Loath as every traveller must be to turn his back on Capri and lose sight of Sorrento lying on its black cliff by the sea, yet it is a rare moment when first one tops the mountain barrier and sees the Gulf of Salerno far spreading at one's feet, with the Islands of the Sirens just below, and away over the blue distance the plain of Pæstum, once a rose garden, now a fever-stricken flat, hemmed in between the mountains and the sea. The road, traversing the plain as far as Meta, in the shadow of St. Angelo, commences to ascend by long convolutions, winding perpetually through orange groves and orchards of amazing richness and fertility, mounting continually, gaining every moment wider views over plain and mountain. Directly in the path rises the sharp cone of Vico Alvano, precipitous and rugged. It seems to block the way, but suddenly the road sweeps towards the right, the ridge is gained at last, and all the Gulf of Salerno lies spread out below.

"So I turned to the sea, and there slumbered

As greenly as ever

Those Isles of the Sirens, your Galli;

No ages can sever

The three, nor enable the sister

To join them—half-way

On the voyage, she looked at Ulysses."

300

There is no escaping the spell of this ancient legend. At every turn it confronts one, testifying to the passage of unnumbered years since the first ships sailed upon this lovely gulf which in its time has seen such mighty armaments. It was shipping which made the power of the cities on the gulf. By the sea they rose, and by the sea the noblest of them fell. For Amalfi has been torn away yard by yard; wharf and palace have been alike engulfed; and now there remains so little of the ancient city that one must guess and guess again before discovering where its splendour lay. Its greatness has departed as utterly as that of Pæstum, and though it still teems with people, while the city of Neptune is desolate and silent, there seems no more chance for one than for the other that the spirit of old days will return to animate the present, or set the modern energies towards a goal which fits their past. What is it, in Heaven's name, which filches from so many splendid cities the desire to excel, and leaves them content to see the weeds grow over their past achievements?

I have said already that the mountains of the peninsula show their sternest face towards Salerno. The road which is carried along these precipices is of astonishing grandeur. From the very summit of the mountains the cliffs fall by wide steep slopes to the deep water washing round their feet. Farms or cottages scarcely exist; the ravines seem inaccessible. Beaches there are none, save at three or four points in the long distance to Amalfi; few fishermen dwell on this barren coast. Only at one or two points are the tunny nets spread upon the sea; and one may trudge for miles without meeting any soul but travellers whisked along by their quick-trotting ponies, or here and there a knot of soldiers lounging, 301rifle in hand, outside a guardhouse. The cliff is red and yellow; the grass slopes and the jutting crags which break them are odorous with rosemary. The road follows a course meant only for the sea-birds, now buttressed out over the very face of the abyss, guarded only by a low, crumbling wall, now driven through the flank of some great headland which could not be turned. Every yard reminds one that the road is modern, that no trodden way led along the faces of these cliffs in mediæval times, and when one comes at last to the ravine of Positano and looks down on the old brown town, clinging like a hawk's nest to the steep sides of the gulley which gives access to the sea, the first thought which occurs is that here was a site of wondrous strength, secure from all attack save that which came across the ocean, and faced the perils of a landing on the narrow beach.

Positano feared nothing from the ocean so long as the banner of Amalfi flew. For this strange cluster of half abandoned houses, looking now as if some giant had gone through the streets poking holes in the baked clay of the walls, was a member of that group of towns and havens which to the world outside the gulf called itself Amalfi.

Positano, Prajano, Conca, Pontone, Scala, Ravello, Minori, Majori, Cetara—all these and other communes supplied the hardy sailors and keen merchants who packed the city with the silks and spices of the East, who, though traders, retained their nobility, like the gentlemen of Venice, and whose regard for discipline and social obligations was so keen that the sea laws they had evolved in their two centuries of admiralty became the wonder and the pattern of the world.

The standing puzzle on the Riviera d'Amalfi is to discover the original impulse which gave birth to this commonalty. Whence came the high spirit and the 302desire of greatness which burnt so brightly, and flickered out so utterly, these many centuries ago? If the belief of some historians be true, Positano, which originally was a monks' town, a mere cluster of houses in the shadow of a monastery, was made populous by an influx of refugees from Pæstum, fleeing across the gulf from the pirates who, in the ninth century, gave the *coup de grâce* to that dying city. The tale is not improbable, and it may be that men born in the shadow of the splendid ruins which we see to-day carried with them to their new settlement some tradition of past greatness, which was stung to life again by the shock of their misfortunes. But the virile energy which made Pæstum feared upon the sea must have been almost a forgotten memory even then, and doubtless one should search elsewhere for the spirit which breathed life into the growing state.

Whencesoever it came, there was once a high audacity among the seamen of this small port, little as it counts among the harbours of Italy to-day. It is here that Flavio Gioja dwelt, by whom, as is boasted at Amalfi, the mariner's compass was given to the world. It is quite certain that the polarity of the magnet was known before Gioja lived, if live he did; but though he was assuredly not the first of mankind to observe the properties of the needle, it may well be that he did bring back the knowledge from some trading voyage to the East, and make it known in his own portion of the earth. If so, was he not entitled to the honour which his country claims for him? At the end of the thirteenth century, to which his lifetime is ascribed, discoveries of science were not noised about the world as they are to-day. The knowledge of one man radiated only a short distance round his birthplace. Those strangers who 303had the wit to appreciate it and carry it elsewhere earned scarcely less honour, and by as just a title.

The priests have their own legend in explanation of the name which the town bears. Over the high altar of the church is a picture of the Virgin and Child painted on a panel of cedar wood. This picture was rescued— so the story goes—from the fury of the Iconoclasts; and when the ship which bore it from Greece was nearing Positano, on its way, I suppose, to Rome, a miraculous voice was heard upon the sea, saying over and over again, "Posa, posa!" till at last the sailors heeded, and brought the ship to land, and called the place Positano in memory of the event.

The road goes down the ravine beside the town of Positano, yet the old houses go on lower still, to the very edge of the blue sea, where the water laps in shadow on the beach. There is a fine cascade rushing down the hillside opposite the town, and high up on the towering skyline the crag of rock is pierced by a natural arch. The road, always grand and beautiful, becomes still wilder when the town is passed, and for a great way it hangs like a ridge of swallows' nests midway on the face of such precipices as defy description. The villages come rarely, and the jutting headlands which cut off all prospect of the different towns increase the solitude of this wilderness of mountains. When one has passed Vettica Maggiore, where the women sit plying distaff and spindle in their doorways, one comes in contact with the degraded and persistent beggary which makes the peasants of this coast abhorred of strangers; and having rounded the great cliff of Capo Sottile, one sees far down in a beautiful gorge the small beach of Prajano, where two or three boats hauled up on the gravel, with a cottage under the cliff, make a picture of homely industry which is indescribably refreshing 304after the savage grandeur through which one has come for hours. Ere long one sees the beautiful headland of Conca, with its castle on the cliff. That point is one of the boundaries of the Bay of Amalfi; and when it has been rounded one comes ere long to a bridge thrown across the deep gulley of Furore, so named, it is said, from the wild surging of the waves through its rocky hollow in rough weather; and so, passing by many a grotto and overhanging rock, which seems to totter to its fall, one attains at last to the ancient city of Amalfi.

A long beach of white and grey gravel, facing full south, lies sparkling in the sunshine. Here and there the strand is littered by great boulders which have fallen from the cliff, and the sea washes in among them, cool and translucent. Long lines of net, brown and red, are extended on the gravel, and here and there a man sits patching it, while great numbers more sprawl idle on the warm stones. The main road, descending the hill through a long tunnel in the cliffs, crosses the Marina. Half the width between the houses and the beach is occupied by sheets of sacking, on which yellow rice and macaroni are spread out to bleach. A couple of brown-legged boys in brilliant scarlet caps sprawl over the half-dried goods, spreading them to catch the sun more freely; while all the throng of sailors, women going to the fountain, children pestering visitors for alms, carriages rattling at quick pace across the stones, crowd up and down the narrow remnant of the way as best they can.

The mountains drop so steeply on either side of the ravine, and form with the sea-front a triangle so narrow, that there is but little space left for the city. The houses are crowded in strange confusion. It is a town of long vaulted staircases, branching into 305dark alleys, out of which the houses are approached by flights of steps. For several hundred feet one may climb up these eyries, now tasting the fresh air and catching a glimpse of the blue sea or the many-coloured campanile rising out of the huddled town below, now dodging to avoid the refuse flung from some high window on the stair, till at last a breastwork is attained which sweeps round a corner of the ravine, lined with houses and protected by a low wall. On a level space below are orange trees, growing freely among the housetops; and over all tower the vast mountains, cramping the space on every hand.

Where, one asks oneself, is old Amalfi? In what region of this dirty, squalid town of idlers are we to seek the relics of that proud city for the accommodation of whose Oriental trade, brought out of Asia by the ancient trade route up the Volga and down the Don, a whole quarter of Constantinople was an emporium not too large. The banner of Amalfi floated over hospitals for pilgrims in Jerusalem long ere any other Christian power was able to protect them, and for the better defence of the sacred places she called into life the noblest of all military orders, the Knights of St. John of Jerusalem, who first at Acre, then at Rhodes, and lastly on the rocks of Malta, sustained the cause of Europe against the Turk with a passionate devotion which might well have shamed the monarchs into imitation. Where are the palaces of those senators and doges, the council halls, the exchanges, the noble colonnades such as one sees in other cities not more famous? What has happened to the churches, and the monasteries? And where in this small harbour, fit only for the accommodation of a few coasting schooners, could anchorage have been found for the fleets which sought out the furthest corner of the East, and 306flaunted the banner of Amalfi in every port from Alexandria to Trebizond?

There is no doubt about the answer. All those splendours, all the apparatus of this once great city, lie beneath the sea. That which we look upon to-day is not Amalfi, but a shred of it, only the small segment which the sea has not yet taken, and the crumbling cliff has spared from the ruin of its landslips. Look at the western point of the small harbour. There is just room for the road to climb round between the mountain and the sea. When one stands at the curve of the highway, underneath the ancient watchtower that guards the entrance, one sees the deep creek of Atrani, a town continuous in these days with Amalfi; and beyond the limits of that creek a wider, broader indent into the mountain wall, making an open valley, on the further side of which the town of Majori lies under the vast shadow of the Monte dell'Avvocato. Such is the aspect of the coast to-day, and one watches the boats plying in deep water from one point to another of the cliff. But the chronicle of Minori tells us there was once a beach from Amalfi to Majori! If that be so, if an alteration so immense has occurred in the aspect of the coast-line, of what use is it for us to marvel where the argosies lay, or to guess what may have been reft from us by the encroaching sea?

It is futile to ponder over what is lost. That which remains is rarely beautiful, a miracle of colour, and of noisy, seething life. Under the watchtower of which I spoke there is a broad stone seat, which makes a pleasant resting-place, if only the greedy beggars of the town will be content to hunt their prey at the Marina, where the crowd is thickest, and to leave a moment's peace to the traveller who desires nothing less than their obtrusive help in discovering what it is 307worth while to see. From this point one looks across the beach from hill to hill, and sidewards up the ravine to the brown mountain-tops. In the very centre of the town rises the campanile of the cathedral, having a small cupola roofed with green tiles; and on the hill which closes down on the further side of the town, approached by a stair of many flights, stand the long, low buildings of the Cappuccini convent, now a home for saints no longer, but for sinful tourists, a noisy hostelry alive with the tongues of many nations, all caring more for cookery than heaven.

The convent was the work of Cardinal Capuano, a noted ecclesiastic of Amalfi, on whose name one may pause awhile, if only to recall the fact that it was he who found the body of St. Andrew the apostle, and brought it from the East to the cathedral, where it rests beneath a gorgeous shrine—for ever, we may hope, since the days are past in which even dead cities are rifled of the bones of saints. It is a strange fate which gives tombs to two apostles on this coast at so short a distance from each other as Amalfi and Salerno! The good Cardinal was at Constantinople shortly after the Crusaders sacked it. All his life he had been eager to find the body of St. Andrew, patron saint of his native city. He knew it rested in the city on the Bosphorus, whither it had been carried from Patras centuries before; but where the shrine lay no man could tell him. At length, after many fruitless searches, going one day to the Church of the Holy Apostles to pray, he was approached by an old priest, who revealed himself to be his fellow-townsman, and declared the treasure which he sought was in that very church.

At this point the historian Pansa, from whose learned work I extract this pious tale, is less precise than could be wished. The Cardinal, he tells us, 308watched his opportunity, and got the body of the saint, with several other bodies, more or less complete in their several parts. But how? Churches rarely give up relics willingly, and it must have cost much trouble to abstract so many bones. Some interesting act of theft is here glossed over. One would like to be quite sure, moreover, that the relics were authentic, though after all there cannot really be much doubt of that, for St. Andrew had lain at Amalfi scarce three centuries and a half when he did the town most signal service. The corsair Barbarossa, often mentioned in these pages, having been driven off

85

from Pozzuoli by the Viceroy of Naples, conceived the idea of revenging himself at Amalfi; and would certainly have accomplished his fell purpose, the sea power of the city being long since dead, had not St. Andrew, out of a clear summer sky, raised such a tempest as taught the pirate once for all that he could not flout a saint with safety.

I wish that the powers which scattered Barbarossa's ships had been exerted to hold back the ruin which crashed down on the end of the long buildings of the Cappuccini some six months ago. As I sit looking across the harbour to the hillside where the convent stands, my sight is drawn continually by a ghastly scar in the rock at the further end of the buildings, and beyond it, down to the very level of the sea, is a hideous ruin—a wild confusion of gigantic boulders projecting from steep slopes of rubble and débris. One might look at the wreck of this evident convulsion a hundred times without guessing what was there six months ago—indeed, what lies there still, crushed and hidden by the fall of the overhanging cliff.

Just at the entrance of the town the road passes through the Grotto of St. Christopher. At the 309mouth of the grotto is a signboard, bearing the words, "Hotel e Pensione Santa Caterina," with an arrow pointing to a narrow path cut round the cliff towards the face of the projecting headland. The path goes nowhere now; after a few yards it ends in nothing.

At that point one can see no more; but from this seat on the opposite side of the harbour one looks towards the headland, formerly most beautiful. For the overhanging cliff was topped with brushwood; it was chiselled into slopes and hollows, where the shadows lay superbly. Midway up its height stood the white buildings of the Pensione Caterina, with its terraced garden; and a winding footway cut below the Pensione was the access for sailors to a quay and a pretty strip of beach, where a few boats were hauled up and the larger barks of fishermen lay moored in safety. So it looked on that December morning, when, with little warning, all the face of the headland slipped away and crashed down upon the shore, carrying with it nearly a third part of the Cappuccini Convent, and burying the whole of the "Santa Caterina" as completely as if it had never been.

Since that awful catastrophe, in which two ladies and several fishermen lost their lives, the ruin has lain untouched. Probably it will continue so, until time has covered up the scars with moss and lichen, and softened the piteous tale of the two lost ladies with all the grace and charm of folklore. Landslips and encroachments of the sea have dealt hardly with Amalfi. Perhaps it is scarcely strange that a people so buffeted by fate should lose their hope of greatness, and conceive no interest save the pillage of their guests. Returning to the centre of the town, I turn off from the marina by the first archway leading to the piazza, just where a tablet on the wall calls on Mary by the name of Stella Maris, 310"Star of the Sea," to aid all sailors in peril of the deep; and ere quitting the shadow for the sunlight, I stand in wonder at the beauty of the prospect. The piazza is irregular in shape, roughly triangular, following the conformation of the ground. In its midst is an ancient statue round whose base the pavement is stacked high with vegetables, piles of lettuces and carrots lighting up the grey shadowy space, round which stand the high, irregular houses, with quaint alcoves and dark stairs climbing to the higher stories. There is a deafening babble of tongues, swarthy, broad-browed women kneeling by their baskets and screaming ceaselessly at the purchasers, who themselves are no less voluble, while the confusion is increased by bawling children, of whom some one is every moment at the traveller's elbow, pestering him with "Signurì, u' sold'," and clinging like a leech, in spite of the angriest "Vattèn" which stranger-lips can speak.

It is a striking, many-coloured scene of full and vivid life, material, not to say degraded, in its aspect. But beyond this crowd of unaspiring humanity, passionate of gain rather than of any unsubstantial thing, rises the splendid front of the cathedral, set upon a height, as the temple of the Lord should be. A long and noble flight of steps, the haunt of squalid beggar children, gives access to a portico of many arches, rebuilt in recent years, but resting still on some of its antique pillars; while on the left rises the many-coloured campanile, its four small turrets clustered about the central lantern like the apostles standing round the Incarnate Word, so Volpicella puts it. Ruined and restored, altered by hands of men who could not comprehend the strivings of the ancient builders, this lovely structure still bears witness to the spirituality which dwelt here, as elsewhere 311in Italy, seven centuries ago. High over the babble of the degraded town it towers in its old majesty of form and colour; while higher still the mountain-slopes behind it rise in terrace beyond terrace into the silent regions of pure sunlight and fresh, untainted air.

It is the only spot in Amalfi where soul still triumphs over sense. The interior has been badly modernised, and is less striking. The sub-church, as happens so often in south Italy, is but little changed, and its five apses suggest tolerably clearly that the upper church must at one time have had double aisles. Indeed, one of those aisles exists still on the north side, though walled off so as to form a distinct church.

There are many things worth notice in this church, but I shall speak chiefly of the doors of the main entrance, the great bronze doors of workmanship so fine that the most careless visitor cannot pass them by unnoticed. These doors were given to the cathedral by the great family of Pantaleone, before the year 1066. They are not of Italian workmanship, but were wrought in Constantinople, with which town, as I have said before, Amalfi traders held a constant intercourse. It is not a bad way of realising the extent and importance of that trade to stand in front of these very beautiful doors, to consider what their value must have been, and then to reflect that the family of Pantaleone gave to Italian churches no less than five pairs of similar doors. These were their first gift. Others were presented to the Church of San Salvatore a Bireta at Atrani, where the doges of Amalfi were elected. It is interesting to compare them with these of the cathedral. Another set went to Rome, but do not now exist; another to Monte Cassino; while for another benefaction still the Pantaleoni reached 312across the peninsula to the Adriatic shore, and presented bronze doors to the Church of the Archangel upon Monte Gargano, that great and solitary mountain shrine which in mediæval days was all and more than all that Monte Cassino and Monte Vergine are to-day, visited with at least as much rapture of devotion and far more famous in the remotest parts of Christian Europe, being indeed the mother church of Mont St. Michel and our own St. Michael's Mount.

Monte Gargano looks down on the Apulian coast towns, Trani, Bari, Barletta, and half a dozen more, all of which, by their situation facing to the east, are and have always been the chief gates of Oriental trade passing into Italy. Travellers of to-day are apt to forget the importance of the Adriatic coast throughout Italian history. It may well be that a great part of the trade between Amalfi and Constantinople was conducted by sea; but certainly also much traffic must have passed across the country from coast to coast; and it is certain that Ravello and Scala traded chiefly with the Apulian coast towns, maintaining important settlements in every one, and so securing a share in the Eastern trade at second hand. Thus it is not surprising to see in the cathedral at Ravello another pair of bronze gates, about which there is this interesting fact to be noted, namely that they are not of Constantinople workmanship, though of that school, but were wrought by Barisanus of Trani, who also made a similar pair of gates for the cathedral of his own city, and another for that of Monreale.

Thus the art practised in Constantinople had passed over sea to one of the most important of the Apulian towns, and in its passage it had gained nobility. For the work of the Apulian craftsman is finer and more dignified than that of his Greek 313master, and indeed Schulz, who was no mean critic, declared roundly that the Ravello gates were unmatched save only by those which, by a miracle of craft, Ghiberti wrought for the baptistery of Florence.

Upon the summit of the mountain which rises behind the cathedral stands a very noticeable tower. It is of well-authenticated history, and the guide-books will give all the truth about it. Thus I need concern myself only with the fable, which I do the more gladly since it brings on the scene an old acquaintance, no other, indeed, than "La Regina Giovanna," whom we left behind on the Posilipo. I do not know of any historical warrant for connecting either Queen Joanna with Amalfi, though doubtless both visited a city so important in their day. But the peasants, intent as ever on localising their folklore, repeat upon this spot all the legends of the luckless Queen, her lovers and the fate which she reserved for them. I wish some traveller of leisure would make it his business to collect out of all southern Italy the various traces of this myth. It has bitten deeply into the heart of the people from Sicily to Naples, if not further, and in Provence, which was included in the dominions of the first Joanna, the tradition is said also to exist. "Si' comme 'a Regina Giuvanna!" is a taunt which strips the last rag from a woman's character. In Sicily it is said that the Queen visited her stables nightly and chose her lovers from her grooms. There is in existence the strangest possible dialogue in Latin between the Queen and an enchanter, who conjures up a spirit to foretell her end. It dates from the first half of the fifteenth century, and embodies what were doubtless the current traditions when the dissolute life of the second Joanna had revived and deepened the memory of the failings of the first.314

The way to the mountain fastness of Ravello is wild and beautiful. It turns up across the hill beyond Atrani, and having surmounted the ridge, drops down again into the valley of the mills, a silent, shadowy ravine, between the brooding mountains, through which a pretty brook splashes down from leap to leap. The road winds upwards steadily till at last the old brown town of Scala is seen on the further side of the ravine, and a little later the towers of Ravello face it on the nearer hill. Both are inland villages, deserted in these days by almost all save peasants. But when Amalfi was great these mountain cities were great also; and of Ravello a tale is set down by Boccaccio, which sheds a flood of light on the pursuits of the dwellers on this coast five centuries ago.

"Near Salerno," says the prince of storytellers, "is a hill country looking on the sea, named by its inhabitants 'La Costa d'Amalfi,' full of little cities, of gardens and of fountains, as well as of rich men, eager in the pursuit of commerce. Among these cities is one named Ravello, wherein, just as there are rich men in it now, once dwelt Landolfo Rufolo, who was more than rich, but, not content with his wealth, tried to double it, and went near to lose the whole."

Landolfo, it appears, had conceived the idea that a large market lay open in Cyprus for certain kinds of wares, and accordingly he realised all the capital he could command, bought a large ship, laded it deep with goods, and set sail from home, but when he reached Cyprus he found the markets glutted. Prices fell to almost nothing, and he had almost to give the goods away. Thus he was cast down in a single day from wealth to poverty, and saw no course open to him but to die or to turn corsair.

Of these alternatives the natural man would choose 315the last, and Landolfo was frankly natural in all his acts. He sold his heavy ship, bought a light one, fitted it with all things needful for the trade of piracy, and set sail once more, intent on pillage,—of Turks especially, but by no means only those, for pirates must be practical. In this vocation Heaven helped him who helped himself, so that within a year he had not only regained what Boccaccio quaintly calls "his own," but much more also; and being minded not to push his luck too far, set sail for home, where he meant to live in peace.

He had got as far as the Greek archipelago when he met a storm, and put into a small creek for shelter. In that creek two Genoese ships were lying, and the Genoese, being of like profession to Landolfo, made a prize of him, sacked his ship, and scuttled it.

These Genoese were God-fearing men, and having got Landolfo's goods, by no means desired to deprive him of his life. Thus when the storm abated the citizen of Ravello, now once more a beggar, set sail for Genoa on his captors' ship. For a whole day the sea was kind and smooth; but the storm came back, the two ships were driven far apart, and the one in which Landolfo was a prisoner, driving on a reef off the island of Cephalonia, was shattered like a glass bottle flung at a wall.

The ship was gone; it was dark night; the sea was strewn with floating wreckage; and Landolfo, who had been calling all day for death to relieve his sorrows, saw the grisly shape awaiting him and did not like it. Accordingly he caught at a table which went swimming by, and getting astride of it as best he could, held on with a grip of desperation. So he went on, up and down the hills and valleys of the sea, till at last he became aware of a huge chest floating near him, which threatened every 316moment to surge up against his frail raft and sink it utterly. He fended the chest off with his hand as best he could, but presently there came a mighty squall of wind, raising a sea so great that the chest drove down and over the luckless merchant, tore him from his perch, and sank him in the sea.

When he came up, gasping and half drowned, his raft was so far off that he feared to make for it. But the chest was close at hand, and across it he cast himself, and so was tossed up and down all that day and the next night. But when the light returned, either the will of God or the force of the wind drove him to the shore of the Island of Gurfo, where a poor woman happened to be polishing her household pots among the sand; and she, seeing a shapeless thing tossing up and down in the surf a little way from shore, waded out and dragged it ashore.

Much warm water and judicious rubbing brought back the departing life to Landolfo's body, and in a day or two he thought himself well enough to go. The old woman thought so too, and gave him a broad hint to be off. So the ruined merchant gathered up his rags, and being in no want of the chest, thought of giving it to his hostess in return for her Christian care of him. But like a prudent merchant he first took the precaution of opening it when alone, and found it filled with precious stones, set and unset, of great value.

Landolfo, though somewhat stunned by this fresh caprice of fortune, yet saw clearly how improper it would be to give all this wealth to the old woman. So he packed the whole of it about his person, gave her the empty chest, and departed with tears and blessings. On some fisherman's boat he got across to Brindisi, and so up the coast to Trani, where he found merchants of his own town. Note once more 317the close relations between Ravello and the Apulian cities. These friendly merchants clothed him, gave him a horse, and sent him home, where he realised his wealth and lived in honour all his days.

This Rufolo family of Amalfi was one of the greatest in all Italy, though unhappily it has been extinct these many centuries. So far as can be ascertained, the name of Landolfo does not occur among their records. But Boccaccio's story has the marks of truth. It is all quite possible, and its incidents entirely in keeping with the manners of the age. One writer, I see, calls it a "brutta storia," but we need not use hard names about what we ourselves should certainly have done had we lived in the twelfth century. The greedy vulture Charles of Anjou was often indebted to the wealth of the Rufoli for loans. In 1275 Matteo Rufolo and fifteen other nobles of this neighbourhood held the royal crown in pledge! What wealth there must have been in the decaying palaces of these hillsides! The Rufoli had a villa on the seashore at a spot called "La Marmorata," set by a stream which flows down through groves of oranges and lemons to the sea. In this villa they feasted the monarchs of the House of Anjou right royally; and the peasants still say that at the end of every course the silver dishes were flung out of the window into the sea, to show how little the wealthy Rufoli recked even of such precious wares as those. But it is added that the canny nobles did not really lose the dishes, for nets had been laid carefully beneath the sea, into which the silver fell, and out of which it was recovered when the guests had gone.

This tale sounds too remarkable to be invented. Yet it is in fact only a variant of a myth localised also in Sicily, and doubtless in many other places. 318The Palermo version is worth noting. It is a pendant, of course quite unhistorical, to one of the traditions of the Sicilian Vespers. After the massacre, the Pope laid an interdict on Sicily. The churches were closed and the bells silent. The people could not live so; something must be done. So they built a ship, and a group of gentlemen went on board, carrying with them all the silver cups and dishes which they possessed. They sailed to Rome, and having reached the Tiber, they feigned the speech and manners of some strange country, and on the deck of their ship they sat banqueting, while as each precious vessel served its turn they flung it overboard, where it fell into a net concealed about the vessel's keel. The fame of these reckless strangers soon reached the Pope, who came down to see the marvel, and, being very curious about the matter, was easily induced to step on board. Whereupon the strangers shot out their oars and, rowing quickly off, carried the Pope to Palermo, where he was soon persuaded to relieve Sicily of the interdict.

Such tales as these blow about the world like balls of thistledown, lighting now here, now there, and securing at each resting-place a passionate belief. What is the truth of the fact common to both these tales, and in what age and place are we to seek for it? The age of Mediterranean folklore is past guessing, and the variety of races which have dwelt upon the shores of the great inland sea should make it the richest in the world.

Whilst we have been discoursing of the Rufoli the road, having climbed over the shoulder of the hill above Atrani, has been slowly mounting the valley of the Dragone, and at last it emerges on the small piazza fronting the Cathedral of Ravello. By the time he attains this plateau on the mountain-top 319the traveller will have seen enough of the approach to set him pondering by what fact it happened that Ravello ever grew into an important city. For nothing is more certain than that the course of trade is not determined by caprice. Chance has no part in it, and any man who wishes to understand the causes of the rise or fall of cities must ask himself in every case what convenience brought trade thither, or what inconvenience checked it. Now the inconvenience of the situation in which Ravello lies is manifest, and as the existing road was made out of a rough muletrack only in the present generation, the difficulty of access either to Ravello or La Scala must have been immense. Yet that difficulty did not deflect the trade. Both cities were undoubtedly rich. La Scala is said to have possessed one hundred and thirty churches, a statement which seems incredible to-day, even if the outlying towns of Pontone and Minuto be included in the number. D'Engenio enumerates no less than twenty-five families of undoubted nobility at Ravello, and adds to his list the words "et alii." At Scala he mentions only twelve. All abandoned these hilltops centuries ago, leaving their palaces to decay. That is scarcely strange. It is easy to understand why trade left this half-inaccessible eyrie. The wonder is what brought it here. The city had a great reputation for the dyeing of stuffs. Why did not the dyers establish their vats at the foot of the hill, profiting by the constant intercourse of Amalfi with other cities? I can see no other reason for the growth of Ravello and La Scala than the paramount necessity in the early Middle Ages of safety from sea rovers. It will be impossible to verify this guess until some really scholarly man, probably a German, elects to spend his learning in elucidating the dim and tangled history 320of this most interesting coast. It would be a noble task, and it is strange that some fine scholar has not been attracted to the work ere now.

Probably the visitor who has just arrived in the cathedral piazza may not immediately see with how great beauty Ravello has been adorned. It is certainly no more than the wreck of what it once was. But this can be said of so many Italian towns that the point may be scarcely worth making. The cathedral once possessed a beautiful porch, approached from the piazza by a double flight of seventeen white marble steps. It has none now. Within is a lamentable scene of desolation, a church once filled with glorious works of art among which rather more than a century ago a bishop was allowed to work his will. An Anglican rector with a passion for encaustic tiles could not have wrought more mischief. The bishop's conception of beauty lay in the whitewash pot. This simple ideal he worked out with such thoroughness that in all the church only two half-figures remain of the noble frescoes which were once its pride. The bishop looked round, saw that it was well, and began on the mosaics, which were priceless and beyond all praise. The most beautiful of these was probably the baldacchino which surmounted the high altar. This the energetic bishop got rid of altogether, unless it be the fact, as some suppose, that a few scraps of it are embedded in the bishops throne. There were fifty-two choir stalls of carved walnut wood. They dated from the year 1320, and anyone who surveys the relics of the great beauty with which the founders of the church equipped it may guess that the choir stalls were rarely lovely. Not one chip remains of them. By the time he had done all this the bishop had made much progress towards bringing his lovely cathedral to the condition 321of some Bible Christian chapel in a country village. But the church was full of marbles. Out they went, no one knows where. The pulpit was among the most exquisite of man's works. He began to deface it, but something stayed his hand, I cannot guess what, for such a man must have been impenetrable to remorse. The man who did us this intolerable wrong was called Tafuri, and I hope visitors to Ravello will not forget him.

By some providential accident the pulpit remains but little hurt. Its western end is carried on six slender spiral pillars, each a twist of exquisite mosaic, and supported on the backs of lions and lionesses of strong, fine workmanship. The body of the pulpit is a marvel, a superb blend of rich soft colour with the purest carving in white marble. It is wrought with the most delicate fancy and restraint. It lights up the whole desolated church, and makes one's heart burn for the rare beauty which was shattered and destroyed by the ignorant Bishop Tafuri. And, more than that, this pulpit is an object which sets one pondering whether southern Italy in the great age of the Hohenstaufen, or their first successors, can have been so destitute of great artists as is maintained by certain critics, among the rest by Crowe and Cavalcaselle. It is true that scarce any paintings in Naples can be attributed to the native artists of that period save those which have been retouched so often as to be of no value to the argument. But granting this, it is surely fair to say that the existence of this pulpit proves the possession of a sense of form and colour so noble that it must have produced fine painters. The craftsman was Nicolo di Foggia, again an Apulian town, unless it be the fact, as I see some say, that a family named De Foggia was settled in Ravello. But art so beautiful as this is begotten of a 322long tradition; it is an inheritance from many predecessors of less merit. It does not leap into existence in the full blossom of its beauty. The ideals of Nicolo, and in some measure his attainments also, must have been those of others in his day, and it cannot be that some of them did not express their conceptions with the brush. The last four centuries have wrought almost as much mischief in southern Italy as a barbarian invasion, yet the cathedral at Ravello remains one of the spots at which we can best perceive the greatness of that which once was; and few men who ponder on the grandeur of the doors and the soft wealth of colour on the pulpit, the ambo, and the bishop's throne, will be disposed to deny that there was once a tribe of artists in these regions who earned immortality of fame, though destiny has snatched away their crown.

89

It is but a stone's-throw from the cathedral to the gate of the Palazzo Rufolo, which, by the unselfish courtesy of the late Mr. Reid and his widow, is freely opened to the inspection of any stranger anxious to examine its rare beauty. The palace, though lovingly repaired and tended by Mr. Reid, is but the wreck of itself, having suffered sorely not only by the waste of time, but also by cruel barbarity in the last century. Yet it remains a most important example of the Saracenic taste which crept into this country from the middle of the ninth century, affecting profoundly both its life and art, and perhaps carrying with it the seed of ultimate destruction. It is true, at all events, that the rulers of this coast began in the eleventh or twelfth century to lay such stress on purity of blood as to suggest that they discovered peril in the blending of Italian blood with Moorish. It is not easy to realise in what degree Saracens dwelt freely in the land. It was in the year 842 that a rival claimant for 323the great Lombard Duchy of Benevento called in the aid of Saracens. Not long afterwards the followers of the Crescent established themselves at Bari. They pillaged Sant'Angelo, the sacred city on Monte Gargano, both in 869 and 952, while before the ninth century closed the Dukes of Naples, Amalfi and Salerno were in league with them for the plunder of Roman territory. The Norman kings, when they founded the realm of Naples, made no effort to exterminate them. Frederick the Second loved their art and science, spoke their language, and was often taunted with adopting their religion and manners.

Clearly, then, there is no ground for surprise at finding on this spot traces of Saracenic influence on architecture. Doubtless, if we had records of the life led by the founders of this palace, we should find that it also was largely Saracenic, and that from Bari, Lucera, Salerno, and elsewhere, many a turbaned scholar or merchant brought the grace and luxury of the East, and fired the latent sense of beauty in Italian hearts much as in olden days the Greeks had touched the selfsame strings.

Many parts of the Palazzo Rufolo show the lovely fancy of the Saracen builders, but more than elsewhere it is displayed in the remnants of the courtyard, where one arcade is still intact of arches so delicate and graceful as make one wish that the same principles of building might have permeated all the country and transformed the palaces of other nobles also into dwellings as beautiful as the Palazzo Rufolo once was. From the court one passes to the terrace garden, which lies on the very brow of the mountain, commanding what is surely among the loveliest views of the whole world.

The curious penetrating charm of this terrace garden, the marvel of its view across the fabled sea 324which was cleft by the galleys of Ulysses and Æneas, appealed so strongly to the most romantic spirit of our generation that Richard Wagner, signing his name in the visitors' book of the Hotel Palumbo, added the words, "Klingsor's Zaubergarten ist gefunden."

Destiny is sometimes overkind, or she would not have added to a spot so rich in memories all the associations which are called up by those four words,—the lovely songs of the flower maidens, most exquisite of all our age; the strange passionate seduction of the enchantress Kundry, plucking chord after chord of memory; the wild ecstasy of spiritual purity reasserting its dominion over the guileless fool, the magic spear hurled at him from the battlements and caught harmless in mid air, the crumbling of the castle walls like the unsubstantial fabric of a vision. Many an age will go by before what is noblest in the heart of man will cease to be uplifted by this great fable. And it is to Ravello that our thoughts must turn whenever *Parsifal*exalts them. It is on this mountain-top that the great temptation was trodden underfoot.

Beyond the Palazzo Rufolo the old mountain city prolongs itself into what was once its most exclusive quarter, the "Toro." The nobles of this privileged spot held themselves aloof from their fellow-townsmen, and assumed the privileges of a ruling caste. On the Piazza in the centre of this quarter stands the Church of San Giovanni del Toro, of which Pansa said that it was the most beautiful seen in many hours' journey along this coast. Like the cathedral, it has been sorely used; yet of late years something has been done for its preservation. The crypt with its interesting frescoes was ruined and inaccessible when Schulz visited Ravello, but is in tolerable order now. There is a mosaic pulpit, less beautiful than that of the 325cathedral, but still magnificent, and traces of fine frescoes remain to show how the keepers of the church interpreted their obligations to posterity.

More than one of the old palaces in this quarter retains some of its old splendour. Among them is the Hotel Palumbo, to which I have referred already—a quiet, comfortable resting-place, in which a kindly hostess not only speaks English, but understands the habits of the English far enough to make her house a charming memory with all who stay there. I do not know of any more beautiful or pleasant spot, even in Capri, and certainly there can be none healthier than this mountain town, perched high above the exhalations which strangers dread, though indeed less justly than they should fear their own prudence. The hotel was formerly the bishop's palace. Its comfortable salon was once the chapel, and a little door opening from one corner gives access to a narrow stair by which the bishop descended to his meditation chamber. The holier men are, the more the foul fiend plagues them; and that is doubtless how it comes to pass that in this meditation chamber there are ladies painted on the walls, temptations which no doubt the bishop caused to be depicted there in everlasting memory of his triumphant victory over the intrusive fiend.

The terrace of the hotel commands what is practically the same view which is seen from the garden of the Palazzo Rufolo. The light is failing, and the great bulk of the Monte dell'Avvocata is growing black. I know not how many ages have passed since the Virgin, clothed in light, appeared to a simple shepherd on the mountain-side, saying to him, "If thou wilt stay here and pray, I will be thine advocate." The man did stay to pray, and on the spot where the mother of mankind became his advocate he built a 326hermitage which these many years has lain in ruins. But still the mountain retains its name, for faith lingers yet upon these heights, where life is simple, and forces up no problems. My friend Mr. Ferard, staying at the Hotel Palumbo about the time when the autumn evening darkens down early over hill and valley, was called out by his hostess to the terrace to listen to the bell of Sant'Antonio chiming from the ancient convent near the town. It was the first hour of the night, an hour after Angelus; and as the peal of Sant'Antonio floated across the steep hillside, it was met by the answering chimes from the cathedral churches of Majori and Minori, lying far down by the base of the mountain near the sea. Presently a number of small lights began to glimmer in the valley. They were the lamps and candles set outside their houses by the peasants when they hear the chiming of the bells, and kept there till the ringing ceases. But why, or with what object? It is because every Thursday evening, at the first hour of the night, our Lord who redeemed the world comes down out of heaven and passes through the street. He must not pass in darkness, and the lamps are set out to light Him by. The chiming of the bell through the brown autumn air, the lights twinkling like little stars out of the deep valley, the simple act of faith and reverence, leave a deep impression on the hearts of those who witness a ceremony so little tainted with the modern spirit. One is carried back into an earlier age, when many a lovely vision occupied men's minds which left the world the poorer when it fled from the earth. And so I leave Ravello, while the lamps are set outside the windows still and the chiming of the bells announces that on this mountain-side faith is not dead, nor the homes of the peasants yet left comfortless.

CHAPTER XIV

THE ABBEY OF TRINITÀ DELLA CAVA, SALERNO, AND THE RUINED MAJESTY OF PÆSTUM

327

The arms of the ancient city of Majori are the most apt that could possibly be devised. Upon an azure field the city bears a sprig of marjoram—in token, surely it must have been in token, of the rare and memorable beauty of its mountain-sides, where a sea so blue that nothing out of heaven can surpass it laps about the base of cliffs which in spring-time are from top to bottom and from end to end one fragrant field of aromatic and delicious odours. The scented myrtle is knee-deep. The rosemary and marjoram root themselves in every cleft, and a thousand other herbs growing rank along the mountain-side catch every breeze that blows and fill the air, especially in the morning when the shadows are still wet and the day has not yet grown languorous, with thymy fragrances blown out of every hollow and ravine. Meantime among the grass and herbage of the cliffs the flowers glow like an Eastern carpet. The white gum-cistus stars the hillside thickly, and the anemones cluster in soft banks of colour, while up and down the banks crimson cyclamens burn little tongues of flame, and over all waves the graceful asphodel.

It is when one climbs the hill on the Salerno road 328beyond Majori that these sweet sights and odours are encountered. But first the way passes through Minori, dipping down to the sea-level at the marina of that little town, which now has no industry but fishing, yet once harboured ships and traders from the East. No one of these townlets is devoid of interest, yet when a man travels by this road he is afire to reach the greater beauty further on, and will not tarry to collect the broken fragments of an old tradition at this point. The road emerges from the houses, and in a little way it frees itself from the hills and enters the wider valley of Majori, running out on a wide, pleasant beach, where an avenue of trees gives shelter from the sun. On the right-hand the fishers are drawing up their nets, women hauling with the men, while on the left the ancient town lies open in a broad, straight street, surmounted by the castle which in old days could not save it from the Pisan onslaught, and in modern ones has nothing left to guard. It is not, however, this landward castle which lingers in the memory of the traveller as he turns his memory back upon this beautiful and breezy beach. It is rather the tower, not near so ancient, which juts out to the sea at the very point of the cliff formed by the downward slope of the Monte dell'Avvocata. That vast mountain wall descends so steeply that it seems to forbid access to this pleasant valley from the outer world; and just where the dark and shadowy rock touches the blue sea the castle is approached by three high and slender arches carrying a bridge. It is one of the coast towers erected as a refuge from the incursions of sea-rovers, belonging to the same group of fortifications as the Castello di Conca, or the Torre dello Ziro at Atrani.

The castle stands out finely in the shadow of the hill. The blue sea is warm and soft. Far away 329towards Salerno a dim gleam from time to time betrays the mountains of Cilento, snow-capped and wreathed in clouds. The road climbs upward from the beach, winding round the headland with continually growing beauty. The rock forms are superb; and as the way rises on the flank of the sweet-scented mountain it passes ravine upon ravine, each one cleft down to the blue water's edge, a shadowy precipice fringed by the soft spring sunshine. The road mounts. The ravines grow deeper. The washing of the sea dies away to a pleasant far-off murmur; and at last one attains the summit of the Capo d'Orso, and pauses to absorb the immense beauty of the prospect.

As one stands upon this height one perceives that the creek upon which Amalfi is built has receded into its true position as no more than a single inlet in a wide bay which extends from Capo di Conca to Capo d'Orso, at least five miles as the crow flies, and includes other indentations of no less size.

91

It is by the size and importance of this bay that the old consequence of Amalfi should be measured rather than by what stood upon the city site itself. The historian Hallam, when he visited this coast, doubted the tradition of commercial greatness, remarking that the nature of the ground and the proximity of the mountains to the sea can never have admitted the growth of a city whose transactions were really vast. He does not seem to have realised that Amalfi was a group of cities, of which, perhaps, no one was very large, but each had its own vigorous life, each one contributed some distinct element to the strength and valour of the commonwealth. Doubtless, also, all vied together to promote the glory of the whole.

After crossing Capo d'Orso the road descends, and its beauty decreases, until one sees Cetara, the old 330cliff town which was the limit of the Duchy of Amalfi, and for many years a nest of Saracens; and further on Vietri, standing quaint and beautiful upon the sea.

At Vietri we must turn inland, for though the greater beauty of the sea coast has led us away from the high valley of La Cava, yet the ancient abbey on the mountain-side above that summer resort is famous by too many titles for us to pass it by. A pleasant road leads inland from the pretty little port. Ere long the highway up the valley is abandoned for a winding lane, which climbs and climbs till it comes out at last on a small white village, nestling under the slopes of higher hills. The air is keen upon this lofty ground. Spring has not yet advanced so far as on the coast, but all the brown coppice on the mountain slopes is flushing into green, and the serrated ridge that jags the skyline is lit and obscured by flying light and shadow.

All the air is musical with streams and fragrant with the scent of fresh-sawn wood. Plodding cautiously along the mountain path come the mules laden with sawn boughs for vine-poles; and on a stair which mounts to the level of the abbey out of the deep valley-bottom children are carrying up long bundles of fresh-smelling laths. The abbey stands half-way down the narrow valley, a solitude of wood and mountain. The church is of the period when piety proved its zeal by destroying fine building which it was unable to replace, but beneath it are many remnants of the ancient beauty, and even in the church itself, glittering with gold and undistinguished paintings, one may see in the south-east chapel a fragment of primæval rock covered with rough frescoes, which recalls strangely the memory of an age in which the monks sought heaven by 331a ruder path than that which they tread now. If one descends into the crypt, that austere impression grows the deeper. Here is nothing splendid, but construction which is simple, solid, and severe. There is a noble courtyard and a cavernous crypt, in which lie the bones of Lombard princes loosely stacked with those of others of less note, all equal now, the greater undistinguished from the less. Some came hither humbly clad as pilgrims; and indeed in early days, when faith impelled men forth on pilgrimage from every land, this great abbey, lying so near both to Amalfi and Salerno, must have heard the orisons of those who spoke in many tongues.

Pilgrims who sought the Holy Land travelled very frequently on ships belonging to this coast. They came sometimes in penance and sometimes in love. Some travelled laden with fetters made of the steel with which they had slain a neighbour, some bore no other burden than the staff and scrip; but both alike came over the Alps from northern countries in astonishing numbers, and all were cared for as they came or went by that abounding charity which is the great glory of the Middle Ages. "In richer places," declared an ordinance of the Emperor Lewis the Pious in the year 816, "two-thirds of the wealth given to the clergy shall be set aside for the poor; in poorer places one-half." Out of these funds hospitals to shelter pilgrims were placed on every lonely tract where they might be stayed by the necessities of travel, on mountain roads where night might overtake them far from hospitable dwellings, by bridgeless rivers which might be made impassable by flood. Churchmen and laity vied with each other to ease the way of these wanderers of God, and the care with which edicts were issued relating to the maintenance of the hospices testifies to the greatness 332of the numbers which, but for the piety of the faithful, must have perished in the wilderness.

In this passionate devotion to the sacred places originated the kingdom of the Normans in southern Italy and Sicily. For a band of Normans returning from the Holy Land on a ship of Salerno were still in that city, then a Lombard duchy, when the Saracens landed to exact the tribute which they extorted at certain or uncertain intervals. The proud pilgrims resented the insolent demand, and at the permission of the duke attacked the followers of Mahomet and drove them off. Then followed the usual tale of profuse gratitude, territorial concessions, and ultimate subjection to the stranger. Thus it is not for nothing that Norman pilgrims are recalled to our memory at La Cava.

The abbey has rendered to the world priceless services by the careful preservation of its records. Manuscripts of inestimable value lie stored in the long presses of its library; and for the last two centuries have formed the chief resource of historians of southern Italy. Lying as La Cava does on the edge of the ground over which Lombards, Saracens, and Normans wrestled for dominion, her records have an absolutely vital interest, and many a scholar turns his mind towards that quiet library among the mountains with reverence almost as deep as the ancient pilgrims felt for the abbey church.

There is not very much of interest upon the way from the abbey to Salerno, saving only the exquisite beauty of the sea, which grows bluer as the day increases. But in approaching the old city, which was once so famed among physicians, one passes by the arches of an ancient aqueduct, which reminds me that I undertook to explain why the Isles of the Sirens are called "I Galli." You think the 333moment has gone by for speaking of the islets? By no means. This is the proper place, for in this city of Salerno dwelt an enchanter who knew more about their origin than any other man.

This enchanter was called Pietro Bajalardo—there are other forms of his name, but we need not be exact. The aqueduct reminded me of him because he is said to have built it by his magic powers just as Virgil with the same black art constructed the Grotto of Posilipo. It may have been the success of this great feat which inspired him with the idea of rendering to Salerno a service even more important, and providing it with a good safe harbour. This is a thing which all Salernitans have desired ardently from very early days, and on the possible construction of which they have based such hopes of eminence that, as they say—

"Si Salerno avesse 'o puorte
Napule sarria muorte!"

This neighbourly aspiration it was which Pietro set himself to encourage; and he asked of the eager townsmen one thing only, namely, that they should forthwith slaughter all the cocks in the city, so that when his legions of fiends were engaged in their gigantic task they might not be disturbed and frightened by that sound which all sinners have loathed since the days of the Apostle Peter. So light a condition was complied with gladly. All day Salerno was filled with the sound of expiring cackles; and night descended with the comfortable belief that for once her stillness would reign unbroken by the officious trumpeting which bade her go.

Pietro was at work in the window of his high tower. Through the dark air legions of devils came and went to do his bidding. Fast they sped over 334the silent sea, carrying huge blocks of limestone from the Punta di Campanella. The sky was crossed and recrossed thickly with wondrous potencies and powers, while all the city lay and held its breath. All, that is to say, save one old woman, who loved her cock too much to slaughter him. The harbour was very little to her, the cock was much. So she hid him under an old pan, and went to bed hoping he would be discreet. But the bird smelt the approach of dawn in his confinement, and announced it with an indignant screech. Away flew the demons, tumbling over each other in their fright. In their haste to be gone they let drop into the sea the big blocks they were carrying, and never by any art could be induced to take up their task again. The blocks they dropped are now the islands of "I Galli," that is to say, "The Cocks," and if any man is so incredulous as to doubt this tale, he may very fairly be asked to keep his incredulity to himself until he has found another explanation of the name.

In the cathedral of Salerno many men will be interested in many things. Some will delight in its beautiful forecourt, arcaded with antique pillars and adorned with marbles brought from Pæstum. Some will marvel at the fine mosaic of the pulpit, others at the ancient chest of ivory kept in the sacristy, while some will even take pleasure in the gorgeous decoration of the lower church, with its huge statue of St. Matthew, or rather its two statues set back to back, so that the apostle turns a face toward either altar, thus giving point to the local gibe, "He is double faced (tene doje facce) like San Matteo." But I set aside these things and others with a passing glance, and go straight up to a chapel in the eastern end of the great church, on the south side of the choir, where, slumbering in a peace which rarely blessed 335him while he lived, lies the greatest of all popes, Gregory the Seventh.

GOSSIP—NAPLES.

In the Duomo at Naples we paused before the tomb of Innocent the Fourth, who fought and won the last battle between Papacy and Empire, the last, that is to say, which really counted in that long and awful rivalry. Never after the victory of Innocent did the Emperor, the great world Sovereign, occupy the same pinnacle in men's minds again. The theory of his position was not altered; but in practice the Pope had demonstrated its futility, and set himself, Christ's Vicar upon earth, supreme at the head of all mankind. Once or twice the Empire flickered into life, but the issue was unchanged.

This overthrow of the Empire by the Pope is one of those events which have profoundly modified the history of Europe and the world. If Innocent completed it, Gregory began it. He, first of all popes, dared to initiate the fight. His clear brain, his high, stern courage, planned the complete release of the Papacy from dependence upon the Empire. With a quick perception of the legal weakness of his cause, he linked the support of privilege with that of chastity, and thus appealing to that which mediæval men esteemed the loftiest and most saintly of all virtues, gave his attitude a moral greatness which it did not derive from inherent principle. He attacked the Empire while it was still near its highest power, clothed in the traditions of Charlemagne and Otho the Great. He did not fear to question the prerogative of the lord of the world, the King of the Romans, who made or unmade popes. When the Emperor resisted, he dared to declare him dethroned; and ere long after the issue of that declaration the great Cæsar had crossed the Alps a suppliant for pardon, and stood bareheaded, clothed in the woollen 336garment of a penitent, in the courtyard of the castle at Canossa, waiting humbly till the Pope should admit him to his presence.

There, prostrate in the snow, lay the only power which could measure itself against the Pope. There fell, once and for all, the supreme dominion of the Empire. Three days and nights the Emperor waited upon Gregory's will. It was an awful victory, the humiliation of the lord of kings, the temporal head of all mankind became the footstool of his spiritual brother. In vain that very Emperor ere long abandoned his humility, and drove Gregory to exile in Salerno, where he died. In vain many another Emperor fought and struggled for the old supremacy. The world had seen the Emperor a suppliant waiting in the snow, and could not forget it. This, for good or evil, was the deed of Gregory who sleeps here at Salerno. "I have loved justice and hated iniquity," he said in dying, "therefore I die in exile." Did he in truth act only from those pure motives? It may be so, for indeed he and other popes of the same age were great idealists. He died in exile thinking his cause lost, when in fact it was absolutely won. There are those among us who look on the Papacy with fear, and some with hope; but all alike, if they think at all, regard it as big with destiny, and charged with most potent influences on the future of mankind. Therefore this tomb in the Duomo of Salerno is one of the most interesting upon earth. In days far distant from our own the bones of him who first lifted St. Peter's chair to world-wide supremacy may be cursed or blessed, but forgotten they can never be.

We men and women of to-day, regardful only of the accomplished fact, contemptuous of the power of ideals, and profoundly careless of the teachings of history, dismiss these matters very lightly from our 337minds as having been settled in the "Settanta" when the Italians entered Rome. This is a mere error bred of ignorance. The old strife of Guelf and Ghibelline is raging still. Once again the Papacy is at war with a monarchy, with one, moreover, which is by no means founded on the rock of Christ, as was the Holy Roman Empire, nor supported by the prescriptive glories of Charlemagne or of the Cæsars. The rival which possessed those vast advantages was brought to stand humbly in the snow at Canossa. What will be the issue of the present contest? It is idle to speculate. Faith and asceticism, two strong weapons of the mediæval popes, no longer stir mankind to action. We can only sit and watch, remembering that thirty years are but as a day in the judgment of the oldest of all human institutions. Kingdoms rise and fall. They change their form and develop into other constitutions. The Church of Rome is the only organism on earth which neither changes nor develops. How should it do either, when it claims to be a mere expression of eternal law?

It was a weary journey which one made in old days from Salerno through Battipaglia to Pæstum. The plain which in Greek hands overflowed with fertility has long been but roughly cultivated, and fever has wrought its fatal work with little check among the dwellers on the neglected flats. It was an unsafe journey too, for the main road through the lonely country was infested by brigands who, though they practised chiefly among the native proprietors, yet rejoiced greatly when they met a wealthy stranger unattended by carabineers. The years following the expulsion of the Bourbons in 1860 witnessed a terrible recrudescence of the scourge. Manzi was the most ferocious of the bandits in this region. He haunted chiefly the oak forest of Persano, on the further side of 338Pæstum, and on any alarm his band used to disperse to hiding-places which they only knew among the mountains. But now the brigands have been hunted down, and the land sleeps in peace. The fever, too, is less, thanks to the eucalyptus, whose red stems and glossy foliage spread far and wide across the swampy ground beside the milky rivers. The time may yet come when Pæstum will be a rose garden again, though never more, so far as human intelligence can make a forecast, will the crafts or eager life of a crowded city displace the husbandmen from the wide plains between the mountains and the sea. The Italian races, compact into one strong people, have fixed the centre of their life on other spots, and the day of Pæstum will no more return.

How great a day it was! Time, which has dealt so hardly with the cities of the Italian mainland, has preserved here, in solitary grandeur, the evidence of splendours which elsewhere are but a dream. Cumæ is a rubbish heap, Sybaris and Croton have perished everlastingly. Taranto is overbuilt into the semblance of a mediæval if not a modern city. Brindisi is paltry and Otranto dead. At Pæstum only on the mainland, thanks to the expulsion of the last handful of its citizens eleven centuries ago, three temples stand erect out of the waste of herbage which has strewn itself over the ruined streets and market-places. There alone we can comprehend the lost greatness of that Hellenic people whose submersion by barbaric onslaught must be counted as the greatest misfortune which has befallen the human race.

It is no great wonder that the Greeks, having once overcome the terrors of the ocean on the night side of the world, crossed over in large numbers to the fair coasts which are in sight from the Albanian mountains. So short a ferry must have been constantly 339at work. There are still Greeks in Italy—not Greeks by descent alone, nor of Greek origin mixed with other elements, but Greeks of pure blood and speech. No less than twenty thousand of them dwell in two colonies in southern Italy, one in the Terra d'Otranto, the other some twenty miles south-east of Reggio. Neither maintains communications with the other, nor does either possess traditions of its origin. Both maintain themselves apart from the surrounding people, whom they call "Latinoi." Their language is unwritten. It differs from modern Romaic, and is apparently not derived from the Greek spoken in the cities of Magna Grecia. The colonists are probably descendants of immigrants who came from Greece not later than the eleventh century, or perhaps in those earlier days when refugees crowded into Italy for shelter from the fury of the iconoclasts.

But whencesoever these mysterious colonies came, they have shown not a trace of the great heart and spirit which animated the earliest settlers of their race upon Italian shores. Pæstum, or rather Poseidonia, to give it its Greek name, was a city less ancient than Cumæ. It was not founded by settlers direct from Greece. It was a colony thrown off by Sybaris, that great city of Calabria which became a byword of luxury while Rome was young and counted for little in the Italian land. Five centuries before Christ was born that mighty city was destroyed by its rival Croton, destroyed so utterly that the River Krathis was led over the ruins; yet Poseidonia, its distant colony, still remembered the greatness of her origin, and grew and flourished splendidly, till she became the mightiest town of all this coast, powerful upon sea, potent to thrust back the swarming tribes which looked down enviously from the mountains on her wealth.340

All the city's life is lost and forgotten. What we know of her greatness and her beauty is revealed by no records, but by the tangible evidence of indestructible things. Her coins are numerous exceedingly and of the purest beauty. They prove her abounding wealth. Whence that wealth came is suggested by the fact that the city gave her name to the whole gulf, which could scarcely have happened had she not been great upon the sea. Poseidon was the tutelary deity of the city, and on her coins he appears brandishing his trident, a mighty emblem of sea empire. These coins prove, too, the perfection of the art for which the city was renowned. When Phocæan Greeks founded the once famous city of Velia, some twenty miles away, it was to Poseidonia that they came for instruction in the art of building, drawn doubtless by the desire to match the superb temples which we see to-day, the envy of our builders as of theirs, though we, less fortunate, can summon no citizen of Poseidonia to teach us what our hearts and minds cannot of themselves design.

It must have been a proud and splendid life which throbbed itself out upon this spot. At last the savage mountaineers stormed the city. Greek aid from Epirus gave back its liberty, but to no purpose. The mountain warriors returned and were quelled at last only by the onward march of Rome, which imposed on Poseidonia another servitude and changed its name to Pæstum. Thenceforwards nothing was left to the Greek citizens but their regrets, which they wept out yearly in a mournful festival, telling over the greatness of the days that had been. Even the mourning has been done these twelve centuries and more, yet still the temples stand there silent and deserted, and the walls mark out the empty circuit of the city.341

Virgil, when he came near the end of his poem upon husbandry, and, perceiving the limits of his space, sketched out briefly what other subjects he might have treated, spoke of the twice-flowering roses of Pæstum as if the gardens where they bloomed were the loveliest he knew. There are none now. Only such flowers grow at Pæstum still as flourish in a rough, coarse soil, or can exist in the scant foothold of mould which has collected on the friezes of the temples. High up, where the shattered reddish stone seems to touch the cloudless sky, the blossoming weeds run riot. The mallow flaunts its blood-red flowers on the architrave, and the ruddy snap-dragon looks down into the inmost places of the temple. Over all there is a constant twittering of little birds. The lizards, green and brown, flash in and out among the vast shadows of the columns. They will stop and listen if you whistle to them, raising their heads and peering round in delight with any noise which breaks the long, deathly silence of the city. Beyond the shadow white oxen are ploughing languidly in the thick heat, and across two fields the sea is breaking on a shore as lonely as it was when the Greeks from Sybaris first beached their galleys there. Perhaps they found a city there already. Lenormant was inclined to think so; and it is certainly strange that the Greek name was so completely driven out by the Roman, unless the latter be an older name revived. But though all men use the Latin appellation, and though their scanty knowledge of the city is largely gained from Latin writers, yet the glory of the place is Greek, and neither Roman nor barbarian added to its lustre. Some day men will excavate upon this ground, of which the surface has been barely scratched. They will unearth the tombs outside the city gate, in some of which remarkable 342paintings have been found already. They will lay bare the foundations of all the crowded city, houses, streets, and temples, and declare once more in the clear sunlight how great and splendid was this city of Neptune, which the course of time has reduced to three vast temples standing in a lonely waste.

The grandest of the three temples is that assigned, probably enough, to Poseidon. It cannot be much less ancient than the city itself, and out of Athens there is not a nobler example of Greek architecture, unless it be at Girgenti, where the Temple of Concord is perhaps as fine and somewhat more perfect. It is Doric in style. Its fluted pillars, somewhat short in proportion to their mass, give the building an aspect of gigantic bulk; its heavy architrave, the austerity of its design, the dull red hues with which rain and storm have stained the travertine, all combine to leave a rare impression on the mind. The space within seems strangely narrow. One realises why the early Christians rejected the Greek form of temple, designed for acts of worship paid by individuals singly, and took the model of their churches from the Basilica, in whose spacious hall the congregation which professed to be a brotherhood might assemble at its ease. No congregation could have met in this vast Neptune temple. From the busy market-place outside, the central spot of all the crowded city, worshippers slipped in one by one beneath the shadowy colonnade.

There is a so-called Basilica here, but the name is of no authority, and the building is probably a temple. Wide differences of opinion exist about its date, but none about its beauty. The third temple shows marks of differing styles, and while in part it may be coeval with the foundation of the city, it was probably retouched during the period of Roman rule.343

Such are the visible remains of Pæstum. In all Italy there is no more interesting spot. Not Rome itself, which ruled the habitable world, has cast over mankind a spell so mighty as these Greek cities, which scarcely aimed at rule beyond their walls, and cared nothing for the lust of wide dominion. Conquest was not in their hearts, but the desire of beauty burned there more passionately than ever before or after, creating loveliness which has gone on breeding loveliness and wisdom which has not ceased begetting wisdom, while kingdoms have crumbled into dust and conquerors have earned no better guerdon than forgetfulness; so that still men look back on the life of the Greek cities as the very flower of human culture, the finest expression of what may be achieved by heart and soul and brain aspiring together. The cities perished, but the heritage to mankind remains, kindling still the desire for that beauty in form, thought, and word which was attained upon these coasts more than twenty centuries ago. And if the heritage was for mankind, it was first of all for Italy, that noble land which has been the scene of every kind of greatness, which has been burdened with every shame and sorrow that can afflict mankind, yet is rising once more into strength which will surely dismay her slanderers and shame those who seek to work her ruin. And so I lay down my pen, with a faith in the future which turns ever back to the noblest song yet sung of Italy:—

"Salve magna parens frugum, Saturnia tellus,
Magna virûm; tibi res antiquæ laudis et artis
Ingredior...."

APPENDIX

Page 6. The story of the French knights who misunderstood the warning shots from Ischia is told in Brantôme's Life of Dragut, No. 37 of the "Vies des Hommes Illustres." Concerning Vittoria Colonna there is, of course, a considerable literature. A pleasant and readable account of her life is contained in *A Decade of Italian Women*, by T. A. Trollope (Chapman and Hall, 1859).

Page 7. The tale of Gianni di Procida is Novella VI. of the fifth day of the *Decameron*.

Page 9. The common tale about the origin of the Sicilian Vespers is that Gianni di Procida, who is sometimes spoken of as having suffered in his own family from the lustful dealings of the French soldiery, and sometimes only as sympathising with the islanders in their intolerable wrongs, went through the island in disguise, beating a drum and capering up to whomsoever he met. If it were a Frenchman, he screamed some mad jest in his ear; if a Sicilian, he whispered some information about the projected rising, which was to take place at the signal of the Vesper bell ringing in Palermo. But for this tale there is no historical authority. Procida had certainly some connection with the revolt; but so far as can be discovered, the actual outbreak was unpremeditated, and the name of the Sicilian Vespers is applied to the massacre by no writer earlier than the latter part of the fifteenth century. The great authority on this subject is of course Amari, *La Guerra del Vespro Siciliano.*346

Page 9. Virgil the enchanter. See note on p. 55.

Page 21. It is impossible to give separate references to all the authorities which I have consulted in writing this chapter. The work which I have found most valuable—incomparably so—is the *Campanien* of Beloch, which outstrips both in learning and in judgment all works known to me upon the Phlegræan Fields. It may be said, once for all, that with hardly one exception, the best works upon the region of Naples are by Germans. English scholarship does not appear to advantage. If a man will not read German, he may seek information usefully from Breislak, *Topograpia Fisica della Campania* (Firenze, 1798). Other useful works are:—Phillips, J.,*Vesuvius* (Oxford, 1869); Daubeny, C. G. B., *A Description of Volcanoes* (London, 1848); Logan Lobley, *Mount Vesuvius* (London, 1889); to which should be added the "Physical Notices of the Bay of Naples," by Professor Forbes, in Brewster's*Edinburgh Journal of Science*, vol. x. All these works treat of the Phlegræan Fields, as well as of Vesuvius.

Page 24. The treatise of Capaccio will be found in the collection of chronicles which bears the name of Grævius, but was, in fact, completed after the death of that great scholar by Peter Burmann. The collection is an honour to Leyden, where it was published full half a century before Muratori commenced his work.

Page 26. This gossip about the Grotta del Cane is derived chiefly from a small guide to the locality, published early in the present century.

Page 37. Petrarch's account of his visit to the Phlegræan Fields will be found among his Latin verse epistles (*Carm.* lib. ii. epist. 7).

Page 41. Upon the theory that Cumæ was founded so early as a thousand years before Christ, I translate as follows from Holm (*Geschichte Griechenlands*, vol. i. p. 340), the most recent of authorities, and perhaps the most judicious:—"It is scarcely credible that an organised Greek city existed in these regions in such early times. But it need not be questioned that scattered settlements of 347Greeks were already established on the Campanian coast a thousand years before Christ; and it cannot be doubted that Cumæ is the earliest Greek colony, recognised as such, in the West.... Cumæ also became the mother city of Naples, but at what precise date cannot be determined."

Page 45. The dyke of Hercules. See Beloch, *Campanien.*

Page 52. For the Villa of Vedius Pollio, as well as for all the other antiquities of this region, see Beloch, *Campanien.*

Page 53. The story of the Grotta dei Tuoni is one of the interesting pieces of folklore collected by Signor Gaetano Amalfi, to whose unwearied labours I acknowledge gratefully many debts. It was published in the periodical called *Napoli Nobilissima* in 1895.

Page 55. For the stories of the enchanter Virgil, see Comparetti, *Virgilio nel Mediævo.* The tale of the plundering of Virgil's tomb in the reign of Roger of Sicily is taken from the same work, where it is told on the authority of Gervasius of Tilbury. It was a widely credited tale, and will be found also in Marin Sanudo, *Vite dei Dogi*, p. 232 of the fine new edition of Muratori, now (1901) being issued under the direction of Giosuè Carducci, an enterprise which is remarkable both for scholarship and beauty, and deserves the more praise since it emanates from no great city, but from the printing house of Scipione Lapi at Città di Castello, on the upper valley of the Tiber.

Page 65. The traditions of Queen Joanna are well set out by Signor Amalfi in *La Regina Giovanna nella Tradizione* (Naples, 1892), a little work which, though no other exists upon the subject, the British Museum disdains to purchase. Mr. Nutt procured me a copy, though with some difficulty. The book is not as complete as it might be; it contains, for example, no reference to the traditions of the Queen at Amalfi.

Page 71. For Alfonso of Aragon, see Guicciardini, *Istoria d'Italia*, lib. i. cap. 4. Most of my history is taken from this writer.348

Page 72. For an account of San Lionardo, as well as for the subsequent tale of the Torretta, see *Napoli Nobilissima* (1892).

Page 81. Niccolò Pesce. See *Nap. Nob.* (1896). Schiller's ballad, "Der Taucher," will of course be found in any collection of his works.

Page 88. The best book on the Hohenstaufen is Von Räumer, *Geschichte der Hohenstaufen*, a very fine and interesting work. Frederick loved more than Arab art, unless history is unjust. Amari speaks of him and his grandfather, King Roger, as "i due Sultani battezzati di Sicilia."

Page 97. Upon the vexed question where Palæopolis stood, or if it stood anywhere at all, Beloch seems a little wilful, arguing stoutly that there never was such a city. "But," says Mr. Hodgkin, "in the face of Livy's clear statement (viii. 22) as to the situation of the two cities, and the record in the Triumphal Fasti of the victory of Publilius over the 'Samnites Palæopolitanei,' this seems too bold a stroke of historical scepticism" (*Italy and Her Invaders*, vol. iv. p. 53).

Page 108.et seq. See Camillo Porzio, *La Congiura de' Baroni.*

Page 121. Upon the churches of Naples there are two works which surpass all others—namely, *Documenti per la storia, le arti e le industrie*, by Prince Gaetano Filangieri, a monument of vast learning; and *Denkmaeler der Kunst des Mittelalters in Unter Italien*, by H. W. Schulz, whose work forms the basis of almost every guide-book published on southern Italy.

Page 123. This tale of the graceless Duke of Calabria is in Giannone, *Storia di Napoli*, lib. xxii. *ad init.*

Page 126. Those who desire more information on the everyday life of Naples will do well to seek it in Kellner's work, *Alltägliches aus Neapel*, the tenth volume of the well-known series, "Kennst du das Land," which is sold everywhere in Italy.349

Page 137. The account of this storm is in book v. epist. 5, of Petrarch's letters. The storm may, or may not, be the one which destroyed Amalfi. I know of no evidence pointing either way, save the improbability that two tempests should have wrought such devastation.

Page 140. Fucini's work is called *Napoli a Occhio Nudo.*

Page 141. Any history of Naples will give the facts of the struggle between Frederick the Second and Innocent. See especially von Räumer or Giannone.

Page 143. La Colonna della Vicaria. Signor Amalfi quotes from Voltero,*Dizionario filosofico, s.v.* "Banqueroute," the following passage:—"Le négociant*fallito* pouvait dans certaines villes d'Italie garder tous ses biens et frustrer ses créanciers, pourvu qu'il s'assit le derrière nu sur une pierre en présence de tous les marchands. C'était une dérivation douce de l'ancien proverbe romain, *Solvere aut in aere, aut in cute*, payer de son argent ou de sa peau" (*Tradizioni ed usi*, p. 123).

Page 146. The facts about the descent of the Turks upon Otranto in 1480 will be found stated briefly in all the histories. But they are sufficiently curious to make it worth while to consult the admirable and detailed report made to Ludovic Sforza, Il Moro, by the commissary who served him in his capacity as Duke of Bari. As ruler of the chief Apulian coast town, Il Moro was of course painfully anxious for exact information about the proceedings of the Turks. The report will be found in volume vi. of the *Archivio Storico*, published by the "Società di Storia Patria," of Naples.

Page 150.et seq. The story of Conradin's expedition and death is told best in von Räumer, *Geschichte der Hohenstaufen*. It will be found also in Amari, *La Guerra del Vespro*. The two historians report the circumstances of Conradin's death with some differences of detail, having relied on different chronicles. The variations are not essential.

Page 158. Details concerning the examination of Conradin's tomb will be found in Filangieri, *op. cit.*350

Page 161. For the story of Mas'aniello's revolt I have followed Sign. Gabriele Tontoli, *Il Masaniello, overo Discorsi Narrativi. La Solleratione di Napoli*, printed at Naples in 1648. I selected this work (1) because it is rare; (2) because it is full of detail; (3) because it is the narrative of an eye-witness.

Page 178. The literature of Vesuvius is immense. As general references, I can only indicate again the works named in the note on page 21.

Page 182. Braccini's narrative was published at Naples in 1632 under the title*Dell'Incendio fattosi nel Vesuvio.*

Page 190. Palmieri's account has been translated. *The Eruption of Vesuvius in 1872*(London, 1873).

Page 196. Herculaneum. Once more it is well to refer to Beloch, *Campanien.*

Page 201.et seq. The work of Signori Comparetti and de Petra was published at Turin in 1883, under the title *La Villa Ercolanense dei Pisoni*. It is one of those monuments of patient, well-directed learning and research which fill one with high hopes for the future of Italian scholarship. I presume the British Museum acquired its copy shortly after publication. I may add that I cut its pages in July, 1900—a fact that says worlds about British scholarship.

Page 209. The translation of Mau's *Pompeii, its Life and Art*, was published at New York in 1899.

Page 217. The only works worth mentioning about the pictures at Pompeii are those of Helbig, *Untersuchungen über die Campanische Wandmalerei* (Leipzig, 1873), and his earlier *Wandgemälde* (Leipzig, 1868). A summary of Helbig's conclusions will be found in *Promenades Archéologiques*, by Gaston Boissier (Paris, 1895).

Page 223. On Stabiæ a work comparable only to that cited above on Piso's villa has been written by Signor Michele Ruggiero, *Degli Scavi di Stabia* (Naples, 1881).

In connection with the Roman country life, I might have 351mentioned the recent excavations at Bosco-reale, where the villas were doubtless similar to those upon Varano. The first discoveries on that spot are set down by the superstitious peasants to the credit of a priest, who is said to have indicated a place where treasure would be found by digging. The real fact is that about the year 1868 a small proprietor named Pulzella discovered, while hoeing his field, the entrance to a buried chamber. He enlarged the aperture, and found a second room; but could not penetrate further without entering a neighbouring property, which belonged to Signor de Prisco. Of this discovery he said nothing for twenty years. In 1888 the ground passed into the possession of the de Prisco family, who, learning what had occurred, continued the excavation, found in 1894 all the apartments of a bath, and in one of them a great treasure of money and silver plate of exquisite workmanship, which was bought by Baron Rothschild and presented to the Louvre. A full account of the villa then unearthed is given by August Mau.

Six years passed, and recently the excavations have been resumed. A larger villa has been unearthed, near the former one. No treasure was found in it, nor any portable articles. Possibly the owners had been able to return and recover their property, or more probably they had fled on earlier warning. But the interest of this new house lies in its frescoes, which are of great beauty, both architectural and figure pieces. There can be no doubt that we are on the verge of a great expansion of our knowledge of Roman life; and it is to be hoped that the works at Bosco-reale will be vigorously pushed and carefully supervised.

An interesting account of the discoveries, with illustrations, will be found in the Italian magazine *Emporium* for December, 1900.

Page 229. Trade routes in the Sorrento peninsula. I cannot discover that anyone has written with scholarship on this most interesting subject. There is none more important to a clear comprehension of history, nor any more generally neglected.

Page 230. Santa Maria Maggiore. Gsell-Fels gives a good account of this remarkable church, based on that of Schulz.352

Page 231. Catacombs at Castellammare. I regret that the passage in Schulz,*Denkmaeler der Kunst des Mittelalters in Unter Italien*, vol. ii. p. 224, referring to these catacombs, did not come under my notice in time to admit of my making a personal examination of them. They appear to be so completely forgotten that several well-informed persons to whom I applied denied their existence. They do exist, however, upon the road to La Cava. I cannot indicate the spot exactly, nor does Schulz do so. I translate from him as follows:—"To the largest grotto one goes by a broad passage hewn in the rock, in whose sides are squared niches, apparently designed for flasks, lamps, inscriptions or children's coffins. The uncertain line between ancient and modern alterations makes decision difficult. Then one goes through a sort of rock gateway of more modern construction.... In the background of the grotto, which has five niches on either of its longer sides, there are more graves under a vault. The greater number of the pictures are on the left as one enters. In the first recess stands a woman's figure in the Norman-Greek style of painting, badly damaged. Near her is a smaller figure of a saint holding a book. Higher up, in a disc set with white pearls, hovers the figure of Christ with a nimbus; and by it are other circles, with busts of angels. Over the upper one is written 'RAFA' (Raphael), above another 'MICAH, SCS VRVS' (?). The painting is in the ancient style with black, white, and red—that peculiar dark brown-red of early Christian pictures, as in the lower church at Assisi, the catacombs of Syracuse and Naples, etc.... The inscriptions, mostly white on a green ground, are in characters of the twelfth and thirteenth centuries, or yet later times," etc., etc.

I cannot too emphatically express my sense of the great value of Schulz' work. Much is changed since 1860, when he wrote; yet still his survey must be the starting-point for every other writer.

Page 236. La Madonna di Pozzano. I take this legend from *Storia dell'Immagine di S. Maria di Pozzano*, written by Padre Serafino de Ruggieri. It was published at Valle di Pompeii in 1893.353

Page 237. The facts about the Iconoclasts will be found in any Church history; *e.g.* Milman, *Hist. of Latin Christianity*, bk. iv. chap. 7.

Page 238. My chief authority for the stories of madonnas in this chapter and the next is Signor Gaetano Amalfi, whose invaluable work, *Tradizioni ed Usi nella Penisola Sorrentina*, forms volume viii. of the "Curiosità Popolari Tradizionali," published by Signor Pitrè at Palermo. Those who are acquainted with the bookshops in Naples will not be surprised to hear that I searched them vainly for a copy of this work, great as its interest should be for all visitors to the city. The book is largely written in the local dialects, and would be of little use to those who cannot read them.

Page 241. The old road from Castellammare towards Sorrento. Breislak, who wrote so recently as in 1800, says, "Le chemin est le plus mauvais possible, et ne peut se faire avec sureté qu'à pied."

Page 245. Quaresima. I refer once more to Signor Amalfi, *op. cit.*

Page 255. These various scraps of folklore are from the same work, as are also the legends in this chapter.

Page 260. For the tufa of Sorrento, see Breislak, *Voyages physiques*.

Page 270. On the archæology of Sorrento the best work known to me is that of Beloch, *Campanien.*

Page 273. Not much has been written well on Capri. *Storia dell'Isola di Capri,* by Mons. A. Canale, is sold throughout the town, but has little value. *Die Insel Capri,* by Ferdinand Gregorovius, is a book of great beauty and merit; the reputation of Gregorovius stands in no need of praise. Kopisch' narrative, *Die Entdeckung der blauen Grotte,* is volume 2,907 of Reclam's "Universal Bibliothek."

Page 301. It is much to be desired that some German or Italian scholar—I fear none other would have the necessary patience—might undertake to elucidate the history of that collection of communes which passed by the name of 354Amalfi. Two histories exist—a modern one by Camera, an ancient one by Pansa. Both comprise interesting facts, but neither attempts to solve the puzzles which beset the traveller on every side. Nor will it be of any use for other writers to attempt solutions without long study; yet for one who might be willing to bestow the labour, there will certainly be reserved a rich reward of fame. Probably there is scarce any spot where thorough investigation might teach us so much of the tangled yet splendid history of Italy in the Middle Ages.

Page 305. The Knights Hospitallers of St. John were settled at Cyprus for a time after their expulsion from Acre; but were not long contented to remain vassals of the king of that island, and accordingly obtained the Pope's permission to turn their arms against the Greek Empire, from which they took Rhodes on 15th August, 1310. Finlay, *History of Greece,* vol. iii. p. 410.

Page 306. No one need concern himself with the works of Volpicella. They belong to the bad period of archæology, when sentiment overcame both reason and sense. Schulz remains the safe and trusty guide; it being remembered always that changes have occurred since he wrote.

Page 311. The bronze doors at Amalfi and Ravello. Schulz remains the chief authority on this very interesting subject; but there is a good article on the subject in Lenormant, *À travers l'Apulie et la Lucanie,* under the heading "Monte Sant'Angelo."

Page 312. Monte Gargano, one of the most picturesque and interesting spots in Italy. There was a shrine for pagan pilgrims on this mountain in Strabo's time. He describes the crowd who came to consult the demi-god in his cavern, and lay sleeping in the open air around the cave, resting on skins of the black sheep they had slaughtered. In due course the heathen demi-god was replaced by a miraculous apparition of the archangel Michael, and Christian pilgrims came in crowds. It was the common process. The priests recognised a tradition of pilgrimage which they could not check, and legalised it by a Christian legend. See Lenormant, *À travers l'Apulie et la Lucanie* (Paris, 1883).355

Page 330. Vietri is of great age. Strabo, quoted by Camera, indicates it under the name Marcinna as the only city between the rocks of the Sirens and Pæstum. Possibly he looked on Salerno and Vietri as one.

Page 331. The facts about pilgrims are from Ducange, *s.v.* "Peregrinatio," and Muratori, Dissertation 37.

Page 338. The best account of Pæstum known to me is in Lenormant, *op. cit.*

Made in the USA
Charleston, SC
10 September 2015